Irina Ratushinskaya

Born in Odessa in 1954, Irina Ratushinskaya is one of the leading contemporary Russian poets. She spent four years in a labour camp for 'anti-Soviet agitation and propaganda' where she managed to smuggle out her poems. They were published in the collection NO, I'M NOT AFRAID. After a series of hunger strikes, Irina was released and came to Britain. Her story is told in GREY IS THE COLOUR OF HOPE and IN THE BEGINNING. She and her husband now live in London.

D0452975

SCEPTRE

The Odessans

IRINA RATUSHINSKAYA

Translated from the
Russian by Geoffrey Smith

SCEPTRE

Copyright © 1996 Irina Ratushinskaya
English Language Translation Copyright © 1996 Geoffrey Smith

First published in 1996 by Hodder and Stoughton
First published in paperback in 1996
by Hodder and Stoughton
A division of Hodder Headline PLC
A Sceptre Paperback

10 9 8 7 6 5 4 3 2 1

A CIP catalogue record for this title is
available from British Library.

ISBN 0 340 66563 7

Printed and bound in Great Britain by
Cox & Wyman Ltd, Reading, Berkshire

Hodder and Stoughton
A division of Hodder Headline PLC
338 Euston Road
London NW1 3BH

Acknowledgements ∫

I would like to express my gratitude to all old Odessans who have never got tired of telling their stories and mercilessly expected the youngsters to listen. Had I not been one of those youngsters, I would never have learned about some of the pages from my country's and my city's history.

Warmest thanks to Richard Cohen for giving me the idea to put it in writing.

PART ONE

1

The check has to be made while it is still dark – has there been an overnight dew? And, if not, then the 'broad' wind can be expected. The waves get warmer, a murky off-yellow is added to their green, and, on land as on water, all who understand the sea know before light that the 'broad' is coming. It is a trusty wind. It is a beauty of a wind. For the fishermen, it is the best wind. Now they can go after the large mackerel that swim in close to Odessa each May, just as they will go on doing for many years to come. And, whether large or small, the boats lying anchored offshore set their course for the north-east.

Meanwhile, the rest of Odessa can sleep on. Then, closer to sun-up, the outskirts start stirring into life. A bit later comes time for the central streets to wake up, too. Unless, of course, anything out of the ordinary has happened.

But this was 1905, and with their daily cries of 'amazing news' about strikes, student unrest and terrorists, the newspaper boys had managed to shriek themselves hoarse, and by now everyone was tired of hearing them. Events were somehow cheapened, people had grown used to them, and this morning Odessa was in no rush to wake up.

Maxim Petrov, however, was another case altogether. In the house on Koblevskaya Street he was the first to spring into action. And even as he opened his sleepy eyelids, he knew with delight that some treat was in store for him. Because, whenever you opened your eyes and saw a flash of green light (which only happened in bright sunlight), that meant it was bound to be a happy day. Then he remembered, smiled and hid his face in his pillow. Today was his fifth birthday – so that's what it was! Yesterday evening he was four, and he had been four through the night, but then he got up and found that he was already five. Now he was a big boy, and everyone would wish him a happy birthday, and his presents would be waiting for him on the living-room table . . .

Until he had actually seen his presents, the best thing was to go on dreaming about them for a bit longer. But he could not possibly hang around in bed any more, because he started feeling sick somewhere just above his tummy. Maxim jumped down on to his favourite rug with its troika of horses. Just like every other morning, he was careful not to tread on any of the horses so as not to upset them. And he marched over to his observation post at the window-sill, admiring his bare legs as he went (they were already five years old!). But, on this occasion, he did not reach the sill. Something black and white had been left neatly folded on the chair with the buckled legs, and lying on top of it was a sailor's hat! Even before he had torn the wrapping off he recognised what it was. It was a real sailor-suit! With long trousers!

When his mother came in to wake up her son and wish him a happy birthday, she found him panting to do his trousers up. Because the way to put on real sailors' trousers was turning out to be quite different from the way that short trousers were put on. But he had to do it on his own, or else it would be too shameful. His mother could, nevertheless, help just a little, for she never laughed at Maxim. As usual, they greeted each other by kissing one another's palm. It was something which they never did in front of anyone else, however, for this was a secret which they kept to themselves.

'Mummy! How lovely you look! That's a new dress you've got, isn't it?'

'I've got a new dress, Max dear, and you've got some new clothes, too. Let's go downstairs and show ourselves off,' said his mother, smiling as she swallowed a sigh. She took one more look into her younger son's eyes and, as so often before, was amazed at how blue they were. Everyone else in the family had grey eyes. Yes, he was the youngest, and, yes – it was impossible to hide – he was her favourite, too. Well, and what of it? After all, who else in the house ever told her how lovely she looked?

Father was downstairs having his morning tea and read of the newspapers, and he showed his approval when his son came running in, though there was still that faint wrinkle between his brows which Maxim found daunting.

'What a fine fellow! Happy birthday, son. Turn round, now! Every inch the sailor. Now, sir, I wonder which ship you're from? What do you mean, you don't know? What's that name you've got written on your hat? Come on, read it out.'

'A-li-mi . . . Alma . . .' Maxim started bashfully. He had put his foot right in it! What he should have done was to take his time and work it out back in his room, but now that his father was quizzing him like this, he would never make it out. What were those two small horns stuck on the end there?

His mother was trying to signal something without being spotted. But then his father looked round and she had to stop. Everything was happening over Maxim's unfortunate, and now also sweaty head. And the birthday that had started so happily might have ended in tears, had not his brother and sisters – all three of them – suddenly come rushing in. And, to Maxim's relief, they immediately span and whirled him round, admiring his hat, as Zina casually read out, 'The *Almaz*! So you're on the same ship as Uncle Sergei, are you?'

Their father frowned in annoyance, but it was too late to stop her. Besides, since when could looks stop Zina?

The children eagerly gathered round the table with the presents, and peals of delight rang out. After a while they called their mother over, and, with an apologetic smile, she went and joined them, leaving the father to himself and his newspaper.

Ivan Alexandrovich Petrov. A nobleman. A householder. A happy family man. Here he was, happily celebrating his son's birthday in the midst of this, his loving family, he kept goading himself. He knew just how silly he was being, and that it was pure chance that everyone else happened to be in one corner of the room whilst he was in another, and that not one of them could have possibly known what had just happened to him. But, all the same, was it really asking too much for one of them to summon sensitivity enough to stop and take a proper look at the father of the house? With the children it was understandable, but what about Masha? He was so used to being greeted by that look of hers – 'Is all well with us?' But this morning, just when that look was the one thing he most needed (the sight of it usually annoyed him), she had behaved quite differently. As if she were too busy admiring herself. He rolled his shoulders and deliberately took stock of the situation. What, in actual fact, had happened to him? Coming out of the blue like this, it was bound to be some nonsense, as any doctor would have told him. Now, if he were to take another look at his newspaper, everything would go back to normal, and he would laugh at himself.

But, just as before, the newspaper's lines kept swimming out of focus, and, except for the headlines, Ivan Alexandrovich could read nothing. So there really was something the matter with his eyes. It came on all of a sudden, half-way through a line. So it was true that a man of his age should expect these nasty surprises. What next? Glasses? A pince-nez? How revolting. Ivan Alexandrovich was renowned as a good-looking man, and he was used to this role. In fact, it was all that he had ever done with his life. After his marriage, he had been able to give up the idea of having to work for a living, and was secretly amused that his brother Sergei belonged to the Tsar, to the navy, to his ship – to whoever, but not to himself. And what had come of it? Now Sergei was out in the Far East somewhere, and the whole of Russia was going mad over the gallantry of the troops at war with Japan. But who knew Ivan Alexandrovich? Well, he was known in the Odessan Assembly of Noblemen, and there were the ladies at the opera . . .

Imperceptibly, his estate had one way or another been mortgaged off, then remortgaged, until finally it had ended up in the hands of some stranger. In fact, there was little now left of it – just enough to prevent them from having to change their style of life. And that couldn't be blamed on Masha. Nothing ever could . . . He suppressed his irritation and went on thinking. What was he left with? Four children. There, one might have thought, was something to be proud of. Yet what was their attitude to their father? At least with the elder two, Pavel and Zina, there was some reason for this. They had been old enough to understand something of what was going on when there was that episode with Annette. And they had clung even closer to their mother, who brought them up as she thought fit, spoiling them, of course, though he had not dared to interfere, as he had been contemplating a divorce. But then, after all, it had blown over, and just where did children of their age acquire such rancour? Marina, his darling, a girl with a heart of gold – now she, of course, did love her father. But, there again, she loved everyone, whether it was the nanny Dasha, the yard-sweeper, or even a stray dog out on the street. She was that kind of child. As for Maxim, he was just wary of him, though whatever for? He had never once struck him, nor even shouted at him. This was just the time to ensure that he, at least, was properly brought up. A man's hand – that's what the boy needed. But Masha had somehow imperceptibly put a distance between him and the children . . . Stop it. He had already made enough hullabaloo over his eyesight, and he was not about to allow himself any mean thoughts. He was guilty enough towards her as it was.

She loved him, and she would have died for him. That evening he would tell her about his eyes, and she would be frightened, and then start comforting him, and he would see just how ludicrous these earlier thoughts were. If it weren't for Masha, these bouts of irritation would have been the death of him long ago. No, he had to be a man! So come on, father, go to the children and guests who are waiting for you to join in the festivities.

It was a long day, and for some reason it was to remain fixed in the minds of all the Petrovs and, years later, they would recall it as one of the last days when time still moved evenly, and was considerate towards people, without making any wild leaps, or coming crashing down on top of their heads.

Maxim was jumping up and down, thrilled with his new pistol, while Pavel showed him how he should load the pink cap-rolls, and the blue gunpowder smoke went flying out of the window and settled on the tender paws of the horse-chestnut trees. Then the guests arrived with their children, and even Zina, who already attended the gymnasium, forgot her adult condescension, and became excited and flushed as she kept organising new games. The mother was left in peace, as Zina was the one for whom they kept calling.

Now don't get overexcited, little sister, thought Pavel, trying to raise himself up to his usual tone of superiority with the youngsters. And who would have thought she knew how to play the irreproachable little miss? But then he promptly dropped this tone and obediently ran off to fetch a glass of water.

'Ready, steady . . . go!' shrieked the youngest children excitedly, and, in a flourish like Cleopatra, Zina tossed a crumpled little ball of grey paper into the glass. Immediately and in front of their very eyes a spiral of small petals unfurled as it slowly opened out into torrid crimson, blue, and white marvels.

'Chinese flowers! How beautiful! They're incredible! Again, Zina, do it again!' rose the delighted yell, and the glasses were arranged in a row across the festive table-cloth, like a complete Chinese garden.

Then came the ride from the French Boulevard to Nikolayev Boulevard, with the Petrovs' carriage, the Serdyuks' carriage, and the two hired cabs. A surf of pinky-white horse-chestnut blossom beat against the pavements, and the 'broad' kept blowing, as the women laughed and clung on to their hats.

To Maxim, it all seemed wonderfully new, as if it had just been made: the blue expanse of the sea, the May smells, and the clouds that were damply dispersed across the whole sky, as bright as Chinese flowers. Towards evening he became worn out with happiness and, when a game of 'living pictures' was being organised, he suddenly burst into tears and ran off to his room. Marina noticed immediately and, as she went running out after him, she managed to glance at her mother. 'I'll go and join him for a while, but you pretend nothing's happened, and send Dasha up, then you come when it seems right' – her mother understood, smiling as the eight-year-old diplomat left.

Dasha, the nanny, found Maxim crying to his sister all about something he had just thought up to explain away his tears and his misery. It turned out that what he really wanted was a kitten, and he had had all sorts of presents, but not a kitten. By now he actually believed in this misfortune himself, and all that remained for Marina to do was to press her young brother's head to her body, as she quickly added in a convincing whisper, 'Maxim, now don't cry, Maxy dear, you'll get your kitten, Papa will let you have one, and everything's going to be all right . . .'

'He's ever so tired. It's been such a long day for him,' Dasha affectionately kept saying, as she prepared his bed. 'Come on, sweetie, it's time for prayers. Ooh, now look how wet you've gone and made Marina's lace dress.'

But Maxim kept clinging to Marina's crumpled dress, until he broke off a sob and unexpectedly fell asleep on her shoulder.

Downstairs, there were only a few guests remaining in the living-room. Those with children had already left. The conversation was quiet and somehow concerned nothing, as can happen when people have known each other for a long time. Over on the plush green sofa in the corner, Pavel and Zina looked at one another and burst out laughing.

'Why are you laughing?'

'I just am. We've spent the whole day fooling around like kids, so I thought we'd better crawl off under the piano to avoid being spotted and sent up to bed.'

There was a sharp ring on the doorbell, and everyone looked round, because by this time no further guests were expected. Briskly, and without even smoothing the crumples which his hat left on his grey head of hair, in strode San Sanych, a retired naval officer and an acquaintance of the Petrovs. Everyone could see from his eyes and his manner that something was up, so greetings were dealt with smartly.

'A dispatch has come in from Petersburg. It's just arrived. Andreyev told me about it. The squadron's been destroyed. Twelve ships are lost, for sure. As for the rest, nothing's yet known. It's the most terrible rout of the whole war.'

'Dear God! And what about the *Almaz*?' gasped the hostess.

'My dear Maria Vasilyevna, I've told you all that I know. Andreyev says there's still no news on the *Almaz*. The *Oslyabya*, *Navarin*, *Uralets* and *Kamchatka* have gone down, as well as two anti-torpedo boats, and two, if not three transport ships. Admiral Nebogatov's been taken prisoner along with three thousand of his men. If anyone ever wanted to find the best possible way of ruining Russia . . . We're done for!'

'But is it definite? Who told Andreyev?'

'He got it straight from Zilotti. It's definite, unfortunately. Who ever heard of such a thing – sending a squadron to face certain death?' said San Sanych, flaring up. 'The fleet was a hotchpotch, and what did they do to ensure they had enough coal? Rozhestvensky even telegraphed some while ago . . . and next thing is he finds that he has to load his coal out at sea, which is why he went and got himself stuck in those straights at Tsushima, because he couldn't go round them.'

San Sanych was already using the mouthpiece of his pipe to outline on the table-cloth the direction in which the squadron had been sent, and showing how they should have gone round such a narrow spot. All the others followed his gestures in silence, but without really taking in what he was saying. From the entire squadron and the entire war, the matter of greatest concern to the hosts was the fate of the *Almaz*, on which Sergei was serving. The others, however, grasped the full gravity of the news immediately: Russia had lost the war. This time the defeat was final and irreversible. It was unthinkable. It was something nobody wanted to believe in.

'Even if you're right, San Sanych, is all really lost?' persisted Nikolai Nikitich, the librarian at the Commercial Assembly. 'I mean, we've had Port Arthur, and Liaoyang and Mukden, but even so . . .'

'Well, it's all over now, old chap! This time it's worse than all the rest of them put together. You simply can't understand it, you're not a naval man. But I've spent thirty years in the navy. Oh, what shame the Lord has let me live to see! Once they'd let the navy get into such a state, what on earth made them go and get involved in this war? They were too used to banking on sheer force of numbers . . . Maybe they could have got away with it on land, but at sea – come off it now! And as for that ghastly good-for-nothing bay at Port Arthur, what the heck did we need that for?' declared San Sanych indignantly.

'What did we need it for? What about the Yala concessions?'

Despite the tragic nature of the news, a ripple of laughter passed through the living-room. In Odessa the real cause of the war was regarded as an open secret. San Sanych went on to explain something further about the paramount role of the torpedo in modern warfare, and how proper account should have been taken of that, rather than laying such stress on the ships' guns when they had been equipping the navy, but by this stage Pavel could bear it no longer. He ran upstairs and slammed shut the door of his room. Here it was as though Russia had not been crushed, and everything was just the same as before – the scratched table, the rug and the light-blue wallpaper with seagulls on. The only light came from the oil-lamp under his grandfather's old icon. Pavel did not bother to light the main lamp. What, now, was the point?

For the first time in ages, he knelt down and ardently began addressing the almost indiscernibly dark face in the silver frame. 'Oh Lord! I ask you this as I have never asked you for anything ever before. Do something to make it untrue! And let us, let Russia crush Japan. The whole of Japan, once and for all. Oh Lord . . .'

He could feel that he was crying, but he still kept whispering something, making vows and oaths – anything, so long as Russia won.

He stood up exhausted, yet strangely calmed. This time it seemed to Pavel as though God, who was always remote and never easy to understand, had seen and listened to him.

Downstairs, after getting over the initial impact of the horror, everyone was now able to speak again.

'So what will become of it all, gentlemen?'

'Why, a constitution, of course! After all, things can't go on like this . . .' said Nina Borisovna, a teacher at the gymnasium, mounting her hobby-horse. She was renowned in Odessa as a radical, and for the outspokenness of her views on the government. This was why she had recently had to give up her place at the state-owned girls' gymnasium and take up a post in Mrs Krol's more liberal private school.

'Every sensible person has known for ages what a dead loss the monarchy is. All the more so, as you can't tell who's more incompetent – the Tsar or his ministers,' she averred, nervously straightening her only ornament, a medallion on a velvet ribbon which had turned over the wrong way. 'They've destroyed the second squadron, and if anyone shows they're at all bright and comes up with any ideas of their own, they stifle them . . .'

'Well now, ma'am,' said San Sanych, unexpectedly joining in, 'and just what did your bright people with ideas of their own get up to at the beginning of the war? Chucking bombs?

Organising disorder? A fat lot of good that did the country . . .
Give them freedom, and—'

'So what's to be done, seeing as any attempt to get things
changed is outlawed? It isn't that I support the terrorists, but,
if you think about it, they're giving their lives for Russia,
as well.'

'And there you have our tragedy, gentlemen,' interceded Dr
Dulchin. 'Everyone's ready to give their lives for Russia – why,
they're even yearning to. The terrorists think they're giving their
lives for Russia. And so do the people they're killing. Mere kids,
students who haven't even finished their courses want to go off
to war and die for Russia. So who's meant to save the country
– the dead? What you must realise is that, until we've learnt
how to work for Russia, rather than die . . .'

That night it was not until late that the last guests left the
Petrovs. The general opinion was that a constitution and some
major changes could now be expected.

Ivan Alexandrovich, a modern-thinking man, did not pray at
night. His attitude towards religion was one of formal decorum:
he attended church twice a year on the major holidays, and
considered that, for his part, this manifested a reasonable level
of tolerance. However, he found it necessary to encourage piety
in women, and it pleased him that Masha spent a long time
standing in front of the icon each evening. He was sure that he
could guess what she was praying for, and would have been very
surprised to discover how wrong he was. This evening, however,
he was not wrong. She was, indeed, praying for Sergei.

A few days later came definite news confirming the defeat.
But, even before then, all-knowing Odessa was seething with
indignation. There was pity for Admiral Rozhestvensky, who
had been sent to face certain death, and it was perspicaciously
thought that there would be an attempt to blame everything
on him. There were reports that Yung, the captain of *The
Eagle*, had shot himself together with his senior officer; that
half the sailors had mutinied – what else was to be expected of
'reserves'? – and that they had had to be tied up, leaving too
small a crew to continue the fight. There was outrage at the
fact that four ships had been surrendered to the enemy intact.
It was obvious that the regulars had mutinied as well: the city

knew the commanding officers involved, and the general view was that they were incapable of such a thing. The reports that Rozhestvensky had slipped through to Vladivostok proved to be unfounded. It was the *Almaz* that had broken through to Vladivostok. She was the first to report what had happened.

Sergei was alive.

The war was lost.

Shortly thereafter a rescript was published in the name of Grand Duke Alexei Alexandrovich, announcing his retirement from the navy. Before he had even received any decoration, Sergei Alexandrovich Petrov, a senior officer on the *Almaz*, resigned his commission. His pretext was a minor wound. It was not until half a year later that he calmed down enough to talk about his real reason.

Just as before, there continued to be a ridiculous Japanese soldier in the middle of the collapsing figures on the rifle ranges, and a good shot sent him reeling back head over heels. But the figure was no longer the target of fun that it had been.

2

A long booming noise was coming from somewhere above and it was growing louder and louder. It made you want to duck your head or get down on the pavement. Vladek's throat contracted and he held himself upright. Pavel was just about to huddle up when he saw his friend and threw out his chest. The next moment all the air round them shattered like a bowl of glass, the sky crashed down, and they heard and saw nothing else.

By the time they came to, they found themselves sitting on the blue cobble-stones, and someone was shouting, 'Hey, some school-kids have been killed!' And just then a second boom scudded over Nezhinskaya Street. It was the first time that the boys had ever heard shells fired, but once was enough to teach them that, for the time being, they'd better keep low. Away in the distance there was another roar, and then they got up and brushed down their light-grey summer uniforms. A bearded man wearing an apron with a badge (whom they vaguely guessed to be a yard-sweeper) was for some reason shaking them by the shoulders.

'Still in one piece, eh? That was the Lord's doing, what saved you then! Missed you by a hair's breadth, that did!'

And, after satisfying himself that they were no more than stunned, he promptly set off to join everyone else by the corner of the nearest building. As such, it had no corner. Dust and smoke were billowing up from it. Nearby on the road a horse lay floundering and rolling its eyes. A bewildered cabman was stamping up and down, trying to untangle the horse's harness. From the sympathetic murmuring of the crowd Pavel and Vladek realised that the horse had been hit by a piece of stone.

'Crikey! What a blood-bath!'

'It's gone clean through the vein. Get something to bind its leg, you idiot!'

'What on earth's going on? She could flatten the entire city!'

'Very easily. Those are nine-inch guns, you know. They can level anything to the ground.'

'She', of course, was the mutinous battleship *Potemkin*, currently anchored off the coast of Odessa. As to what had caused the mutiny, everyone had their own version. But it was common knowledge that the sailors had killed their officers, hoisted the red flag, and were now demanding something from the city. The boys had heard this last night, when they thought there wasn't even the slightest chance that their parents would let them go out.

Until bedtime Pavel stayed with his nanny Dasha. Every now and then Dasha started crying, as her son Vasily was a sailor on the *Potemkin*. But she had no idea what was happening on the *Potemkin*, and only lamented, 'Oh, my dear son, what is to become of it all?'

Her wrinkled cheeks quivered, and Pavel suddenly noticed that she had become an old woman, and was no longer the same cheerful and agile Dasha who had brought up all four of them.

This morning Pavel naturally said that he had been invited to see his class-mate Vladek Teslenko. Vladek told the same lie about Pavel, and they met on Nezhinskaya Street to go down to the port and find out exactly what was going on. As it turned out, their detour was pointless. The parents of a third friend, Yura Nezhdanov, had urgently sent him away to his grandfather at the German colony of Lilienthal. The Nezhdanovs had decided to stay put there until everything settled down. Poor old Yura, missing out on all this lot!

The bombardment appeared to be over. The streets were full of excited Odessans. But the panic, it should be said, was of a light-minded nature.

'Who fancies their luck, then! All right, folks, need a bit of luck, eh? Come on, Yasha, we can't have this lady fretting over trifles – fish something out of that lucky dip for her!' hollered a shabby-looking organ-grinder in a fit of inspiration. He had managed to pick a spot where he was sure to be in everyone's way. The small parrot Yasha started poking around among some little rolls of paper. As the lucky dip was faring so well, the canny organ-grinder had hiked up his ticket prices.

The boys cut across the Cathedral Square, where some mounted Cossacks were positioned. There was a lacklustre look in the Cossacks' eyes, in readiness should they have to disperse the crowd. The red stripes on their trousers rippled as the horses moved. Some people claimed that they were the ones at whom the *Potemkin* had, in fact, been firing. Others confidently dismissed this as nonsense. The real target was the City Theatre, where a military council headed by General Kaulbars was being held. In any event, the battleship had missed, and both shots had landed in housing areas.

'Regular marksmen, eh? Managed to hit their officers, all right!'

'Criminals, taking pot-shots at people like that!'

To Pavel it seemed as though the entire city, which until only an hour ago was still brimming with sympathetic curiosity, now hated the unfortunate *Potemkin*. He felt sorry for Dasha and her Vasily. But maybe Vasily was the one who had done the firing?

Pavel and Vladek did not mind the bombardment. It was far too exciting for that! They had reached Red Alley when Vladek tugged at Pavel's sleeve. 'Nosey!'

They both dived into the nearest gateway.

'Did he see us?'

'Who knows? Don't worry though – we'll soon know if he did.'

Nosov, the gymnasium inspector, was a niggly man. Of course, if he had spotted them they were done for. Not only would he send them straight back home, but, what was worse, he would escort them himself, and then hand them over to their parents in person. They held tight for a few minutes in a cosy little yard with some small Grecian verandas entwined in ornamental vine. But they were in luck, for when they cautiously peeped out, the inspector was no longer to be seen. Without any further adventures they reached the boulevard, with its red flower-beds now looking more and more parched beneath the June sun.

The battleship had three funnels, and how white and small it looked against the harshness of the blue. It stood far out to sea, in between the lighthouse and the end of the breakwater, and its appearance was anything but terrible. It seemed incredible to think that it could have flattened the entire city in an hour. Slightly disappointed, Pavel and Vladek set off back home. The streets were lined with carts and cabs that were cram-packed with possessions. The Nezhdanovs were clearly not the only ones who had decided to leave the city.

To Pavel's relief, his father had no intention of going. Back home, there was, of course, a scene, what with the place coming under fire and the boy going missing like that.

'But I told you where I'd be, Mama! I was next door with Vladek's family. We were looking at some books. How was I meant to know what was going to happen!'

'What took you so long, then? You knew how worried we'd be.'

'I'd have come straight home when the firing began, only Vladek's father stopped me. He said I had to stay put until he was sure the bombardment was over.'

'And thank God for that. He's an absolute saint,' said his mother, calming down.

However necessary it was for him to lie like this, Pavel still disliked it. He and Vladek had become friends back in the preparatory class, and now they were both in the fourth form, although never once had Vladek invited him to his home. They would accompany each other as far as Papudov's house, in which the Teslenkos rented their apartment, and then Vladek would say goodbye and Pavel head off home down Koblevskaya Street. There was some mystery here. Vladek was tall and thin with long eyelashes and a dimpled chin, and his standing in the class made it unthinkable to go pestering him with enquiries.

Whether it was because of his eyelashes or his refusal to take part in some prank, it was back in their first autumn at the gymnasium when the strapping Shmukler had called him a little girl. Vladek blanched and stood up. The ensuing fight drew blood, thus making it one of the gravest offences known at the gymnasium. A teachers' meeting was convened, and, in a quite unheard-of manner, a delegation of 'preppies' went to petition on Vladek's behalf. The idea was Pavel's, and he went to see the headmaster of the gymnasium in person and, with his throat parched in horror, he made a courageous speech. Attired in his dress-coat with its two rows of gold buttons, the headmaster was a gentleman as straight as a stick and with sideboards, and he had found it hard not to burst out laughing. Now, why was it that all the 'preppies' had ears that stuck out like that? To Pavel it seemed that the headmaster was having difficulty in keeping his temper, and that at any moment he would explode, and what might happen then was too ghastly to contemplate.

One way or another, the petition had its effect, and Vladek was rusticated from the gymnasium for a week. For a week there was no sign of Shmukler, either, though for a different reason. Pavel, of course, never said anything to Vladek about his role in all this. But when Vladek came back into the class a hero, it somehow seemed natural for them to share the same desk together, and – although they did not bother to ask their old desk-mates if it was all right – no one dared to object. Pavel was flattered, but there was still some sort of distance between them, and he felt slightly hurt by this.

The following morning, after some complex diplomacy, the friends managed to slip away from home. By now they realised that the harbour was the real focus of interest. That was where the body of the murdered sailor had been taken, and where the public rallies were taking place. Hordes of people were descending on it.

'He's on the Platonov Pier, I've just come back. Not a pretty sight, though, lying there butchered like that. There's blood all over the place!' the passers-by learnt from a gentleman of unkempt appearance (or a vagabond?), who was wearing odd boots and frayed trousers.

It turned out that he had been lying, for the real place to go was the New Pier. But the boys heard that the Cossacks had cordoned it off and were letting no one through. They went all the same, only to find that there was no sign of either soldiers or Cossacks. In fact, there was nothing to stop them from pressing on right the way to the end of the pier, where a makeshift tent had been pitched. It was in here that the sailor had been laid.

His face was grey, and his moustache wheaten-coloured. He looked very calm, and there was no sign of his wounds. He had a piece of paper pinned to his chest. This was the second time that Pavel had seen a dead person. The first time was when their class-mate Seryozha Sazonov had died of scarlet fever. All of them went to his funeral, with the snow and the piercing wind blowing in off the sea, while Seryozha had a strange smile on his face and was dressed up in his little coat that the gymnasium pupils wore as their best uniform. Pavel then realised that the dead looked like dolls, only they were not painted up. However, he was shoved aside before he had the chance to get a proper look at the sailor. But even if he had got a proper look, what difference would it have made? Pavel had never seen Vasily, and could not have recognised him even if it had been him lying there.

A spritely dark-haired sailor read out the appeal, as the sheet on the murdered man's chest was called.

'Comrades! The sailor Grigory Vakulenchuk was brutally murdered by an officer just for saying the bortsch was no good . . . Vengeance on the tyrants. Cross yourselves, and you Jews do it your way. Long live freedom!'

Then the people in the tent yelled 'Hurray!', and down the length of the dockside hundreds more voices took up the cry. The hatred of the previous day was quite forgotten. Or perhaps it was simply a different crowd down here in the harbour? This crowd had the smell of the docks to it – salt, wheat dust and dry roach. Here vagabonds mingled with the smartly-dressed. Some sort of gentleman in a cockaded military hat took it off even before he had set foot on the pier. Not so much out of respect for the dead, Pavel realised, as to hide his cockade. Here there was a collection bowl for the sailor's funeral expenses, and money kept pouring into it like rainwater.

Pavel had a ten-kopeck piece, and he gave it to Vladek. 'You're closer – chuck it in.'

Pavel knew from the gymnasium that Vladek never bought

any bread rolls or meat-balls for his breakfast. He just had a cup of tea.

Some long-haired young men were making a speech to the crowd, trying to persuade them to wait for instructions from the battleship and not to disperse. 'They're S-Ds,' Pavel heard the girl standing next to him say. But he felt silly asking what S-D stood for. And nothing else happened, though they were quite happy to go on waiting. Over and over again the appeal kept being read out to fresh cries of 'Hurray!'

It was not until several hours later that they managed to get away from the pier, and saw from above how many people were making their way down towards it from the city. There were students, railway workers, fishermen, women in headscarves and young ladies from the women's higher education college. It was a strange feeling – everyone was on the move, and they were with them.

When he reached Greek Street up at the top, Pavel suddenly saw Dasha in a dappled dress and raced over to her.

'Dasha! It isn't him!'

'Who isn't him?'

'The murdered sailor. It isn't Vasily, it's Grigory. Vakulenchuk. It's him they're collecting money for down there, so Vasily must be alive!' Pavel breathlessly blurted out.

'Oh, my darling! So that's where you raced off to!'

And, without pausing for thought, Dasha planted a kiss on his forehead in full view of everyone. If anything like this had happened before, Pavel would have burnt with shame. But now everyone was behaving unusually, and he saw everything in a different light. He even found Dasha's kiss pleasant. He assured her that no harm would come to the sailors, as there were not even any police there, and the people were all on the side of the mutineers. Vladek stayed patiently waiting, and Pavel did not see any trace of a sneer in his eyes. They reached the corner, where they usually said goodbye to each other, but felt that such an important day could not end so simply. They had to do something else, something that would match the tone of the solemn tragedy down in the port, the white battleship flying the red flag that was scarcely visible from the shore, something that fitted the stern wording of the 'appeal', and even its incoherent text.

'Vladek, let's . . . I know what – let's take an oath . . .'

'Yes, let's swear that, whatever happens, we'll always be for the sailors as long as we live!' Vladek exclaimed ardently.

Pavel immediately started mulling this over. There was something not quite right about it, and he had to hurry up and figure out just what it was. Given the way things had turned out, 'for the sailors' meant against the officers. But then what about Uncle Sergei? And what about General Kondratenko, who had been killed in Manchuria, and whose funeral the whole city had recently mourned? He had been brought up from the port on a gun-carriage, with his horse being led behind, and there could be no doubt that he was a hero who had given his life for Russia.

'Let's not say only for the sailors, but let's put it like this: always to be for the people!' he said, finding the right wording.

Vladek did not argue, and he even preferred it this way. So then and there, beneath the moulting acacias, they shook hands with one another. Now their lives were fixed. They could cross Cathedral Square feeling slightly shattered, and resigned to the leisurely rhythm of the summer evening. The florists on the corners were selling some peonies and early roses. The flowers swam in their heavy enamel jars, as if idly swishing their fins. The vast body of the cathedral looked more massive than ever against the background of the bright, though now deepening, blue of the sky. If only I could meet a girl with eyes that colour – Pavel thought for some reason.

Vladek also had something on his mind, and then he unexpectedly suggested, 'How about coming to my place?' And, clearly taking Pavel's astonishment for hesitation, he quickly added, 'Not for long. I know you're expected back home. I'll just introduce you to my family, seeing as we're virtually there now, anyway. And tomorrow evening you can come and have tea with us.'

The Teslenkos lived in a small second-floor apartment that was very clean but plainly showed that they were not well-off. As he was being introduced, Pavel for some reason felt embarrassed, although he was greeted as if he were a long-standing acquaintance.

'Pavel? We've heard so much about you,' said Vanda Kazimirovna, Vladek's mother, breaking into a smile.

For some reason Pavel thought Vladek did not have a mother. He had seen Vladek go to Christmas and Easter services at the same cathedral which his own family attended, and he was accompanied by a tall gentleman, probably his father, a girl with bright plaits, and a small boy who was about the same age as Maxim. But they never had a mother with them.

'You see, our mother's a Polish Catholic. But our father's Orthodox. They used to live in the Kholm region, but the Catholic and Orthodox communities there get on so badly that they simply never had any peace. Just like the Montagues and the Capulets. That was why they moved here. Mama goes to her Polish church, and we go to the cathedral. Of course, she worries about it,' explained Pavel, as he accompanied his friend home. 'But she shouldn't. No one bothers about that sort of thing here. All that really upsets her is that we're not Catholics – I mean us kids. But mother and father were the ones who wanted it this way. They reckoned we'd be better off like that. But if it had been left to me, I'd much sooner have Scripture classes with the Catholic priest than old Medvedev.'

Pavel burst out laughing. The entire class heartily loathed the Orthodox priest Medvedev, who pitilessly gave 'highly unsatisfactories' whenever his pupils made the slightest mistake in their Scripture texts. The Catholic pupils had the same lesson with Gubinsky, an old Catholic priest who never upset anyone and loved telling stories about Rome. He had been there twice and intended to go back and see it again. The rest of the class were jealous of the Catholics. But it was even better for the Jews because they simply had no Scripture classes whatever, and only had to get to school in time for the second lesson.

At home Pavel's mother was glad that he could at last give a coherent account of Vladek's family. The father was an engineer on the South-Eastern Railways, and the mother was a great music-lover who played the piano, while his sister was a really quiet (he took a meaningful look at Zina) and modest girl. Zina burst out laughing.

'And she's called Anna, and she's in the same class as me, and of course she kept quiet. You talk so much and never let anyone get a word in edgeways, especially if you're trying to charm someone. Now I'll tell her that you've been eyeing her up in the cathedral!'

Pavel was so indignant that he was left speechless. Vladek's sister was one of Zina's class-mates, and she had never even said a word about it! So that's how cagey the girl was – why, it was dreadful! And she was meant to be his sister. Now, Vladek had obviously struck it lucky. You could tell straight away that his Anna would never stoop to such a thing. Here he finally recovered himself.

'You know what you should do – copy your class-mate's example!'

The next evening, when Pavel was going to the Teslenkos, now as a guest invited for tea, he was vexed at how anxious he was, and, before ringing the bell, he wiped his sweaty palms on his trousers. But when Vladek came out to greet him with such candid delight, Pavel forgot all about his embarrassment. All the more so when Vladek immediately dragged him off to his room. It was roughly the size of a cabin, and the first thing that struck Pavel was a yellow wooden rocking-horse.

'That's Basya,' laughed Vladek. 'She used to be my horse, but now she's Antos's. He and I share this room together. But Anna has her own room,' he proudly stressed.

Wide-eyed Antos was thrilled to have a guest.

'Are you Vladek's friend? Have you got one of those school-hats with leaves on, as well? Here, I'll show you what I've got.'

From somewhere he dragged out a tall hat made from lambskin.

'It's a real Cossack *papakha*. And it's really old, too. My papa gave it to me, and his papa gave it to him!'

Antos clearly had his own plans, and was determined to press-gang the guest into going along with them and introduce him to all his treasures, but then tea was called. Vanda Kazimirovna gave her guests Polish *mazurkas* – home-made dried almond biscuits.

'Mama does all the Polish cooking herself – she doesn't trust the cook,' said Vladek with a wink. 'She doesn't trust Anna, either, and quite right, too!'

For some reason Antos burst out laughing, whereupon so did Anna.

'I tried doing them once,' she said. 'But Antos was the only one who could get his teeth into them. So he ended up with the entire lot!'

After tea Ivan Timofeyevich, the head of the family, kissed his wife's hand. 'Our most humble thanks to the lady of the house.'

This struck Pavel as very beautiful. His own father never kissed his mother's hand after supper. It was probably some Polish thing ... But Ivan Timofeyevich was Ukrainian. So maybe it was Ukrainian.

'Papa, are you going to sing to us today?' asked Antos, jumping up from the table.

'Another time, son. I'm tired today. We've had some trouble at work.'

'Was there a strike?' asked Antos, knowingly.

'Not yet. But I don't want to talk about it! I'd sooner have Anusya read to us for a while.'

And again Pavel was taken aback at the way in which he talked to the little boy. It was as though he were an equal. His own father never talked about his affairs with any of them.

The only light in the room came from the one green lamp – the same ordinary lamp that half of Russia used, with its heavy base and arched glass shade. Without either refusing or making a fuss over it, Anna went and fetched a book. It seemed that the members of this family just never got embarrassed, and were as comfortable with each other as they were with themselves.

'Where did we stop last time, Antos?'

'Where the Jew dressed Taras up and led him out on to the square.'

This was Gogol's *Taras Bulba*, a book which Pavel was himself fond of. But it was obviously the first time that Anna had read it, and she found it disturbing. She tried to read it in a steady voice, but when she got to the point of Ostap's execution, Pavel felt how hard it was for her. Her voice shook, though she immediately steadied herself and bravely went on. Antos was listening with blazing eyes, but their parents' minds were elsewhere. By now Anna had reached the last pages.

'But the cruel Cossacks heeded none of it and, lifting the babies up off the streets with their lances, they hurled them, too, into the flames. "That's in memory of Ostap, you accursed Poles," said Taras.'

At this point she sobbed, jumped up and, leaving the book lying open on the sofa, ran out of the room. Pavel could hardly breathe. He could scarcely race off and follow this strange girl up to her room to wipe away her tears and then stay by her side until a smile returned to her face. This was the first creature that he had ever wanted to protect from all the world's tears, but what could he do about Gogol? Why had he never noticed what a cruel book it was? Of course, all that the Ukrainians and Poles ever did in it was to go round killing one another, and, really, what sort of stuff was that for a girl from a family like this?

The way to Koblevskaya Street was so short that Pavel took a detour. Then he took another. He did not feel like going home, where everything would be as drab as ever. Could she really be the same age as Zina, that Anna? She seemed so much older. She was a friend's sister, and maybe that was all there was to it? A friend's sister.

3

It took them a long time to smash into the small shop, as it had a strong door and a grille over the window. The befuddled yells with which they started breaking into it were soon replaced by a short and business-like exchange.

'Mitro, wrench it with the crow.'

'It won't give. Ah, these pampered Yids with their bloody locks!'

'Come o-on. Hold it . . . the poxy thing's coming!'

Even if they did look flushed, these men were not drunks, and they worked briskly. Their immediate concern was getting at the goods rather than having fun, for this was a jeweller's shop.

Isaak Geiber stood lifeless. Perhaps that was why nobody noticed him. He had been ignored both by these men, with their strong necks and boots spotlessly polished since first thing in the morning, and by the horde of vagabonds and shrieking women whom they had driven away from the booty, and by the mounted Cossack patrol that had gone studiously riding past in full dress uniform. All that remained of Isaak's hopes was now ruined. The move to Kishinyov, a place at the gymnasium for Yakov, his position of respect at the synagogue, and a decent tombstone for Shimek in Odessa's Jewish Cemetery.

A fight broke out by his smashed door, and some woman in a crimson headscarf had managed to grab hold of a clasp mounted in blue velvet. But Isaak stood still, and just his eyes – the only feature that he had inherited from his father – went on dying.

His little son Yakov was meanwhile merrily running home, and so excited that he occasionally jumped up in the air. And with reason! Today was the first time that he had seen a kite fly, and for a brief but blissful moment he had even been allowed to hold the string.

'Little Yid, little Yid – what's your age, funny kid?'

There was an unpleasant, menacing tone of endearment in this voice, and Yakov froze on the spot. But it turned out that the towering owner of the colossal shadow cast over him was someone he knew well, the cobbler Simonenko. Yakov had occasionally been sent to get shoe-laces from him, or some polish, and the cobbler always smiled and sang something, and on one occasion he even gave Yakov a green sweet in the shape of a cockerel.

Yakov smiled timidly.

'Uncle Simonenko, it's me, Yakov!'

To his horror, however, Simonenko was a different man today, and he had a strange and terrible smell to him. They were the only ones in this quiet back street with its yellow burdocks. Yet Simonenko did not recognise him. Or he pretended not to. Yakov was terrified by the silent Sunday sun and Simonenko's gleeful white eyes.

'You're lying, you're not Yakov, you're a little Abram. So out with it – what's your age, little Abram?'

'Six, Uncle Simonenko. You know that . . .'

Yakov felt that he had to keep answering. He had to smile and keep this strange game going. If he put a foot wrong, by breaking into tears or calling for his mama, then something terrible would happen – even more terrible than this.

'I'm not your sodding uncle. Now what's little Abram got in that bag there?'

'A bay leaf. My mama sent me to get it,' Yakov found he had to explain. 'We've got guests coming today.'

'So his mumsy's got guests, has she? Ooh, isn't that ni-ice, and what dances there'll be!'

Simonenko grabbed hold of the little bag. A few hard leaves fell on to the white dust. He tried to screw up the ones that were left into some sort of objects.

'You know what these are, little Abram? Pigs' ears. You do like pigs' ears, don't you? Here – let's try them on.'

He grabbed Yakov by the hair, and took his time as he set about shoving something hard and prickly into his ears. It hurt, but Yakov put up with it and tried not to blink. If he did as he was told, all would be well. What he was most afraid of was wetting his pants. And Simonenko really did let go of him.

'That looks better! And now, little Abram, dance!'

Yakov was sensible enough not to try and run away: under his arm the cobbler had a stick with an iron hook driven into it, and now he took a better hold of it. Yakov forced a pained smile and started jumping as best as he could.

'Hop-tsa-tsa! Hop-tsa-tsa,' Simonenko sang along. 'Come on, little Abram, look lively there!'

He was trying, Yakov vaguely felt, to work himself up into the right mood for something. But he had not yet reached the required pitch. Yakov was now jumping over the stick more and more often. The hook was painfully catching his legs. Just so long as it did not tear his new suit. If that happened, then all was lost.

And at this point a third person appeared in the back street: Simonenko's wife. Her woollen jacket was undone, and she was breathing heavily.

'So that's where you are, you curse of my life! Over on Okhotnitskaya Street everyone's helping themselves to boots, and linen and shawls. And here you are fooling around with some little Yid! They're about to lug the entire lot off up there! Mikhaila's had to fetch a cart for his load, and what is it you get up to? Lord, what some wives have to put up with!'

'Coming, Katya, coming. I'll just give little Abram here a goodbye kiss. By-ee!'

Simonenko thrust his open snout forward, but at this point Yakov screamed and made a determined dash for it. It was the right moment. Simonenko saw no point in racing after a boy when he would sooner hurry off to Okhotnitskaya Street, where anyone with any sense in their heads was busy helping themselves to the goods now up for grabs in the Jewish shops.

Gasping for breath and running all the way, Yakov kept whimpering, 'Mama! Mamochka . . .'

But when he got home he found that it, too, was terrible and unrecognisable. Just like Simonenko and everything else had become. Some strange grown-ups were busy smashing the windows. A fat woman was coming out from where the door used to be clutching a bundle wrapped up in an orange velvet table-cloth. And something white kept flying around, and it stuck to his suit and clung to his eyelids. This was another world from the one in which Yakov had lived before.

So that was how God punished boys who went dashing off to watch Vaska fly his kite instead of running straight home once they had got their bay leaves.

He no longer knew where to run to, and his tears prevented him from seeing properly. But, even so, he had not made a mess of his suit. Good Lord, had he really not made a mess of his suit? Apparently not, because there, as he rounded the corner, by now deafened by the terror and noise, he saw his mother running along. And he burst out crying loud and proper, and buried his head into her soft tummy. Rakhil grabbed her son in her arms like a baby and carried him off somewhere, and after that Yakov probably fell asleep.

That morning it had not sunk in when Rakhil first heard Madam Dombach, the wife of the telegraph-operator, talk about it. What pogrom? How – I ask you – could there possibly be a pogrom, now that there was the Tsar's manifesto, the constitution, and everyone had become equal? And where could she go, if she had to leave home with the fish still in the oven, and Isaak about to bring home his guest, and her boy not yet back from the shop?

But the dim hubbub from somewhere down on the streets below was getting louder and louder, and by now shooting could also be heard. She had to save the children, and only then did Rakhil realise what was happening, and she rushed over to kiss the hands of Madam Dombach, who lost no time in saying, 'Hurry, hurry. I'll take the girl, and you find the boy and then come and join us straight away. Your husband will guess that you've come to us.'

Rimma, who was always an obstinate girl, now obediently followed this Russian woman, while Rakhil went tearing round the local streets. An eternity passed before she found Yakov. Now, behind the life-saving little gate with a cross chalked on it, behind the windows crammed full of icons, she could at last turn her attention to the child.

'He'll soon get over it. Someone gave him a nasty fright,' said the hostess, reassuringly.

'I'll bring some vinegar.'

She had already dressed Yakov's temples, and the boy really did start sobbing as he came round again.

'Vera Nikolayevna! What a saint you are!'

'Knock it off, Rakhil. Give him a hot drink. The samovar's over there. Well, how are you, dearie? Any better? Now, there's a clever boy. And good for your Rimma – what a brave girl she is!'

Eleven-year-old Rimma was quietly sitting as told, and her eyes were livid and blazing. From the distant streets shooting could be heard. She had learnt from Vera Nikolayevna that the youngsters from the Jewish community had formed a self-defence group. And several students who happened to be in the city were also there, including the Dombaches' son. They were trying to stop the thugs. Oh, if only she could be there with them, and have a shot at those ugly goyish mugs . . . That was no way to think. The student Dombach was also goyish, from one of the houses with icons. But, as for the rest – shoot the entire lot. Every last one of them should be killed. Oh, why wasn't she a boy? She would have gone running off to join them, she would have been there helping them, she would have . . . At this point their mother, who had calmed down over Yakov, embraced her, too, and the three of them sat together like this, waiting for it to end. In the same little room, with its single window out on to the yard – the most secluded place in the house – there was also the hunchbacked glazier Shaya and his family, along with their neighbour, Etel, and her baby girl. Vera Nikolayevna smiled cheerfully as she gave some biscuits round to her guests. The children took them without lifting their eyes, and ate them carefully so as not to get any crumbs on the parquet floor.

'What wonderful, quiet children you have, Shaya!' Madam Dombach observed in delight.

'Don't talk to me about these little bandits. It's taken nothing short of a pogrom to make that lot quiet. That's life for you, Madam Dombach, we were there in Kishinyov for that earthquake – you remember the one, they even reported it in the papers? But no, the earthquake wasn't enough for this lot. It's the first time in my life that I've ever seen them quiet, if you want to know,' chuckled Shaya.

Lucky Shaya considered that he was obliged to keep the others entertained: his entire family, including even his aged grandmother, were here with him. But what could he do for the women who had a son, or husband, or possibly – like Etel – a father now out in the thick of the street-fighting? So he cracked his little jokes, and the women dutifully smiled.

Now Rakhil understood that Isaak was unlikely to have guessed that this was where she had come to hide, and she just hoped that he was sitting tight somewhere, and Shaya promised that later on he would go and look for him. But it was almost the evening of the next day before everything quietened down. Either the authorities finally intervened, or else the October rain that had been falling since Monday managed to cool the passions of the town of Nikolayev.

It was not until the Tuesday that Isaak was found, by which time they were with the cabman Meyer, whose home had remained intact. It was old Meyer himself who brought Isaak in by the hand, like a child. He was shaking his head and looking about in surprise, though he came obediently. Rakhil gasped and began wailing. Isaak smiled absent-mindedly.

'Is that you, Rokhl? And the children are here, too. How nice. You clever girl. But what about Shimek? Where's Shimek?'

'Isaak, for the love of God, think what you're saying! Don't frighten the children like that!'

Shimek, the Geibers' first son, had died from meningitis when they were still living in Odessa, and he had been buried before Yakov was born. But Isaak could no longer remember any of this.

'Rokhl, tell me the truth. Where's Shimek? Have those goyim killed him?'

Huddled together in the corner, Rimma and Yakov watched as their father kept walking round the room and bumping into the chairs. His broad shoulders brushed some little vases off the chest of drawers and on to the floor, and he kept breaking away from their mother's arms. Then he embraced the bedside table with the spiral oak stand and pressed it to his cheek.

'Shimek, my boy. Look at Papa. How you've grown. You're

not going into the army, you can play better than Misha Elman
. . . The Tsar's written a manifesto all about you . . .'

Isaak was burning all over, and it took Meyer and Rakhil,
who was now speechless with grief, no small effort to put him
to bed. God was gracious to Isaak. He did not suffer for long.
Just before the end he almost came to and managed to say
something to Rakhil. Though no one heard what.

Yakov, who was now the man of the family, did everything
just as Rabbi Movshe had taught him. Not once did he falter as
he read the Kaddish over his father's grave. He did not cry, and
he held his mother by the elbow as they left the cemetery. And
he broke the Sabbath bread when his mother lit the candles on
that, their penultimate evening in Nikolayev.

The steamboat went through some yellow water, and that
was the Bug. Then came the Black Sea, which really was black,
because by then it had grown dark. Then a bright ruby-coloured
light began twinkling. This was the lighthouse. Beyond it began
Odessa – the fabulous city about which Yakov and Rimma had
heard so much from their parents. Their father used to be a
balagula, with his own cab and horse, but later stopped making
such long journeys and started taking the cargo to the port.
There the men amused themselves with bets as to who could
lift the most sacks in one go, and the women were incredibly
beautiful. It was there that their amazing brother Shimek had
mastered the violin by the age of five, and the name for that
was 'wunderkind'. He had toured various cities giving concerts,
and papa got rid of his horse and carriage and went on tour
with him. They had been in Warsaw, and Vilno, and Vienna,
and Shimek had earned piles of money in his black velvet suit
playing his special little violin. But then Shimek died, because
a boy like him was too clever for this world. And then mama
and papa left Odessa. But now here it was again. Above the sea
hung a vast number of lights, and that was where they were
going – in the direction of those lights.

Nobody met Rakhil, despite the fact that Meyer had written
to some acquaintances in Odessa. But, although it was late,
there was still a crowd of cabbies down by the jetty. Rakhil,
who had spotted an unmistakable Jew among them, with his
locks flowing down from his hat, started haggling with him. The

only boarding-house with a decent reputation that she knew of in Odessa was on Dalnitskaya Street.

'Are you crazy, woman? Dalnitskaya's miles from the port. You know how much that's going to cost you?'

The cabman quoted an exorbitant fare, and Rakhil planted her hands on her hips.

'I would be interested to know,' she began with deceptive meekness, 'whether you have already renounced your Judaism, young man, or are merely toying with these Christian ways?'

'Now why get shirty with me, madam? I give her the best advice possible, and she goes and gives me an earful!'

The cabman went over to the defensive, but Rakhil's voice was gathering the strength of her youth.

'So, if you haven't sold out to the goyim, let our Jewish God send you some of our Jewish luck! For shamelessly fleecing a widow and her two children.'

Rakhil was already aware that the money that had been collected for her in Nikolayev was unlikely to last for three months, as she had calculated that it would. She had forgotten what these Odessan prices were like. Yet she was in no position to make concessions, so the cabman was the one to yield. Without daring to utter a word, he drove them right across the city.

Yakov was thrilled. It wasn't every day that boys were taken out on cab rides, and, what's more, through such smart areas! To him it looked like a city in which no one ever went to bed. And it had such wonderful roads! And so much light! To crown it all, there in the distance over the shoreline, and rising like a fantastic star, was a rocket. It flew in a gently sloping arc, throwing out spectacular clusters of lights. Beyond it, three large flares suddenly started whirling round. All of them went twisting up into the sky. And then there were so many colours which appeared so magical that Yakov did not know where to look.

'What's that? Mama, what is it?'

'Fireworks. I'd like to know quite what they're celebrating,' Rakhil answered briefly.

The smart areas gradually receded, and Monya Shpayer's boarding house, where the compliant cabman unloaded their things, proved to be wholly unlike the palace that the children were expecting. Rakhil, however, was satisfied. She found out that, although there was a room for them, Monya himself would not be there until tomorrow, and she slipped a deposit to the bearded manager, put the children to bed, and sang them their favourite song about a nanny-goat, some raisins and some almonds.

She did not regret leaving Nikolayev for a minute. Her exhausted heart was pounding with maternal distractions. Here, in Odessa, a decent city, she would be able to set the children up on their own two feet. Even if no one helped her. She gave no thought to what she would do, but she had no doubt that something would come along. And it was the first night since that Sunday that she fell straight into a sound sleep.

4

It still looked dark through the windows, and it was somehow an unpleasant darkness. Not a deep blue, but a dank grey, and it also looked as if it was raining. At any rate it was foggy. The clippety-clop of French verbs . . . The Punic Wars – the First, the Second . . . Just counting them was enough to send you to sleep. To sleep. What's the French for marmot? What nonsense – they don't have any marmots there, Anna thought angrily and she finally woke up.

From her brothers' room Antos's little voice could be heard singing: 'I've wandered far in many lands, And with me went my marmot . . .'

The next thing to be heard was a scuffle and some laughter. Well, that was obviously Antos waking up Vladek and being fought off with a pillow. Anna was quickly weaving her plaits and thinking how nice it would be not to have to go to the gymnasium. Lucky Antos! And he did not even know his own luck, getting up at the crack of dawn. Just so he could have his morning tea together with his brother and sister, as if he were big now.

For part of the way Vladek and Anna shared the same route. But previously Vladek always used to be in a hurry to get off and was keen to say goodbye to her by the gates.

'Because men walk quicker,' he explained. Only now it was the opposite, and he accompanied her almost the entire way to the Butovich Gymnasium before leaving her and heading off to the Richelieu Gymnasium. Anna did not know what had got into him. But it was simply that their father had had a word with Vladek on a matter that was to be kept secret from the ladies. He had told him that these were now times when nobody knew what to expect. There were anarchists with bombs – for example, for no reason at all Dietman's café had been blown up, and the police-officer Panasyuk had been murdered, and the railways brought to a standstill, and goodness knew where those hordes of tramps out on the streets came from. Not that Anusya had far to go, of course. And, by and large, for the time being it was safe. But, even so he, his father, would be obliged if Vladek would keep an eye on his sister. His father had sounded sombre and looked tired.

For the time being he had stopped going to work. Reluctant to get caught up in politics, he was not supporting the strike, but neither had he been involved in any arguments with the workers, until the occasion when all the switches at the Odessan Goods Station were disabled. That was something Ivan Timofeyevich could not stand: such barbarism! And he took an active part in establishing the circumstances, and, at the same time, getting the system back to work. A brick thrown from the dark by an unidentified assailant had broken his collar-bone, and he had been given sick-leave from work. But the family's entire well-being depended on his earnings, and, although his parents bravely kept on smiling, Vladek felt their alarm. For the first time he noticed that his father's hair had turned grey. Well, that meant it was time for him, Vladek, to grow up. He swallowed hard, and agreed to do as his father had asked of him. His image of the pleasures of adult life had certainly not included keeping an eye on his sister. And what would Pavel think about being left with no companion?

However, it soon became clear that guarding the fair sex was something that Pavel took seriously. Without fail he would meet her at the corner of Koblevskaya Street, and the minute he set eyes on Anna he would grow an inch in stature, preen himself, and generally, as Zina put it, 'start posing'. But he remained taciturn. Just as anyone would have been in Zina's presence, with those enormous mocking eyes of hers. Yet how could he shake her off, given that she and Anna went to the same classes?

So they had to go as a foursome. Now why couldn't she go and fall in love with Vladek, Pavel thought spitefully. It would serve her right. Vladek was well-known as a 'ladies' man', and, as he freely admitted to Pavel, he fell in love roughly once every three weeks. Each time keeping a respectful distance, and each time for the rest of his life. His last sweetheart had worked in a circus and performed somersaults on the back of a horse. But she had recently fallen off her horse and the circus hand who came rushing to hoist her back up had, by chance or design, brushed the blonde wig from her head. And beneath her wig the beautiful lady had turned out to be bald, with a few sparse tufts of black hair on her naked skull. The spectacle was more than Vladek's heart could endure, and now it had a position vacant – until the next one came along. But it did not look as if that was going to be Zina. She and Vladek were forever cracking jokes about one another and everything else in the world, as if they were the ones that were brother and sister. Come to that, maybe Zina, with her impossible character, was incapable of falling in love with anyone? The way she's going she'll end up punished as an old maid, thought Pavel with satisfaction.

Anna knew nothing of all these complex reckonings. She just walked along in her little green school coat with its black cape, nattering with Zina while keeping one ear on the boys' discussion of football. They were all absolutely mad about football, they called shoes 'boots', and running about 'sport' – thank goodness that a ball, at least, was a ball, rather than anything else. She realised that she was slightly envious, and she burst out laughing.

Hanging on the wall by the corner there was a scrap of paper that was sodden through with light rain, but they paid no attention to it.

'To mark His Majesty's manifesto granting civilian freedoms, for the next three days there will be no classes at the gymnasium,' the class tutor told the girls after they had curtsied and sat down. 'You are all to go home, and do try not to get as overexcited as the grown-ups.'

As far as Anna could remember, she never smiled, their 'Madam Bonton'. Laughter only ever appeared in her eyes and voice.

'Well, that figures,' Zina remarked to this, 'the grown-ups have probably got their freedom for ever, whereas all we get is three days of it!'

They took immediate advantage of their freedom: they flew down the gymnasium staircase, although this was most strictly forbidden. The rain had stopped, and a cluster of people had gathered around the sodden scrap of paper. Someone even started singing the 'Marseillaise'. Anna and Zina would have liked to go and see what was written on it, for by now they realised that this really was a government manifesto. Yet, for all their new-found freedom, they still felt it unseemly to go barging in amongst the crowd. So they went to Zina's house, where they could ponder at leisure on how to take best advantage of this stroke of luck that had so unexpectedly befallen them.

The Petrovs' home was already in the grip of that excitement about which 'Madam Bonton' had, presumably, been warning them. It was not that the Petrov parents had really taken in the likely significance of what had happened. But there was a kind of unsettling thrill, a sense of great occasion. Russia would never be the same again, and it was going on at this very moment, in front of their very eyes! That evening, of course, the guests would be coming. Maria Vasilyevna was giving instructions to the cook. Ivan Alexandrovich went pacing round the living-room singing something from *Tosca*, but then he could bear it no longer, and he put on his coat and announced that he was going out for a stroll.

The girls slipped into Zina's room without the younger children noticing them. It would have been silly to start asking the parents questions now. Such phrases as they had heard of the manifesto were not very intelligible. They made themselves comfortable on the crimson sofa with its enormous number of round cushions.

'Anya, what do you think freedom of conscience means?'

'I don't know. Nina Borisovna said it means everyone praying as they like, each according to their beliefs. We Russians pray to our God, the Jews pray to the Jewish God, and then there are the Muslims, who pray to Allah. But best of all, she said, would be if no one prayed. Though I'm not sure that I understood her properly, because anyway she never crosses herself when she walks past an icon. There must be something more to it.'

'She obviously got a bit muddled somewhere. Everyone has always prayed as they like, and there are different churches, and mosques, and synagogues. What's it got to do with freedom?'

'That's just what I think,' sighed Anna. 'If it's a matter of conscience, then what's freedom got to do with it? That's forbidden, this is forbidden, go there, do that. And if you try to ignore it you're eaten up by that very same conscience, and you lie awake crying at night. And you know what Natasha told me about why Mila Stetsko in the sixth class has eyelashes like that – you know why? She smears them with Vaseline! She smears them when she goes to bed at night, and then in the morning she wipes them clean again and nobody ever knows anything about it.'

'So how come Natasha knows?' asked Zina sceptically. This subject kept them busy for a long time, and they did not notice the commotion, excitement and exclamations going on downstairs.

When, finally, they went down to the living-room, bursting with plans for the next three blissful days, they came to a sudden standstill, blinded by an apparition from the doorway. For there, in the living-room, was a magnificent-looking naval officer. He was wearing a uniform with gold braid, and had an astounding moustache. And he was laughing at something, with Maxim already settled on his knees and playing with his dirk, which looked like a black crucifix with gold.

'Uncle Sergei!' shrieked Zina, and she went tearing over towards him, but, becoming embarrassed, she came to a halt in the middle of the room.

'My God. Can it really be Zina? And already in school uniform ... So you're going to the gymnasium? Wait a minute – how old are you?' the officer asked in surprise. He got up, for some reason awkwardly cradling the back of Maxim's head, as though he were a baby.

'Eleven. But nearly twelve. Hey, Uncle Sergei, you look so ... I mean you look just like a real naval officer!'

Uncle Sergei had, of course, turned out to be the most remarkable adult that they could possibly have ever imagined. He formally introduced himself to Anna, treating both of them, and even Marina, as ladies, and naturally omitted to ask any such dreary questions as 'how are your studies?'

Throughout the entire evening Ivan Alexandrovich glowed with festivity, although, in the depth of his soul, he felt that his brother had unwittingly relegated him, the man of the house, to a position of secondary importance. Naturally, they had guests, all of whom were in high spirits as they discussed the manifesto and felt they were participants in a great historical turning-point. For some reason Sergei shunned these discussions, although it was he, more than anyone else, to whom everyone addressed their remarks.

It was not until after midnight that the brothers got down to any real talking, when they were left on their own together.

'I don't see what you're so cock-a-hoop about, Ivan. Can't you see what all this is leading to?'

'My dear chap, you always were a sceptic. It's a wonderful manifesto, and it's a pity it was such a long time in coming. This is a victory for free thought in Russia, or the first victory of any substance, at any rate.'

'But free thought must at least have some idea of where it's heading, surely? This is the beginning of the end!'

'So you're prophesying the end of the world, are you?'

'Just the end of Russia. It may be dragged out for a time. But it's irreversible. And it's the Tsar's doing! I'll admit I wasn't expecting it.'

'Sergei, what's this I'm hearing? You're the one who's always been the family monarchist!' said Ivan with an ironic grin, stubbing out his cigarette.

'That's precisely my reason! Because I revere the monarch as God's anointed, and believe that he has the right and duty to determine the fate of Russia. Duty, you understand? And if the Tsar lets the country slide into ruin, then he is in breach of that duty. We can all of us be blind, but he has no such right! Unless, that is, the Almighty has decided to make him the instrument of Russia's demise. Which is possibly no more than we deserve – I won't argue with that. But to make whoopee while we dig our own grave?'

Sergei's face was faintly illuminated by the desk lamp, and the shadows of his straight nose and deep eye-sockets almost made him look like an old man. And here he was talking of graves . . . Watching his tortured face, Ivan suddenly felt a heart-rending longing to see the cheerful, long-legged Seryozha peer out from it, that same brother, only a year his junior, who just before they used to go to sleep would invariably come and sit on Ivan's bed and happily natter about important and unimportant things. Not that there were any matters lacking importance back in those days. So now Sergei really had become a sailor, and one way or another, Ivan had not become an aeronaut.

'Come on, Seryozha, old chap, why so gloomy?'

'Let me tell you then. I'll say this now, and then never come back to it again. Don't worry, there won't be any "I told you so's". But now listen. The country's in a state of ruin and disorder. Who's unhappy? The peasants are burning the estates – yet there isn't a word about land in the manifesto. As for the Socialists – well, nothing will ever satisfy that lot. And the Jews – well, the Pale of Settlement still hasn't been done away with, has it? So everyone that's unhappy now is going to stay that way. This isn't a revolution yet. But it's a foretaste of it. It's a trial run at those bloody and drunken outrages that our intelligentsia have been itching for. And now they're here they sweetly pine away, like some damsel. What's more, the manifesto gives the impression of having been forced on the government. And that's exactly how it'll be seen. As a timid retreat and an invitation to yet more revolts in future. Come on, lads, it's all right now! Everyone who supports the revolution, as well as those who are opposed to it – and I take it you agree that there are quite a few such opponents? – will now go and fight it out amongst one another on the streets. And the next thing we'll have is the troops, police and Cossacks trying to keep them from one another's throats. Inevitably, there will then be a backlash against the government – "as victim ye fell in the fateful fight" – and the whole lot'll be blamed on the Tsar. They'll claim he promised freedom and never gave it. And it'll start tomorrow. Not in a figurative sense, but literally.'

'What day is it tomorrow? The nineteenth of October? Just you wait and see. And I'd advise you to take Masha and the children and come and stay with me out at the Fountain for about three weeks. I've already had the place heated and tidied up. I sent Nikita on ahead to get it ready for my arrival.'

'Well, you could at least have told me?'

Ivan was almost affronted. All the time that Sergei had been away at sea, Ivan had been responsible for looking after his brother's house at the Fountain. It was true that he had not spent long there himself, but he had kept himself abreast of the servants' reports to ensure that everything was kept in order.

'I didn't even know myself that I would be coming back so soon. After all, I was expecting to go and make a report on battleships to the Naval Ministry. I thought they would listen to me as I've just seen them in action. And what sort of guns pierce what sort of armour – I actually know. But not a bit of it! Imagine, they're going ahead with another two battleships with the same old seven-and-a-half-inch armour . . . But I can see you couldn't care less.'

'No, no, not at all . . . go on, Seryozha.'

'What is there to go on about? I thought I'd be there for another week, manage to collar someone or other and then get what I was after. But then I realised I was wasting my time. Well, gentlemen – if you're bent on destroying the fleet, then go ahead and do so without me. And then I came straight to you, out of the blue. Where are you going to put me to sleep?'

'Come on then, your bed's made up and waiting!' laughed Ivan. 'I've heard more than enough of you and your Apocalypse – but how good to see you!'

They made their way upstairs to the bedroom by the corner. Despite the fact that the double frames had already been put over the windows, the sprawling horse-chestnut could be heard tossing in the wind, the same tree that the children believed to be a hundred years old.

'Shall I stay up here with you till you've gone to sleep?' asked Ivan, and they both burst out laughing.

'I can scarcely clamber into bed with you nowadays. You have a wife! She's lovely, and the children are so wonderful, too. Listen, you don't believe a word of what I'm saying . . . Well, let's put it like this: if anyone gets killed in the city tomorrow – no matter whose side they're on – then let's have no further argument: I'm taking you all to my place.'

'Seryozha, just think what you're saying. The children still have to go to the gymnasium, haven't they?'

'There won't be any classes at any gymnasium anywhere!

And there's no point in their being here to see the start of it all. And even less to hear it. Enough. So that's settled – I have your word.'

In the morning there was a rumour that several Jews had been killed on Dalnitskaya Street. It was claimed the killings had been carried out by policemen in disguise in retaliation because the Jews had stamped on the Tsar's portrait in a tavern somewhere. The city governor had issued a plea for calm. Shortly before lunch the all-knowing Dasha informed her employers that a patriotic demonstration was on its way up from the port into the city, and that the Jews would be buried beneath red flags right there, in Cathedral Square, and that the Duma had supposedly authorised this. It was, of course, rubbish. But if it were believed for so much as a minute, then it meant that the demonstration and the funeral procession were about to meet head-on virtually outside their house, and they were reluctant to imagine what the likely outcome of that would be.

Ivan gave in and let Sergei make the arrangements for their departure, while he went to issue instructions to the servants who were to stay behind at the house.

5

It was amazing – they were there, living right by the seaside
smack in the middle of autumn. As Pavel imagined it, the sea was
always something associated with holidays and summer-time.
Not, of course, that it disappeared anywhere in winter – he
could see it from Nikolayevsky Boulevard. But then it was
simply somewhere that he didn't really think about. There
would be days when people said that 'the bay's frozen over'.
There then followed the strictest parental ban on running down
to the port and getting any ideas about testing the ice. And there
wasn't even any temptation to break this command. There was
ice at the ice-rink, the Palais-Royale. And, by and large, real
life took place in the city, where there was the circus, the
gymnasium, and Christmas. There were a lot of holidays in
winter and autumn. The small multicoloured lights that lay
strung out between the trees were lit. The damp, black branches
trailed off into the mist, and the next row of lights made the mist
itself look green, pink and blue. The city became smaller, more
toy-like, and cosier. It was good to read books about faraway
journeys and doze off to sleep in a warm room over a map of
America.

But out here it was simply another world. There were deserted
precipices all covered in wormwood and gorse, and the house
miles from anywhere. And the main feature of this world was
the sea. It was there, right next to them, beneath the precipice,
so close that you could smell it. And it was constantly audible.
It sounded as if an enormous animal were heaving its heavy
sides and forever making unsuccessful attempts to get itself
comfortable. The moment they arrived Uncle Sergei said there

would be a storm that night, and that he would take them down to the shore to watch it. Their mother was so taken aback that she was unable to find any objections.

They were all, even Maxim, wrapped in heavy waterproofs that smelt of gutta-percha, and they made their way down the stone steps with a lantern – downwards, into the darkness and the roar. They had got as far as the cliff, which smelt pungently of the sea and, for some reason, gunpowder, when Uncle Sergei said they should go no further. So there they stood, on the cliff. Sergei extinguished the lantern, whereupon it turned out that it was not so dark after all, and they could see everything. The waves were pitch-black and kept pounding into the shore like artillery fire. Then everything exploded in white foam and went climbing up to an astonishing height. The sky was invisible. To Pavel it seemed that at any moment he would find that he was flying, that in fact he already was flying – into this bliss, and terror and roar. Uncle Sergei burst out laughing and yelled something, but Pavel was deafened and he neither understood nor wanted to understand. He and the sea now belonged to each other, and nobody – not even Sergei – could come between them.

And later, when they had returned to the city, Pavel still continued to feel this new bond: between the sea and himself. Had he been told this was love, he would have been very surprised. It was more like a taut length of rubber that allowed him to go on with his life and move about, yet constantly kept tugging him back to the same spot. To that cliff. To that flight. He did not yet know that this was to be for ever.

Back in the city, it transpired that Pavel had missed out on a whole stack of goings-on.

'There was one heck of a shoot-up here!' said Vladek excitedly. 'Imagine, the red flag was flying over the Duma, and everyone was saying the Jews had seized power, but then the port rose up in rebellion, and what a right old shoot-up that started. Some were firing out of windows, others through windows, in volleys. And there were machine-guns, too. Some sort of Jewish newspaper office was torn apart – evidently *The Southern Review*. That's where they were shooting from. And then they came in off the farms to sack the city, they said – only not to get the Jews, this time, but everyone. Well, that's when the soldiers showed up, of course, and then things really started hotting up! I tell you, mate, I went and saw the students, and they'd got themselves organised as a proper band. I mean a real fighting band!'

'So what did you do once you'd got there?' asked Pavel. He was trying not to show that he was burning with envy. 'Did they give you a gun?'

'No,' sighed the honest Vladek. 'Up until then nothing had happened, so they told me to hang around and said I may be needed to run some errands for them. But then later on, when they started bringing in the wounded, a medical student had a go at me. A second-year medic, bossing people around like that. Worse than old Nosey, he was. I was led off home like a primary schoolkid, and – with the railway out on strike – my father was there. And he wouldn't let me out of the house again. Then came the pogrom, and everyone put icons in their windows, so Anna and I weren't even allowed anywhere near the window. Although we didn't have any shooting outside the house here. And at Romanovka, they say, hundreds may have been killed! And you know that madman, Grisha the Horse – well, he's outside the cathedral, weeping. He's yelling that now they've been defiled the icons will abandon Russia.'

'And how about Anna?' asked Pavel with an effort. Just to think that while the city was being almost sacked she had remained here. Well, with her parents, of course, and Vladek – but even so. She was such a delicate girl, and people were being killed in the city.

'Anna's all right. To begin with she was all wide-eyed and quiet as a mouse, but then she spent the whole time looking after little David, who had an upset tummy or something. She loves babies.'

'Which little David is that?'

'The little Gurvits boy, the one who can still only crawl. One chirp – and that's his lot. You know Gurvits? He runs the tobacco stall just next-door to here, the same place we bought our exercise books from. They holed up here for a couple of days. Our house was left untouched – the yard-cleaner hung an icon out on the gates. It was weird, you know: a household icon, and then all of a sudden there it was – out in the rain.'

It was difficult for Pavel to believe that this had all taken place scarcely two days ago. Their street looked just the same as usual: there were no pools of blood, or frightened faces, or ruins anywhere. Only vibrant glaziers all over the place, yelling 'Win-do-ows!', and little boys out in the yard swapping used cartridges and cartridgecases, swearing that they were live ammunition. But believe it he must.

'Then everyone felt sorry for them,' said Dasha under her breath, casting a look round at the door. She doubted that Ivan Alexandrovich would approve of such stories, but she could not disappoint her darling. 'It's one thing not giving the Yids power over the people, but, really, it wasn't right to go laying into all of them like that, was it? At Moldavanka they were cut to ribbons, they were – and a lot of them were perfectly innocent. Then the Cossacks came and carted them out of the city, and fed them bread – I saw it. And there were little kiddies there too – what a sorry sight it was! Poor things.'

She wanted to say something else, but hesitated. Then she leaned right up close to Pavel. There was a smell of her favourite floral soap and, just as he had in his childhood, Pavel pressed his cheek to her shoulder.

'Don't tell anyone, Pavlik . . . Promise me now!'

Pavel silently crossed himself.

'Vasily called by. He's still in one piece, some students hid him here in the city, and then so did some of his other friends, too. He's just left for St Petersburg – he says he's got some business to see to up there. I didn't ask him what sort of business, of course. I just kept quiet and cried. But he laughed it off, gave me a hug and said 'Don't be sad, Mama, there's work there and it isn't dangerous, I've been fixed up with new documents. Good times are just round the corner, he said. And he was well dressed, and not hungry. He didn't even eat any of my cakes,' she added with a certain air of grievance.

A life that was so ordinary it was depressing set in: the gymnasium, home, lessons. Lighting-up time was earlier. It was late autumn, and as it grew dark Pavel would occasionally hear the steady toll of a storm-bell coming from the direction of the sea.

Rakhil's money was coming to an end. It became known that

Mirlits, who was indebted to Isaak, had gone off to America. As for such few of her acquaintances as were still in Odessa, they had little with which to help her: the affairs of virtually all of them were in disorder. Who would ever have thought that there would be a pogrom in Odessa at the same time as in Nikolayev? She had heard something of the sort even before leaving, but had disbelieved it: this was a decent city, it was impossible. Yet it turned out to be true, and now she did not know how she was supposed to go on living.

Shpayer did not evict her from the house, even though she was three weeks in arrears with her rent. The area round here had not suffered: the local boys were not lightly to be messed with, and, without uttering a nasty word to anyone, they had placed some machine-guns up on the roof-tops. So Shpayer could not draw on the pogrom as an excuse. But, even so, what did the future hold?

'Madam Geiber, there's somebody here to see you!' the drayman Yankel yelled from the yard, and, in a state of alarm, Rakhil went to the door.

There in the doorway stood a respectable-looking gentleman in a coat that could have come from London, exuding an air of self-assurance and looking wholly out of place in Monya Shpayer's boarding-house. An entirely Russian gentleman. With entirely Jewish eyes.

'Rakhil, dear girl. Don't you recognise me?'

And then Rakhil did recognise him, and she felt like sitting down on the spot, right in the doorway. But she simply clung to the doorpost and stood in silence. She did not know what to say, or even what to call him. After all, now he was probably altogether different from the Moisei that he used to be.

Many years earlier, when Rakhil was still a little girl, her father had come home looking completely pale and with his entire face shaking. He had carefully taken off his shoes, sat down on the floor in his socks, and said to her mother, 'Betya, we no longer have a son.'

And her mother had sobbed and howled, and Rakhil became frightened and she, too, started sobbing. The family mourned as if he had died, and his name was no longer mentioned in the house. There could be no greater shame for a Jewish family than to have a son who had adopted Christianity! It was surprising that, after that, anyone had been prepared to take Rakhil as a wife.

And now here he was, standing there smiling, her brother Moisha, who had been a skinny, intelligent little boy, the pride of his father, of whom neighbours had foretold that he would be a rabbi, and who was now goyish and could not even be allowed into the house. Once again the damp wind tore into Monya's yard and whirled around, beating against some tarpaulin covers. Heavy rain started to pour down, and Moisei grabbed hold of his hat, though he made no move to step inside. And he remained standing like that, with the water pouring down his cheek. And if Rakhil never let him in, there he would remain standing, with his face wet . . .

Rakhil sobbed and embraced him. Oh, how sweet it was – to cry on her brother's shoulder, and have him mutter something and comfort her, and to smell the wet fur on his collar, as well as something else that was Russian and unfamiliar. She dragged him inside her little room, where there was a table with an oilcloth, and an iron bed with a frame. The painted floor felt a bit sticky to walk on. It even took Rakhil a little time to realise where to sit her brother: he seemed so big, and both the stools were so shaky and had such thin legs, and were constantly threatening to fall apart.

But having to see to the essential womanly chores saved her from confusion. She had to get a move on and boil the water and make the tea – there was still something in the green tea-caddy. And she had to lay his coat out on the bed to let it dry, and sweep the crumbs from the table, and keep turning Moisei's face to the light and see what sort of man he had become. Rakhil did all this at once, and she talked and talked for both of them. Because if both of them should suddenly fall silent, that would renew all the old whole heartache, and they would each think they no longer had anything to talk about with one another.

She told him about all that had happened to her, peppering this with questions which he did not, in any event, have time to answer. Only then did she feel that what she had needed all this time was someone to open her heart to, but there was no one! Of course, here in Odessa there was always someone to talk to, even if it was just her neighbour Sonya, or that sweet old couple the Lotmans, or Monya's wife, who had so many children and was forever bustling about seeing to the housework. And she had visited some old acquaintances of Isaak, all of whom were kind and welcoming people. Yet somehow she had been unable to bring herself to tell them what she had been through. It was not that they objected to her, but that they would immediately start talking about what had happened in Odessa, and then it became clear that here it had been far worse than in Nikolayev. These stories sounded terrible, and Rakhil constantly had the impression that they derived a certain incomprehensible satisfaction from them. She would become annoyed, herself growing frightened at her annoyance, and try to change the subject.

But Moisei was listening just as she wanted. As kin should listen. And, from the way he kept changing his face, the way he kept repeating 'my poor child', and the way he absorbed every detail, she already knew that he was kin. Christian or not, he was her brother, and not some stranger.

At last she calmed down, feeling drained and no longer frightened of the two of them having nothing to say to one another. Moisei embraced her and, gently rocking her to and fro like a little girl, started to say something. Rakhil barely listened, as though she had known what he would say before he even said anything. Yes, of course he would pay Monya and take them away from here immediately. He had a major business in Odessa and, together with another man, he was joint owner of several houses that they rented out, and she would have a nice little apartment in a decent area, and she wouldn't have to worry about earning her living any more, and for as long as Moisei remained alive, she would not have to worry about anything else, either. Nor was there anything to fear from what people would say, because this wasn't some little backwater, and it had a lot of clever people who wouldn't make a world tragedy out of trifles, but thought as Europeans. To call Moldavanka Europe was, of course, stretching it, but she would be living in the real city, rather than here – and there could be no doubting that it was Europe, and free of all prejudice.

At that moment the door slammed (how many times did she

have to ask her boy not to slam the door like that!) and the children ran in with some great news.

'Mama, you know that Bobik that belongs to Sanya the cabman – well, he isn't Bobik at all, but Bobka, and now she's gone and had puppies, four little puppies!' yelled Yakov as he was still by the doorway. Then he saw Moisei and clammed up. Rimma did not utter a word, but simply stopped and waited for an explanation.

And Rakhil felt that an explanation was called for. What with one thing and another she had been getting more and more worried about the girl lately. Yakov somehow took everything more straightforwardly: for a while he had grown thinner and more adult, but that hadn't lasted long. And about a month and a half later he went back to being the same happy little boy he had always been, and he stopped waking up at night and crying. As for Rimma, she had become rather withdrawn and, although on the face of it she was a lot more obedient, for some reason Rakhil could not help permanently feeling guilty about her, and this angered her. Then she realised what it was: the girl's eyes had become insolent! And now it seemed that all of this was about to come flooding out into the open.

'Children, this is your uncle Moisei,' said Rakhil, sounding as confident as she could manage.

'O-oh, Uncle! So that's your fur-coat, is it? Did you come in a cab? I'm Yakov, and I'm already seven years old, and I can read everything. Is that a watch you've got there?'

Yakov was already milling around near the smiling Moisei and striving to get a better look at the chain of the pocket-watch that was hanging from his black waistcoat with a dull gleam.

'Uncle? But I thought Papa didn't have any brothers,' said Rimma, speaking her mind and sounding highly suspicious.

'This is my brother. And this is Rimma, Moisei – she's my eldest.'

'A wonderful girl. How old are you?' Moisei asked fondly but he received no reply.

'Papa said you hadn't got any brothers. You had a sister, but she died, and Papa said you had a brother, too, but that he turned Christian, and that's the same as if he didn't exist. So you're the one that went Christian?' she asked point blank of this strange man who had made himself nice and cosy by the table. At the same time she noticed the alarm growing in her mother's eyes and the stranger becoming embarrassed. She liked that: let them get embarrassed!

'Rimma, curb your tongue!'

'Let her be, Rokhl. Why shouldn't the girl ask? Yes, Rimma, I am – I'm your mother's brother that turned Christian. Is that why you're so mad at me?'

'No, why should I be mad at you? I don't even know you. I just don't understand why you're an uncle to me now. You're probably not even Moisei any longer. I've heard people like that go in for new names when they get christened. So what are you called nowadays? Ivan?'

'Mikhail,' her uncle acknowledged. To Rimma's bewilderment, his embarrassment had now passed, and his eyes were becoming more and more cheerful. 'And my surname is now Katsenko. Do you have any more questions? Don't be shy. I won't be offended.'

For Rimma this was the limit: as though she were concerned about trying not to offend this goyim! Suddenly she was seething with a fury that she had never previously experienced, and already she felt that this Mikhail-Moisei was guilty for everything: for the pogrom, for the death of her father, for their wretched life here in this much-vaunted Odessa, for how coarsely the cabmen swore out in the yard, for the fact that she, her mama and Yakov had to share the same room together, and had an oilcloth instead of a table-cloth, and that for days on end her shoes had been rubbing on her feet, and she had been afraid to tell her mama – because in any event she didn't have enough money for a new pair. And to crown it all now along came this man, interfering and sneering!

She could not remember what she said, only that she tried to be as cutting as possible: had Uncle Mikhail taken part in the pogrom, had he been well paid for turning Christian, and something else besides that was every bit as offensive. With horror she felt that she was unable to stop, while her uncle kept quiet all the time and made no answer until she ran out of anything else to say to him. Then, all of a sudden, and surprising herself, she burst out sobbing – right in front of him!

– and the shame of it made her start shrieking and stamping her feet.

Then, as calm as you like, this Mikhail lifted her up in his arms (his arms were, in fact, very strong and – it seemed – tender?), put her down on the bed and covered her with his coat. She was trembling all over, and no longer resisted, simply keeping her face hidden in the sweet-smelling brown, smooth fur. Her mama put a damp towel on her forehead, and Rimma suddenly started feeling astonishingly well, like a little girl, even though she did still feel slightly ashamed.

As she half-slept she caught snatches of conversation: the timid voice of her mama, and the male, confident voice of this new uncle.

'I'll take you straight over to Koblevskaya . . . You've had a terrible time . . . How can I be offended, Rokhl, the girl has a man's head on her shoulders . . . To the gymnasium . . . Well, let's get a tutor to prepare her . . . A good private institution . . . Butovich . . . Don't argue, Rokhl, the best education possible – for both the children . . . No worse than anyone else . . . We have to be Europeans . . . Get your things.'

Then, to Yakov's delight, they were being driven somewhere in a cab, and were taken into a rich street with a cobbled drive and there, right in the drive, was a little garden with trees. And the windows of their new apartment looked out on the trees. Three rooms with parquet, and one of them even had a piano in it! And Uncle Moisei kept promising to put everything in order and make the apartment a 'sweetie' for them. He was not in the least angry with Rimma. He said he would explain everything to her later, including about God, too (here for some reason he grinned, as though he were not at all afraid of Him), and that a girl of her intelligence would understand it all. So Rimma went to sleep with a feeling that now the real Odessa had begun, one that at last resembled the fabulous city of her mama's stories. Now there would be a new, interesting life, in which everything was possible. And for girls, too.

6

When thirty girls stand up, it looks like birds taking off. Fr-r-r! Identical birds, with black-winged pinafores. No slamming desk-tops, now. It's unseemly. And if you slip up and the wretched top does make a wooden clatter everyone looks round, and the class mistress treats you to that special look known in the class as a 'Gorgon in syrup'. Then for half the lesson you're left with glowing cheeks. So, you just have to fly up and immediately freeze. Thirty watching one – that's how gymnasium starts if you arrive in the middle of the year.

'Meet our new pupil. Rimma Geiber. Make her welcome and help her in getting to know our routine.'

'Madam Bonton' always spoke as if she were reading out a dictation. It took several months of getting to know her before realising that she was, essentially, harmless. The new girl, who was in the same black pinafore as everyone else, held herself very straight, and even smiled bravely.

'She's pretty,' was muttered from somewhere in the back row. And, indeed, she was pretty, this Rimma, with her bright brown eyes and black curly hair. Though it was clear she could not claim to be the foremost beauty in the class. That position was firmly held by Zina.

During the first break the new girl was, in the customary manner, surrounded and subjected to questioning.

'From Nikola-a-yev? Oh, how provincial!' drawled Lyolya Gubinskaya with a shrug of the shoulder. Lyolya was not the class favourite. There was nothing wrong, of course, in the fact that her papa had given so much money to the Evangelical Hospital. That was seen as decent, and anyone who did anything for the city could be sure that it would be the talk of the whole of Odessa. But obviously not the person himself or his family members! In Lyolya's shameless conversations on the subject there was also something demeaning for the city: as though, were she not to make such a hullabaloo about it, Odessa would forget to be grateful. The girls felt that this was worse than ordinary boasting, although they gave no real thought to exactly why it should be worse. They were even more indignant about Lyolya's excitement over the magic lantern that she had been given for Christmas. A magic lantern – it was almost a miracle, and it was better not to think about it. To avoid having to admit that you privately envied Lyolya!

Rimma could know nothing of all these relationships, but she felt that she had clearly won the sympathy of the class, and she took a disdainful look at Lyolya's crumpled hair-ribbon.

'Have you ever been there? To Nikolayev?' she ingratiatingly asked.

'Of course not!' said Lyolya, jerking her chin up as if she had had her plait yanked from behind.

'Then it must be provincial,' Rimma cheerfully agreed, and the girls burst out laughing.

How spirited she is! And bright, too, with a quick tongue, thought Anna, deciding to take the new girl under her wing. Which could yet prove necessary, because Lyolya had no intention of climbing down.

'So what made you leave Nikolayev then?'

Oh, at this point Rimma could curb her tongue no longer. She had latched on to the fact that no one would now dare to laugh at her, or refuse to display at least some sympathy towards her.

'My father died there. In tragic circumstances. And my mother couldn't go on living there.'

'Why not?'

By now Lyolya was herself regretting that she had started picking on this newcomer, but she was unable to stop herself. At the very least she needed some way of ensuring she could save face!

'Because she loved him. But you're probably still too young to understand about love.'

This was like a slap in the face. None of the girls in the second-year class at the gymnasium could possibly let themselves get away with not understanding about love. Everyone took Rimma's side, and now Lyolya could expect pity from no one.

'Of course she doesn't understand. Come on, Rimma, let's go and I'll show you where we have tea,' said Zina, putting her arm round the new girl. And they went to celebrate Rimma's victory over the tea and rolls that were usually sold during the first break.

It turned out that Rimma lived in the same building as the Petrovs, but in a rented wing. This was seen as an amazing stroke of fate, and, after just a few weeks, Zina, Anna and Rimma duly became close friends and were inseparable at the gymnasium.

It was not, for some reason, the birds that were the first to feel the onset of spring in Odessa, but rather the cats. Suddenly some February night would explode in belligerent caterwauls, victory calls and a totally wild, animal clamour. Apart from the household cats, which also forgot their attachment to civilisation, there were countless hordes of footloose vagrants that had had no difficulty in surviving the mild southern winter, and were now busy hollering themselves hoarse. From the shabby roofs of the city's outskirts to the roof of the city governor's palace, a cat's chorus poured forth, and for all their infuriation the cleaners would remain powerless to do anything as the most vociferous bandits, rumour had it, proceeded to stage a spring concert on the sculptured roof of the Opera House.

Next morning the city would awake to the new air of spring. It made you feel like either sleeping or else getting up to tomfoolery of some sort. And vernal, too, were the conversations, and the look in everyone's eye, and there was a certain confusion in the most mundane of things. From Shrovetide right through until Palm Sunday everything was somehow peculiarly muddled, and Anna could never work out whether this interim was interminably long or, on the contrary, flew by quicker than she would have liked.

On the way back from the gymnasium it was possible to buy some early violets, to grab them from the icy water in the flower-sellers' jars and laugh at how your fingers immediately turned red with cold. The best and cosiest place in the whole world was that little crimson sofa in Zina's room, where the three of them could settle down and discuss matters that were important, compelling and slightly shameful.

'Are you going to get married then? I certainly won't! Zina, you horrid girl, what are you laughing at now?'

'It's a sign: whoever says that will be the first to get married.'

'What rubbish.'

Rimma smiled condescendingly, just as her uncle Moisei did when he was talking about provincial prejudices.

'Just you wait and see. You'll be in a white dress, with flowers in your hands, and we'll congratulate you and be frightfully, frightfully envious because Anna and I will still be single whereas you'll already be a lady. In a hat from Paris.'

'Yes, yes,' said Anna, warming to the subject, 'and then you'll have a baby, with such curly hair, and we'll give it toys.'

'Not for anything on earth! I'll be a singer, and go to Italy and sing in Milan. And all the men will stare at me, but I won't look at a single one of them.'

'That means you'll get married to an Italian. Which makes it even more likely your baby will be curly-headed.'

'Why do you keep harping on about me having a baby!'

Rimma's eyes blazed with fury, but the two girls burst out laughing together so concordantly that not even she could restrain herself. Discussions of this sort always ended in laughter, as the subject was, for all that, dangerous, and it was better either to joke or talk about other people. Love was like a rather terrifying game, or an illness for which there was no cure. It made men shoot themselves, and women take poison or throw themselves beneath trains. The more terribly it ended, the more beautiful love seemed. Furthermore, if books about love ended in marriage, then obviously nothing else worth bothering about ever actually happened, which meant it was all over anyway.

'Well, have you ever read about a husband and wife loving one another? Just take Tolstoy, or anyone else you like. You remember Count Nikolai explaining to his wife Marie that he didn't love her, and that he regarded her as a finger he couldn't cut off. Yuck – how ghastly!'

'No, Zina – wait a second. I'm not arguing with you, because you're right in what you say, but there are exceptions, you know.'

Rimma was concentrating on running her finger over the round embroidered cushion, as though counting how many yellow petals there were in the protruding cross-stitches.

'For a start, that Nikolai was a fool. Like most men. But take the Count of Monte Cristo – you can't deny that he loved his Greek girl. Because he was a remarkable man.'

'What's so remarkable about him!' Anna cried indignantly. 'He spent his life going round being horrid to people.'

'But that was for revenge!'

'Well, what's so good about that? Again and again he took revenge till he ended up being cruel himself, and a cheat, and a slave-owner. And as for loving the Greek girl – well, for a start, she wasn't even his wife, and, secondly, in the end he was bound to drown her or slit her throat.'

'What do you mean – "in the end"? We know how it ends – with them sailing away together, and the sail's the last we see of them.'

'Well, you think about it. I always think the plot through past the end. Once he'd decided to execute the people who'd wronged him, he couldn't stop, could he? And he would have found some way in which she'd wronged him once he got bored and had nothing better to do.'

'But never slit her throat!'

'And definitely slit her throat!'

'Girls – what's all this I hear? Who's going to slit whose throat?'

Maria Vasilyevna had opened the door.

'I go down the corridor, and what do I hear but three well-raised young ladies plotting bloody murder, and what's more, loud enough for the servants to hear.'

She immediately regretted breaking up their discussion.

The girls blushed and became confused, as if they had been caught red-handed at the scene of some crime. How funny they were at this age. Here they were, on the verge of becoming young ladies, yet sometimes when you looked at them they appeared just like kittens in a basket. What would they be like in three or four years' time? She was, of course, unaware that the girls already had this all planned out: they reckoned that it was at the age of about sixteen that real life started. But would she still be here to see them in three or four years' time? She smiled as nonchalantly as possible.

'Now downstairs, girls, there are some strawberries. Fresh in from the Bugayevskys' greenhouse. So let's go and feast ourselves!'

Strawberries in April – oh, that was far more important than the fate of the unfortunate Greek girl and all the marital love in the world. From the dining-room enlivened voices could already be heard, but Maria Vasilyevna was in no hurry to follow them downstairs. She probably needed to get something that had been left behind on the girls' sofa. Dr Vilme had just left, and he had insisted there was no danger. It was only the right lung, and just the top of it. It was not yet consumption. And, besides, how could she die, a mother with four little children to look after? It was too silly – it was just a woman's nervousness. She would leave for Yalta right away and, once the classes at the gymnasium were over, Ivan would bring all the family and come and join her. They would have a wonderful summer. Dr Vilme gave such sound advice. There, in Yalta, nothing short of miracles took place.

'Ivan, of course, won't like it. Well, that's too bad,' she heard the whisper of a lingering, youthful arrogance from the warm velvet. She was the one who was ill, and it was for her to decide what to do and how to do it. But she was taking Maxim with her. Yes, yes, Maxim would go with her immediately.

Thus calmed, she went downstairs, so Maxim never found out that what he owed the happiest journey of his life to was really the crimson sofa. He left with his mama and nanny Dasha, and the rest of the family all came and saw them off, and he even felt slightly sorry for them, especially, for some reason, his papa. But anyway it served them right – as for us, we were about to go sailing off on a white steamer.

And they were in Yalta, yes, they were in Yalta – in May, when it was hot and people could already go swimming, and, out of all the crowds of holiday-makers his mama was the most beautiful woman there, and people turned their heads to admire her, whereupon Maxim, in his little white suit, would assume a stern and knightly posture.

For the first two weeks Maria Vasilyevna was constantly trying to remind herself that the reason she had come was anything but cheery. It made her somehow uneasy simply delighting in the cypresses, the freedom, the remarkable bathing-huts and her new acquaintances. But she stopped coughing so quickly that she even felt guilty towards Yalta's celebrated Dr Asmeyev. For, although Asmeyev had ruled out the possibility of consumption, he still insisted that she should spend the entire summer in Yalta.

'Until September, at the very least. Ca-te-gorically! You have to build up your strength. Otherwise you may suffer a relapse!'

These two words – 'categorically' and 'relapse' – somehow calmed Maria Vasilyevna, for she felt that she was merely doing as she had to, and that there was nothing wrong in this illicit delight she was enjoying. She and Maxim went for donkey rides together, gathered pebbles on the sea-shore, bought a number of knick-knacks, including a coral necklace that was quite useless to her, and played shuttlecock in the city park. On several occasions she was mistaken for Maxim's elder sister. She liked her rejuvenated and more slender body, she liked being slim and light again, going for long swims and, in the evenings, leaving Maxim with Dasha while she went off to a concert beneath the open sky, or took a stroll along the sea-front, knowing that, apart from her elderly Odessan acquaintances, there she would also meet some new, carefree and witty people.

In 1906 the brilliant Yalta society, which was comprised almost entirely of trippers and people taking a break, was deriving pleasure from permitting itself an informality which back in the salons of the capital cities would have been viewed as perilously close to vulgar. Furthermore, whereas throughout the rest of Russia the done thing was to discuss politics, world problems and questions such as 'where is it all leading?', here, in this special world of the resort, the unwritten law forbade this. Maria Vasilyevna liked this, too. Now she became aware that, more than she had realised, she had grown sick of all those conversations in her own living-room about strikes, demonstrations, the liberalisation of society, emancipation and the execution of terrorists. Now, finding herself outside the circle in which these conversations were endlessly repeated, she recalled them easily and with amusement and a light mind.

Naturally, she had her suitors, and she liked having them, too. For some reason, she took particular pleasure in never letting the courtship go too far, and so it amounted to no more – though, in fact, it did – than dancing, or a game together. So, when for the first time in her life she was unfaithful to her husband, it was easy, and she was even cold-blooded about it – and very surprised at herself. Not so much because it had happened, as at her own shameless lack of remorse.

She understood that, in the depth of her soul, she would not be troubled by a guilty conscience towards her husband (for some reason, ever since leaving for Yalta she had thought of Ivan with a certain irritation). But should not the vulgarity of a seaside love-affair have offended, if not her conscience, then at least her sense of taste? Yet she felt nothing vulgar, either in herself or the youth who, barely out of university, was undoubtedly in love with her, demanded nothing and was as meek as a little boy with her. She knew what day he was leaving, and she let it happen only once, on his last night. Then off he went, trembling with happiness and anguish, but not daring to violate her prohibition. And she had known that he wouldn't dare to: he would not look back, and he would not return.

Next morning she and Maxim went chasing one another, and this new quality of hers – that of a fallen woman – only forced her to laugh and clown about more than usual. It would, of course, never happen again – of this she was certain. For her, once would suffice for the rest of her life: it was not a painful, but rather a sweet memory. A little treasure in her life, an isolated transgression that she must safeguard from everyone and not demean by repetition.

When Ivan Alexandrovich arrived with the children in July he was flabbergasted. 'Masha, darling, you look just like a young girl!'

'That's me, Papa – I've been looking after her,' interjected Maxim importantly.

Maria Vasilyevna was glad to see her husband in a way

that she had not expected. Truly he had missed her, that was obvious, and when that same evening he whispered to her out on the veranda, 'I can't live without you – I was going out of my mind,' she knew that that, too, was true. She was slightly embarrassed that she now behaved differently with her husband – brazenly, as she thought to herself. Guilty of nothing towards him previously, she had usually acted and answered as though she were guilty, and been frightened of angering him. Now that there was guilt, it had to be kept hidden and the proper place for that was inside, in Maria, the handmaiden of God, of whose existence Ivan Alexandrovich had never even been aware. The more independently and confidently the outer Maria Vasilyevna behaved, the more, to her surprise, her husband simply liked it. Just as he liked her change of perfume. To suspect that this may have been caused by anything other than her total recovery never even entered his head, and he blamed himself for failing to send Masha to the resort a great deal earlier, instead of letting it reach the stage of having to call in the doctor.

The happy Petrov family left Yalta in September and returned to the staid life of Odessa. During the Advent fast of the Nativity of Our Lord, Maria Vasilyevna confessed her sin to the priest, and the liberal-minded father forgave her without imposing any church penance.

7

December 1908 was wonderful: snowy and windless. The exhilarated Odessans, who were not spoilt with snow every winter, made the most of what they had missed out on, and did all they could to hoard this enjoyment away for long into the future. The entire city, or at any rate the whole of what the Odessan newspapers called 'the entire city', was on the move somewhere, delighting in their sledges, in the picturesque blue snow-drifts along the sides of the pavements, the shops with their Christmas decorations, and the special, wintry, furry softness and the hush. The Advent fast of the Nativity of Our Lord meant that there could be no question of any wild revelry, but a number of Odessan charitable societies vied with each other in arranging something each evening: be it a concert in the hall of the Stock Exchange in benefit of ex-prisoners and the homeless, or a jumble sale with tea in benefit of the orphans' homes, or candle-lit vocal evenings.

Vanda Kazimirovna, who was renowned even among the demanding Odessans as a 'musician of divine grace', and especially as a refined accompanist, divided these days between the Catholic Church and evenings giving resounding grand-piano recitals. These grand pianos stood in every house in the city that received visitors: they were properly tuned and well cared for, and each one of them was as quirky as a thoroughbred horse. 'Madam Teslenko is our treasure,' they gasped in the Women's Charitable Society, which was renowned for its pitiless manner of coercing any visiting celebrity into service. There was no point in resisting: Mazzini, Tamanio, and Giraldoni, and even the divine Battistini had not refused to help the poor, or at least so claimed the insistent ladies of the Society. Vanda Kazimirovna would accompany all the 'prisoners of war', as she jokingly called them, and all were happy, and kissed her hand when acknowledging the applause.

Vladek, who had always adored his mother, felt this to be a doubly festive time of year. First, there was his mother's Catholic Christmas. The star of Bethlehem was reflected in the stained-glass windows of Rome and Warsaw, and his mother would bring their reflection back from the church and into the house with her. Then the star seemed to fade and gradually disappear over the horizon, until thirteen days later it again shone forth – this time for the Orthodox Christmas, gleaming on the chasubles of the priests and the bulging golden bells.

By now seventeen years old and in his last year at the gymnasium, with a black-collared grey overcoat and a wheaten, stubbly down over his upper lip, Vladek proudly and diligently accompanied his mother to the service in Ekaterinskaya Street. He found the church steps and the angels on the ceilings that he could see through the open door luring, although, being Orthodox, he was not allowed in. Not that it was forbidden (he could have gone in), but each time his mother would squeeze his hand by the door and then let go, as if tearing herself away from him. And that was as far as he dared to go. She went on alone, to meet the Infant Jesus, holding herself upright and stern, in black and lilac that flounced lightly as she went up the steps. And he would stay behind, with all his sins and impure thoughts, neither a boy, nor yet a man, though still his mother's son, with her eyes and her colour of hair.

On the Catholic Christmas Eve the entire family would decorate the Christmas tree. And that was far better than in the other homes, where the children were not allowed in until later, when everything had already been got ready. Their father brought it home dripping wet, and Antos became so excited that he even kissed it, smack on the damp prickles. Their mother went and fetched some boxes out of the pantry, and from these, from within the dusty, greying cotton-wool, impatient hands would grab at their favourite baubles. Then, when everything was in place, their father would light the candles while their mother played Chopin, and the Christmas tree started to smell and quiver with gold and lilac thread.

Out of respect for the mother of the family, no one ate until the star had appeared. Ever since the age of five, the boy had declined all blandishments with the Polish '*Nie chcem*' – 'I don't want to'. Then their mother would lay the table with the crackling table-cloth and the Polish fasting dishes – the same as her grandmothers and great-grandmothers had known. That night the children would lie awake until late: the festivity was on the frost-laden windows, and in the empty dining-room, where the Christmas tree was unable to go to sleep, and even in the smell of the specially starched bed linen.

Naturally, their mother continued her fast until the Orthodox Christmas. She would greet them after the midnight service, when they were thrilled and deafened by the bells and the singing, and give each of them three kisses and wish them happy Christmas. And, in the proper fashion, she would cook the Orthodox wheat, honey and poppy seeds. And then at last it was morning, with the presents waiting for the children, and the parcels ready for the charwomen and the boys who came and sang in glory of Christ, as well as for the yard-cleaner and anyone else who cared to call in and wish them a happy Christmas. And this was only the start of the feast that would continue until all were exhausted: the theatres would open, and the circus and the ice-rinks, too – along with everything else that the Christmas holidays brought with them. And only then would the New Year come, and so came 1909.

From their parents the Petrov children received one present for all: a plump little book of tickets to go and see *Captain Grant's Children*.

'I'm already worn out with all this theatre-going,' said Ivan Alexandrovich, pulling a comical face. 'Why don't you take all your friends along with you – the grown-ups and the children – and go yourselves. You won't all fit in with Fedko – we'll have to hire another cab. And I'd like you and Vladek, as young men, to look after the children and the girls,' he said, addressing his son.

In a voice that was already breaking into a deep baritone, Pavel briefly replied, 'Of course, Papa, thank you,' but he was unable to control that rather childish smile which the house had given the name of 'bu-bu'. The show was, of course, really meant for children, but he was going to look after them, so there could be nothing out of the ordinary about that.

'Ah, children,' sighed Maria Vasilyevna, 'so this is your first trip out into the world, when you'll all be going off on your own together, like grown-ups. And it could very well be your last: our Pavlik is about to go off to university. Really – can't you grow a bit slower!'

It was a pity it was such a short trip to the theatre: the sledges scarcely even had time to get up speed before the lights of the theatre porch came into view. Here the snow-drifts were swept away, and there were even some motor cars parked outside. It took Vladek and Pavel no small effort to keep Antos and Yakov from rushing over to examine them: to a child's mind the motor car was in those days the ultimate human dream. Maxim was the only one of the boys who regarded motor cars with contempt: what was the point of a machine if it didn't fly? The future plainly belonged to aeroplanes, and he had no intention of letting his adamant heart be divided in two. He also felt contemptuous towards people who regarded eight-year-olds as little boys, but at the moment he had no time to explain all this to his elder brother. He kept glancing at Yakov, trying to make up his mind: should he immediately feel jealous because of Antos, or should he let him become the third member of their gang? He had known Antos for ages, they were both studying for the entrance exam for the gymnasium, and at home the younger Teslenko was generally treated as one of the family. And, as for this brother of Rimma's, even if he did live in a rented wing next door, what was the big deal in that? Rimma had never previously brought him to see them, and she was, all in all, a snooty sort of girl who payed no attention to younger children, and Maxim disliked her for that. And now, in front of his very eyes, something akin to treason was taking place: his closest friend Antos was talking with this long-nosed boy as if they had known one another for ages – about motors, about foreign makes of car, and as though he, Maxim, might as well not have bothered to come.

Then the warm, theatrical air flooded over them, with its

perfume and that other, special aroma that is only ever found in theatres. It was the first time that Yakov had been to a theatre, and he was immediately intoxicated by the lights, the gilded mirror frames and the cherry-coloured velvet of the boxes. Yes, yes, they were in boxes – no less than two, all to themselves, and he was lucky enough to have wangled his way into the one without Rimma, so he promptly stuck his elbows up on the ravishing velvet parapet, and then summoned the courage to peer down over the top and survey what was below for as long as he liked. He was happy, he loved everyone, and he blissfully looked at his new acquaintances. The younger daughter of the rich Petrovs, who was there in the same box, smiled at him. 'Are you Yakov? How nice that you've come, too, because I knew Rimma had a brother, but no one's ever introduced us. Would you like to have a go on my binoculars?'

This Marina struck Yakov as a quite extraordinary girl, for she was just like a grey-eyed princess, even if she was wearing a school uniform. Could she really be older than him? They were roughly the same height as one another. To be on the safe side, however, Yakov raised himself slightly up on tiptoes. But the fact remained: she was already at the gymnasium, whereas he still had to get through the entrance exam. And there was more than a year to go before he could take it.

'You've got those binoculars the wrong way round,' interjected Maxim, 'that makes everything look far away. You're meant to look through the little holes.'

Yakov gladly accepted the patronage of this broad-shouldered boy, though he had noticed that he, at least, thank goodness, was no older than himself: he was in a sailor-suit, rather than a school uniform.

'I suppose you probably go to the theatre rather a lot, do you?' he asked, and, immediately placated, Maxim had enough time to tell him that he was indeed rather a regular theatre-goer, and that he even went to the opera, and was already getting so carried away that he was about to start fibbing, but then the lights started fading and the curtains suddenly whooshed open.

It was not yet the show: some children from the orphans' home sang the national anthem, 'God Save the Tsar'. This was the tradition at any show raising money for charity. Maxim managed to whisper to Yakov that they were orphans, and Yakov was surprised: there was nothing poor about the way these boys dressed, nor anything gloomy about how they sang, which was how he had imagined orphans ought to sing, and how the organ-grinders' children sang out in the yards. Even so, it was a thrilling build-up to the show, and Yakov wished that they could have gone on singing for a little longer.

By the time of the intermission the children's cheeks were burning, and they clapped gratefully and conscientiously, enjoying joining in the applause. The elders looked much amused at the little ones, but even they were suspiciously flushed.

'Look! Uncle Sergei!' exclaimed Zina in delight, and Pavel really had spotted Sergei making his way into the stalls accompanied by two other gentlemen.

'Who's that with him – you don't know, do you, Pavlik?'

Well, really – only a girl could ask a question like that! There beside Uncle Sergei, and causing the floor to all but sag beneath him, was Ivan Zaikin, the wrestler who was famed throughout the whole of Odessa, and possibly the entire world, and who, furthermore, was the only wrestler who had ever learnt how to fly an aeroplane. Vladek recognised the other man. 'That's Yura Morfessi!'

Yes, of course it was, although, in the flesh, Yura did not look too much like the man of destiny of the sort depicted on his posters, but even so, there was no call to doubt it. The celebrated king of gypsy song was here in the theatre.

'Pavlik, introduce me!'

Pavel and Vladek exchanged glances. Even if they were still pupils at the gymnasium, they were, nevertheless, acquainted with the members of their future departments at the university, and knew just what great things the university students had planned for this Yura Morfessi. What an opportunity! They left the box, and Maxim realised that all the rest of the party would probably now have to go without the ice-cream that he had been so looking forward to.

In the meantime, Anna, Zina and Rimma were busy recalling all the legends about Yura that had for so long been circulating round Odessa.

'His grandfather was a real Greek pirate, and buried an

enormous amount of treasure somewhere, but then he perished without ever managing to tell his family where it was hidden.'

'What's treasure to him! He's been a singer ever since he was eight years old. He's travelled half the world, and in Petersburg he's never off the stage.'

'No, at the moment he's performing in Moscow. He's brought out some gramophone records. They say he sang to the heir to the throne at Tsarskoye Selo. And the Grand Duke patronises him.'

'Which one?'

'Nikolai Konstantinovich – the one in Tashkent.'

'Ah, that one . . .'

'Well, even so!'

'Is it true that he recently beat up a couple of Germans single-handedly for speaking badly of Russia?'

'I don't know. It's probably rubbish. He's a singer, not a bandit.'

'Not that singers are always so restrained – just look at Shalyapin.'

'Shalyapin's a peasant, whereas Morfessi is a man of culture – there's no comparison.'

Sergei, in the meantime, was busy introducing his companions to both Pavel, who was blushing furiously, and Vladek, for whom, as usual, embarrassment was the last thing on his mind.

'Two longstanding admirers of yours, Ivan: my nephew and his friend. So far as I am aware, they haven't missed a single one of your matches, and have forsaken breakfast at the gymnasium for their tickets. As the gymnasium doesn't lay on supper, they were unable, Yura, to accord you quite the same attention. You should perform at the circus, my friend!'

'What a splendid idea!' laughed Morfessi. 'We could start with Ivan and I singing together, and then have Ivan pin me in a full nelson! That would certainly rake in a bit of money! But I'm very glad to meet you both. We may yet become great friends. After all, as I understand it, next year you'll be students, won't you? So what have you chosen to study?'

'I'm going to join the department of medicine, and Pavel the department of physics and mathematics. He intends to be an aircraft designer,' Vladek deferentially replied.

'Right up your street once again, Ivan!' grinned Sergei. 'Now here's a fellow who could design the sort of machine that not even you would manage to crash, and keep you from driving Antara bankrupt.'

Arthur Antonovich Antara, the owner and director of 'The Odessan School of Pilots' had, indeed, granted his favourite Zaikin total freedom in his business – for which he had also paid with several machines, until, to the delight of the whole of Odessa, Zaikin successfully completed his first circle over the city.

The boys were a little disappointed by Zaikin's handshake, which, despite the size of his hand, turned out to be not at all bear-like, but plain courteous. Morfessi went on cracking jokes and, on learning that the gentlemen from the gymnasium had left some girls behind in the box, he immediately asked to be introduced. He was amused by the idea that the ladies seeking his attention would spend the entire intermission watching him conversing with some girls in school uniform. All the more so as the girls were nice, one was actually pretty, and the other, the dark-eyed one, was looking at him, Yura, with that speechless adoration of the kind that only schoolgirls are capable of.

Working in both capital cities, as well as touring the provinces, Morfessi came to Odessa to relax and enjoy the lively company, and now, with his old friend Ivan, he was having a whale of a time. Ivan Zaikin wasn't doing too badly, either: right there in the box he offered to let these little chaps, who were utterly charmed as it was anyway, take it in turns standing on his outstretched, knightly palm, and all three of the boys had time for a go before the bell rang for the second act. Yakov was in seventh heaven, and was only surprised at why, instead of asking if she could herself have a go, Rimma kept staring at the Greek crooner who, even if he was descended from pirates, was still a perfectly ordinary-looking black-haired gentleman, to say nothing of his being rather fat, when beside her was Ivan Zaikin!

Under his breath Pavel asked his uncle if it was a good time to ask a favour of Mr Morfessi, one which he knew the students at the university had been meaning to ask, but never previously had the chance to. The scheme was to stage some show to help impecunious students, and if Morfessi himself were to agree to take it on, then success was guaranteed. Sergei said that this was quite acceptable, and the magnanimous Morfessi promised that the very next day he would receive a delegation of students in the London Hotel and finalise the matter with them then.

Rimma knew that when people fell in love they necessarily didn't sleep at night. So the minute she got home she told her mother that she was tired and went off to bed to be free to dream to her heart's content. From the adjacent room came the sound of Yakov's voice, who was simply unable to calm down until Rakhil could say for sure which parts of the book had, for some reason, been cut out of the show, and he was saying what a shame it hadn't lasted longer, and what a remarkable man his new friend Ivan Zaikin was, and that Maxim Petrov had invited him and Antos to go and see him the next day, and that they might go to the circus together next Saturday. Then there were some arguments with his mother about whether he could go to the circus on a Saturday and, by now in a weeping voice, Yakov was trying to get his way by arguing: 'But it's all right for Rimma to go to the gymnasium on Saturday?'

Rimma, however, could no longer hear him, for she was immersed in recollections of her encounter with the great Morfessi, which she now saw as fate. What a commanding look he had, and what a voice – not loud, but as though he held your entire soul in his hands. And how he had kissed her hand – so carefully, and with such hot lips, though her hand had been more like a lump of ice . . . Yes, he had talked to her quite differently from how he had talked to the others, and she was the only one he had asked if she studied singing. Why hadn't she thought of taking up singing before – after all, she had a perfect musical ear! Uncle Moisei hired a woman to give her piano lessons, and he would probably agree to replace her with a singing teacher! She was fourteen years old – it still wasn't too late to start. And, after all, she had once longed for nothing more than to be a singer! One day she would be famous, and give performances on the same stage as Yura Morfessi, and then he would realise that he had not been wrong, but had spotted her talent right from the start. And the two of them . . .

She got up and went over to the mirror. Yes, she had an inspired face. Her chin was too pointed, though she would fill out in time, once she stopped growing. But she did have eloquent eyes. She had read that there were some women with eloquent eyes, and that these were *femmes fatales*, even if their mouths were a bit big. She threw back her head and tried to make herself look *fatale*. It wasn't a bad result, either. But to pass a sleepless night proved too much for her. Without noticing how, she dozed off and the next morning felt ashamed. So maybe it still wasn't love?

Life's difficulties were discussed, not on Zina's sofa, but in Anna's little room at the Teslenkos. It may have been rather more cramped there, but apart from the snow-white bed in Catholic taste and the little pine table, there was just enough room for the wonderfully old-fashioned, grey-green armchair with its plush upholstery, which could fit both of them even with their legs up. This armchair stood right up by the window-sill, and beyond the high window a knightly plane tree stirred, almost lurching into the room and blocking out any view of the rather drab back street that it looked on to. In summer it lent the room a green light, but now it made it blue and snowy, and it seemed as if the armchair were itself rocking with the branches of this colossus, or had itself sprouted out of one of its branches. Here, on Anna's shoulder, it was possible to cry, to bemoan fate and feel sorry for yourself – and, for some reason, without feeling in the least bit ashamed of it. There was no one who could sympathise like Anna, and everyone knew it. In class she was jokingly known as 'the sister of mercy', but when the joking was over it was to Anna that they went, to her plane tree and her armchair, both of which were called 'grandads', and both of which knew how to keep a secret: even before she arrived, everything here seemed to have been got just right for Anna.

Just as now, for Anna was in the dining-room busy loading the tray with tea and biscuits, while Rimma had got herself cosy in the familiar armchair, and the 'grandad' made some reassuring, creaking noises and muttered as though it were half-awake. This made her feel instantly better, and by the time Anna came back, Rimma already felt that all things were possible: both her career as a singer and her extraordinary love. Anna was not at all surprised by her friend's story. 'I always knew you would lead an extraordinary life, like no one else.'

'Do you think so?'

'Of course, you don't see it yourself, and, mostly, no one sees themselves as they are, but there's something special about you, Rimma. It wasn't for nothing that Yura Spiridonovich looked at you that way – I mean differently from how he looked at Zina and me. He's an artist, and they have to feel these things immediately.'

'Do you think he looked at me differently?'

'Oh, no question. You were understandably excited, but I could see. And remember that we were all three of us there, and neither I, nor Zina fell in love, although he really is a remarkable man. Of course it's fate.'

To Rimma this argument seemed quite irrefutable, and she let out a deep sigh. 'That's how it struck me, too. Though what if he doesn't love me, but just happened to notice me?'

'Then there's nothing you can do about it, and your love will be unhappy. And it'll make you into a singer, or something else, but you'll still be a remarkable woman, and then, perhaps, he will love you, though it'll be too late.'

And they decided to leave it at that. The entire city was at the time plastered with posters announcing the forthcoming staging of part of The Beautiful Helen, directed by Morfessi and with the participation of the following personae: 'Achilles – Zaikin; Calchas – Kuprin; Ajax – Giacomino; Menelaus – Morfessi himself.'

This was unheard of, and Odessa was gripped with excitement. A wrestler, a writer and a clown – all celebrities, all city favourites, but the idea of them all sharing the same stage together was just unimaginable. Furthermore, if the director were to be Morfessi himself . . . This would raise monstrous amounts and, if the truth be told, the large-spirited director had not an inkling as to who exactly – from all the city – most hankered after the infeasible dream of playing the Beautiful Helen in this show. So instead he devoted his entire attentions not so much to rehearsals as to attempts to restrain his fun-loving friends from libations to Bacchus.

The whole scheme struck them as a wonderful ruse quite in keeping with the Odessan spirit: they would have some fun on stage and, at the same time, add a few thousand to the meagre student funds. Only Morfessi had the professional nous to sense the ghost of scandal in the air: frivolity was one thing, but if the audience were offended, then the whole thing would turn into a disaster, and for that the city would never forgive him. Odessa had been known to give the bird to celebrities who thought too highly of themselves, and these southerners knew no happy medium: a show was either a runaway success, or else a total flop.

The theatre was full, and there were not even enough wall-seats. Not only pupils and students, but also somewhat older gentlemen stood meekly in the gangways. All our youngsters were here. They had gone to particular pains to see this show: irrespective of their age, pupils from the gymnasium were forbidden from attending public spectacles without the prior permission of the school inspector, and such permission was granted no more than twice a week. But at the Butovich gym-nasium once was considered enough – and that, furthermore, during the theatrical season! Nevertheless, Vladek, who had not been given permission, was by some miracle here too, hoping that he would pass unnoticed in the crowd. This was risky, for good old Nosey was himself an inveterate theatre-goer, and in the evenings he managed to combine duty with pleasure: by seeing every decent show that was on in the city, and, at the same time, catching any miscreants from the gymnasium. That posed some very nasty threats, even for the last-year class. But, as is known, art demands sacrifices.

Up on stage, meantime, the magnificently attired Kuprin – Calchas – had departed from the script and, with an imperious look, was making it up as he went along. This was not only noticed by Morfessi, who was backstage clasping his head, but it was also felt by the audience. In the electrified atmosphere of the crammed theatre one whistle would have been enough to bring the whole, grand venture down in ruin, burying the director's reputation with it. Rimma was more dead than alive. But then Kuprin smiled – almost mockingly, almost coyly, and this smile, Morfessi sensed, somehow saved the situation. For the youngsters Kuprin was an idol anyway. Morfessi made an expansive sign of the cross and went out on stage with a feeling that all would be well. Rimma was not entirely right in later claiming that he had 'kept the entire show going on his own'. What did it matter if some heathen priest talked gibberish, for that, ultimately, was what heathen priests were there to do, but who had ever previously seen Kuprin in bed-sheets? The boards trembled beneath the enormous Achilles, his shoulders were clearly bursting out of his armour, and he astounded the imagination with his magnificence – and who really cared that he growled rather than sang?

The audience was utterly won over. The energy that had seemed to be building towards a riot erupted in interminable applause. To the further delight of the auditorium, as Achilles took his bow to the ovation the buckle of his Household Cavalry armour finally burst open.

The following year Vladek became one of the students to get help with his tuition fees from the unheard-of amounts that were raised by the show. Having reached a final decision on her fate, Rimma did not find it particularly difficult convincing her mother and uncle that she had to study singing. She was by this time the top pupil at the gymnasium, and it would have been strange to try and keep the girl back from studying what she had set her heart on. Yakov was the only one to take a critical view of 'these solfeggios', and on a number of occasions he disrupted his sister's musical home-work by emitting a protracted 'miao-aow', note for note copying Rimma's roulades. She then had to break off her singing and go chasing her evasive little brother through all three of the rooms. Yakov loved these chases, and on these conditions he agreed to put up with the music that he was so sick of hearing around the house.

8 ∫

Throughout the whole of Russia the preparations for Palm Sunday began identically: the Lent services were held in the churches, while out on all the roads carts and entire convoys of trucks lumbered towards the local Palm Fair. The squares in which the great festival was to be held were cleared and tidied up. By April it was already warm in Odessa and, after drying out following the spring showers, the field of Kulikovo basked placidly in the sun in anticipation of the forthcoming fun and festivities.

As Pavel and Vladek were now students, the priest at the gymnasium – the one whom they so disliked – no longer had any power over them, although, judging from the stories of their younger brothers, he had lost none of his austerity. In any event, he considered it necessary to give the 'preppies' a special talking to on the subject of the festival of Palm Sunday.

'Let me r-r-remind you, gentlemen, that this is a time when the Church expects you to fast and be penitent, and not to indulge in frivolous, and indeed, frequently sinful forms of entertainment. If the gymnasium lets you off class for a week, it does so in order that each one of you may fast in the proper manner, rather than treat this as an extra holiday. And if you fail to attend so much as a single church service, then don't expect that the gymnasium – at which you have so recently had the honour to be enrolled – will continue to look so kindly upon you. In particular, I want to warn you about the so-called Palm Fair. Although pupils from the gymnasium are not forbidden from going there, you must, nevertheless, remember that these are days when we shall be preparing ourselves for the great festival of our Lord's entry into Jerusalem, and, according to church tradition, it is for precisely that reason that we Orthodox greet this festival with pussy-willow branches, in token of the palms with which our Lord was greeted in Jerusalem. Petrov, what is the name given to the palm branches in the Scriptures?'

'Baion, father,' replied Maxim, standing to attention.

'Correct, but in future kindly take the trouble of giving a full answer. You may sit down. So there we have it – that is exactly why pussy-willow is sold at the fair. Garlands may also be bought, along with decorations for icons and Easter gifts for friends and relatives. But it is unwo-o-orthy for a Christian, and furthermore, a young person who already bears responsibility for the salvation of his soul, to spend these days amusing himself with all sorts of tin whistles and waxwork shows, and especially with images of the devil in bottles. Knowing of your childish frivolity, I want to warn you of this in par-ti-cular: once you have confessed your sins to your Holy Father, try to restrain yourselves from committing new ones – at least until Easter Day has been celebrated.' He unexpectedly smiled.

As usual, now that he had smiled, the austere Medvedev thawed and started talking more cordially – of how wisely the Lord had arranged all in his care in Russia: this was a period when there were no flowers to be seen anywhere, not to mention palms, but the pussy-willow was in bloom, bringing solace to the Orthodox. True, as he surveyed the class during his discourse on the special role of children in the forthcoming festival he even succumbed to doubt, though he finally bade them peace, and dismissed them without giving bad marks to so much as one of them.

The 'young people responsible for the salvation of their souls' came tearing out of the class with relief and no small clatter, feeling somewhat perplexed by the role of the pussy-willow. The fact that a pussy-willow, rather than anything else, was the thing to take into the service on the eve of Palm Sunday was something they had known since birth, and it was so pleasant to come out of church carrying them, when it was already night; the branches all in their tender down, and the equally tender candle flames, and the smell of pussy-willow and wax blending into a surprising, festive aroma. What was the point of exchanging flowers and palms in this part of the world? In southern Odessa in April the flowers were already out, and virtually every house had palm-trees in tubs, while in the rich country houses and some of the gardens they were growing straight out of the earth, where they had simply been wrapped for winter and boarded for warmth. Did that then mean that Odessa wasn't Russia?

'Medvedev was talking rubbish, wasn't he?' Antos asked Maxim when they were outside, squinting from the spring light.

'Who's to say? It's roughly like that in the Scriptures, but there are flowers all over the place, and the pussy-willows just come out once a year, so there's no comparison. The way he goes on you'd think the only one who's got it right is Grisha the Horse – so maybe we should copy him and tear down the palm branches in Arcadia?'

They both laughed. Grisha the Horse was a local madman who had been given this nickname because of his loud, and always unexpected neighing. No one knew where he lived, but usually he could be seen in the parvis of the cathedral or inside the cathedral itself during a service. On the eve of Palm Sunday he would invariably drag in a pile of palm branches and try to distribute them to the boys, but that was because he was mad. In the same mad way the friends thought they could get through the festival without their favourite toy – a little glass devil in a jar. These little devils were sympathetic, with their little horns, paunch bellies and hooves on bandy-legged paws. They merrily swam up and down, spinning somersaults in the spirit, and were not at all reminiscent of devils to be feared, so that any child who was left without one of these little devils and a painted tin whistle during Palm Sunday had every right to feel hard done by. It would have been quite different had Medvedev said the boys were too big for fun of this sort; then, from the advantage of their ten to eleven years, the gentlemen of the gymnasium would indeed have given it their consideration.

The friends, however, had enough to consider as it was. To miss out on the festivities was unthinkable, all the more so as it was the first time that their parents had let them attend the festival alone. The only one for whom it was hard was Yakov:

as a Jew, Medvedev's hints about the possible repercussions did not apply to him, although, on the other hand, neither did Rakhil understand why a Jewish boy could want to go to a goyish fair. But Yakov could easily make up some lie about being invited to visit a rich friend, and in these situations Uncle Moisei always stuck up for him and Rimma. He called this 'the children cultivating their contacts', and encouraged it at every opportunity, thus giving them a chance of getting their way in any arguments with their mother.

But where could they get the money from? Back in November the three friends had finalised their decision to escape to America. The date was fixed for June, or July at the latest, and a terrible oath had been taken that all of their money – down to the last brass coin – was to be set aside for the enterprise, for they would have sizeable costs to face. Yakov honestly contributed even the Hanukkah money that his uncle had generously given him. Maxim and Antos did what they could not to lag behind. They spent Christmas heroically: they had plenty of presents, and could get by without any money. In spring they even sold their skates to the stall-holder Shleme at the New Bazaar, for in America no one went round on skates, but on mustangs, as everyone knew. And by the time it was 1911 they would already be in America to greet it. Come to think of it, what sort of winter did they have over there? But to be left without a brass coin for the Palm Fair – and perhaps the last one in their life . . . That was really taking things too far . . . After talking it over, they decided to permit themselves some fun, but not to spend more than fifty kopecks a head and then make up for it by not even having any tea to drink at the gymnasium.

On the day of the main festival the sun was such that it even made your head ring, and colourful circles constantly seemed to be whirling in front of your eyes. Over on the field of Kulikovo a brass band had already struck up, tin whistles were chirruping, and there was a steady hubbub from the countless human voices. Quietest of all were the horses, but even they occasionally became excited: it only took one of them to start neighing to prompt a response from every corner of the square. The boys split up, agreeing to meet again in an hour's time outside the tent with the waxworks show. Each of them wanted to enjoy their recently acquired freedom on their own.

Yakov strolled blissfully by the hawkers' trays with their mounds of paper roses and tubs containing pussy-willow, on past the countless tents with waffles, tin whistles, toys and all sorts of bricabrac. He was restraining himself, and persuading himself that on no account should he spend any money on anything before having a proper look at everything – as though that were possible in an hour. To make his struggle with these temptations more bearable, he took his time over buying a chunk of lemon jelly wrapped in lace-paper, and, after safely tucking his precious purse away in an inside breast-pocket, set about calmly devoting himself to contemplation.

'Uncle, you've not come across a five-kopeck piece around here, have you?' a plaintive voice was heard. 'It was brand new, with a nick down the side . . .'

Yakov saw a skinny, black-haired lad who was dressed no better than a newspaper boy and roughly the same height as himself. The boy kept blinking and was clearly on his last legs with the strain of holding back his tears. Yakov's heart overflowed with sympathy. It was plain that this five-kopeck piece was all the boy had, and now he had been silly enough to drop it and, try as he may, he would never find it beneath the feet of a crowd such as this. Nor would anyone else, and, even if they did, they would not go looking for its owner. Yakov could not bear to see such anguish, so he rummaged about in his purse and, afraid of changing his mind, quickly held out a coin to the boy.

'Look what I just found. It's probably yours,' he magnanimously lied, feeling proud of himself.

But, rather than showing any delight or gratitude, the boy angrily pushed Yakov's hand away, furtively whispering, 'Mind your own business! And let me get on with mine!'

Yakov was so flabbergasted that his mouth fell open, and the mysterious boy softened his attitude. He put a rather grimy mitt on Yakov's shoulder and, now adopting a friendly tone, said, 'Come on, mate – don't take it bad. It's not that I'm not grateful. You put your five kopecks away – to me that's peanuts. You know nothing about life – I can tell. I could teach you, if you fancy – only don't stick so close to me. You've fouled my pitch here, so let's move on to some other place. Stand over to the side there and watch.'

Some twenty yards further on the same thing was repeated, with further anguished enquiries about a five-kopeck piece with a nick down the side. Yakov noticed that the boy was not asking people at random, but addressing himself exclusively to well-dressed men with ladies. The first man merely sympathised and walked past, but when it came to the second, the lady gave him such an expressive look that he promptly delved into his pocket for some small change. The smallest he had proved to be a twenty-kopeck piece, and he then spent some more time in trying to persuade the boy to take it. The boy beamed with gratitude, showing his stunted front teeth with their childish jags. At this point Yakov realised that his new acquaintance was probably younger than he was. But by now the artful collector of small change had made his way over to another spot, closer to the organ-grinder, and he earned something there, too, before again moving on . . . Yakov followed as if spellbound. Very soon the boy condescendingly turned to him, 'Get the idea? A rouble plus ten kopecks – what's that make? What do they teach you at that gymnasium?'

'Is this your own idea?' asked Yakov respectfully.

'You bet. I've no rivals, either. And I'm showing you 'cos I know you won't go and ape me. You're a gormless schoolkid – that sticks out a mile. Oh, you were lucky I never caught you in the Botanika!'

The 'Botanika' was what Odessan boys called the abandoned botanical gardens above the sea, an area that had become wild and overgrown – it was an attractive spot but if ever the street urchins, who lived by their own laws, caught any of the boys from the gymnasium there, they would beat them up.

Yakov was perfectly aware that he was not himself cut out for this walk of life, but he sincerely admired Andreika, as his new friend was called. Andreika, as it turned out, had also grown up without a father, and his mother was a washerwoman, but was 'poorly nowadays', though it was plain that Andreika would always manage to look after himself.

'Know how I make my living? What I make at the fair is hardly worth bothering with – but tonight and tomorrow, I reckon I'll clear about ten roubles – just doing this. Know what sort of voice I've got? I'm an alto, and our choirmaster says he'd do anything to get me into Faig's school next year, or find someone else to put up the money, just so long as I don't go and join another choir.'

It turned out that Andreika sang in church, and he went on to tell Yakov what a fantastic amount of vodka the basses managed to get through, how Temlyakov from their choir used to sing at the Imperial Theatre, and how much you could make out of rich funerals, along with a lot of other useful bits of information.

And it was only natural that, in due course, the two of them found their way to the waxworks show: today Andreika was in more of a mood for having fun than getting down to any serious work. The happy Maxim was already there, and was whiling away his time by trying to get his little devil to perform a triple somersault in its oblong jar. Soon Antos came and joined them. He had a party-blower, and it was, he assured them, the longest 'mother-in-law's tongue' that could possibly be found. It was, indeed, a splendid 'tongue' – violet with a mischievous curl and a squeal. To make sure that Antos was not exaggerating they immediately tried it out, blowing as hard as they could. In the meantime, everything around them thundered on.

'A panoramic kaleidoscope for the little 'uns! Twenty thousand images! Hey, little 'un – want a look see? Now there's a smart kid! Madam, don't upset the boy – give him a golden childhood!'

'Buns, sweet sugared buns!'

'A twentieth-century miracle, a cardboard frog that jumps on top of a living man!'

The boys had just enough money for four tickets into the waxworks show. Andreika was, naturally, also invited to join them, and he too was riveted by 'the genuine skull of Alexander the Great as a boy', the mermaid that had been caught in the Southern Seas, and the pink, heaving bust of an eternally dying Cleopatra with a small, black snake clinging to her. The greatest pleasure, however, was yet to come. As they came out of the tent, Andreika was generous enough to announce, 'Let's go and have a shoot at "Monte Cristo's"! Come on – it's on me.'

This was unheard-of generosity, and the boys deferentially

followed him into the improvised shooting-range where, in a moment of blissful possession, they were each given a real gun and five precious little bullets. Maxim, who had already once fired from his uncle's gun and been taught how to hold his breath, was sure that this was just the chance to show his metal. But all that he managed to do was force some stupid windmill to spin round, and even that was a fluke: what he had really been aiming at was, of course, the Japanese samurai. He did, however, have enough sense to keep that to himself. It was Yakov who turned out to be the best shot: one after the other he sent five tin figures whirling head over heels, and a cluster of onlookers burst into applause.

'Hey, young fellow, it must be the man of the sea himself who's helping you,' grinned the stall-owner, with his pomaded moustache, and he solemnly gave Yakov his prize: a funny little monkey with twisted wiry legs on a bit of elastic.

The fun ended with a drink of seltzer water, and then, surprising even themselves, the friends let Andreika in on their great plan of escape. It was assumed that their new friend would, naturally, consider his involvement in the enterprise an honour. But, to their amazement, Andreika did not express any enthusiasm.

'What's all the fuss about America? It's all baloney. I've been in port I dunno how many times when they've got grain for America – just grain, and loads of it, too! I reckon they must be starving over there, but look at us – loads of everything! And as for them Red Indians – well, big deal! We've got Greeks and Italians here, and Bob Hopkins, the dancer, you know him? – black as boots and married to a Cossack girl. We've got all sorts over here – and if anyone hasn't come here yet, they will – where else is there for them to go? Everyone comes to Odessa.'

'A lot of people go to America, too,' objected Yakov.

'No comparison! They're the failures. They've had no luck over here so, obviously, they go off to America. But who comes to Odessa? All sorts of famous people. You just think about it. Maybe Legodé first got to know about how to make trams run back in Belgium, but once he wised up – where did he come?'

The trams were, of course, a strong argument. At any moment

now they were due to start running in Odessa, and the boys hoped that they would be able to see this great occasion before the time came for their escape. But, whether or not they did in fact, the plan still had to be seen through, and even such a patriot as Andreika was no longer able to make them change their mind about it. Not that he tried all that hard.

'Why not go then, if that's what you fancy? See for yourselves. Maybe I could spend a year there with you but, if I went my mother would lose her only bread-winner. Know what,' he said, flaring up, 'all this boat-talk is daft – you'd be better off on the *Vladimir* – you know the one, don't you, the ship that takes the convicts?'

'Where to?'

'Where to, he asks . . . Sakhalin, of course! You're still wet behind the ears, you are! It goes via Constantinople, and it's loading up tonight. Hop on, and you're away! Stow away and it'll take you to Constantinople, no problem – and then take it from there. The port there's hu-u-uge!'

This advice was business-like, and the friends later regretted not following it. But for now they did not want to change their plans as they went along: seeing as they had decided to buy a boat and cross the Black Sea in it, that was what they should stick to. Andreika did not even bother to argue with this, asking only how much money they had, and letting out a whistle.

'That isn't enough for a row-boat. Or maybe you fancied buying a scull?'

It almost sounded like an insult: the tiny 'sculls' had many virtues, but only an infant could have ever imagined getting much further than the light-house in one. Andreika promptly advised them to invest their money in business.

'Otherwise you'll get nowhere. You obviously know nothing about business, and you don't need to, either. Tell you what: at the moment you've got twenty-two roubles – you give them to me, and I give you my word of honour that at the start of June I'll bring you back forty. I've got some very promising business on the go right now. It's good for you, and it's good for me.'

The boys looked at one another, and the decisive Antos was the first to say, 'Deal!'

Neither the financial genius of Andreika, nor his honesty –

at any rate, with them – were in doubt, for it was true that otherwise they would get nowhere. They suddenly saw the entire adventure in a new light, through the eyes of Andreika. Those parts of the plan that they had not thought through properly were, of course, shamefully childish. But all the keener did this make them long to show themselves and the world just what the three of them were capable of – and without the help of any grown-ups.

The money was solemnly handed over to their new friend, and shortly after that they had their exams, so there was no time to worry about anything else. On the very first day of the holidays Andreika whistled outside Yakov's window and, when he came out, he thrust a packet in his hand.

'Here, count it. If you need a boat, tell me – I know where to get one.'

But they had already chosen a boat from a fisherman from Peresyp. He was a solid, middle-aged man, and swore that 'this vessel' could even get them to China, let alone America. It was a good boat, with a tarred sail, and the fisherman had also promised to give it another coat of paint before it was due to sail, and not charge a single kopeck extra for doing so. All that remained for them to do was gather their things and fix the day. The prairies awaited. Lazy waves came gently lapping in off the Black Sea, and there clearly was not going to be a storm on it that month. Their mothers – hoped the travellers – would weep for a time but then they would get over it, and in time they would come to be proud of them.

9

The appointed day came, and the fisherman Fomich was to sail the boat to an agreed little bay near Langeron by five o'clock that evening. The money had been paid the day before. Fomich had said the boat 'needed leavin' to dry out for a bit', and any time earlier than five was quite out of the question.

Throughout the entire morning Yakov never left his mother's sight. He had gathered his things, the packs were hidden, and there was nothing more to do – except wait. Rakhil, who was glad that today, at least, the boy was not conniving to go tearing off first thing, felt happier. They were good children, really. Perhaps it was silly of her to feel so frightened that they were about to embark on a life of their own, quite separate from hers, and with various friends of their own. Perhaps Moisei was right, and there was nothing wrong with those 'goyish ideas of fun', such as football, 'living pictures', and trips out to sea? It was, of course, terrible to lose control over the children, but, there again, she was an uneducated woman, and even in Moisei's living-room she always felt ill-at-ease, as though she were somehow dressed wrongly and did not know how to discuss topical issues. But the children – they were getting a proper education, the likes of which neither she nor Isaak had even dreamt of, and their acquaintances were all children from decent homes, and they were so polite. Rimma, however, was rather cold towards her mother, but that was just her nature, and besides, what could you possibly say of a girl who was top of her class at the gymnasium and studying singing? Take today, for example, when she had her last exam – could Rakhil honestly doubt what mark the girl would bring home? And, as for Yakov, although scarcely a day went by without him getting carried away with some new madcap scheme or other, he still had a heart of gold. He was so affectionate and, even if he was frivolous, he was only eleven years old, after all! And a healthy boy, thank God. How he used to cough when he was little, when she had to force him to eat his food and keep his chest covered, whereas now – what an appetite he had, and he was already looking so tanned . . .

The two of them spent a lovely time sitting at the small table by the window. Yakov had popped down to the corner to get some early cherries, and was now building a pyramid of pips on his blue saucer, quizzing Rakhil as to what Papa's horse had been called, and how Mama and Papa had met, and what sort of wedding they had had – about everything that his mother loved to relate, and he loved listening to time and time again.

She felt easy about letting him go when he said that today he was going with his friends to Langeron, and, once again, she was touched at how affectionately he kissed her. As he left the yard, Yakov looked back. It would be a long time before he saw the house again. But no serious thoughts came to mind, for he was more concerned in case he had forgotten to pack the beads that were to be exchanged with the Red Indians. Through each of his veins a sweet shiver of the forthcoming journey was already coursing, and everything around looked so ordinary and languid in the summer heat that he had not the slightest regret at leaving.

The cosy little bay exuded the warmth that had accrued during the day, and the friends made themselves comfortable on a little rock that was shaped like a cockle-shell and jutted out into the sea, and from where they could immediately spot Fomich arriving in the boat. None of them had a watch on, but the time was drawing near: they knew from the shadows. Fomich, however, was late, and Maxim was the first to get worried.

'What if he doesn't come today?'

'What do you mean "doesn't come"? We had an agreement, remember!' Antos indignantly remarked.

But it was already getting dark, and there was still no sign of the familiar boat. They began peering closely at every sail, but not one of them looked even remotely recognisable. Then even the sails grew invisible, and all that could be seen were occasional lights out at sea. Down below, in the dark, the warm water could be heard dragging on the shingle. It was obvious that Fomich was not coming. Could he have swindled them? They had not yet come across human baseness on a scale quite such as this, and were reluctant to believe it. But suddenly it struck them that they did not even know where to look for him. He was from Peresyp – he had told them so himself, though they had met him at Langeron, and that was also where they had inspected the boat . . . By now they already suspected that they would never again set eyes on the man at Langeron. Nor would they be able to get hold of so much money again, either. And what would Andreika say if they, the intrepid fugitives to America, came across him in the city gardens, as though nothing had ever happened?

Yakov suddenly burst out laughing, 'What fools we are!'

'I don't see what you find so funny about it!' said Maxim indignantly.

'So you'd sooner I cried, would you? One day you can tell your grandchildren what a great adventurer their grandad was!'

For all his heart-felt anguish, this unexpected notion of Maxim's grandchildren made Antos snigger, too, but he recovered himself, and said sternly, 'Right – here's what we do: for the time being we must go home, even if it is shameful, of course. I hope, gentlemen, you understand yourselves – not a word to anybody. This matter must go no further than ourselves.'

'Ye-eah, so how are we meant to get back at this time of night? It's already late. And what are we going to say when we get home?' Maxim started whingeing.

But the friends quickly shut him up: what had happened had happened, and they must take it like men. They might be able to think something up later – but, for the time being, they had to go home and keep their mouths shut! The return home was not pleasant. In reply to the severe questioning of his father as to where he had been idling away his time until late, Antos firmly replied, 'Papa, I've done nothing wrong. But I gave my word to my friends that I wouldn't talk about it.'

Knowing his son, his father realised that he could not get any sense out of him now. The boy was distraught, though he still looked him straight in the eyes, and Ivan Timofeyevich merely wished to confirm, 'But you weren't up to trouble?'

'Word of honour!'

After that Antos heroically endured a week of house arrest, and that was an end of the matter. Yakov concocted an entire story about a fire at Blizhnye Melnitsy to tell his mother – only what he found hardest was, not putting up with the domestic scandal, but keeping it all to himself. In his memory the entire incident became embellished with a whole stack of humorous details, and he was bursting to tell at least someone about them. But, for the time being, he endured it. As for Maxim, as soon as he got home, his mother, who was beside herself with worry, immediately embraced him. For the first few minutes it never even occurred to anyone to reprimand him: thank God the boy was safe! And then, still in a state of shock at the injustice he had suffered, he burst into tears and told his mother of his anguish. What dreadful people there were in the world!

Such was his despair that he was not even scolded but sent straight to bed. However, before he fell asleep his mother forced him to swear, and kiss the cross as he did so, that never again would he run away from her, and, being very worked up, Maxim gladly did as he was bid. Next day the Petrov parents were already laughing the adventure off at Sergei's country house, and the guests merrily recalled how they had themselves run away and got into trouble as youngsters. Dr Dulchin had even developed an entire theory of his own on the subject.

'What is to be done – that's Odessan children for you! They're born poets and adventurers, and that's what they grow up to be. And do you know why? It's all a matter of astrology and acacias! Yes, ladies and gentlemen – acacias! It's all down to the acacia tree!'

This gave a new turn to the conversation, and the guests, who were accustomed to Dulchin's paradoxes, already knew that they were about to be treated to something rather fresh and out of the ordinary that would be pleasant to repeat to their acquaintances on some later occasion. In Odessa the acacia bloomed with the force of an act of God: it was all over the place, and its sweet and sinful smell permeated the entire city for weeks on end, the branches of the trees were laden with its blossom, vases were filled with it, boys would eat handfuls of its wet, creamy-coloured blossom, and ladies pin it to their dresses. After they had bloomed and dried out, the flowers would go spilling down the carriageways, and horses would rake at them with their hooves. Like now, for although the blossom was coming to an end, with each gust of wind Sergei's open veranda exuded such a strong smell of acacia that it was even slightly giddying.

'Do you know, ladies and gentlemen, what this smell does to people? We need not go into details . . . But I tell you as a doctor: the birth-rate in Odessa reaches its peak nine months after the acacia has bloomed. I even have my own statistics on the subject, so let's have no argument about it. And that means – depending on the year – that if they are born under the sign of Aquarius, they become entrepreneurs, adventurers, travellers and generally highly active people. Or, if they are born under the sign of Pisces, then what you have on your hands is children with stardust in their eyes. They become artists, poets, musicians, and generally people with a feel for beauty. This, I say again, is the majority, and it is they who give the city its physiognomy. It is they who make Odessans what they are,' Dulchin concluded with satisfaction, lounging back in his wickerwork Marseille armchair.

The theory was more than vulnerable, if only because the boy who had inspired such universal mirth had been born in May. But Dulchin was not a man to argue with: at the time mysticism was in fashion, and everybody was pleased to learn that there were solid grounds for Odessa's exceptional character.

There were jokes about the earnest Christian feelings with which Maria Vasilyevna would now pray for the scoundrel Fomich, who had so wronged her son and, at the same time, evidently, managed to save his life. And, for everybody except Sergei, that was an end of the matter. He, better than anybody, was aware of the value of youngsters enjoying themselves at sea. Not having any family of his own, he had become very attached to Ivan's family: he was respectfully tender towards 'our angel Masha', he spoilt the children, and was regarded as one of the family. However, he could see that, apart from himself, there were also others who spoiled the children, and that, unlike their parents, ahead of them there lay a hard life. Masha and Ivan naturally did not understand what all this was leading up to, and it was pointless trying to explain. He was horrified to discover that in 1905 Ivan had given a sizeable sum of money in support of the Social Democrats, simply because it had been the done thing and a lot of others had been making contributions. Every attempt to clear the matter up with his brother came to nothing. Well, in that case the only thing he could do was to toughen the children up. The time would come when they would be grateful to him for it.

And he suggested to the Petrov parents that the children might come and spend the whole summer at his country house: he had horses on which they could go riding, and a yacht, so why not arrange 'a home-based cadet corps'? They could invite their friends and he, Sergei, would ensure that at night the entire party would be so exhausted that they would be ready to collapse. Discipline, fresh air and no wool-gathering!

'What do you mean, Sergei – the girls, too?' was all Maria Vasilyevna could think to ask.

'Masha, dear, the girls are quite capable of their own wool-gathering! Emancipation, tragic love and all that sort of stuff – God forbid. They're better off riding and swimming – and it's good for their health, too. Zina will be our little housekeeper, and Marina will pick up a decent sun-tan, instead of spending her time weeping in front of the mirror.'

Everybody burst out laughing. Marina, who was already thirteen, and promised to be a good-looking girl, was suffering because of some spots on her forehead, and considered that she was hopelessly disfigured. As the adults knew, for a girl of her age the only available remedy from this misfortune was sunburn.

And everything was arranged accordingly. Maria Vasilyevna visited Rakhil and the Teslenkos and promised that she would take personal responsibility for looking after the girls and that, as far as the boys were concerned, there was no need to worry as they would be with Sergei.

'Shanks! Slacken your shanks!' the anxious uncle would ball out, as Maxim, sweaty and exhausted, came flying out of the saddle yet again. Sergei, who was mad on horse-riding, thought the initial instruction should be conducted without stirrups: a good horseman could grip with just his knees. His one concession was for the girls: they exercised on the placid mare Brysya, whereas the boys were kept exclusively to the jolty Arap. However, for those fond of adventure Uncle Sergei's favourite, Strelets, was also at their disposal, and he had the nature of a thoroughbred Kirgyzian stallion.

They had even greater fun on the water: for a start it became clear that Yakov was unable to swim. God alone knew how he had managed to keep this hidden until now, but it showed that he would sooner have gone to America like that rather than own up to this. Now his friends were too busy to mock him: for the life of him Antos could not get the hang of rowing in time with the others, and every now and then his oar would send up a splash, while Maxim, it transpired, suffered from seasickness. Sergei was quite merciless about this: he took all his protégés down to the sea when the 'broad' was blowing and showed them 'once and for all what a good shake-up's all about' – it was a cruel method, but it was effective. In no time Maxim and Yakov were longing to die as quickly as possible, while Antos sat proud and pale, and Marina, who for some reason was not at all seasick, sympathised as best she could, agilely working her way round the yacht with wet towels. To their delight and surprise, however, it really did put an end to their seasickness once and for all, and, by the time it came to their next major sea outing, so great was Yakov's appetite that he distinguished himself by eating his way through the entire ration of biscuits.

'The gentlemen students' – Pavel and Vladek – were spared from Uncle Sergei's schooling: they were, he thought, passably well trained enough as it was, or at any rate, with them he felt it 'looked presentable from ashore'. Nor, in fact, did they stay at his country house: Vladek was spending his summer holidays at the Andreyevsky Estuary, coaching the son of the grain-trader Valiyev for the gymnasium entrance exam. And Pavel became mad on the idea of wireless communications, and had crammed his room at Koblevskaya Street full of piles of wires and home-made induction coils. Fessenden's fame gave him not a moment of peace. They were both occasional visitors to the Fountain and, as Sergei put it, both were 'free-thinkers', and would laugh encouragingly as they looked at the peeling noses and worn palms of the young 'cadets'. Their arrival brought the feminine half of the house to life, for with it came the promise of longer and more entertaining evenings.

Zina, who was by now accustomed to her role as housekeeper, would serve everyone tea, and Rimma, after brief promptings, would sing romances, while Vladek, who had jokingly cast himself as Marina's knightly protector, would tease Yakov, who evidently aspired to the same role. Just as Sergei had promised, however, by evening the 'cadets' were already nodding off to sleep and went to bed almost without protest. Maria Vasilyevna, who herself always attended such evenings, kept a close eye on the youngsters: here she was responsible for the girls and, furthermore, in her opinion girls who were in their penultimate year at the gymnasium needed to be watched especially closely. For, as was well known with these country house evenings, before you knew what was what everyone was falling in love with one another. Her elder son, she had noticed, was excited by the blue eyes of that Teslenko girl. They were good eyes, and clear, but weren't they both a little young for that sort of thing?

> 'When first we met, and the last times too,
> How lovely the voice of my sweetheart true . . .'

sang Pavel in his young baritone, while Sergei, with his head lowered, dwelt on thoughts of his own. Marina, who was always quick to sense the mood, rested her slender hand on Uncle Sergei's sleeve, and he gratefully kissed her childish little paw. For some reason, it struck him that this fashionable 'romance' had a secondary, prophetical meaning. As if they were all leaving Russia, or Russia no longer existed, or that they had themselves ceased to exist, and never again would anything be as it had been in the past – neither this lamp, nor the warm smell of gillyflower, nor the white table-cloth, nor these young faces which so readily changed from thoughtfulness to laughter. And the reason they were happy was precisely because they thought their chief happiness still lay ahead . . . and here he sat, with his doom and his gloom, imagining that he knew everything that the future held. 'I'm getting old and sentimental,' thought Sergei, grinning wryly.

The youngsters had already finished singing and were now arguing heatedly about the Russian tsars: had there ever been so much as a single progressive one amongst them? Was Peter the First the one exception? They knew that it was audacious to discuss the monarchs so freely in the presence of Uncle Sergei, but that was precisely what egged them on.

'Yes, Peter was a fine one, too – killing his own son!' said Vladek, with an indignant shrug of the shoulder.

Once again, it was time to set them straight, and Sergei quietly pointed out, 'So, in your opinion, Vladek, that was unprogressive, was it?'

'Really, Sergei Alexandrovich, what is there to discuss? Murder is murder.'

'After all, it wasn't just his son that he killed. You must agree that the entire story goes way beyond ordinary domestic violence. After all, he killed someone with a claim to the Russian throne – and, however you look at it, that makes it political.'

'But, Uncle, whether or not it was a political killing, there is still no justification for murder!' interjected Pavel.

'So that's what you think now, is it, my friend? But I recall how three days ago you, Vladek and Rimma were all in favour of Vera Zasulich, and the fact that the jury acquitted her, although she was the one who shot Trepov. I understood you to be in favour of political killings, and now all of a sudden it's unprogressive . . .'

This was a telling blow. They had nothing to come back at him with, and Pavel, who was blushing, only asked, though already by way of self-defence, 'But then three days ago, Uncle Sergei, you raised absolutely no objection, if I remember rightly?'

'Of course not, my boy. I'm not yet so old as to fail to understand that in arguments such as these you are not in the slightest bit interested in the opinions of old uncle miseryguts, or anybody else's for that matter, other than your own. Don't think I'm reproaching you: youth has rights of its own. I was just the same when I was your age. That's why I didn't argue with you. I can only oppose your opinions with opinions of your own. And, given that, I hope you will at least put them into some sort of logical order.'

'But even so it's not an entirely apt parallel,' objected Rimma, still trying to keep up the resistance. 'After all, Zasulich did not kill Trepov!'

'Yes, I recall how at the time you regretted that she hadn't,' remarked Sergei, courteously bowing his head. 'So what's the difference? Whether or not Trepov had survived would have made no difference to your principles, would it?'

'Uncle Sergei! Really now, that'll do – this is becoming more like the slaughter of the innocents. As housekeeper, I order you: stop it!' laughed Zina. In her heart she was happy to see Pavel and Vladek put down like this, but she could see that Rimma was about to flare up, though there was no call for this.

'Aye-aye – leave off slaughter of innocents!' Sergei jocularly responded. 'Would you care for some refreshments, my queen?'

The youngsters gladly took up this offer of refreshments. A marble-like water-melon was cut open, and compliments were duly paid to it, although by their demeanour the gentlemen students let it be known that they had expected refreshments to mean something rather stronger.

As she was combing her hair before going to bed, Rimma mercilessly yanked on the comb. Why did she feel so irked by that uncle of Zina's? He was a middle-aged crank who was incapable of thinking in the modern way. He had almost certainly not read Kropotkin. He had been in the Russian navy, and now he was a Russian landowner. But what arrogance! It was as if he were mocking her all the time . . . and all the others, too. But he was, at the same time, a cordial host, and so attentive to everyone. Yakov followed at his heels like a pup. And he was tender with Yakov. But to her, Rimma, there was no telling what he felt. And what, really, did she care how he felt about her? There was an impenetrable wall of good manners around him, and he paid polite compliments to her singing, though no more. With irritation she felt that for some reason it was important to prove to this man . . . Prove what? Why did she have to prove anything to him? Why had she ever mounted that crazy Strelets – just so that this Sergei Alexandrovich could marvel at how brave she was? Well, he had marvelled – so what? How delicately he always spoke with Anna, and how he always smiled when she wasn't looking – as though she were some kind of wonder! With Zina he was always joking, but that was understandable – they were relatives. But with Rimma – the wall. Was it a nobleman's attitude to a Jewess? But then what about Yakov – he showed no coldness towards him, for she could feel things like that. Should she have a word with Anna? But Anna would not understand, for as far as she was concerned everyone was always nice . . . a somewhat original attitude to people! Zina, as ever, would simply burst out laughing. There was just about nothing that she took seriously. A nobleman's daughter, and, what's more, a beauty – why should she trouble her head thinking? From the day she was born she had had everything she ever wanted. This world of horse-riding, mirrored shop-windows, yachts and polite servants – she was at home in it. No, that wasn't it. The shop-windows and yachts – all that sort of stuff could be bought with money. Uncle Moisei was rich, too, but he would never have the same status as Zina. How freely she gave instructions to her uncle's Nikita, and he would all but leap into action, even though she was still just a girl. Was he a toady? No, he was not – sometimes he would even grumble at Sergei Alexandrovich, who would just comically shrug his shoulders . . . They were fond of Nikita, and that was all there was to it.

But she, Rimma, was not at home in this world. Yakov could do what he wanted, but not her. Though surely it was possible to love other people's worlds? Take Morfessi – he wasn't Russian either, but he was on good terms with Sergei Alexandrovich. No, he was Russian, all the same. A Russian Greek. Then why was she in love with him? That had nothing to do with it, ideas like that simply confused you. One thing was clear to her: she would either have to love the world of these Petrovs, or else hate it. And it did not look as though it would be love.

10

'Attempt on life of Minister Stolypin! Shot in the arm and liver! Sensational details!' yelled the newspaper boys one clear September morning, all but throwing themselves beneath the wheels of the cabs. Odessa, which was by that time already incandescent with the merchant seamen's strike in the three ports along the coast, gave vent to political passions that had seemed to be quietening down.

'Uncle, what do you think – will there be any pogroms?' asked Yakov.

'Now where d'you get an idea like that from?' asked Moisei, grinning.

'Then it's not true that Bogrov is a Jew, is it? That's just what I said at the gymnasium, but they—'

'You, chum, should button your mouth at the gymnasium. Silence is golden, don't you know? Bogrov is a Jew, so he's obviously no fool. He wasn't shooting at the Tsar, after all, although he would have been just as successful if he had been. Of two monarchists – if, of course, Nikolai can be considered a monarchist – he went for the more dangerous. Had he assassinated the Tsar, then of course there would have been a pogrom such as never before. But no one will bother about Stolypin. Even Nikolai, they say, is not particularly upset.'

'So who's going to replace Stolypin now, Uncle?' interjected Rimma, who had been anxiously listening to them.

'Rasputin will have something to say on that – don't you worry.'

When Moisei spoke, everything seemed clear: there was nothing to worry about, this probably called for no more than a dismissive little witticism. It was a storm in a tea cup. However, that very evening Rimma heard Moisei talking with her mother, only seriously this time. He was intending to transfer all his capital to Vienna and eventually to go and settle there. The monarchy would soon collapse, which was all it was fit for anyway. But what was the point in hanging around to be buried by its ruins? Who could predict what would come next? Universal brotherhood, he was sorry to say, was somehow scarcely credible in this country. Rakhil also had to think about the future. But there was still time, it did not have to be decided overnight.

For Rimma, however, this was unconvincing. The Tsar was on his throne, and in two years' time they would celebrate three hundred years of his dynasty – so why should this monarchy collapse if people just hung around waiting for it to do so? Imagine having a chance to assassinate the Tsar – and then fluffing it? This Bogrov had probably missed. It was hard shooting from the auditorium of a theatre. What if it were done from the stage, when you have the entire auditorium right in front of you! Why hadn't anyone thought of that before? The performers weren't searched, after all. Now what about going out on stage with pistols – she and Morfessi – and having a shot at the monarchy: there, that's for your Pale of Settlement! That's for your censorship! That's for your Cossacks with whips and the searches and the secret police! Let them later hang her for it, let them tear her to pieces. What bliss to perish together with the man she loved for a just cause. Russia's finest people had been the Decembrists, the members of the People's Will, Lieutenant Schmidt – had not this been what they, too, had dreamed of?

There was no one to share this with: it was hardly a subject to discuss with her relatives. Nor with her friends either, for they had bourgeois views, after all. Or rather, there was no telling whether, in fact, they had any views on anything. As for Zina, at least she had some imagination, and something to her, a certain unpredictability. But Vladek had been right in dubbing her the Snow Queen: no one ever knew what she had on her mind, and she would always do everything in her own particular way, and force others to do so, too. As for Anna, she was straightforwardly decent. The only thing for a girl like her to do was get married and have babies and cultivate potted ficuses. But how could she get on a stage from which to fire the shot? The Tsar spent most of his time in St Petersburg – who would let her go there, across the Pale of Settlement? How lonely she was. This was not how it ought to be: there were revolutionaries, after all – in other circles. She had to get to them: Odessa was like some kind of bog. They were out-and-out fun-seekers who never took anything seriously, and in 1905 they had merely been playing at revolution. Well, she would soon finish at the gymnasium. She definitely was not going to the Conservatory here, but would instead go to Kiev. And once she got there everything would become clear – from then on everything would take care of itself.

And, indeed, she did manage to persuade her mother to let her go to Kiev, and in the autumn of 1913 she started her studies at the Conservatory there. To mark her departure the girls arranged a party for her, and she cried sincerely as she bade her friends farewell. What a time of it they had all had together – fooling about with 'Madam Bonton', crying over the same books, teasing their brothers, inventing special words of their own that none but the three of them could understand. There was still a great deal to look forward to, but now all of that had gone for ever. Now they were embarking on a new, adult life.

'Mama, come and sit with me awhile.'

Vanda Kazimirovna smiled and let out a sigh. They both loved this 'come and sit with me awhile'. It was almost before Anna learnt to speak, and possibly even earlier, that the two of them used to sit together in the old armchair, with the mother in the seat, and Anna on the arm-rest. Here they had sung Polish songs together, here Anna – looking over her mother's shoulder – had learnt how to read, here her mother had answered her countless childish, and then no longer childish, questions. Her little girl, her little daughter. With the boys it was all different, but it had been possible to dress this one up in lace, and kiss the dimples in her cheeks, and put curls in her hair, and buy straw hats – over and over again, until she grew up. But she had grown thin – where were those dimples now! – and she had a lady's hair-do, and a grey dress without any lace. She had her course studies to be thinking of. And her mother already felt that today's conversation would be a difficult one. Anna had been anxious of late, she had become withdrawn, and been eating virtually nothing – her waist-line appeared to reveal a good deal more than just worry. Well, the girl was eighteen years old. Had she fallen in love? If only that were it! Oh Lord, preserve us and have mercy on us!

Anna, as always, pressed her cheek against her mother's shoulder, but then raised her head.

'Mama, I'm so afraid of hurting you . . . But you should know about anything important, shouldn't you?'

Vanda Kazimirovna nodded bravely. Anna continued to embrace her, and she felt her daughter's hands stiffen.

'Mama, it seems I don't believe in God.'

So that was it! Now just be sure not to start shouting or crying. Gently, gently. Maybe it was not all so awful. For at least she still took it as important.

'Is this someone else's doing, Anusya?'

'No, Mama, it's not that. If it were just a matter of thoughts – are you with me? – well, ideas and all that sort of stuff, then of course it would be possible to argue until eternity. But I know all these arguments off by heart. You know, to me it seems that whenever I listen to anyone, they're right, and then someone else says something – and they're right, too, and you don't know who to agree with. But anyway I always end up coming back to my own way of thinking. I'm probably too stupid for anyone to make me agree with them. I'm not a believer – not with my head, I simply don't feel anything. Before I used to be – but not any more. And in church I feel ashamed, as if I'm lying, and I go up and take communion like a thief. It's just dishonest, isn't it – going to church if you don't believe?'

'Is it a private shame, Anusya, or is it shame because of what others might think of you?'

'Who do you mean, Mama?'

'There's no need to explain, child, you know what I mean. You have some new acquaintances – there, on your course, and you have your own circle of friends, and there are young people there – students, and not only students. Most of them, I know, aren't believers, and they regard going to church as backward. You think that you also don't believe – that with them you'd be ashamed to behave differently? Or is it that you'd like to believe, but don't feel any faith, and that's what's troubling you? Don't answer now, if you don't want. But the first one is a great sin. As for the second – that happens to each and every one of us, at some time or another. It's the Lord testing your faithfulness.'

'Mama, I don't know, I've never thought of it like that. You think that one day I'll believe again, do you?'

'I will pray very hard for it. And you pray, too, even if it seems that you're praying into the emptiness. Anusya, my girl! Just don't refuse, my faith alone will be enough! I'll pray for it as long as I live, and then I'll die – and I'll go on praying in that other world – the Lord won't turn his back on you, just don't refuse . . . Anusya . . .'

They were both crying now, and Vanda Kazimirovna felt relieved that the most important thing had been said, and that there was nothing further terrible to face. It was like a hand on her shoulder – not that of her daughter, but another hand – a sign from God. Even before she had offered up her prayer. The girl would be saved – of this she could not have been more convinced even if she had just that moment heard a Voice.

'Mama, forgive me. How shameless I am – how sad I make you. It would be better if God existed and punished me for this.'

'Some time ago, Anusya, I made my own mama sad in just the same way. And I was about the same age as you, too. You're not to blame for it, it's just the way families are: everything that we do, our children in turn do – both the good and the bad: differently, but they still do it. And that'll be true of your children, too.'

'You're talking about the time you ran off with Papa, aren't you? But Granny later forgave you, didn't she?'

'Yet, even so, she was very hurt by it. And as far as her forgiving me's concerned – I'll also forgive you everything, just as you will with your children.'

'But what if she hadn't? After all, Grandpa . . .'

'It's enough if anyone takes it all on themselves. Any sorrow, any sin – take it on yourself to forgive, and that will put an end to it, and nothing more will be left of it, you understand?'

'Yes, it's true. But I'll never run away from you.'

'Are you sure?' Vanda Kazimirovna smiled.

'But you do like Pavel, don't you?'

'Ah, so you've already decided, have you? It's nice of you not to forget to tell me.'

Anna shook her head. 'We've decided nothing. Rather the opposite, in fact. You see, he made me a proposal, and I said that, for the time being, there was no need to talk about it. He loves me, I know, but it's myself I still don't know about. It's all somehow too ordinary.'

'Well, you clever girl, not rushing into anything. He's out of his mind: he's still a student, and already proposing . . . In our time a man used to make sure he could stand on his own two feet before he thought about marriage.'

'No, he meant in future, when he has qualified.'

'So, before that happens he wanted you to commit yourself by giving him your word, did he?'

'I didn't like it, either. You know, I don't want to marry him at all. Only I feel that that's what'll happen anyway . . . Silly, isn't it?'

'If marriage is what you want, then that's what you'll get. Just don't go hoping your parents will help out by forcing it upon you,' said her mother, bursting out laughing.

'Some hope. You see, Mama, I thought that if I told you what I thought about God, you and Papa would drive me out of the house.'

'Anusya, how many mad-hat ideas have you got in that head of yours?'

As always after crying, neither of them any longer had it in them to discuss anything serious. They wanted to natter and joke, and they suddenly felt like something to eat.

Pavel was furiously spurring Strelets faster on over the drooping sweet clover. He had already been riding off the road for a long time, and now all about him was the steppe, with its bird cries and wild smells. She had been right to refuse him. What a boy he was, what a fool! What gibberish his shyness had made him come out with, it was shameful to remember. It all came back to Pavel and he shook his head and groaned. He thought that, once he had taken the decision, it would be like plunging into water – and that once he found himself on the spot the words would come of their own accord. Fine one he was! He wasn't the sort of student who was going to discover gunpowder – Professor Novikov was quite right. What would the future hold? A career as a mediocre academic? He could become an engineer, of course – but then why bother going to university? The polytechnical institute would have been more appropriate. To Anna, of course, it wasn't important . . . but what was important to her? What was he like – generally, as a man? Neither one thing nor the other . . . He even lacked spiritual nobility: what, in all conscience, had made him go and talk about the future like that with her? He had been frightened that, now she was no longer a child, someone more interesting and intelligent than he, Pavel, might come along – and take her away from him. And then Pavel would lose her for ever. That would be just awful. He should have kept his worries to himself, nonentity!

He should have gone straight from the gymnasium into the navy. His uncle had been wrong in urging him not to. So what if the fleet was disintegrating? All the more reason for him to be in it. Well, so that made it his uncle's fault. Why did they all have to go heaping the blame on to somebody else? It was true of his father, Maxim, and himself. Did it run in the family? Why, for example, was he now ruining his uncle's horse? Was he taking his fury out on the animal? Ah, to hell with it all! He saw a little ravine that was densely overgrown with gorse, and sharply ordered the horse onwards. Strelets obediently jumped over it, thought very nearly catching his hind legs. This sobered Pavel, and he slowed to a trot.

Strelets had been on the verge of high spirits, but now he gave a disrespectful snort. Just as the fun was starting, the rider had gone all mopey. Strelets loved nothing more than to run flat out, when it was no longer possible to tell where was the rider's will and where that of Strelets himself, when the rider had no pity for him, but was also not anxious about being disobeyed, when they both thought as one and merged into a single being: the man almost a beast, and Strelets almost a man. For this Strelets was ready to submit, but only for this. His owner he understood, but why did he allow anyone that came along to use his beast? Strelets pretended that he had not immediately understood the command, and from a gallop he abruptly switched to a mocking saunter.

'Hey, quit messing around!' yelled Pavel, and turned in the direction of the Fountain. For some reason the awareness that life would never go his way made him feel easier. There was no point in trying to guess ahead, and things were so good now. From Strelets came the smell of hot horse flesh, over his right shoulder the sky had already started to darken into evening – Pavel was riding obliquely towards the sunset, and each little blade of grass cast a sharp shadow. He was young, he was alone – and that in itself gave him an impression of immortality. Whatever would be would be. And now he could see the sea, too. He did not stay and spend the night at his uncle's, but rode on into town, to Koblevskaya Street.

At home the smaller children were playing an old game of which Pavel was himself very fond: 'where's the sea?' Everyone took it in turns to be blindfolded and spun round by the shoulders. Once you stopped, you had immediately to point in the direction of the sea, and anyone who made a mistake was penalised. Pavel never made a mistake in this game, and he let them tie the fold over his eyes with pleasure. As she tied the fold Marina smoothed down his hair, and he suddenly felt how much he loved this house – it had always been the same and would always remain so, with its potted philodendrons, its grand piano, the clatter of crockery in the evenings, and its newspapers in a pile on the little hexagonal table.

But the Petrovs' house had by this time changed: now the children had grown up, they had, without even noticing it themselves, brought a new tone to the family. This had started several years ago, and it was Zina, of course, who was behind it. Ivan Alexandrovich had at the time been furiously indignant about Pavel's fascination with football, and had flatly refused to let him go to a match at the gymnasium.

'What sort of scoundrels' game is that – hoofing the ball round with your feet?' he thundered. 'And this unbelievable jargon – backs, forwards, and some sort of dribbling . . . And the dress – it's almost like underwear. The Sporting Club, they call it . . . I know every decent club there is in Odessa, and there's no such club! Where does this happen? What do you mean "behind the French boulevard"? It's a wilderness there! It's a place for convicts, not children from decent families!'

'Papa, do you really want to be more conservative than Wolf-Lamb?' Zina unexpectedly piped up.

'And who might that be?' asked her father, spinning round.

'Sorry, Papa,' smiled Zina, 'I meant the inspector of the Odessan Educational District, Mr Shcherbakov. You know, without his permission, this match . . . what match is it, Pavel? That's the one, the final of the inter-gymnasium competition – it simply couldn't have happened.'

Ivan Alexandrovich looked at his daughter and saw an almost adult, understanding and crafty look. And that manner of tilting her head . . . A girl, good God, who looked just like him! What a gang they had grown into! He realised that now she would be able to do as she pleased with her father – manipulating him with her little hands, and he, what was more, would be glad of it. How was it that he had never previously understood which of the children was closest to him?

'Wolf-Lamb, you say?' He asked with a wry smile.

That was something he could relish telling his acquaintances – the nickname that the pupils at the gymnasium had given to Shcherbakov, who was renowned for his conservatism. It wasn't bad: Wolf-Lamb.

Pavel looked into Zina's laughing eyes and understood that this vile snake of a little sister might have some sense in her head after all. From that day forth they became friends. And their father had become so amenable to all the novelties of the time that when his sons became 'fans' of Utochkin – the maddest of all the Odessan madcap sportsmen – not only did he not try to stop them, but even joined them standing in the crowd, beside himself with delight, as everyone watched the red-haired hero ride down the Potemkin stairs on a bicycle. A hundred and ninety-two steps! It was simply the largest set of stairs to be found anywhere in the city, so after that Utochkin had no choice but to become an aviator instead, and once again delight his admirers by describing a circle over the city and the sea.

The very word sport was then still new, and Ivan Alexandrovich became carried away with it – naturally, not as a sportsman, but as a patron. He made new acquaintances, he donated a certain amount to the Odessan Aeroclub, he became an *habitué* of the hippodrome and took great delight in holding forth on the advantages of the Russian school of riding as against the English.

For the first time Maria Vasilyevna grew worried that her husband might ruin the family at the races, but this did not happen: Ivan Alexandrovich gave his word that he would place no large bets, and he kept it. He himself, it seemed, had become younger, and relationships in the house became more frivolous and straightforward. The atmosphere of a storm that simply would not break, which in the past had so tormented Maria Vasilyevna, cleared. Their father had but to knit his brows for the children to go racing over to the bronze barometer in mock horror. The barometer was hopelessly ruined, and required no more than a tap of the finger to send it pointing to 'clear'.

The Teslenkos' material situation picked up. The father received a pay rise. Vladek, who worked as a tutor, managed to keep himself, just like many other students. The professors at the medical faculty were regarded as virtual Black Hundreds, and at the time were renowned for their merciless demands on the students. In the very first exam on anatomy Vladek all but failed a question on cranial bones, and since then he had no more time for the riotous student life seething out in the corridors and at the meetings of the local associations. The vice-chancellor, Kishensky, was himself a professor of medicine, and was considered reactionary, and barred students from holding meetings: 'This is not 1905, gentlemen!' And if any meeting did take place, then the medical students simply had no time to take part in them, for the lilac-lined buildings of the medical faculty were too far away from the main building.

Vladek quickly got over all a medical student's usual passions: he found that he had every disease described in his textbooks, he abused the word 'colleague', and at anatomicals he shied away from the corpses whose state of decomposition sometimes caused their muscles to contract. After a while, however, with horror he came to understand how little medicine, which he had previously regarded as all but omnipotent, could actually do.

'Yesterday, colleagues, I participated in the autopsy of a five-month-old baby. I regret that you could not have been present: it was a police enquiry. The story is banal: a peasant woman came to the city in search of work, she gave birth to a child and, as they say, she "overslept" it, in other words, she appeared to have accidentally suffocated it in bed. There was naturally a suspicion of murder,' said Professor Telesin with relish, raising his large white hands. 'I checked the lungs, the blood vessels – no signs of cyanosis. There was no poisoning in the stomach. It was a perfectly healthy baby. The cause of death remained a mystery. Imagine my predicament: I had to write up an official report, but as yet no diagnosis had been made. The reason I'm telling you this is so that you might know – not how to save such "overslept" babies, but that medicine is, for the time being, powerless to explain this phenomenon. A dilemma: should I take the sin on my own conscience, have pity on the woman, and write something about congenital pathology? Or write what had actually happened, and thereafter leave the investigation to take its own course? No, I shall not tell you what I did. A doctor is not God, but God is a doctor's only judge. In future, colleagues, bear that in mind.'

Vladek already understood there were two types of medicine: one for the uninitiated – with medical luminaries, amazing cures and eternal hope in the powerful and confident doctor, and the other for the doctors themselves, who were capable of so pitifully little and were themselves aware of this.

'Doctor, sew my arms back on!' a worker from the rope factory had pleaded in semi-delirium.

'Everything will be all right, dear chap,' Dr Golovin had said reassuringly, and the students, who had been brought in to see a typical case of blood poisoning, proceeded to the next patient. The man was, they all realised, beyond hope.

Vladek knew that he was an idealist. All that remained for him was to let himself sink into unmitigated cynicism, or, alternately, to overcome it, to become familiar with all that medicine currently knew, and leave the impossible for some later time. If no one knew how, then he must find a way himself. Now he was frightening his parents with his sunken cheeks and the fanatical fire in his eyes. At night he would sometimes mutter in Latin, and then Antos would unceremoniously poke him in the ribs.

'I'm so worried about him, Holy Father,' said Vanda Kazimirovna to the black-eyed Catholic priest Orylsky, a friend of the family.

'The boy's red-blooded, *pani* Vanda, the boy's red-blooded. You remember what I say – such a son will lead you into the sin of pride,' smiled the priest, taking a saucer with apricot jam.

One day in December 1913 Nikita woke the Petrovs up. He was crumpling his cap with trembling hands. The snow was melting on his boots. He senselessly looked on as Ivan Alexandrovich came running out in his dressing-gown.

'The master . . . He's died . . .'

Sergei, who had never had anything wrong with his health, had failed to wake up that morning, and although Dulchin came immediately there was nothing he could do to help.

'Say what you will – it's still the most merciful form of stroke,' he tried to persuade Ivan Alexandrovich in an undertone, taking hold of his shoulders. 'He didn't suffer, he wasn't stricken with paralysis . . .'

Sergei was buried in the Second Cemetery. The uniforms of the naval officers, his friends, looked black against the pale blue snow. The wind ruffled the wreaths, and the petals on the ones made of living flowers contracted in the freezing cold. The old priest sang in a faint voice – or so it simply seemed when the choir lapsed into silence. And the grave into which Sergei was lowered was as black as the naval uniforms. Pavel dimly watched as the mound grew steadily bigger. A crow with a fluffy grey hood settled on the adjacent grave, where his grandparents were buried. It kept a curious eye on the dish with the funeral fare. Someone placed a hand on his sleeve. Pavel knew who it was. He gratefully squeezed her cold fingers in his palm – for some reason she had no gloves on – and he felt the torpor had passed, and tried to hold back the tears.

By evening Nikita was already back at the empty dacha. From now on, he realised, this house would belong to the other Petrovs, and there would be a new way of life here. He went off to the stables and hugged Strelets's warm neck. And so the two of them stood, mourning. Strelets was the first to cry.

PART TWO

'Pavlik, you've gone mad!'

His mother slumped lifelessly back in her wickerwork chair.

'Mama dear, everything will be all right. It's an excellent regiment – normally they're not keen on taking volunteers, but I'm a physicist, and they need educated people. Remember – this is the artillery, not the infantry. They've really got everything worked out, you know. I'll be an ensign there till the end of the year. And it's getting easier to win promotion nowadays. It could hardly have worked out better for me, and there you are, moping away. Tomorrow I'll be issued with a uniform – so soon, just think of it!'

Pavel was unusually animated and with his eyes blazing he was recounting to his mother the advantages of serving in the artillery, reiterating that the war would soon be over and that it was perfectly feasible for him to complete his university course the following year – and anything else that might reassure her and keep her from tears. The tears he had foreseen – but what could he possibly do, given that there was a war on, and that he was a man? He certainly couldn't go on sitting at his university desk, pleading exemption from military service! Why, he would have died of shame.

'Masha, don't worry, my dear,' sighed Ivan Alexandrovich. 'But what am I talking about? With the sort of children we've brought up, how can we ever be anything but worried? You can't hold them back . . . It's in the Petrov blood.'

'Papa, how wonderful and clever and remarkable you are!' said Zina, rushing over to embrace her father. 'Now where has my papa got grey hair? Here's one . . . and here, and here . . . all because of his bad, disrespectful and disobedient children. First they don't eat their porridge, then they get bad school reports, and next they're off to war – and only then do they come to their senses.'

She was frolicking about, kissing her father on the head, and Ivan Alexandrovich suddenly felt that his eyes were becoming slightly watery.

'Well, thank goodness that you, at least, you mischievous girl, haven't gone dashing off anywhere yet. Dulchin told me that the hospitals here have plenty of work to keep everyone busy. So you should be glad . . . sister of mercy indeed!' he said, jokingly pushing Zina away.

'Papa, even if by some miracle she gets through the exam, she'll be the most merciless sister anyone could possibly imagine! And I should know, if anyone!' Pavel chimed in, glad at the turn this heavy-going conversation had now taken.

At that point Maxim came running in and excitedly informed them that some soldiers and some Serbs were being carried shoulder-high down Pushkin Street, and that everyone had been shouting 'Hurrah' and throwing flowers down from the windows, and that there was going to be a procession with the portrait of the Tsar, and a band – and it was coming right past the house before going on towards the boulevard. And indeed, after a while the blare of a helicon and a roll of drums were heard. Then trumpets were sounded, and with this silver fanfare playing it seemed to the Petrovs that all was right and well with the world. The Tsar had appealed to Russia, and Russia had risen up, and they would, naturally, win this war, and everything would be wonderful.

At the student party that was held in honour of Pavel and Vladek, the punch was made in the most proper fashion: a head of sugar resting on swords, rather than a prosaic trellis, had been placed over the punch-bowl with the wine, the rum had been warmed before being poured on to the sugar, the electricity was turned off and a flickering blue flame was the only light in the room. Yura Nezhdanov, who was himself going off to war as a volunteer, was keeping an eye on the flame and whenever it flared too high he would dampen it by pouring on some champagne. The entire company was seated on rugs round the punch-bowl, and they watched the large golden drops of burning hot sugar with approval. Slowly, and with a furious hiss, they kept dripping down into the wine. Soon it would be time for farewells, and everybody was aware of this.

'Vladek, if I ever end up in your hands on the front, then – as a favour for an old chum – could I please ask you not to cut off my arms and legs?' pleaded Yura in mock horror.

'The first thing that needs treatment is your head – by dowsing it with cold water. How about starting now?' replied Vladek, grabbing hold of a ladle. He was going to work as a medical orderly on a hospital train, and was disappointed not to have become a surgeon's assistant. But in order to get a special pass in the exam to become a surgeon's assistant, he first needed to have his papers from the university, and Vladek's department had categorically refused to do anything to help him.

'You, young man, must complete your course. Our most promising student – and now he suddenly takes it into his head that he wants to go off to the front! Youth, idealism – I understand. If it was anyone else, I would let them go, but you – never! Don't expect me to kill such talent with my own hands . . .'

And, having got up from his desk, Professor Antonov let it be understood that the interview was over. The rector Kishensky had also turned out to be an unsympathetic man, and, in a huff, Vladek had decided that he could get along fine without the university: they were crying out for medical orderlies, and no special education was called for, either. Very well, he would be feeding the wounded and shoving bedpans under their backsides. But, once he was there, he would show them what he was capable of. Vladek did not doubt for a minute where his proper place was, now that there was a war on: after all, the Germans were already advancing through Poland! It was a pity he could not have become a soldier, like Pavel and Yura. But now that he had committed himself to medicine, Vladek could not possibly renege on it: that would have been treason. He shook his head and started listening to a loud argument between some friends who were by now rather tipsy.

'So, now they're holding special services for the victory of Russian arms. And the English and the French are doing exactly the same thing. And, you can bet, the Germans are praying that they'll win, too. And they all think they're Christian,' Pavel was arguing. 'What I'd like to see is just one person praying as God commanded – for everyone, not just for our men, but for the Germans, as well. Then I might expect something decent of the Church.'

'Well, you go ahead and pray then, seeing as you're so righteous! Pray for the Germans, and the Romanians, and the Yids and whoever else you fancy! But as for us – we'll stick to the old way of praying for Russian arms!' Yura retorted angrily.

'I'd like to pray myself. Only I don't believe in God,' grinned Pavel.

'Well, stop pontificating then. You'd do better to give me your glass – and what about a song, gentlemen! Tatyana's song!'

Saint Tatyana was regarded as the patron saint of all students – believers or otherwise – and the entire student community observed Tatyana's name-day and had written innumerable songs in her honour.

The party broke up shortly before first light, with promises that they would, of course, not lose touch and would write to one another. Pavel was, he thought, not in the slightest bit drunk. His head was extraordinarily light, he no longer felt sleepy, and that beloved sense of his own immortality gave him an agreeable feeling of cold in the pit of his stomach. It was, of course, disconcerting to be gladdened by war. Not that he really was glad. But how could he fail to be aware that, ever since the war had started, everything in his life had changed for the better. What had he been just a week ago? Yet now he was a volunteer and on his way to the front. Behind him he was leaving his family and his sweetheart – under his protection. How right, and even righteous it was, and how calming. Everything was falling into place: if he were killed, Anna had made him no promises, and would be under no obligation to honour his memory. If he were to return, then he would do so as a hero and she might, perhaps, look on him with fresh eyes. In the depth of his soul he did not believe that the war would be over by Christmas, as the newspapers had predicted. He still had plenty of time – indeed, now he would have time to do everything that he wanted in life.

The fresh August night was rapidly melting away, changing its hues. At any moment the birds were bound to burst into song. And then, immediately, without any break, the summer heat would start to intensify. The 'Moldavan' wind would start blowing, but without promising any relief. The dehydrated gorse on the cliff-tops above the sea would rustle dryly, the roses on the balconies crumple up their petals and, when the heat was at its highest, even the vociferous housewives in the Odessan yards would be reduced to silence. The only ones who could be heard yelling then would be the tireless babies of 1914, along with the constant brass voices of the military bands playing out on the field of Kulikovo.

It wasn't hard to pass the exam to become a wartime nurse. There were short courses and some practical work at the Odessan military hospital, where, at the time, the senior doctor was good old Dulchin – so Anna and Zina couldn't possibly fail. If Vladek had not been so hot-headed he could have become a 'brother of mercy' himself just as quickly, and after all, that was still better than being a medical orderly. But Vladek had already gone, and goodness knew where he and his train had got to. Pavel had been seen off, and now his letters were awaited from Poland. And Anna, who had been made a surgical nurse, became shamefully confused when, for the first time in her life, she saw a man without any trousers on the operating table. She did not know where to put her eyes – all the more so as, quite independently of her own will, they kept looking back towards that sunken yellow stomach, and the sort of enormous bluish bags beneath it, beyond which there was the bloody mash that had, evidently, once been a knee.

'Nurse! What do you think you're doing – picking daisies? Scalpel – immediately! Get some gauze ready!' bellowed the doctor, and Anna, burning with shame, focused her attention on the instruments. The hospital was a good one – the wounded had only recently started being brought here, and this amputation was performed under chloroform. All the more horrifying, therefore, did Anna find the sound of the saw on the bloodied creamy-white bone, and the unexpectedness with which the man's leg came away from his body and suddenly shrank and shrivelled, and the way in which the medical orderly tossed it into some tray in the corner. It made a hollow thud, and already the doctor was sewing the stump up into a tidy bag, and Anna was as tidy and as lifeless as the stump. As if she had herself had something sawn away from her and discarded. She found it difficult to talk to Zina that day – her lips seemed to have frozen stiff – and it was not until later that night, when she got back home, that she burst into tears. Over a trifle, really: Antos had given the wooden horse Basya away to some little boys out in the yard and, as she was crossing the yard, she noticed Basya, now with only three of her legs, being ridden into attack by a general of about six, covered in mud and glory.

But she soon became inured to the smell of blood, and to the sight of exposed innards, and to her own, scarcely recognisable self – swathed in the white nurse's cap that made her look like a nun. Zina was having an even worse time of it: not once did she show any sign of nervousness and, to begin with, the doctors could not praise her too highly, but in time the smell of bedsores came to sicken her, and this, of course, became evident the moment that wounded men with bedsores started coming in. Dulchin comforted her, saying that this, too, was something that she would get used to – and he was right. For three weeks Zina was confined to bandaging, and, as though it had been removed by hand, her torpor lifted.

'Don't hold back, nurse, if you feel like being sick,' a middle-aged soldier with his buttock completely torn out comforted her. 'It makes me sick, too.'

'Now then, dear, it'll heal. It's just a flesh wound,' Zina replied spiritedly as she approached him with a solution of corrosive sublimate. 'Now this will burn . . . if you want to scream, go ahead.'

For Zina this was the first time that a wounded man kissed her hand after she had dressed him. Her hands, with their slender blue veins, were so used to worldly kisses that she paid them no heed, yet this was different, and she grew embarrassed, and it stuck in her mind for a long time.

Shortly thereafter Anna and Zina decided to apply for a transfer to the front, and so they appealed to the All-Russian Land Union, for the time being saying nothing about this to their families. They were, of course, hoping to be posted together.

By now it was October, and life in Odessa was still exactly as it had been before the war. True, wounded men were being ferried from the station, and true, also, that the newspapers were publishing lists of officers killed in action, and that the first widows and mothers had been seen in the blackest mourning – now it was accepted to call on them and express your respects. But the theatres were open just as before, and people were having fun in the restaurants and clubs, and the scope for such enjoyment was now even wider than it had ever been. It was a fine autumn – dry and warm. According to the newspapers, somewhere out there, in the middle of Russia, there were even forest fires. And peat-bog fires. Down in the south, however, there was nothing to burn: the sea could not be set ablaze, unless, perhaps, it were done by the blue tit in the fairy-tale?

Yakov had stopped believing in God a long time ago, but he had fallen into the habit of jokingly praying for whatever he felt like. This was made all the easier and more agreeable by knowing that there wasn't really anyone there to make you get embarrassed. And the lower classes at the Richelieu Gymnasium had learnt off by heart a prayer in verse that he had written, beginning with a plea for all Latin teachers to be stricken with plague, and ending with the hope that lessons would be cancelled owing to an earthquake. It was in roughly the same spirit that he prayed before the start of the second lesson, in which there was to be a geometry test, and, furthermore, one with the local school inspector sitting as invigilator. But the class had scarcely stopped banging its desk-tops when there was yet another bang, this time more protracted. Novitsky, who was the class tutor and mathematics teacher, was just about to shout 'That'll do!' when there was another bang, and it became plain that this was no prank by the fifth formers, but something rather more serious.

Were they being shelled? But the front was a long way away, and it was out of the question that anyone could be shelling Odessa. Was it a revolution? For a moment Yakov's hopes soared, but they were soon dashed. Since the outbreak of war the revolution had somehow petered out. The students had been going on patriotic marches singing 'God Save the Tsar' – as Yakov had seen for himself in August, and since then he had resolved never to let himself be surprised by anything ever again.

'Kindly keep calm, gentlemen,' instructed Novitsky, and it was clear from his face that he still wasn't sure what to do next. Should he lead the class over to the assembly hall? Or take them outside? Or send the duty boy to the headmaster for instructions? He had thirty boys in his care, no twenty-nine – Sinyukhin was off ill – and already that boom was getting closer, and there it was again. He had to save the children! But how could he get them from the gymnasium to safety if the city was being shelled? It was vital that there should be no panic . . . But his boys would never panic. They were fifteen- to sixteen-year-olds, at an age when they could be frightened of anything, only not death. How their eyes blazed, and each one of them was bursting with a desperate curiosity and a yearning to perform some great act of valour. Already one boy was asking, 'Please may I run over and find out what it is, Fyodor Andreyevich!'

'There's nothing to find out, Geiber, it's heavy naval guns firing. Gather your things everyone. And keep on your toes. We, gentlemen, are responsible for the younger classes. They're little boys. Any minute now they'll burst into tears and start calling for their mothers. I declare this class to be under martial law. We are going downstairs – to the preparatory and first classes. Once we get there, you are to stand in the corridor and await further instructions. Ustimovich, you're on duty today! It's up to you to ensure discipline!'

Yakov watched the transformed Novitsky in a state of rapture. Where had that snappy and commanding voice come from? Why was the chalk-stained sleeve of his jacket no longer funny, nor the jacket itself, and why were the buttons on it now shining with such military gleam? Oh, now they were prepared to follow Novitsky into fire and water, and from that moment on his nickname at the Richelieu Gymnasium ceased to be 'Sinus', and instead became 'the Colonel'. And so it was that this nickname would find its way into his case file in 1918, and that it would be under this name that he was shot as a counter-revolutionary.

The boom sounded as if it were coming from over by

the Prakticheskaya pier. It no longer looked like a case of straightforward shelling, but more as if a battle was commencing – there, out at sea. The younger pupils were sent home under escort. Strictly speaking, members of the fifth class were not regarded as seniors, but Novitsky had arranged things in such a manner that each of his pupils assumed the responsibility of a senior boy. Yakov sternly knitted his brows and was cursing his shortness as he led two youngsters from the preparatory class through the agitated streets. One of the boys proved to be surprisingly perky, and kept trying to slip off in the direction of the port. Yakov had to grab hold of the little devil's paw, which was ink-stained and covered in something sticky, and even threaten to turn him straight over to a policeman.

The police, however, had quite enough on their hands as it was: on the corner of Sadovaya Street some cabbies had created a blockage, leaving the street now virtually barricaded off. So they had to wait, and, as they did so, they learnt the news.

'We're under attack from the Turks – I've just got back from the port. The pier's been blown to smithereens – honest to God! And they've sunk a French ship.'

'It can't be the Turks! We're not at war with them!'

'Come off it, madam, you don't expect the Turks to bother about declaring war first, do you? They'll blast away for a good hour before getting round to that! It makes no odds to those heathens. When have you ever heard of Turks behaving decently?'

'Heavens above, the Turks are all we need now! Lord have mercy upon us . . .'

'Steady now! They'll be repulsed in no time.'

'Come on, gentlemen, let's get this lot cleared out of the way! Turn that horse's shaft round to the right, you blockhead!'

'No need to shout, my good man, this horse of mine gets some funny ideas sometimes . . .'

The following day the newspapers came out: 'Odessa, Novorossiysk and Sevastopol shelled . . . Perfidious attack by Turkish fleet . . . Russia takes up the challenge . . .' A week later it was announced that brilliant victories had been won on the Turkish front, and that, virtually without meeting any resistance, the army was now advancing deep into Turkey.

'Well, it's high time this business of Constantinople and the Straits was sorted out,' said Nina Borisovna in the Petrovs' living-room, herself now a die-hard patriot.

'This could well prove to be a problem with our allies,' drawled San Sanych thoughtfully.

'Oh, come on! Where would those allies be without us? And who would Paris belong to now if it weren't for our men on the Western Front?' said Nina Borisovna heatedly, kneading the next of the cigarettes that she always seemed to have to hand.

'Well, now we've got another front, too. We mustn't over-stretch ourselves,' sighed Ivan Alexandrovich. He had noticed how, ever since Sergei had died, he was assuming the role of sceptic with increasing frequency – as if his brother had bequeathed him his turn of mind.

At this point Dulchin could no longer contain his indignation. 'So what would you have us do, given they were the aggressors? Let them have Odessa, hey – is that your idea? So much has been written about German atrocities – and now you fancy we need some Turkish ones into the bargain, do you? Gentlemen, my colleague Samarin is presently stationed near Lvov with a field hospital there, and really – the things he's written me!'

'What? What has he written?' asked Maria Vasilyevna in alarm, and Dulchin realised that he had made a gaffe, for the Lvov region was precisely where Pavel's last letter had come from.

'Oh, it's much as ever, Maria Vasilyevna, my dear . . . nothing new, really . . . it's what you'd expect of the Germans. Now don't you worry, our army has never been stronger. All our best people are out at the front, you know. The flower of Russia!' Dulchin loved using such beautiful expressions, and, until the retreat of 1915, they didn't sound so peculiar, either: all the intelligentsia spoke and wrote of the war in somewhat high-flown terms.

'Well, it's all very well talking of flower . . .' said Ivan Alexandrovich, shaking his head, 'but the thing is to ensure that the rear doesn't let them down.'

'Well, we'll certainly try not to, my friend,' replied Dulchin, raising his red and sleep-starved eyes, and Ivan Alexandrovich realised how tactless he had been.

Anna and Zina received their long-awaited postings on the same day: Zina was to be sent to a hospital train carrying wounded from the Western Front, while Anna was to go to the seventh vanguard detachment of the All-Russian Land Union, which had been ordered to the Turkish Front. Although it was a pity that they had to leave one another, Anna realised how incredibly lucky she had been: usually it was only Red Cross nurses who were sent on such responsible postings. They were considered to have the professional experience, and this was felt to be a task that the special wartime nurses simply weren't up to. It was emphasised to Anna that an exception had been made in her case. This was flattering and, at the same time, demeaning. To mark their farewell they had their photograph taken at Bruyevich's studio – and they looked strangely alike, in their nurse's caps coming down over their necks and foreheads, with both of them smiling, and both twenty. Anna knew that Zina would send the little photograph on to Pavel, and she bitterly regretted that it had come out making her look as if she had a broad nose and shadows under her eyes. But, really, it wasn't worth the bother of having it done all over again!

12

Everything was turning out wrong, wrong and wrong again
– not at all as Vladek had wanted. And all because he had
acted so hastily. The Union of Cities was, after all, a civilian
organisation, and its relationship with the government and
the army was not entirely clear. Although its activities were
officially sanctioned, authorities of which Vladek knew nothing,
and which were now co-ordinating the complex machinery of
wartime health care, regarded all its initiatives with a certain
suspicion. Indeed, the hastily organised structure of the Union of
Cities was itself riddled with confusion. Firstly, Vladek had been
put on a hospital train in the rear, and secondly he had found
himself having to make journeys from Moscow to Tambov, or
Yaroslavl, or Saratov. Vladek suspected that this was all part of
some plot. The hastily recruited student volunteers, who had
not yet even got round to taking off their student caps, and
wore them with their soldiers' uniforms – a liberty that would
have been inadmissible in an army at the front – evidently failed
to inspire any great trust, being seen as potential mutineers and
propagandists. So they were farmed out to the rear – safely away
from the front line. Somewhere out there Lvov had already been
taken, and the name on everyone's lips was that of Brusilov.
Already Samsonov's army was advancing on the Mazursky
Lakes. Already Soldau-Tannenberg, previously known only as
geographical place names, had acquired a sinister ring, and
Vladek was meanwhile busy lugging buckets of boiling water
and cabbage soup. This called for almost circus-like dexterity:
two hands to deliver two steaming buckets at the double so
as to prevent them from getting cold, on top of which the

doors leading from the carriage out to the carriage platform had somehow to be opened and closed, and this had to be repeated on the way through into the next carriage as the train jostled about over the points – and how many carriages you had to get through was a matter of sheer luck. Vladek, need it be said, was not lucky: he had to make his way through as many as forty-two, or even forty-six doors in a single direction. Why were there so many blasted doors to a carriage, and why were they built so differently?

> 'Write that my darling is Vova,
> He's the one that I most long to kiss,
> I've an Austrian helmet from Lvov
> For the boy that I so dearly miss . . .'

– a voice could be heard singing in the officers' carriage to the accompaniment of a guitar. It was plainly someone with a light wound, for his voice was robust, and he was neither straining or short of breath. But Vladek rushed on past – on into his own carriage for other ranks, back to his own forty. Half of these men, and sometimes more than half, were unable to get up off their backs – and they were all in his care.

There was little sense to be had from nurse Zalesskaya, who had eyes like a frightened little girl. Even now she was still scared of hurting someone while changing their bandages for them, and it was pitiable to watch the timid state of fluster that she got herself in. When she had been on the point of running off to the senior doctor about a soldier with a perfectly innocuous wound, Vladek became livid. Oh, but his temperature had unexpectedly shot up – and what if he suddenly contracted gangrene? And all this without even checking his dressing. True, it was a complicated dressing – being made of solid plaster, which meant that it shouldn't, really, be changed in the train. This was too much for Vladek, and he ordered the nurse to stay where she was. She meekly obeyed (itself typical of the woman!), and Vladek simply went up and smelt the man's plastered shoulder: if inflammation had set in, then nothing was simpler than to diagnose it by the smell. There was plainly nothing wrong with the wound, so it didn't take a genius to figure out why the man had a temperature. After exchanging a few words with him, Vladek went up to Zalesskaya and, with pointed coarseness, said, 'He's spent the last five days constipated! What are you waiting for, nurse? The senior doctor to come and give him an enema?'

Zalesskaya's transparent and slightly foxy eyes became bigger than ever, and she was clearly on the verge of tears. So Vladek just snapped, 'Leave it to me then.'

Zalesskaya took this in the broad sense, and left Vladek to do almost all her work in the carriage. He did not get angry at this: there were only a few nurses in the train, and she was already in enough trouble with the others as it was. And, besides, he liked the sense of being absolute master of his work, and simply wanted to be left to get on with it. He always kept his carriage spotlessly clean, and saw that the men got their food and drink on time, and were all properly washed, and it was also left to Vladek to look after the bandages and medicines. Of course, the senior doctor Korotin had noticed that medical orderly Teslenko was exceeding his authority but whenever he passed through Vladek's carriage, he simply muttered vague noises of approval. Virtually every medical orderly in the train was a student, and there was only one qualified medic, and Korotin – had it been left to him – would have made Vladek a surgeon's assistant straightaway, but for the time being he made a point of treating him as if he had some special status. Vladek was aware of this, and so it made him all the more annoyed if the wounded asked to see the 'little sister'. And ask they did, with incomprehensible insistence.

The snow clung to the black windows, and the train was passing through an area so forsaken that no light could be seen anywhere. And the soldier in the far berth, the one who sounded as if he came from Ryazan, was forever moaning that his arm felt itchy, and calling for Nastya to come over and see him. Vladek did not even immediately realise who he meant, for he had never taken any interest in nurse Zalesskaya's Christian name, but he had to pander to the patient's whim before he woke the entire carriage up.

'Little sister – oh, it's burning! What is it there? Have a look for me, little sister. Sprinkle some water on it . . . water . . .'

So nurse Nastya brought some water, not for his arm, which did not exist, but for him to drink, and she held her palm to his hot forehead and uttered some tender remark – quite what, Vladek could not hear.

'Oh, that's better! Don't go away, little sister. Have a look outside and tell me where we are, can you? Have we reached Ryazan yet, or not?'

'It won't be long now. So you've got someone in Ryazan, have you?' asked Zalesskaya, as though, having been woken up in the middle of the night for no good reason sleep was the last thing she felt like, and that she was instead interested in talking about Ryazan.

As he tried to catch something of their quiet conversation, for the first time Vladek suddenly became aware that the constant noise in the carriage – the sound to which he was by now so accustomed – was not only the wheels, but also a viscous, quiet moaning and muttering. During the daytime the other ranks tried not to moan, and were generally less capricious than the officers. But in their sleep they whimpered – helplessly, like children. And what they needed was precisely a woman – if not their mama, then at least a nurse: to show them affection and pity. And this was precisely the ability that Vladek lacked, whereas for Nastya, like all these other girl-nurses, who were so inexperienced and unprofessional, and frightened of hurting patients, it was an ability with which they had been born. They could not yet know that they were the nurses in a war that would later, when many of them were no longer alive, come to be known as World War One.

Outwardly Vladek did not alter his attitude to Zalesskaya, but already the very sound of the name Nastya had become surprisingly associated with this snow-bound central Russia, and with hanging about on the sidings in small towns, and the neglected gardens covered in hoar frost and the wooden houses. He could not be described as having fallen in love: it was enough that, each time he looked at Zalesskaya, he could not help recalling Zina – his 'Snow Queen'. And for some reason this made him ashamed. Their very dissimilarity served as a reminder. Zina could never, in Vladek's imagination, lose her composure or burst out crying, nor was her face at all reminiscent of Nastya's rather simple features, nor had she ever looked at Vladek with such gullible, submissive helplessness. He knew that he could do as he pleased with this girl – yet it was for precisely this reason that she came under Zina's invisible protection. Beneath her white nurse's cap Vladek seemed to see another woman, and he would lower his eyes.

Stolen kisses and overnight romances at the train stops came easy to Vladek over that long winter. He was the same ladies' man as ever, and would merely smile when one of the team ribbed him for this. But if they joked about Zalesskaya, he flew into a rage, and after a while, nobody risked it any more. This joy at venting his fury was in itself a new experience. It called to mind the fights of his boyhood – although that had been so long ago, and it wasn't quite the same, either. The first time that he let himself go was in the buffet car, as they were trying to fob him off with some tepid soup for his wounded. Suddenly he turned on one of them and, with whitened eyes, almost in a whisper, he muttered through clenched teeth, 'Scoundrels! I'll crush you!'

And suddenly it proved effective, and he saw that he could get away with it, and there were certain situations that had to be dealt with in this manner: by demonstrating a readiness to cross a certain line beyond which it was clear that if anyone got in his way he would crush them. The war, which overnight had deprived him of almost every freedom and opportunity, was, it now turned out, also opening up certain new possibilities.

In the spring of 1915 the entire team on the train was transferred to a field hospital, and for the first time in his life Vladek found himself in Poland. It was not at all like the Poland that he had dreamed of. There it was, outside the carriage window – with its little stations, damp fields and storks atop the thatched roofs. Yet, even though far from all of the girls who came up to the train bringing cucumbers and milk had golden plaits – as, for some reason, Vladek had imagined that they would – they did all speak Polish. Almost all of the children who waved from the embankments had fair hair, but not the grown-ups. Every now and then he caught sight of crucifixes by the side of the track: crosses beneath a small arch like the roof of a peasant hut. The train was approaching Visla.

'Number two, fire!' bellowed Ensign Kosov, for some reason in a joyous voice. And almost immediately beneath him the earth exploded in black smoke: the Germans had got the range of his battery, but were, for the moment, firing slightly too far to the left. After each explosion it seemed to Pavel that his mouth was full of this earth, and he kept wanting to spit it out. During the lulls he noticed that the three-inch cannon over on the far side lay toppled over with a broken wheel, and it looked as if the ammunition carrier for number two had gone missing somewhere. Ah, poor cannon!

'Number one, fire!'

But then there was another explosion and that was number one done for . . . no, it just looked that way. In fact, two cannons were done for. That left four, and they were still firing, and now a surviving ammunition-carrier came running over to take someone's place.

The retreat was already under way, and it was time for them to get going, too, but – as ill luck would have it – just the day before they'd taken delivery of a fortnight's supply of shells. And it was simply unthinkable to leave without having fired these shells. Even if it wouldn't actually be treason, it would certainly have been a disgrace. And Captain Kavelin's battery could not allow that. Well, every cloud has its silver lining: at least they'd be able to provide cover for somebody else's retreat. And, the way things were shaping up, any moment now they'd be firing at the enemy point blank . . . Was Kavelin stuck up on that hillock? It was a good hillock – one from which you could see everything around, and the ideal spot for the battery commander, too – from here he could co-ordinate the firing. But that was provided they could hang on to their position of cover – and how much longer would they be able to do that for? And by now there wasn't a trace of their communications left.

Pavel sprang up on to Ogurchik and, as so often before, delighted in having such a clever horse. Without waiting to be told what to do, Ogurchik instantly set off for the hillock – and not directly either, but down through the hollow, where Pavel had taken him last time. The hollow was now completely churned up, and all that remained on the slope were some ludicrously drooping bushes with their roots half torn out. Pavel noticed that he was talking to himself, heaping obscenities on the staff and the bastards back in the rear: one minute they'd be clean out of shells, and the next the battery would be ordered to fire no more than three a day – and that was at the front! Then – it beggared belief! – they'd delivered shells just as they faced being cut off with them.

By now he had reached that trough in the hollow where a young fir tree had survived and some spindle-bushes had sprung up. And it was here that the commander's horse, Osman, stood tethered along with the sergeant-major's, Okhalnik. Every horse in the regiment had, of course, a name starting with the same letter. As soon as Pavel jumped down some shots rang out from above. Ah, just as well he did jump! Pavel had no time to tether Ogurchik. He threw down the rein. And took out his Nagan revolver. Then he went up on to the hillock and got behind a boulder that was overgrown with brambles.

There they were – the sons of bitches! A German mounted patrol – so, there were five of them, no, there were only four horsemen. Kavelin must have already brought one of them down. And there he was, sitting on the ground while Dudko reloaded his carbine. Everything was happening slowly, as though the horses were not even running but swimming through a thick jelly – and the sergeant-major went on and on fiddling with his carbine and Kavelin raised his Nagan in his left hand, taking forever over it, as the enemy steadily drew their carbines up to their shoulders. By now, however, Pavel could see that they would have no time to get them up into position before they drew level with the boulder, some four yards away from where he was now – first came the one on the bay horse, he just had to wait and let him go slightly past. As coldly as if he were out training, Pavel found his aim just as the horseman was half-turned around – and then time broke free from its chain and surged ahead at its normal tempo.

Pavel did not hear his shot, but his German came down, and was then caught in his stirrups and dragged off into the hollow by his bay horse. The Germans managed to get off two shots, destroying a gun-rest, and Pavel was now after the second of them, and he saw that his horse had stumbled. Another shot! And another! Just as Dudko fired his shot – and down came the German and his carbine flew away. The two remaining Germans had now realised that they were being shot at from behind the boulder and, having brought down their horses, they were making to turn and face the hillock. Without any compunction, Pavel fired his remaining four cartridges into their backs, and then twice again he senselessly squeezed the trigger. His Nagan obediently clicked: click-click, and these blank clicks were the first sounds that Pavel actually took in. Over on the far side of the hillock there were some wretched pine trees through which the Germans had managed to slip away.

Pavel vehemently shook out the warm cartridge cases. His fingers were now jumping, and he lost a further second on reloading. Only then did he run back over to his own men. They were alive! Kavelin's sleeve was blackened, but he looked clear-headed. There were harsh wrinkles round his mouth, like crushed tin-plate, and he had a strained grimace on his face. He struggled to get up. Dudko was fussing over him with delight in his eyes: they'd made it! The dead German lay with a boyish smile on his face, and his helmet had rolled away to the side. He had his hand under his cheek – his fighting days were over. His eyes were open, and already an ant was crawling over his temple. Pavel had a sudden urge to flick the ant off, but felt it would somehow be wrong. In the meantime the dead man's horse kept thrashing about with a look of pleading in its eyes. Pavel put his Nagan to its ear: well, at least it was better to polish off a horse, rather than a German. How could they possibly have dragged a wounded man from here as a prisoner?

He and Dudko lifted the captain up, and Dudko slung his left arm round the back of Kavelin's neck.

'Gently does it, sir.'

'Timed that one pretty fine, Petrov!' said Kavelin baring his teeth, and then he just made some quiet hisses and screwed up his eyes as they made their way over to the horses. Ogurchik, the beauty, was in exactly the same spot as Pavel had left him, and had not gone bolting off. As Pavel lifted the captain up on to Osman, Dudko grabbed hold of the bay horse, shoving the German out of the way, but hanging on to his carbine. The sergeant-major was not the sort to go leaving any equipment lying behind in the hollow. The German horses were fit and well-fed. And so it was that they eventually got back to their battery with an extra horse in tow.

Ensign Kosov, however, was still out in the thick of it firing off his last shells: he had received no orders from his commander, so this was entirely his own initiative. It looked as if the shells had found their mark, too, for the German shelling had suddenly stopped. Either their observation point had taken a direct hit, or else they were busy changing positions. But this was no place to hang about – it was time to scarper. The battery had three cannons left – which meant they had to get hold of eighteen horses. And what a state they were in, too – lying about on the ground there: the grey was no longer moving, apart from the shuddering of its splattered innards. It was better to avoid looking at those two, but what about that dark bay rascal – he looked as if he had just been taking a nice little lie-down. Dudko immediately set to work on the horses: the ones that were still fit had to be harnessed. Including that new German one: let's see you put in some proper graft with a harness on your back. We'll have you out of here in no time, Captain! Not that the captain had yet given the order to retreat. But then it came.

'Ensign, we're retreating. You take command.'

That was all the captain could say, and then he shook his head and sat down on the ground: he'd been shot through the right shoulder. Dudko immediately lifted him up and carried him over to the gun-carriage. Who, in August 1915, could be expected still to have any clean foot bindings left to use as dressing on their commander? Yet Dudko had: both enough for his commander, and plenty to spare, too. He certainly knew what he was about when he nicked part of the clothings issue. Goodness knows where they came from, but then some towels embroidered with cockerels also appeared. Hey, weren't those from that village he'd gone off to in search of food for the horses? But the ensign had no time to pursue his suspicions of pillage. The commander of the second artillery platoon had been killed, less than half of the men had survived, and now he, Kosov, was the only remaining officer.

'Yes, sir – command taken! Get those wounded on the

gun-carriages! Private Pryanik! That's your responsibility! Sergeant-Major Petrov! Take the observer platoon! You're going on reconnaissance.'

Pavel spurred Ogurchik forward, and four men followed him – all that was left of the observer platoon: three scouts plus Shuleiko the telephonist. Now they had to find the shortest and safest line of retreat – and one that the battery following them could also take – and then stick to it till they got back to their own lines.

Pavel no longer regretted that Commander Kavelin had switched him from the gunners' platoon to reconnaissance. To begin with, however, he had taken it badly, for he had become very fond of the three-inch Schneiders. They were powerful, light and had a modern loading system: unitary and quick-firing. The battery's six gunlayers were, of course, its best-educated soldiers, and Pavel took pride in the fact that he had so easily and quickly been made one himself – after all, he had started off as a mere loader. Shortly thereafter he had been made a sergeant-major and weapons-commander. But it transpired that he was also good at map-reading, and if need be could stand in as the telephonist, and he had a thorough knowledge of how to use all the communications equipment: there had been a number of occasions on which he had mended some simple fault. And this soon caught the attention of the battery commander, despite the fact that Pavel was a student and a volunteer. Then Pavel became his right-hand man – the commander would be stationed at his observation point, determining the angles and lines of fire, and the battery's senior officer, Ensign Kosov, would take charge of the firing, while Pavel saw that their communications kept them in touch with one another. He was finally won round, however, when he was given Ogurchik: the artillery draught-horses were cumbersome, but the ones that the scouts were given were birds, not horses. Fit for an officer.

And, typically, at that very moment Ogurchik was shaking his head in suspicion: he disliked this little marsh, but he still stuck to trotting obediently along the edge. Pavel knew from the map that, if the battery did manage to find a way safely through in between this marsh and the other one over to their right, then they would reach a forest cutting, and from there they could get on to the road to Kovno, which was, he reckoned, still in Russian hands. But the recent rain had all but merged the two marshes into one, and it was touch and go whether the cannons would be able to get through or not. However, if they cut down a few young pines and put them beneath the wheels, then they had a good chance of making it.

Evening was already setting in when, under Dudko's tireless command, the soldiers had managed to lay down enough tree-trunks to prevent the cannons from getting bogged down. The sergeant-major kept wanting to get everything 'nice 'n' tidy', but the ensign was in a hurry, so they pressed on and just managed to get the cannons across all right. They also had to push the gun-trails from behind – but it did the job. And then, once again, came the boom of German shells: from up ahead, and to the right.

'More left, go left!' bellowed Dudko at the top of his voice, his face turning purple. But more to the left was impassable, and by now the first cannon had come to a halt, blocking the narrow passage. From somewhere nearby and off to the right there was a boom that threw up a liquid fountain of mud, and one of the front harness horses started threshing its hoofs and neck in some pinkish shallow water. Ensign Kosov was struck by a falling pine, but the main blow fell on his horse, so, although shaken, Kosov still managed to get back up on his feet.

'The covers! Put the covers under the wheels!' yelled Pavel. It looked as if Kosov was temporarily unable to speak, having been deafened by the blow. Pavel interpreted his weak movement as a nod, and now it was up to him to command the battery. The covers were torn off the cannons and placed down over the mud and logs.

'Shove!'

Somebody had already managed to cut the traces from the wounded horse, but still nothing moved, and then Pavel saw that Kavelin had lifted himself up slightly on the gun-carriage and was almost rolling off the side. And the other six wounded who were still conscious did likewise. And the first cannon moved – and now the ones behind it were free of the weight of seven men. Later on Pavel was unable to remember how they got through this part leading up to the forest cutting – but get through it they did, and from then on the cutting led them off to the left, out of range of the shells. The commander and the rest of the wounded, who were by now caked in mud, had to be carried to the forest cutting and put back on the gun-carriages.

'Sterling stuff, Ensign!' Kavelin muttered to Pavel as he was placing him back on the gun-carriage. And Pavel could not make out whether the captain was so blinded with pain that he'd mistaken him for Kosov. Or had he made him an officer right there on the spot? Although Kavelin was not, of course, empowered to do this. The most he could do was to put in a report requesting his promotion, though now, of course, that was the last thing on his mind. Pavel wanted to slap himself for such thoughts. This was no time to be thinking of shoulder-straps!

After this he kept his mind firmly on the job in hand. They crossed the forest cutting without any particular difficulties, and then Pavel was heartened to see that Kosov was already back on his horse. Even in the twilight his red head was clearly visible, and it was plain that it had not been seriously injured. In all, Pavel had been in command of the battery for half an hour at most, and he wasn't complaining that this was too short. They came out on to the road, along the entire length of which an endless column was trudging back in retreat. But – retreat or not – these were Russians, and Dudko yelled out in delight, 'Hey – boys!'

For almost the next twenty-four hours they continued retreating without a break. By now the road was no longer shot up by artillery, but on a number of occasions some German bi-planes flew overhead, and this was not an encouraging sign. The wounded were handed over to a field-hospital detachment. This detachment consisted of a cart, a small wagon and several men on horseback. These 'fliers', as they were called, made their way along the column faster than anyone: everybody else had to get out of the way for them. Dudko had already found time to foul-mouth the last flier to come along, but this had been mainly for the sake of form: he could see for himself that the carts plainly had no room to take any more wounded. A rumour went down the column that Her Majesty's Motorised Medical Detachment was also somewhere in the vicinity, and Dudko was hoping this might offer a chance to get the commander some proper attention. In the event, however, he had to make do with the first cart that came along with enough spare room on it.

'You ham-fisted imbecile! Can't you see you're bloody well hurting them! Get some straw, you idiot, and lay it down! Here, get your mitts out of it – leave that to me! Ooh, wearing a sword, eh? – damn fool civvy! Do you know who that is you've got there beside you on that cart, you snotty little git? That's our commander! And if anything happens to our commander, you rascal, I'll get you if I have to chase you to the bottom of the sea!' Pavel could hear Dudko's furious cries – and he rode up closer to the cart.

'Take it easy, Sergeant-Major. Don't alarm the wounded,' an abrupt, but strangely familiar voice could be heard.

'How dare you talk to me like that,' flared Dudko.

But then Pavel spotted a tall man in a strange uniform: he had silver shoulder-straps with a little star, and a sword with a gleaming hilt. And he gasped, 'Vladek!'

Vladek raised his uncomprehending eyes to the horseman's unshaven face, with its hollowed pits beneath the cheek-bones, and was barely able to make him out in the twilight.

'Pavel? Is it you?'

'Who d'you think it was!' yelled Pavel with excitement as he sprang down from Ogurchik.

'What's up – do I look different, or something?'

'Oh brother, how skinny you are! And you've got a 'tache . . .'

Vladek was already hugging him, and they both burst into laughter at the same time.

'Well, I'm still kicking, old chap!'

A couple of minutes of senseless natter – jumping from one subject to the next – was all they could permit themselves.

'How's Anna?'

'She's in Turkey, she's fine. I got a letter from home last week. She's in a hospital. No, she's not wounded, you funny fellow – she's a nurse! Your family's all right. And Zina's working on a train round here somewhere.'

'Good Lord! This is no place for her!'

'No, if it was up to me there wouldn't be any women round here. Pavlik, how glad I am!'

'What are you doing in that uniform? It's impossible to tell if you're an ensign or not . . .'

'The Union of Cities issued me with it. Idiots that they are. It's as if they actually meant to rile the soldiers. But who cares about the uniform – I'm obviously not German, and that's what counts.'

On realising that these two clearly knew one another, and that here, after all, was a chance of getting the commander properly seen to, Dudko now started getting pally-pally.

'Now, my good sir . . .' then he realised that to address a civilian with self-appointed stars on as "sir" was overdoing it, and he corrected himself. 'Look, mister doctor's assistant, look after our men, will you . . . Our commander's been through a hell of a time for almost two days now. So I thought maybe you'd like to take a look and see if it's dangerous or not?'

'It isn't dangerous, Sergeant-Major. But we've got to get a move on. We'll get him back and then put some proper dressing on him. Don't worry.'

'But I mean you, personally . . .'

'I promise I'll see to it myself.'

Kavelin shook Pavel's hand: although weak, at least his left arm was working. And he gave a clear smile. How strange it was for some reason, and it took Pavel a while to figure out just what was strange about it. Then he realised: it was simply that it had been so long since he had last seen anyone smile. The dead German had a smile on his face – but none of the living ever did. Vladek hadn't smiled, either: he'd laughed, and then started watching him attentively again, as if he had not quite recognised who Pavel was.

'Move! Get out of the road! Make way for the wounded!' Dudko could be heard roaring from somewhere up ahead and, now back on their horses, the two friends repeated an old prank from their gymnasium days, seeing who had the firmest handshake. Pavel made a secret wish that, provided Vladek did not look round, then all would be well with him. Vladek did not look round.

Only after they had passed Kovno – and that meant getting

altogether clear of it – did the colonel allow a halt. And then, at last, they were back with their own regiment – now reduced to half its former size, but still having managed to hang on to its banner and some of the cannons. They had not been cut off, and – thanks to the position they'd been in – their retreat had been shorter than it had for the others. Pavel realised that the retreat was not yet over, but tonight, at least, could be spent by a camp-fire, giving the soldiers some hot food and with the prospect of a few hours of sleep. A mounted patrol was sent to a nearby farmstead – a *khutor*, or whatever the Poles called it – to fetch some provisions. But the farmstead was abandoned. Evidently in a hurry, too, because the patrol came back with ten chickens and several goats. There was also some hay there, they reported. The farm had not been burnt. The fugitives had, of course, no time to worry about taking any hay with them.

Anyone would think that, the moment their clothes had just about dried out, men that were this exhausted would sleep like the dead. But, instead of this, they sat round the camp-fires, relishing brewing up some soup, and at a nearby fire somewhere they were even singing.

'And so, brothers,' Dudko was saying, after already having been and brought back some of the hay, 'there we were, and I don't mean peeling spuds, either – no, this was an im-pe-rial inspection! All kitted out in parade gear, we were, and our commander, Kavelin, looking like an eagle! And we nailed every one of our targets: direct hits on the lot of 'em. We fired better than anyone else, and there were plenty of batteries there, too! . . . Hey there, you little blighter, it didn't take you long to crawl your way back,' he said, his attention now distracted as he scratched his armpit.

'It's a funny thing, that: they never bite you when there's any fighting, the little beggars!' said the boyish-looking recruit Yefimkin in surprise.

'The louse is a cunning little beastie: he doesn't like shooting. He's a skiver whose natural home is back in the rear. And the minute things quieten down, then back he crawls,' explained Dudko instructively. 'So there you have it, brothers, that's how it was at the inspection: they wanted to see which was the best battery, and up came this Lady-in-Waiting to Her Majesty – in person and with a goblet for the commander. Can you imagine what an honour that is! A silver goblet on a golden platter, and alongside there's the Tsar and all his entourage. No one else could drink anything, just the commander, right there in front of the Tsar! And as soon as the commander got the embossed goblet in his hand, he took a bow and walloped it back in one go – ah, it warmed the cockles of our hearts, it did. Not that we had such a raw time of it, either, of course: once it was all over, the battery went on the razzle for three days.'

'And what was in the goblet? Vodka or some sort of Crimean champagne?' enquired the practically minded gunlayer Zhidkov.

'Come off it! As if the Tsar would give his best officer champagne! It was vodka, brother – don't you doubt it. I later checked up with the commander.'

Pavel walked away from the camp-fire and threw back his head. This was Polish earth, but the stars looked as homely as ever. He remembered Uncle Sergei showing him Cassiopeia and his favourite Orion, and he suppressed a sigh. Something was irking him, and he could not put his finger on what it was. Was it that today was the first time he had killed a man, even two? No, there was nothing at all wrong with that. Anyway, he had probably killed before – just never seen it. After all, what was the artillery for? Was it his untimely thoughts about shoulder-straps? But he decided to forgive himself this: he had been puzzled by Kavelin, and everything had been buzzing inside his head – that's what lay behind it. After all, he hadn't gone to war for the sake of shoulder-straps. Otherwise who had there been to stop him from going to artillery training-school, and a short while later emerging as an ensign, like Kosov? He even preferred fighting as a common soldier, and, besides, in their student circles everyone had looked askance at officers. They'd been regarded as bulwarks of reaction ... God, what fools they had been! Should he have spent more time talking with Vladek? Well, this was certainly no time for heart-to-hearts ... but, even so, that was closer to the mark – yes, he was getting warmer. Only it wasn't Vladek ...

That's what it was! That dead German with the ant – how could he have failed to notice straight away that he looked exactly like Yura Nezhdanov. He had the same light blue eyes and chin shaped like an iron, and his hair was the same colour, too! He could have been Yura's twin brother. Hang on, Yura did have some German relatives, so he must, therefore, have had some German blood, too. Before it hadn't mattered. But did it matter, or not? Where might Yura be now? Maybe he'd already been killed, and had ants crawling all over him. How silly he had been to think it wrong to flick that ant off. But anyway, what good would it have done?

'Well, Petrov, are you dreaming, too?' a voice came from the darkness, and there at his side, crunching a twig, was Ensign Kosov. 'I can't sleep either.' Kosov, who for some unknown reason was jealous of Pavel – was it the attention the commander had showed him? – always treated him with pointed arrogance. Don't forget, he seemed to be saying, that you're not an officer. Not that Pavel really wanted to be chummy with the officers – or the other ranks, for that matter. He was not entirely at ease with either of them but did not aspire to be. But this time Kosov was talking differently, as if to an equal.

'And I bet I know what you're dreaming of, too. Oh, for a woman! But fat chance of that round here . . . Oh, Petrov, you should see the women up in "Peter"! Listen, I had this ballerina once . . .'

Pavel became furious with Kosov. He was almost quaking, almost itching, for suddenly he felt that this was what he, too, needed: right now, desperately. But then why be so furious about it? And, as there weren't any women around, the ensign and the sergeant-major proceeded to talk about them to their heart's content.

13

'Lieutenant, those cows of yours are dying every day . . . and I've got nothing to feed the refugees on. Let me have two cows – it'll make things easier for you.'

'You need written permission for that. Are you authorised to give it?'

'No, the only officer with authority for that is away on duty! There's one authorised officer for eight detachments!'

'Then there's nothing I can do.'

'Well, if you can't, I can!' Vladek bellowed furiously, grabbing hold of his Nagan.

'So you want to shoot it out over some cows, do you?'

'You're off your trolley, Ensign!'

'I'm no ensign – I'm a damn civvy, according to you! But I am a noble. Same as you, I take it?'

The ensign, who was coated in greyish dust, made a move for his Nagan, but then suddenly burst out laughing, 'I like you, civvy! Who issued you with that uniform?'

'Any more questions about my uniform, Ensign, and don't hold me responsible for what happens. We're all a bit mad round here.'

'I can believe it. Take three cows – and then you and your refugees clear off out of here. Mackensen's coming. This time tomorrow the Germans'll be here.'

'So where does that leave you with your herd of cows?'

'One more question about those blasted cows . . .'

They grinned at one another and Vladek instructed two medical orderlies: 'Slaughter them right away, and have all the cauldrons brought over! I'll be back in a minute – I just have to sort the crowd out.'

Vladek, who was now head of a field medical detachment, had been ordered to see to the feeding and medical needs of the refugees. With his knowledge of Polish he was irreplaceable here. The refugees' wagons were all trundling their way towards Kobrin, lagging behind the retreating army. Abandoned corpses could occasionally be seen by the roadside, usually of tiny infants. Vladek sometimes found time to stop and bury them.

'I need ten men – here, now,' he shouted to the crowd of refugees in Polish. 'Stand here, and don't let anyone past that line.' With his sword he drew a line in the grey sand. 'We're going to brew some broth – there's enough for everyone. But they're to stay back till I give the command. Otherwise – so help me God – I'll shoot! Understood?'

'Understood, *pan* Ensign!'

Vladek had long since abandoned sentimentality and civilised manners with people who had been brutalised by exhaustion and hunger. He had not forgotten the first time that he fed them, when someone had yelled 'Let 'em through!' and the refugees had hurled themselves forwards at the cauldrons. He had just managed to spot a child of two being knocked out of his mother's arms, and saw him roll about beneath the feet of the crowd. Beside himself with rage, Vladek fired a shot into the air. That proved sufficient for a moment's pause, and a dishevelled woman managed to pluck the child up from beneath the boots and the bast footwear. Then she had kissed the hands of the '*pan* officer', thus preventing him from keeping an eye on order. But what sort of order could there be, with dozens of hands snatching at each morsel . . . And since then Vladek placed no faith in improvisation, but stuck to a definite system of his own devising. He was further assisted by the fact that an elderly Catholic priest, whose church had been burnt down in Lyatovich, was now tagging along with his detachment.

'*Pan* father, start the service,' ordered Vladek. And as the medical orderlies, with their sleeves now darkened with blood, set about filleting the cows, putting the meat into the cauldrons and skimming the pinkish-grey foam from the top of the broth, the rather frail priest solemnly donned a dirty lace cape and sang a litany, while the subdued crowd sang the refrains. There was something about daily bread, and about the Mother of all who were suffering, but Vladek was not listening. The priest knew his business, and he managed to spin the service out until everything was finally ready. And when Vladek gave the command, he also started distributing the bread, theatrically breaking it up into pieces. And only then were the refugees allowed up to the cauldrons – while Vladek stood by with his Nagan.

On that occasion, everything passed off well, and no one was trampled to death. Vladek knew that in a few hours' time, once they were back on the road, some of them would start feeling sick: that was how starving people usually reacted to meat. And would there be a hospital at Kobrin that could take the sick, or had everyone there already fled in retreat? And where was he to find the food next time? He went to examine the carts. From one came the sound of a groaning woman: it was a mother giving birth. But this was her first labour, and Vladek hoped that he would not have to deliver the child. He figured that she would probably go on screaming for about another ten hours, by which time they would, with any luck, have made it through to Kobrin?

He gave the order to get going once again, and dozed off in his saddle. It wasn't sleep, of course. But every now and then he had surprisingly vivid, though disconnected visions: a yellow-grey puff of shrapnel, poplars of some kind, the operating carriage on the train – which now seemed so cosy, with the blue flame from the burning spirit, and the smells of camphor and carbolic. And the fragile phials of the train pharmacist – so fragile that, for some reason, they were even rather touching . . . And Christmas-tree decorations . . . Then he threw himself on to the sofa, and was afraid of admitting to his mother that he had removed the glass bear from the Christmas tree, taken it to bed with him and accidentally broken it . . . And the sound of breaking glass: there was a Zeppelin over Brest, and people were shooting at it, as it dropped its bombs.

It was already evening, but there was still a glow over the southern skyline. They were burning the crops as they retreated.

Kobrin was virtually deserted: the army had gone, and so had almost all its inhabitants. The field hospital, however, was still only preparing to go, and Vladek managed to get his sick into the last of the little wagons taking them to the train. But it was unclear when the train was departing, so Vladek had to go and accompany them and see they got off all right.

Fortunately, the train was still there on the tracks, flying its two Red Cross flags. Vladek quickly tracked down the senior doctor in order to hand the sick over to him.

'There's a woman in labour. Her contractions are weak, but regular,' he informed a round-faced man with feline whiskers who was dressed in the same wretched Union of Cities uniform.

'My dear fellow, where on earth can I put her?' said the senior doctor, waving his arms. 'We can't take any of these people – we're crammed full as it is, and there's another detachment still to board!'

'Stick them in with the staff! Stick them in the passageways, in the pharmaceutical compartment! And then up on the roof – till you've got all of them on board!' Vladek replied furiously.

'Well, seeing as you're such an expert on loading people on to trains, maybe you'd care to see to it yourself? I've got to deal with an operating room that's blasted with shrapnel, my electricity's off, and – as soon as we leave – I have an operation to see to!' fumed the doctor.

'Well, why didn't you say so? I'll get it done right away. Where's your second detachment?'

'Over there somewhere, on the tracks,' answered the senior doctor, vaguely waving off into the darkness.

Vladek sprang down from the footboard and spent the next half-hour with torch to hand yelling at both his own and the train's medical orderlies, bundling the sick on and off stretchers and, without paying any attention to their moaning, getting them up into bunks, beneath bunks, down corridors and wherever else they could possibly fit.

'It's all right,' he kept muttering out loud, 'I know these hospital trains, they can take double loads – you'll all get away!'

Fortunately, the head of the second detachment chose not to make an issue of it, although he had, in fact, arrived quite a few minutes beforehand. Instead, he quickly agreed that all the sick had to be got on board: both his own and Vladek's. They were just about to depart when from the darkness there came the sound of a woman shrieking and a roar of some sort. Vladek jumped down on to the tracks and, with his lantern, he managed to pick out two bodies thrashing about on the gravel of the track. A shot in the air had not the slightest effect, and Vladek, along with another orderly who had by now come rushing up, started trying to drag the two apart, but to no avail. It was a strapping great man in a soldier's coat who proved to have a grip of iron, and they had to rip a shred from a white nurse's cap that he was clutching before managing to release a half-strangled nurse. Vladek yanked her back up on to her feet, and was surprised at how light she was: it was like lifting a child. She staggered, but remained upright. Vladek left her to sob and, bringing his foot down on the soldier's flailing leg, succeeded in locating a wooden spoon tucked behind his bootleg. That was where they all carried spoons, epileptic or not.

Nodding to the orderly to hold the epileptic's head steady, he thrust the spoon-handle into the man's gaping, wheezing mouth and forced it crossways in between his teeth. And felt a wave of relief – now, at least, he couldn't bite his tongue off. The illness of divine Caesar. Poor girl. There she was, carrying the wounded about, and then who should happen along, but Caesar? Epileptics were the dread of the hospital trains: it only took one to start up for virtually the whole carriage to be at it – with attacks that were purely hysterical, although they looked like epilepsy, and were also accompanied by the same shuddering and yelling. That was why epileptic patients were generally transported separately. But there was plainly no way of arranging that now ... The patient quietened down and Vladek, together with a young orderly whom he had never previously set eyes on – a delightful young fellow, with paws like a bear! – put the man in a passage at the end of a carriage. He was the last one on, and they made it just in time. In the distance shots could already be heard ringing out.

The engine whistled, threw out a couple of streams of vapour, like whiskers, and then twirled these whiskers back down either side of the track. Vladek sighed with relief. And the nurse who had just been all but strangled made the sign of the cross at the departing train and plonked herself down on the gravel. So she clearly wasn't one of the train staff, but was attached to the second detachment. She needed some valerian, but he had left all the supplies back at the hospital.

'Vladek, don't you recognise me?' asked the nurse. Her voice was weak, but Vladek gasped.

'Zina? Zina, good God . . .'

He fumbled about for his lantern. He was being watched by familiar eyes: grey and stern. She pushed the lantern aside.

'Don't look at me now. But you've changed a lot, too. Are you going to the hospital now? We're going the same way, then. Fyodor, get the wagons ready, we're going now.'

This last remark she addressed to the man with the bear-like hands, and he obediently went to turn the horses round. Vladek had to make an effort to move from the spot. He hadn't recognised her! It was dark, but darkness be damned, he had held her by the shoulders, and he hadn't recognised her! Of course, he had never held her by the shoulders before . . . and had a job imagining anyone else trying, either. He had changed, she said. So it must be pretty striking, then. How often had he prayed to meet her – and now it had happened.

At last he was able to take it in, and a warm happiness flooded over him.

Zina was put in the front two-wheeled wagon, and Vladek rode alongside her, bending down from his horse to hear her quiet voice. His hands recalled the sensation of her hard little shoulders, and he caught himself clutching at his rein as though it were something fragile: a kitten, a little sparrow?

The hospital was by now packed and ready to go. All that remained of it were two doctors, a few nurses, and a cartload of medicine. The orders were already being given by the dishevelled Chemodanov, who was the authorised officer, and had a red mark on his forehead from the rim of his service cap. Quite what had come of the cap itself, nobody knew. Now they had to retreat to Slonim. Well, the hospital should be allowed to start the journey immediately, while Vladek should stay back and let the exhausted horses and people get at least a couple of hours of rest. The shooting in the south-west had quietened down, nothing would happen till morning, and the medical orderlies had been without sleep for three days now. The head of the other detachment, a medic from Moscow, gave orders for the supplies to be put on what had once been an operating table: biscuits, tinned meat and some sort of bilberry extract.

'Oh-ho, gentlemen, enjoying the good life, eh!'

'Come and join us, colleague. Hang on, we've got something else here, too. Pure medicinal spirit – I recommend it. I dare say your chaps are also chilled to the bone?'

It was a strange sort of party, illumined by church candles (the hospital was quartered in a deserted Catholic church), and held in a deserted little town from which some people had already fled, and at which others had yet to arrive. There was one doctor for two detachments, a few nurses and medical orderlies, and the elderly *'pan* father', who still hadn't taken his lace cape off. He read out a prayer in Polish, and everyone politely waited. It was necessary to realise that, for an occasion such as this, even the most holy *pan* Jesus would have blessed the drinking of spirit in His house. In the stained-glass window a glow blazed from the darkness outside: it was said that retreating Cossacks had burnt down some warehouses and a synagogue. Flashes through the coloured glass threw blue, cherry and yellow marks on to the vaulted walls, making it look like the northern lights.

Vladek took a swig from some sort of medicinal phial, and did not even feel any burning. His 'Snow Queen' was sitting right by him, elbow to elbow. Goodness knew how she had managed it, but her nurse's cap was now perfectly smoothed out, and it even looked starched. On her cheek, just below her temple, there was a fresh scratch mark – all that remained of her skirmish with the epileptic. This dark mark on her face evoked the same veneration in Vladek as had the running carmine paint on some of the Polish plaster crucifixes – pitiless in their anatomical detail, but for him, still awe-inspiring.

They both reached out to revive the guttering candle, and their hands became entangled. Zina laughed the same happy laugh that Vladek remembered from Odessa. The priest glanced at this young Russian girl, with his lucid black eyes that were untouched by age, and he smiled, as if at a child. Everyone at the table had a sort of understanding look, but Vladek found this more pleasing than annoying. It was as though they were all dancing an old, intricate dance together, and Zina were his partner.

'Let's drink, ladies and gentlemen – for everything good that will remain of our youth once this war is over,' said the Muscovite medic Biryulin, raising his phial, and everyone fell quiet, evidently pondering what that good might be. Then, as often happens, everybody started talking at the same time: of matters familiar but irksome.

'Well, how can it be anything but treason, gentlemen? There's no medicine, and the soldiers are appallingly clothed and hungry. You have only to lift up a wounded man and his coat falls apart in your hands.'

'So, according to the artillery, Sukhomlinov has been taking unheard-of bribes from the industrialists. And selling off all their unwanted junk to the army for them.'

'Well, old chap, of course there's bribery, but what I'm talking about is treason. How, in our dear fatherland, could a war minister possibly not be taking bribes? No, the point is who are the pay-masters? Why are artillery shells exploding inside the gun-barrels? Why was it the front line suddenly ran out of ammunition back in fourteen when – if you remember – the papers were saying we had loads of everything? You've got to look higher than the war minister.'

'Surely you don't mean . . .'

'I don't know. But they're openly saying it's no coincidence that the Tsarina is Alisa of Hessen.'

'Oh, come off it – it's common knowledge that Rasputin is the one behind all the spying! There's nothing new about that!'

Vladek was in no mood to get worked up about these matters. What did Alisa of Hessen, and Rasputin, and even the retreat itself matter now! Zina made a move to get up from the table and, after waiting a little while, he followed her. Everyone was zealously engaged in the conversation, and, naturally, nobody noticed.

Zina was standing by a stone wall that was about half as high as she was. Her thin, distinct shadow lay fragmented on the rather crude cobblestone yard. She did not turn her head when Vladek stood beside her, but simply held out her hand.

'Zina, it must be fate!'

'Yes, yes, fate,' she uttered, as though defying him, and then she suddenly burst out crying.

Again Vladek held her by the shoulders, and all the time she kept sobbing against his chest. This was both painful and sweet – seeing her cry. An unfamiliar sense of burden – it wasn't her weightless body, but what was it? – almost frightened Vladek. Was it love? Was this sense of burden called love? It was as if he had a coat of mail over his shoulders and chest, and it was preventing him from breathing. He was no longer his own man – in this chain-mail – he belonged entirely . . . His lips were cold. He had waited so long to pledge himself, and now it was turning out to be so hard: but the time had come. To pledge himself.

'Zina, I love you. Be my wife.'

'Yes, yes,' she again repeated, and pressed his head to her body.

'How cold your lips are! But your hands are hot . . .'

She whispered something else, besides, and she was laughing, but Vladek was still quite unable to break their embrace. Finally, he recalled himself and said, 'Let's go.'

'Where to, Vladek?'

'To get married.'

'Now? But it's night! Who can possibly marry us now?'

'Let's ask our priest do it.'

'But he's a Catholic!'

'What difference does it make? Where are we going to find an Orthodox priest now?'

'But he's already fast asleep, you madman! Look for yourself – they've even put out the candles. And in two hours we have to leave.'

'That's exactly why. I'll never let you go again. You will be my wife.'

'I will, I will. Only there's no need to wake anyone up. I feel so good as I am now. Let him marry us tomorrow. But now – let's just be alone together. And I won't ever let you go, either. The vestibule's just there – over on the other side. Well, don't be afraid, God will forgive us. I'm not afraid, you know . . .'

Vladek was still kissing her carbolic-burnt hands when there was another explosion somewhere nearby, and the shock through the air made the church bell tinkle. His rosary became caught up with the chain on the cross round her neck, and they quickly disentangled them with impatient fingers. Out in the yard they were already hurriedly harnessing the horses. Fortunately, the hospital was on the right bank of the Muchavets, so they did not have to cross it.

For the next twenty-four hours they remained constantly on the move.

'What a language! I've never heard such gibberish!' Biryulin exclaimed indignantly. 'We've just passed Pruzhany – where are we going now? – to Ruzhany! And I suppose the one after that's gotta be Uzhany, has it?'

'The one after that is Mizhevichi,' said the priest with restraint, and the medics felt awkward. This was his Poland, and they were retreating, leaving the country to the Germans. Of course, they were not soldiers, but even so . . . They were Russians, and they were retreating.

'There you have it – long-promised autonomy,' uttered Vladek with subdued fury. Suddenly, and for the first time since the previous night, he had a sense of where he was and what he was doing. And it sickened him. Why must every happiness be set against a black background? As if it were planned that way . . . As, indeed, it really might be . . .

Zina was sitting in the saddle in a posture of which Uncle Sergei would have approved. Vladek rode beside her, looking at her pale face with anxiety.

'My poor darling! Are you tired?'

'Stop pitying me, will you? I'm happy. "Under a happy star", remember?'

'I remember. That was what the gypsy fortune-teller told you at the pussy-willow fair. And I thought at the time: why does she go and ask a gypsy, when she could have asked me . . . ?'

'Why do you carry that rosary?'

'It has my mother's blessing. She's a Catholic, you know.'

At Smolyanitsa they were joined by yet another party of refugees, and it became impossible for them to continue talking to one another. Despite being busy with his own work, Vladek still periodically noticed Zina bustling about over some women. Several fever victims had been put on the carts. Again reaching for his Nagan, Vladek ordered the refugees to throw some of their baggage down from the carts and let some children on. Then Biryulin called him over to one side.

'It looks bad, colleague. You realise what they've got, don't you?'

'I've had no time to think about it. Typhus?'

'Exactly. Now everyone else will get it, too, but we can't just leave them . . .'

'Well, let's split up then. The healthy can go on ahead, while those with typhus can go behind in the carts with me and – God willing – we should eventually make it. Tell the orderlies I need a few volunteers. Leave me some morphine and camphor.'

'Now steady on a second. Why you? It's a nice idea, but I'm still the doctor round here, and I should be the one to stay behind.'

'Colleague, our only difference is one year of studies. And for typhus, that's neither here nor there. Do as I said.'

'Now you listen here—'

'I'm a Pole. Can't you understand that?' hissed Vladek furiously.

At that moment he suddenly had a firm and clear grasp that, after having thought of himself as a Russian all his life, he was, really, a Pole. Nor was it fortuitous that he had his mother's rosary with him.

They soon split up. The refugees had by now settled down, and made no protest at either the confiscation of their wagons or the firm command given by the *pan* ensign. Only the mothers who remained in the column of carts carrying the typhus victims started howling, trying to prove that their children were healthy, and that they should be taken in the front string of carts. But Biryulin was standing for no nonsense as he sorted them all out. Three volunteer medical orderlies transferred the necessary medicine. The priest, as was to be expected, also stayed behind with Vladek. It was time to say goodbye to Zina.

'My girl, we'll meet in Slonim. I'll try to be there as soon as I can.'

'You mean we'll try to be there as soon as we can. Biryulin's released me.'

'Idiot! It isn't Biryulin who tells you what to do now – it's me. Now clear off out of here and wait for me in Slonim!'

'Don't make a family scene of it, please. You haven't even married me yet, and already you're shouting at me. I'm a nurse, and I'm needed here.'

Vladek realised that it was senseless to argue. And he knew that Zina was right – with that cold rectitude of conscience that pities no one. The priest blessed the departing string of carts with his thin brown hand. And again the expansive sands and deserted fields stretched out before them. Now they were moving slowly. Every so often they would stop to give injections, tie up the delirious, or bury the dead. The priest read the litany for the dead without getting down from his horse. A boy of about three made an unexpected recovery: he had been in the grip of a burning fever, but towards morning he was clearly on the mend. That night his mother died, but the boy did not know this, for he was so delirious that he took Zina to be his mother. Whenever they stopped, Zina tore up some rags and kept him swaddled like a baby. She forced him to drink as much as possible, and he drenched every bit of rag that was put on him. As they were crossing some tiny river beyond Mizhevichi, she even took the chance to get a bit of washing done.

There was now hardly any distance before Slonim, and Vladek was already starting to get over that clinging anxiety that had refused to leave him, and had made his heart go cold. And then Zina reached out and touched his sleeve.

'Vladechek . . .'

One glance was enough to tell him: no, she had not got over it. Those burning eyes and crimson cheeks . . .

'Don't be afraid, my girl, I'm with you.'

Now he no longer even had any sense of horror. It was as if he had known all along. Mother of God, help her. Mother of God, keep her, save her, have mercy on her. He let out no whisper, he did not even move his lips. As he laid Zina down in a cart and covered her with his coat, his heart prayed of its own accord.

'Are you in pain?'

'No, I'm fine . . . I'm floating – blissfully – look at the clouds, how pink they are. Don't worry, I won't die – I'm strong. I'm just thin at the moment, but I'll get over it. I'll get over all this . . . And, when we get back to Odessa, we'll go sailing on Uncle Sergei's yacht, and the water will be green and thick, and it'll rock us, rock us . . . Do you want something?'

'Zina. I'm going to call the *pan* father over so he can marry us.'

'All right, dear. Fine. Only I haven't got a ring to give you.'

'Neither have I. It doesn't matter – we'll get by.'

They had, in any event, to make a stop: to bury two more dead by the roadside. The priest was not at all surprised by Vladek's request. It seemed that, generally, no one was any longer surprised by anything. He got out two dark wax candles which he kept in his bag, along with some holy relics. And from his finger he took a ring with a violet stone.

'Here, take this, *pan* – it's not a wedding ring, but I'll consecrate it. And you can make the other out of grass, if you like.'

'I hope the young lady won't mind . . . I'm a widow – this is no use to me any more,' came a voice from the cart in which Zina was lying. And an elderly peasant woman started struggling to wrench free a ring that had grown into her finger.

'Let the young lady get married and be happy with her *pan* ensign. Jesus, Son of Mary – the young lady's so kind-hearted, like Saint Teresa. May God grant the young lady happiness and many children. I'm an old woman, I know everything.'

Zina smiled, and whispered '*dziekuje*' – the only Polish she knew. It was a short wedding: Zina was unable to stand, and she sat on the cart while Vladek stood by her side. When the priest put the question which had to be answered with a 'yes', he translated. Zina heard everything else as if in a dream. The priest raised his voice and said something straight up into the sky. From that moment Zina understood that they were man and wife. Vladek kissed her, and she fell somewhere. But there, where she fell, it was warm and nice.

After a certain while little Yatsek's crying brought her to again. The orphaned child was not now prepared to lose Zina, and he kept asking to be with her.

'Mama! I want to see my mama!'

'Vladek . . . Let me give him my blessing. You won't give him to the first person to come along, will you? I've been nursing him all this time as if he were our own little boy.'

'I certainly won't give him to anyone. Zina, are you better? We're in Slonim, Zina, and now everything will be fine.'

'I know. Everything will be fine, and you'll never let me go.'

But there was little that was fine. When they reached the hospital, the doctor looked at Zina and said to Vladek, 'Is she your wife? I can take her, of course, but she won't survive being moved again. Feel her pulse. And we're about to move everyone out of here. I'd advise you not to risk it, colleague. Stay here with her for at least another twenty-four hours – the crisis will come at any moment. As for treatment, you know what to do yourself – there's an empty apartment next door, and it has a stove. You can catch us up later in your own good time – but now she needs rest. You can see for yourself how weak she's become. There's one nurse staying behind, a Pole – she'll help you. She's a real treasure.'

Pani Stanislava was, indeed, a real treasure. Notwithstanding all his experience, Vladek was as lost as any ordinary husband would have been, but she set about her work with frenzied energy. Half an hour later Zina had already been put in a clean bed and given an injection, and *pani* Stanislava forced Vladek to drink some coffee that she brewed up in the little pan and nibble some dry-bread biscuits. Vladek did not immediately realise that she had taken under her wing, not only Zina, but also Yatsek. She had evidently decided that he was their child, and was now singing a Polish song to him, and assuring him that his mother was having a little rest before taking him back in her arms.

'*Pan* Ensign! Have you finished your coffee? The child is crying – he's ever so upset. Don't cry, little one, your papa's about to kiss you.'

She plonked the child down on the knees of the dumbfounded Vladek, and the boy cuddled up to him, immediately clasping his small arms and legs around him like a little monkey.

'*Pani* Stanislava! For the love of God! I'll explain everything to you!' interrupted the priest, whom the tireless nurse also gave some coffee.

'Don't worry, my son, let the child calm down a bit, and I'll look after him myself. Yatsek, will you come and sit with Grandpa?'

But Yatsek did not want to go and sit with Grandpa, and it took no small effort to get him finally off to bed.

During the night Zina seemed to get better. Now Vladek could sit with her and hold her hand, and she was no longer delirious, but spoke in a perfectly rational manner.

'Vladek, we still haven't had time to tell one another anything about ourselves. And I so dreamt of meeting up with you and telling you all about everything that's happened: just to complain, like a little girl. You're so strong, and do you know how dreadful it was for me at first? Even in the train it was dreadful, when the surgical nurse fell ill, and I had to . . . And then a soldier asked: "Little sister, where's my arm?" As if he were asking what was done with it once it was cut off. I told him it had been buried at one of the stops. "Along with the dead?" he asked. "No," I told him, "arms and legs are buried separately, in a common grave of their own." And he was ever so serious when he said: "That means I'm partly now buried in a common grave." Later I cried so much, Vladechek, I cried so much . . .'

'My poor darling.'

'And you say that Pavlik is still alive and well? What have we done, Vladek – now he and Anna can't get married any more, can they? Or doesn't it matter, seeing as we married as Catholics?'

'I don't know. It probably doesn't matter. I'll have to ask

the priest. My girl, my joy, you'll soon be better, and then we'll . . .'

'Yes, Vladechek, yes. Who's that over by the stove? Tell him to go away! No, leave him be . . . How silly I am, getting frightened like that. HE has come to us. Oh, how nice! Vladek, what's the matter? Can't you see HIM?'

She died at dawn, and was buried in a small Polish cemetery. The priest conducted her funeral service just as he had conducted her wedding: solemnly and rather sternly. Or was it just the words of the service? Immediately by their side, and with tears rolling down her face, was *pani* Stanislava. There were also some old women, such as are always seen in cemeteries. Vladek was unable to pray. He just convulsively squeezed the finger with the ring that he had been given by Zina.

'Well – what now, my son?' said the priest, when it was all over. 'I'll look after Yatsek – I know that *pani* Zina asked you to see he was looked after. May God bless you. And may He comfort you in your grief and keep you from all misfortune.'

He made the sign of the cross over Vladek, and Vladek kissed his dry hand.

'And what of you, *pan* Father, are you staying on here?'

'Yonder lies Russia, my son. And I'm a Pole, and so is Yatsek. How can we flee elsewhere? We will share whatever *pan* God may send Poland. Farewell, and don't despair – it's a great sin.'

Vladek wandered around the deserted streets of Slonim with unseeing eyes. Where should he go now? He was a Pole, and Zina had died because he was a Pole. She was remaining here, on Polish earth, as his wife. Should he go on into Russia? And abandon Poland? He had not abandoned the typhus victims to the Germans, but what was he to do now?

He tore open the collar of his field shirt and clutched at his rosary. Lord – help, and grant wisdom and guidance! What would his mother say? No, his mother would understand everything. And he was not a military man – he was not bound by any oath. And, besides, his mother had already said it all – back then, when she had sung 'Flow Visla, flow' to Vladek in the cradle.

Yes, he would stay, and whatever fate befell Poland – let it befall him, too. He was needed here, this was where God had sent him. And now he would return to the *pan* father and ask for his blessing.

14

'I swear by the health of my dead mama, Madam Kegulikhes, she told me straight to my face, she did: one rouble! For a mangy old plaice, can you imagine it?'

'Oh, Rakhil, the things you tell me! I've always said people have almost no conscience nowadays, and soon they'll have none at all. So what did you do?'

'Well, I said to her, why is it that back in thirteen you were selling me that same plaice for fifty kopecks? And she says: that's quite some memory you've got there, but we've been at war for over a year now. And then I turned to everyone, and I said: you all be witnesses to what she just said to me! So now they're calling plaice up to war, are they? What have fish got to do with war?'

'You're such a sensible woman, Rakhil. I always find it such a pleasure talking with you.'

To her surprise, Rakhil also found these hours pleasant. Although, to begin with, she had even cried at having to go out and work. But what else could she do? Moisei had gone to Vienna – having, of course, made arrangements for his sister's maintenance. She received the money every month without fail, but now prices were such that you might as well lie down and die. She felt awkward about writing to Moisei to ask him for more money. He was already doing so much for them as it was. Rakhil paid nothing for her apartment, and how important it was to have a solid roof over your head at a time like this. However, in order to make ends meet, Rakhil had taken on a job looking after an old woman. It was a rich family, but they were all taken up with affairs of their own and now the grandma had broken her hip, they had to find someone to come and look after her during the daytime. Officially, Rakhil was employed as a 'reader': it was a clean and inoffensive job. But, although Rakhil could make out what was written on inscriptions, reading out loud was out of the question. Not, as it turned out, that this mattered. The old woman was headstrong and crotchety, and the family was somewhat in awe of her, though she came to love Rakhil almost immediately – not for her reading, but for their conversations together. She found it comforting to learn that times were now hard, and that everything was in such a mess – not at all like it used to be in her own youth.

'So you say they've stopped putting down that paving?'

'Yes, and can you imagine what it looks like? It's a little patch of yellow – right in the middle of Odessa, where everyone can see it, and surrounded by those other cobblestones. They should never have bothered starting on the job.'

They were talking about an artifical German clinker that had been used to start laying the square outside the Duma, but the contract had been terminated because of the war.

'And the papers nowadays are virtually nothing but white: now they've brought in censorship, there's hardly anything for them to print any more. That's why there's all that white paper on sale.'

'Well, at least there's some point in newspapers. Otherwise we'd have nothing to wrap anything up in: before they just used to make your hands all dirty, and everything else, too. So what's your girl been writing to you?'

'Thank God, she's happy in her new place. But I don't understand it, Madam Kegulikhes: she's got such talent – so why all these drama studies, and why does it have to be Moscow? When Shimek was studying he never left Odessa, and he played like an angel, too, and people cried when they listened to him, I swear. But when they abolished the Pale of Settlement, it drove the youngsters mad, that did. They have to be in the capital cities – Odessa's too small for them.'

'Well, do they pay her anything at this studio?'

'At the moment I'm having to support her. Up there in

Moscow, it seems, no one can get by on just singing. But she lives modestly, there's not much that she needs.'

'Thank God, Rakhil. You know what singers are like nowadays. They go gallivanting about in troikas, always with some new lover in tow, and they bath in champagne. What a way for a decent girl to live. It's a good deal better living modestly with the help of your mama, than immodestly with somebody else's help.'

'Hey, what are you saying – my daughter isn't like that . . .'

What Rakhil feared most was that Yakov might find out where she was going, so she arranged her hours with Madam Kegulikhes at the same time that Yakov was away in class. There was no point in the boy knowing that his mother had to go out and earn a living. He was already highly-strung enough as it was: he might pack in the gymnasium at any moment. Only recently she had had to go and buy a new uniform for him, as he had outgrown his old one, with the elbows coming out at the sleeves. And what a to-do that had been. He was sixteen, a nervous age. And it was rather sad, too, for if he'd worked from the age of fourteen, like his father had, and attended the synagogue, then he wouldn't have any nerves to worry about.

The memory of that trip to Alexandrovsky Boulevard for his uniform was no less fresh in Yakov's mind. There, over the lacquered shelves, had hung the lacquered inscription: 'Prices are final'. He tried on a jacket, and then it started. He was told how handsome he looked, and what a charming young man he was, but they were asking such an exorbitant price that Rakhil gasped and started coming out with her lamentations. Burning with embarrassment, he had taken the jacket off and decisively told his mother, 'Right, we're leaving.'

'Young man, where are you off to? Take a look in the mirror: you look just like the next Max Linder in that jacket! Madam, where are your eyes? It's perfect – you see a fit like that once in a thousand years!'

Rakhil went back and offered half.

'I swear by my children, madam, at this price I'm making an outright loss! And I do it only as a mark of respect for such a handsome young man.'

This haggling, with its howls and its imprecations, dragged on for endlessly long, and Yakov was ashamed of his mother, and ashamed that he was ashamed. With burning cheeks he then had to endure the purchase of a pair of trousers (Rakhil had, of course, included them in the same half-price), but, when it came to his coat, in a subdued whisper he promised his mother that he would quit the gymnasium if they did not leave immediately. Coats were not compulsory, and it was just at that moment that his class-mate Kutsap came in with his father, also looking for a uniform – and the shop assistants bowed and brought out a coat along with various other accoutrements. And they held the coat out for him, as he put his arms in the sleeves – rather than flinging it down on the counter as they had with his mother.

Yakov, however, was now above prejudice. He flaunted his poverty, and did not give a damn what these grovelling shop assistants thought of him. His life was now given over to something else – something that had started unexpectedly during the summer, at the 'Humour' theatre. Yakov loved this little summer theatre that was set in the garden of Ekaterinskaya Square. During the evenings, the dusty, wooden structure was transformed: the arc lights shone with a milky purity, the colourful garlands of electric light bulbs flickered enticingly, and the gravel crunched good-naturedly underfoot after its watering following the heat of day. This was where Chernov and Vronsky shone, and in the city it was considered especially chic 'to dress à la Vronsky' – in the same style as the brown-haired beau who was the troupe's leading romantic player. Back in his youth Khenkin had made audiences sob with laughter at couplets which the whole of Odessa later could be heard singing, and each evening he would throw in some entirely new ones. He pretended to be a teacher of dance and good manners surrounded by his numerous children: his family would be right by his side kicking up a dreadful racket as he tried to give a lesson, and they were forever getting up to something that had nothing whatsoever in common with good manners. Yet there was only one man on stage, though it seemed as if the stage was full, and that at any moment someone would come tumbling down into the auditorium.

'Gentlemen, invite the la-ay-dies:
They're the ones with a broach on their chest!
So it's forward quick march, me ol' ma-ay-ties,
And the foot you put forward's your best!'

Yakov was groaning with laughter. He was imagining how successfully these couplets could be adapted to life at the gymnasium. Compulsory military training with wooden rifles had now been introduced, and soon 'forward quick march' would once again be the order of the day. He was acknowledged as the class poet, so who – if not Yakov – could come up with some fitting verses?

At this point a student sitting on the end of the row nudged his elbow, and when Yakov disdainfully turned his head the student looked over and silently drew his attention to two policemen entering the theatre. Then he slipped him some sort of packet, put his finger to his lips, and smartly resumed his seat on a bench at the back. Yakov realised that from this he was to assume that the student was a revolutionary and, feeling flattered, he hugged the rather hefty package close to his body. The alarm, however, turned out to be false: nobody laid a finger on the student. At the end of the show Yakov ambled slowly out into the evening cool of the garden with the packet still on him. He tried not to look round: the student was bound to be following him.

'Now give that back to me, young man. Thank you for your help,' the student finally said, once they were in the trusty darkness. 'Well, you're plainly no coward.'

'Does that surprise you?' replied Yakov. And this was how they struck up their acquaintanceship.

What had Yakov's life been prior to that, and who, really, was he? He had entertained vague dreams of poetic fame, agonised over whether or not he was a genius, taken a desultory interest in the 'Poalei Zion' movement, and been pained by his shortness . . . He had friends who led the same senseless puppy existence as himself: Maxim and Antos. The most heroic thing that they had ever read was the writings of Pisarev – and that was only because he was forbidden reading for the pupils at the gymnasium. The student – he called himself

Comrade Andreyev – cleared up the chaos of Yakov's views and put them into order for him, and everything became wonderfully clear. All this military-patriotic bravado was, as Yakov himself had felt, simply the death throes of a doomed empire. It was time to change the world. Scrap the monarchies, and all power to the workers and whoever would show them the way forward. The propaganda of hatred for the Germans was rubbish, just like all the rest of the national brouhaha. The Germans had given Karl Marx to the world, and Marx had proclaimed internationalism. Yet did Yakov know that in 1905 half of the Russian copies of the *Manifesto* had been printed here, in Odessa? Underground, of course. Was there any vocation higher than working in the underground? Through prison, the scaffold, penal servitude – towards the happiness of mankind!

The student was not just saying this, either, for he had himself been imprisoned for two whole months, and had heard the prisoners sing 'The Warsaw March', and seen them hurl bowls of swill at the guards. He was not a local, Comrade Andreyev: he said 'poorly' rather than 'badly', and 'boots' rather than 'shoes'. Was he from 'Peter'? The comrade smiled mysteriously: he was from wherever the Party sent him. And did Yakov know that Marx had written about Petersburg? 'Without Petersburg and Odessa, Russia would be a giant with his arms cut off.' So these idiots had renamed Petersburg Petrograd at the start of the war – as part of the struggle with all things German – but that wouldn't make any difference. And Marx had called Odessa 'a rising star' – so how could they fail to prove him right? It would, indeed, be a rising star of the revolution. It was from here, from 'Marusya', that Ulyanov himself – Lenin – who was a delegate at the Third Party Congress, came. What, hadn't Yakov heard of 'Marusya'? The Odessan Committee of the Russian Social Democratic Workers' Party. Yakov suspected that Andreyev was an assumed name, and this gave him a sweet thrill. After all, that was how everything in their underground had to be: the secret police weren't dozing, either, so they had to use code-names.

'Ah-ha, is that Aunt Vera arriving?' good-naturedly remarked a grey-haired man with trim hands and dressed in a worker's jacket, of whom Yakov knew only that he was 'the Godfather'. Yakov doughtily declined offers of tea and, having received the precious packet 'for Aunt Vera', set off on his way from the settlement of Kuyalnik back to Blizhnye Melnitsy. The little steam train that crawled back and forth between the city and the Zhevakhova mountain puffed cosily, and Yakov thought how adeptly the paper had been given the name *Iskra* – 'The Spark'. His hands were burning, his heart was burning: such fear and rapture! Should the secret police take it into their heads to search him now, then it was farewell to the gymnasium, and to Odessa, too: this smacked of Siberia, especially now, with the war on. The little house at Kuyalnik had a remarkable room, with an entrance leading directly down into the catacombs and, furthermore, the police were wholly unaware of this entrance. There was no such thing as a complete map of the catacombs: there were many miles of caves and connecting passages with two or three tiers, and some most unexpected outlets to the city and the sea. It was there, in one of these caves, that the underground printing press which reproduced *Iskra* was kept. And Blizhnye Melnitsy was inhabited by workers. Railway metal-workers. This was where 'Marusya' had one of its secret meeting places, and it was from there that Yakov set out for Kuyalnik – off into the blue distance, between the Zhevakhova and Shkodova mountains – carrying the agreeably hefty satchels with the typeset.

Comrade Andreyev and 'the Godfather' were pleased with him, but they kept reiterating what a great honour it was to be a courier for the Party. He had to grow up: to read literature, keep abreast of all that was happening, and, in particular, learn how to talk with the common people. And Yakov tried – but talking with the common people proved to be not such a straightforward matter. His first attempt was simply shameful.

It took place at Goryachka, on the beach at Peresyp behind Vainshtein's mill, at a spot that had long been a favourite with the three friends. Naturally they were contemptuous of beaches such as the ones at Arcadia or Langeron: those were for pampered idlers. You had to pay to get on – three kopecks! – and why, for goodness' sake? They sold little cream cones and gingermen there, and the traders yelled out 'Ho-o-ot, fresh, boiled co-orn', children howled, and sodden, empty cigarette packets and melon rinds floated about in the water. Arcadia was rather more chic, with the sounds of the band from the restaurant, whereas Langeron was rather poorer – but, like all these places for the posh public, they were also rather dull. Svai and Goryachka, however, were another matter altogether! Goryachka was an amazing place: you could swim there all the year round! This was where the hot water from the city's power-station poured out into the sea, and the locals did not even have to spend any money on going to the bath-house. On cold days solid steam hung above Goryachka, and heads – like water melons – could be heard oohing and ahing with satisfaction from within the steam. It was, of course, possible to choose a rather cooler stream, where the water had already mixed in with the sea, and there were sand crabs crawling over the ribbed, sandy bottom. And this was where the local workers, stevedores and fishermen went bathing – merry and unassuming people, all of them.

It was also here that Yakov took it into his head to try and tell an elderly stevedore – after all, the most downtrodden class element that there was! – about socialism. Of course, he realised that there was no need to spout on about it in bookish terms, but rather to choose simple words that would be readily understood.

'Under socialism there won't be any more rich or poor, or Russians, or Jews or Poles,' he said, convincingly painting a picture of universal happiness.

'So then, laddie, it's when everyone's been killed off, is that it?'

'No, why should anyone be killed? Everyone will be equal, don't you see? There won't be any more differences!'

'Now how's that – everyone'll go to synagogues on Saturday, and church on Sunday, eh?'

'But there won't be any synagogues or churches! Religion is the opium of the people!'

'Well, that's just what I reckoned – everyone'll be killed off. So you fancied I'd live to let you clobber my church, did you? You be off now, laddie, and tell your old man to give you a sound thrashing on your backside!'

'My father's dead!' said Yakov defiantly. Usually this was a foolproof ploy: people became embarrassed, as if it was somehow their fault. But this lumbering great fellow with folds in his red neck was devoid of such sensibilities, and he had his own way of sympathising with Yakov.

'Poor little kiddie! Lost his dad, so now he's lost his wits and starts playing the rebel! Come 'ere, and I'll thrash you myself.'

And he reached out to grab the belt from his discarded trousers. It was time to beat a hasty retreat: he was a strapping great fellow, and what if he really wasn't messing about?

Then Yakov acquired rather more experience. He joined Comrade Andreyev on his trips to Barzhana, which was a hostel for homeless port-workers. Comrade Andreyev, who was well turned out and always wore a spotlessly clean worker's jacket, was not embarrassed at how clearly out of place he looked in this hole, with its foul-smelling vapour instead of clean air, and its mattresses stuffed with wood shavings lying about on the concrete floor. He would start by asking about a non-existent Tarasov from Bugayevka, as though he had come to see a friend. Everyone would immediately give him loads of advice about where to look for him, and someone would even remember this Tarasov, and then they would strike up a conversation 'about life'. This immediately induced the workers to start airing their grievances about how they lived, and complaining about prices – and all would agree that they deserved something rather better. And wouldn't it be a good idea to bring Brodsky himself, and Valuyev, to Barzhana, along with the other sugar-refinery proprietors and corn merchants? After that, all Comrade Andreyev had to do was to prime them with some plainly sensible ideas about how this could be achieved. And they would agree: as soon as the war came to an end they must go on strike and throw all those bastards into the sea. No one was prepared to go on strike immediately – but, even so, it was a good beginning.

Yakov watched and noted. Hardest of all was burning his diary. Andreyev lost no time in asking him: 'Keep a diary, do you?'

Yakov blushed furiously and admitted that he did.

'You're all the same, you gentlemen from the gymnasium! "I love Shura, and I suffer for Mura." But when it comes to a search, it's not just Shura and Mura they find written up in there, is it? Burn it – and let's have no more diaries in future.'

Yakov understood that he was right, but it was still a heck of a shame. Not, of course, that it had any Shuras or Muras in it: Yakov was keeping his diary for posterity. It contained outlines of future verses, for example: the drunkard rocks, like a cradle, beneath the street-lights. It also contained some finely observed comments on the evil of the day: the papers were printing lists of the officers killed in action, but there were no lists of the common soldiers. And why should there be – Yakov had written with mordant irony – as the common soldiers' wives didn't even know how to read?

'The whole hardship of youth lies in having to discover whether or not you are a genius,' Yakov reread for the last time from his exercise book in its blue oil-skin cover, 'then – either way – life becomes simpler, but it is no longer so interesting.' Privately, Yakov knew that he was a genius, and that after his death his exercise-book would be found, and published and republished over and again. And, to prevent anyone from guessing why it had been written, he had been cunning: he made notes of the type 'Today it was windy. Had bortsch with spinach.' Now all this had to be burnt. With an effort he tore off the cover – otherwise it would have stunk out the entire apartment! – and slowly, one page at a time, he fed the rest of it into the stove. The pages curled up, as if they, too, found it painful. Then Yakov, excited and relieved, wrote a poem about burning bridges. He wrote it in one sitting, without any corrections.

A posting to Karakalisa – it sounded impressive and dangerous. The nurses and medical orderlies had been warned that it would be dangerous, and for a posting such as this only volunteers were accepted. But what a journey from Igdyr! The mountain passes were still snowed under, so the only way of getting there was on horseback. Anna had started to look wild, with her face wind-beaten and covered in red blotches from the sunburn. One glance in her pocket mirror was enough: what a pretty sight, dearie – the female volunteer. Her lambskin cloak had originally been light grey, but now it had absorbed so much horse sweat that it was no longer clear what colour it was. Her boots were rather too big, and had room enough for her to wrap a couple of foot-bindings over her feet. In Erevan there had been nothing in her size – and where could she possibly find anything now? The detachment was advancing deep into Turkey, and there was nothing at all here, except for the odd puff of smoke from beneath the ground. This was where the Kurds lived. Underground. And when they emerged, they were given to attacking the odd passing convoy. Anna kept some cyanide potassium on her, as did the other nurses. It was said that if the Kurds caught you they raped you – there had been such instances.

Petya the medical orderly was forever struggling with the camels carrying the kerosene, for they disliked the smell. The camels carrying the other supplies were all right – they got up. But the ones with the kerosene refused to budge even if you beat them with a stick.

'Ladies, block up your ears!'

Anna and Natasha, the doctor's assistant, would laugh and block up their ears – but they could still hear. Not that they could possibly blame Petya. The Cossacks at Igdyr had taught the camels some choice obscenities, and now they refused to move until they heard the words to which they had become accustomed.

The mountains were blue, and, up here, so were the flowers. Were those forget-me-nots? No, they were too big. Now those over there were tulips, on short stems – yellow and red. After riding for so long, Natasha's loose native trousers had torn. But Anna had lined hers with leather. Anna had an affectionate mare, quite unlike Strelets back at the Fountain. But she was grateful to Strelets and to Sergei Alexandrovich, for, to begin with, nearly everyone else had groaned, including even the convoy leader – but for Anna this was more like an enjoyable ride in the countryside. She had felt exhausted in Igdyr: all that dreadful bandaging to do! And the amputations, and the cases where there was nothing left to amputate. The Turks used dumdum bullets. She had seen a victim with his skull smashed in, and grey-coloured brains oozing from it, yet the man was still alive, and asking for a drink. Anna had not cried once since leaving Odessa, she just felt tired – Lord, how tired she felt!

If a man was dying, he called a nurse Marusya, or Dasha, or by some other name. He took her for his wife. And the men who called her 'mama' were the unmarried ones. But, if they were still conscious, they all called for Anna, although she could not understand why. There were nurses who were a good deal more experienced and more kindly than she was. Like Natasha, the doctor's assistant, who called each of the men 'sweetheart, my dearie, my little sunshine!' She had been married, but her husband had died. She knew how to get on with the patients, but Anna didn't. Then Petya heard something and when he related it to Anna everything fell into place. It transpired there was a rumour among the Cossacks that there was 'a nurse with golden plaits who raised men from the dead'. And, after completing her training course, she really had stopped cutting her hair, and now she had plaits which, although short, she still felt it would be a pity to cut off. But how had they ever noticed her plaits – that was the mystery! The nurses in the hospital were all identical: they all had the same grey dress and nurse's cap. And the cap had been cleverly designed, not just to hide their hair, but also their foreheads. It made their faces look plump, and as flat as a pancake. This cap came down like a cape, covering their chest and shoulders. There had to be a palm's width between their waist and the point where it ended. So don't stare – there's nothing to stare at. A nurse is a nurse, and that's all there is to it. Yet, even so, they had somehow managed to spot her plaits. The men were so cunning.

And, of course, she did not raise anyone from the dead. Occasionally someone would be on the point of death, and then the next thing you knew they were breathing again, and smiling, and they would go on living. The Cossacks were a hardy people. One of them, who was called Stetsko, was forever asking Anna, 'Little sister, do something, say a prayer at least! Pray that I'll live! It would be a shame for me to die – it can't be that my time is up! I haven't had a son yet – our family name would come to an end!'

And Anna was so moved to pity that she would pray as though

prayer came to her as something that was perfectly natural. To start with, she said all the prayers that she knew, but then she made up prayers of her own: O Lord, do something to stop him from dying! Do something, do something – do something! But afterwards she could no longer remember what she had said.

To everyone's surprise, Stetsko survived, and it became impossible to convince him that it had not been Anna's doing. Oh, come now, Stetsko, where would you be now, if it weren't for surgeon Malinin, who extracted eleven bits of that dumdum bullet from you? What had Anna done – just come along once it was all over and poured in some saline solution. But that's what people are like: he forgot to say thank you to Malinin, yet he brought Anna a lambswool hat with a white top – a must against sunburn! And a shepherd's sheepskin coat that she could use for sleeping on the ground. It was even embarrassing, for the other nurses immediately started gossiping and making jokes about it.

Now that she was sleeping up in the mountains, the coat came in handy. When she had been little, Anna's mother used to wrap her up in a blanket in much the same way, telling her to lie down on one wing, and then cover herself over with the other. And now, once again, she found herself lying on one wing, with her saddle beneath her head, covering herself up and getting snug. The coat smelt of sheep and wormwood, as the nurses had learnt to sprinkle everything with chopped wormwood in order to keep the flees off. And up here the stars were amazing – they appeared low and enormous, and each had its own colour. They were like fruit-drops hanging in the sky. Blink, and you almost brushed them with your eyelashes.

Karakalisa turned out to be a shabby village, and only a few of its houses could really be called such, and even then . . . But it sounded so impressive: the headquarters of General Abatsiev's warring army! And this, it transpired, was one of those same squalid houses. The hospital, however, had to erect tents. There was no electricity here, and kerosene was used as sparingly as possible. And, again, there were those terrible nights, with one medical orderly per tent, and one nurse on night duty. One nurse – for nearly two hundred patients!

Getting tired is like getting into cold water: the prospect seems dreadful, but once you're in and swimming about you no longer feel the cold. When you start getting tired, you feel sorry for yourself, and get annoyed at everything, especially when you're due for a break and then something else suddenly crops up. But by now you know you can swim for as long as it may take – and that eventually it will pass, provided you just stick at it for a bit longer. And then it gets easier, and you can smile, and your body becomes light. Anna had already come to terms with the fact that she was hopelessly selfish, and she simply did all that she could to keep this concealed. There were more typhus victims here than wounded, and the tents were for the various types of typhus – louse-borne typhus, abdominal typhus and recurrent fever. Three times a day the victims were given injections of camphor, especially the ones with louse-borne typhus. But the fourth tent was for the wounded. The wounded screamed less, but the victims of louse-borne typhus were delirious and howled dreadfully. The medical orderly Petya also became infected, but he was cured. He cried all the time as he lay sweltering, and he kept on asking for cranberries.

There was another nurse there called Alexandra, who – it was said – was a countess. Although she had broad bones and hands just like a peasant's. But here was someone Anna could learn from! Goodness alone knew where she managed to get hold of some cranberry extract for Petya. And before anyone knew what was happening she was rearing chickens – she just went straight up to the general and asked him to get her some hens. And – being the dear fellow that he was – he did as he was told. And then she got a cow, as well: and the patients got milk.

'Don't just grab it and yank, Anna! Can't you see she's too nervous to give any milk? Gently does it, you stroke her udder ever so gently, and let her feel all that goodness she's got to give. Come on now, dearie, there we are – let's have some nice warm milk . . .' (this last being spoken to the cow).

Anna's hands became so sore that the pain kept her awake at night. Who would ever have thought that milking a cow was such hard work? But Alexandra took it in her stride – she just chuckled. She said her father had advised her to learn how to milk a cow back on their family estate. Some of these counts were eccentric. Come to think of it, Tolstoy was a count, too. Perhaps she was a relative? But no, she didn't go round in bare feet. So Anna never discovered that this Alexandra was, in fact, Tolstoy's daughter. She was soon transferred to Van, and after that Anna never saw her again.

It did not look as if the All-Russian Land Union had much of a clue about how to manage the medical staff under its command. People were sent off somewhere and then brought back again, and most of the nurses and surgeon's assistants were, for some incomprehensible reason, stuck in Erevan. So Anna was not surprised when she was posted back to Igdyr, where the hospital was being expanded.

They were already through the mountain pass: she and Petya were on horseback, and behind them came the medical orderly, Ivashchenko, with the unloaded camels. Petya was still weak, and was being sent to Erevan to convalesce.

'Anna! Look what a morning it is! Glance up at the sky and you'll see angels! Do you see them, Anna?' said Petya in delight. Convalescents always look like children. Perhaps he really had seen some angels . . .

Anna first saw him clutch at his chest and slump from his horse – and only then did she hear the shot.

'Kurds! Anna, go on – I'll cover you!' yelled Ivashchenko, and then there were more shots, and he stopped yelling. Anna dug in her shanks: rescue me, little dove!

But they were gaining on her, and not shooting, either – and the sound of their hooves was getting nearer and nearer. Anna looked round: there were four of them. In turbans. Yes, yes – so the Kurds really did wear turbans. They were about to catch her, there was no escape. Oh, Mama! Dear Mama, forgive me! The cyanide potassium was not sealed inside the test tube, but the stopper was too stiff and she had no time to remove it. The glass shattered in her teeth, and Anna gulped it down convulsively.

She was torn from her saddle with a terrible, brusque force and hurled face down. Something was throbbing in the pit of her stomach, and Anna started vomiting uncontrollably. Then she found herself unable to breathe, and being whirled round and round – to the right and upwards.

The four men stopped: their quarry was ruined. The one that had thrown Anna across his saddle looked mawkishly down as he gingerly wiped some bloody slime from his knee. And, in the meantime, this devilish woman in loose trousers kept convulsively thrashing about, and vomiting and vomiting. Urgh, unclean spirit!

'Little sister! Can you hear me, little sister!'

It was terribly difficult opening her eyes: how was it done? No, it was too much. And what difference did it make, as she was already dead, anyway?

But the face above her was so pock-marked and stubbly, and so undoubtedly Russian, that she realised – no, I'm still here. It was a soldier. One of ours.

'Little sister, can you hear me, are you alive?'

'She's alive, look! She's blinking. Maybe she was overwrought with fear? She looks in a dreadful state!'

'She's been sick as a dog. Maybe she's pregnant. These things do happen with her sex. Hand me that flask, Mitrich.'

By the time she recovered consciousness Anna was in Igdyr. She was already lying in a hospital bed, covered over with a coarse grey blanket. And just as well, too, for, despite the heat, she was shivering with cold.

'Well now, milady – how are we feeling today?' asked the familiar Dr Malinin, sitting down by her bedside.

'A-all right. I'm just cold. Doctor – but this can't be happening!'

'I agree, it's improbable. You were lucky – like one in a thousand! You were lucky that the Kurds hung about on the road instead of rushing off . . . And lucky that it just happened to be when some of our men had to take some wheels to be repaired . . . You must lead a charmed life. You may be pleased to learn that three of your Kurds were killed, and the one that was wounded is now here in the hospital. As a prisoner of war, filthy scoundrel that he is. I removed a bullet from him.'

'No, that's not the point, doctor . . . I mean, I took some cyanide potassium.'

'Well, well, well . . . So that's what caused the convulsions. That makes it a good deal less surprising, then. All you nurses believe in cyanide potassium as if it were the Lord God. But, in fact, it decomposes in high temperatures. Was the capsule sealed?'

'No, but it had a tight stopper.'

'Aha, so that's it . . . An unsealed container, plus all the heat – and I dare say you've been carrying it around with you all summer? And, on top of that, they threw you across the saddle before you had time to swallow it down properly. Naturally you vomited, and, as it was, we had no more than a bit of a scare to deal with – much to everyone's delight.'

'Is it really that unreliable?'

'Well, what do you want? There's no such thing as a hundred per cent reliability. Have you read the Sarayev case? That was a similar story: a gunman took some of this delightful stuff, but it didn't kill him. He fell into the hands of the police. Just as you've now fallen into mine. You're under my arrest until you've fully recovered. I have some good news for you: you won't suffer any after-effects. Well, your muscles will ache for about a week – and then you'll be right as rain.'

'Doctor . . . What about Petya?'

'Petya – well . . . There was nothing we could do for him. The shot went clean through him, and it severed his artery. Now, now, dear . . . there's no need for that . . . We all go that way in the end. Well, you go ahead and cry – it's good for you after such a nasty scrape. I'll have one of the nurses come and see you.'

When Anna grew stronger she was sent to Tiflis. To convalesce. It was wild seeing electric street-lights again, and shops, and being able to take a hot bath, and even buy a dress. Her present dress now hung down in folds on her. In Tiflis she had to wait for a new posting, so, for the time being, she suddenly found herself without any obligations. It was incredible: she could sleep for as long as she wanted. So she did – but, even when she had fully caught up on her sleep, it still seemed a senseless waste to wake up when no one was actually waking her, and she would try to go back to sleep again. She sent her parents a brave letter, without, of course, any description of her adventures: saying how remarkable the local climate was, and the fruits and medicinal waters.

Vanda Kazimirovna sighed over it: Anna was clearly trying too hard, and the letter came out sounding altogether too jolly. It looked as if the girl was having a hard time of it. But, thank God, at least she had not caught malaria in those outlandish places. Nor had she caught typhus, for she was writing about her plaits . . . Clever girl, not to have cut them off. But there was no photograph – oh, what did that mean? How did she look, and why hadn't she sent a photograph? After all, Tiflis was a civilised city, and she could easily have had her photograph taken . . . Well, praise be to God, she was alive! Though there was still no word from Vladek . . .

But news of Vladek came through a less usual channel. One fine day after Mass the Catholic priest gave her a nod, indicating that she was to stay behind, and for some reason her heart froze.

'*Pani* Teslenko, I have some news for you. Don't ask me where I got it, but it's true. Vladek is alive and well. He asked for me to send you his greetings, and has requested your blessing, but, for the time being, he is unable to write. He is still in Poland.'

'What? Under the Germans?'

'In Poland, my daughter, all other peoples come and go, except for the Poles. You're surprised that he's ended up in Poland, and feels that it is his home? It has also dawned on him to praise the Lord, and he has come into the bosom of our Holy Church. The most holy *pan* Jesus has heard your maternal prayers.'

Vanda Kazimirovna looked up, following the direction of the priest's eyes: was it the dark angels on the ceiling that he was looking at? She automatically made the sign of the cross with her cold fingers.

'Tell me, *pan* Father – in Poland . . . is it very dangerous?'

'He has escaped many great dangers, *pani* Teslenko. And he will continue to do so in future. Men like him are needed in Poland. The war won't last for ever, and neither will the Germans. Now Poland will have a new history, and he will be one of those who will start to make it. Shall I send him your forgiveness and blessing?'

'Yes, yes, *pan* Father . . . may the Lord keep him, and grant him His mercy for evermore. Can you tell me anything more about him?'

'Yes, one more thing. He got married – there, in Poland. To some young Russian girl, but he married in the bosom of our Church. She died shortly afterwards, they hardly had any time together.'

'Vladek got married? Lord, who to?'

'I wasn't told her name. She died, after all, so nothing is known of her. In the name of the Father, the Son, and the Holy Spirit . . .'

He blessed Vanda Kazimirovna and let her go. Only when she was out in the damp December snow did she first wonder how to break this news to her husband.

15

Maria Vasilyevna's fondest possession was a small trunk that was painted in green and had raised brass corners. Here she kept her wedding candles, children's christening shirts, their first ever locks of hair, and some photographs of them with patterned edges, and now looking rather yellow: Pavel in his pinafore, Zina on a pony, Marina and Zina with their dolls, and the five-year-old Maxim in his sailor-suit. Here, too, was a file with their childish drawings, and now also another file – for letters. It was in this file that she kept the letter that Pavel had written after being awarded the St. George's Cross for saving his commander and made an officer, though this letter was kept apart from the others, and was bound in a black and orange striped ribbon. So that it could be instantly located.

After crying and rejoicing to her heart's content, now she would read the letter to every one of her guests, sometimes forgetting that it was the second or third time she had done so. She gently, but firmly, brushed aside an attempt by Dasha to take the letter from her. Well, really, what use was it to her, an illiterate? But Dasha was not offended for long. Marina – the great diplomat – could not bear to see anyone in a huff, and resolved every problem in her own particular way: in a whirlwind of kisses and laughter that it was impossible not to be infected by.

'He was so brave – so why did they just give him a St. George's Cross for other ranks? Yura Nezhdanov got the officers' St. George's Cross, second class, just for some ammunition box . . .' Maria Vasilyevna had initially said, sharing her indignation with her husband. But he simply burst out laughing.

'Masha, my angel – you're such a woman, really! What do you know about medals! The St. George's Cross for other ranks is the highest decoration that anyone can possibly get – believe you me. The St. George's Cross for officers isn't fit to be spoken of in the same breath, and an officer can have no greater honour than to receive a St. George's Cross for other ranks. But it's only ever awarded on the recommendation of a general meeting of the regiment, together with the soldiers . . . Yura would be glad to swap places with Pavlik, I assure you.'

Now Maria Vasilyevna would proudly stress to everyone that Pavel had been awarded, not a plain St. George's Cross, but the St. George's Cross for other ranks. The mood in her salon had changed from its pre-war extreme liberalism to moderate patriotism. Which meant: you could curse all the ministers and the Tsar's entourage as much as you liked, but, for as long as the war continued, no one should even dare take it into their head to doubt the war's victorious outcome, or the valour of our army. Strictly speaking, the Petrovs should have cut back on their guest evenings. Their wealth, which was not, in any event, substantial, could have been wiped out altogether with the devaluation of the rouble. And the food situation was getting harder all the time – in 'Peter' they were on ration cards, and soon they would have them here, too. Was this any time to be entertaining guests? But, once they had got the morning ordeal with the newspapers behind them, could they not, at least, permit themselves some relaxation with old acquaintances of an evening?

And ordeal it had become, for now the papers were carrying the lists of officers killed in action.

Petrov!

Petrov!

Petrov! – each day now the name would lash into Maria Vasilyevna's eyes from the pages of the newspapers. And each time she had to convince herself of the names and numbers of the regiment, and that the Petrovs who had been killed were some other Petrovs – and not Pavlik. It's such a common surname. What Russian name is more widespread than Petrov? Perhaps only Ivanov. Maria Vasilyevna could never hold back her tears for these other Petrovs in the lists. Yet how many more Petrovs must there be – among the other ranks . . . In their minds, Pavel's parents understood that he was an ensign now, and that if he was promoted any further the boy would face no greater risk than he had before. But the risk was so plain to see: every time it was heart-rending. They hadn't received a letter from Zina for ages, but, for some reason, they were much less worried about her. Thank God that, for the time being at least, the youngest children were still at home.

'Masha, dear, you're not sleeping?' Ivan Alexandrovich asked, groping his way round the little bedside table and lighting the candle: he did not feel like turning on the electricity. She could see his head and naked chest in the faint light. Now even the hairs on his chest had turned grey. We're getting old, thought Maria Vasilyevna, but Ivan's still so sprightly, even grey hair suits him. She pressed her cheek to his hand.

'Ivan, nothing will happen to Pavlik, will it? I have this feeling that he's going to be all right.'

'Yes, yes – so have I. Do you remember when he was little and came down with scarlet fever, and we hardly even worried about him, though there was plenty of reason to. Yet we always knew he'd get better – although quite why we were so sure, I've no idea.'

'Yes, and do you remember how the yard-cleaner hewed a little axe from a piece of wood for him, and he took it to bed with him?'

'By then he was already a warrior . . .'

Both the Petrov parents often had insomnia now.

Anna was delighted that she had to report to Moscow for her new posting. That meant she was probably being sent west. It would have been hard going back to Turkey. Now that her exhaustion had gone, she felt even worse: it was a sense of having been defiled. Could that be simply because she was lucky not to have been raped? What a girl who had been raped must feel like she could not imagine, and she chewed at her fingers whenever she found herself unable to banish her thoughts on the matter. Could it be because her attempted suicide had been so ghastly and humiliating – not at all as she had expected. What, essentially, had she expected? The poison to take instant effect, and a dignified end. Surely that was the least a person was entitled to? She knew she would have felt ashamed to see Malinin and the nurses in Igdyr again. She realised that this shame was senseless, but that simply made it burn all the more fiercely. So was this something she now had to live with? It was probably the same feeling that people have after an operation, when the anaesthetic wears off.

Moscow delighted and amazed her with its thick snow, its sledges and swankily decorated horse-collars, the dense steam from the horses and its general state of higgledy-pigglediness. This city had never strained to become a city, as such, and it took pride in having grown from a village, and had done so, not by following any plan, but living its own ramshackle sort of life, without striving to conform to anything other than its own self. Here there was the tolling of countless church bells, and here, too, were posters for the Arts Theatre. It was hard to believe that the world still had any theatres! In order to get tickets it proved necessary to queue in advance, but she no longer had time for that. In two days' time she was due to leave for Zalesye to take up her new post. She could have postponed it, but the apartment where she was being put up with two other nurses was unwelcoming – both in itself, and because the landlady kept a somehow suspicious eye on them. She was forever watching them, with her round pale eyes staring out from her pasty face: anxious, perhaps, for her silverware?

Anna only just had time to see the Kremlin (the cabman drove her in through the gate of the Saviour Tower and, in time-honoured fashion, doffed his hat as they passed beneath it). She went to see the Iverskaya icon of the Mother of God in the chantry, and put a candle there, but she was unable to pray. She did not recognise the face of the Mother of God in this dark image. In their cathedral back at home the icons were different from the Southern Russian school, and the style was not so austere. And the Madonna in her mother's room was beautiful, and had a tender face. Anna tucked her hands a little deeper into her hareskin muff and went out into the falling snow. This was lovely snow – crunchy and with blue shadows. She suddenly had a feeling of loneliness: she was in Moscow – and alone. The Petrovs knew no one in Moscow. Rimma was somewhere here, as Anna knew from a family letter – but where was she to be found? The letter had not even given the name of her studio. And, besides, they were probably away on tour.

It was too cold to walk, too expensive to travel by transport, and the thought of going back to her apartment was too off-putting. The gay life of Moscow, with all its large-spirited hospitality, theatres and concerts, was passing her by, and she found this upsetting. Nevertheless, she did take a ride on a tram that was chock-a-block with high-spirited college girls and students, and also some old women in threadbare coats and gentlemen in beaver coats. On the steam-coated window pane someone had drawn an ugly face with the tongue sticking out, and beneath it was the name 'Grishka'. Then a student by the window drew a noose round its neck and added the name 'Rasputin'. The passengers burst into approving laughter. Here it was as though the war did not exist – it was simply that wounded men could be seen walking the streets on crutches. But no one seemed to pay any attention to them.

The point is this, realised Anna, I've grown used to being constantly needed by someone. Day and night, desperately. But here I'm needed by no one. Not even myself, very much. Well, get used to it, princess! This immediately made her feel easier, for she knew that she had no time to get used to it. Whatever else Zalesye might hold for her, she knew that once again she would have to grab her sleep in snatches, and have no time to wash and dry her hair, and have bruises on her arms – from the clutches of delirious men – and once again there would be the pleas of 'give me a drink, little sister'. This feeling of not being needed by anyone was, in fact, freedom – here in this city she was a stranger to everyone, and it was wonderful. It was a feeling of being protected, as though she were behind a mask.

She went to a ladies' hairdresser and had a short haircut. The hairdresser, who was a rather frail Jew, looked like an Odessan: he strewed his patter with numerous French words, and kept going into raptures over the shape of her face.

'*Charmant, charmant, madame*! I will make you look like Vera Kholodnaya! What an extraordinary colour of hair: it is gold, pure gold! If *madame* will be so good as to look at the back of her head in the mirror . . .'

Anna cheered up: she always felt cheered by having her hair cut. It was a bit of mischief, a bit of masquerade. Maybe it was even true that it was at the ends of your hair, rather than in your heart, that worries accumulated? Cut them off, and they've gone. That's why soldiers have crew-cuts. But she was in no mood for gloom: she liked herself in the mirror. Her eyes were big, and even her thinness didn't matter, for it hadn't ruined her looks.

The hairdresser charged an exorbitant price and, as a precaution, started whining about how he was 'a father to many children'. Anna burst out laughing, settled up and left. She'd started to like Moscow.

In the evening there was a concert for those who were about to leave for the front. Well, at least it was recognition of some sort. A man with closely cropped hair in a black frock-coat drawled out some verses about war. They were quite unlike the reality. A lieutenant sitting next to Anna had a crooked grin on his face, and he started tapping his spur. It rang out in time with the declamation: subtly, mordantly. He and Anna exchanged glances and smiled at one another, like conspirators. Then there was some singing, and things picked up a little. The master of ceremonies said something and Anna let out a sigh: Rimma − no, it was another Rimma. Volynsteva − or was it Volantseva? But no, it was undoubtedly Rimma that came out on stage, with that familiar blaze in her eyes: that was something she could never mistake.

> 'Gee-up there, troika, snow like fluff,
> And all around the frozen steppe . . .'

Anna applauded louder than anyone, and the lieutenant arched his brow in surprise. But she no longer even saw him. Rimma was here! And what a way to show up!

She waited for the end, until Rimma was leaving with some young men, and called out mischievously, in the manner of 'Madam Bonton': 'Rimma Geiber! Irregular verbs!'

And Rimma looked round in surprise, and immediately recognised who it was, and she came flying over to embrace her. She dragged Anna back to introduce her to her colleagues from the studio, but it came to nothing: they were both laughing like lunatics, and it was obvious that they were interested in no one but each other.

When they got back to Rimma's little room, and were munching on some biscuits from the last century, they tried to start talking coherently, but this immediately turned into a conversation about everything, and then – unexpectedly – it turned to a conversation about nothing. While they were recalling old acquaintances, and who was where now, she was like the Rimma of old, with her sharp tongue and ever-ready jokes. But then she became like a stranger, like a woman from some other world.

'What have you got out of all this busy-bodying, Anna? What you've been telling me is awful. And it doesn't suit you one little bit. But how much prettier you look. You've such an interesting face, and you're so thin – you'd be a sensation on the stage. Only how dreadfully you've let your hands go. I understand, carbolic and all that sort of thing. Well, you know what's good for that? Bran! You try it. Now, just wait a moment, and I'll give you some cream – I've got a spare jar, anyway.'

Anna took the cream in some bewilderment and turned it round. Her hands – yes, well, she'd certainly had no time to think of her hands. But by now Rimma was already expounding her views on pure art, and how it was the only thing that was worth serving, and telling her about the studio: how envious some of the girls were, if only Anna knew! The war she called a lot of fuss over nothing – Anna did not mishear this. And she was forever expressing surprise.

'Well, you always were the compassionate one among us. Even back in the gymnasium you were called the 'sister of mercy'. But can you imagine Zina as a nurse? I mean, as far as I can remember, she was a girl with some non-trivial ideas in her head. After all, when all's said and done, it's so unaesthetic: those nurses' caps are awful – they make you look like a nun. Anyway, so much for aesthetics – the main point is: why do it?'

Anna did not know how to reply to this. She had never thought about why she did it. It was simply that she had been working in the only place in which she could imagine herself being. But now it looked as if Rimma's was the only way to live, and that, in fact, all real life took place somewhere quite different. How the idea of art had moved forward over the last two years! How the interpretation of the role of gesture on stage had altered! And, given the new schools and movements that had arisen, how could anyone possibly fail to keep up with them?

'So you've got a different surname now? Are you married?'

'What's that got to do with it? It's perfectly normal to have a stage name. Geiber sounds too drab. But I'm thinking of changing it again, as the name I've got now sounds too much like Vyaltseva. The last thing I want is to have people muddle me up with some gramophone crooner.'

But it was still a good meeting. They enjoyed recalling old jokes and pranks: like the rat in the chalk-box just before the fractions test, and the time they'd got the boys' fishing tackle tangled up in the dacha at the Fountain, and how they'd teased Yakov for bringing Marina those lilacs that he'd broken from a tree in the cemetery! It was already past midnight by the time they parted, and Anna delighted in taking a stroll around the snow-plumped back streets. It was so wonderful walking around a city on her own, and knowing that it was Moscow. There were no Turks or Germans here: it was calm, and there was no shooting. It was deep in the rear. And as cosy as a snow-drift.

Yet, even so, something rankled: could it be that she and this new Rimma were now virtual strangers? She kept trying to persuade herself that there was nothing to be upset about: after all, she was not interested in hearing how the diaphragm supported the voice – so why should Rimma be interested in her affairs? Maybe the same thing would happen when she and Zina met up? Maybe Pavel had changed, too? She shook her head and took a cab to her apartment, for anyway she could not have found her own way back at this time of night. The cabby had a magnificent horse that looked as finely groomed as one of Renoir's women. Anna smiled: that's what came of talking with Rimma – now she remembered that there actually were such things as Renoir's pictures in the world.

'Almonds! It smells of almonds!'

That meant they had to put on their masks: those foul muzzles with the square glass covers.

'Get the horses out of here! Gas! Put on your masks!'

It makes you sick: fear always takes you like that. But it was a good team, and everyone knew what they were doing. The wounded – the ones from the dug-out – had to be got up on to the hillock, as the gas was spreading out over the low ground. But the Germans were pounding the hillock with heavy shells. Well, in that case they'd have to get to the other side of the hillock: God wouldn't forsake them. The horses were already being driven away, and the wounded that couldn't move had been put on the carts – at least, as many as possible of them. You couldn't put a mask on a horse, but if the horses were poisoned then how could the wounded be moved? The hospital detachment had two vehicles that were a gift from the Empress, but the Germans had been targeting them in the belief that they were being used to carry the top brass. Not that the vehicles could have got through to here now, anyway. It was all churned up. As for the other wounded who couldn't walk, they just had to be carried. There weren't enough stretchers, though any moment now some should be coming from the second 'flying detachment'. But that 'any moment now' still had to be got through.

Anna knew that she was strong. But it was only fear that enabled her to carry heavy male bodies on her own like this.

'Legs! Squeeze with your legs!'

But what could he hear if she was mumbling through a mask? And how were commanders meant to give orders through a Zelinsky mask? And so they tore them off in order to shout out, and were poisoned.

The nurses were dragging over the ones who were still conscious, while the medical orderlies were seeing to the rest. A limp body is heavier. They had to be got to the carts – and then they had to go back again, at the double. And it wasn't only the wounded they'd got to see to, but also the men that had just been gassed. Some had torn off their mask in panic, thinking they couldn't breathe. Their faces were a greyish red – you could see the veins on their necks swelling up.

'Where's your mask, nurse?' the woman in charge of the

detachment asked her when she got to the cart. Anna just shook her head: well, I gave it to him. And she sat down by the wheel, while a junior captain was put up on to the cart without her help.

'How did you manage to get him out?'

'I tried not to breathe.'

'You must be mad!'

But she was not at all mad – the wind had simply got up and started to dispel the gas. That's how she managed. And now it was even stronger – it was on their side, the wind, and the yellow-grey haze was drifting back over towards the German trenches. Serve them right, too! And the firing was now concentrated in that direction, too: our men had gone over to the attack, this was no longer 1915. But it was terrible to see how, for miles on end, there wasn't a single living leaf or blade of grass. Everything was yellow and shrivelled. Anna had thought that no weapon could be baser than the new German bombs with horizontal explosion. But now they'd invented gas. This was utterly inhuman, and so was people's reaction to it.

Anna, now in a starched white gown once again, was in her second week at the hospital. The front line had moved over to the west, and things had become slightly calmer. But she noticed how the wounded here were different. They were nastier. And not only the wounded, but everyone else, too. Previously, they had simply been fighting the Germans – 'Herman's fighting us, and we're fighting Herman.' Back in the rear, people had got themselves all excited at the start of the war, rooting out German names, and smashing up German shops. But there was nothing like that in the army. Hatred comes from powerless rage, but a soldier has a gun, and an outlet for action. However, that's for as long as it's gun on gun – but what if you're being wiped out like cockroaches? The good-natured jokes about 'Herman' came to an end, and now they hated him with a vengeance. There were soon rumours that our own side had started using gas as well, but Anna tried not to believe this.

And the overall mood had changed, too. The soldiers that were first called up had been calmer, and they'd gone off to war as if going to work. But how many call-ups had there been since then? And now it was the wrong sort of soldier that came. Irritation had grown, and the hospitals had more patients with nervous disorders. The wounded were rude more often, and many of them kept staring with mindless malice. Anna knew little about the Socialists' propaganda, but she could see for herself that the men were tired of fighting.

It was here, in the relative safety of the hospital, that she evidently came closer to death than at any other time. Her night duty had been quiet, and it wasn't the most difficult of wards, either. Everyone was asleep – only a man with a shattered hip over in the corner by the window kept muttering in his sleep. Anna was quietly reading by her little desk, with her back turned to the patients so as to block out the candle-light and not disturb them. She had found little time to read lately, but the surgeon's assistant had given her a book by Bunin for the night. What he loves most, thought Anna, is dogs and stars. He's always at his best when he's writing about them. But about women, he's not always so good.

Just then she had a sudden urge to look round. One step away from her there stood a tall and puffy-looking man in a hospital gown. And in total silence he was stretching his hands out towards her. Towards her neck. Slowly. Anna froze with horror, but only for an instant. She checked him with her glance, and abruptly gave the order: 'Le-eft turn!'

He automatically turned round, and Anna did not leave it at that, either, 'Forward march to bed!'

Then she went to the door and quietly, under her breath, called over the medical orderly.

A minute later, by the time the sleepy Vasiliev and an unfamiliar new orderly had arrived, the patient was already sitting calmly on his bed and telling Anna all about his great mission. It was a long story whose final details it fell to the surgeon's assistant Kovalevich to hear out: Anna was relieved of her duty. For the rest of her shift she cried like a little girl in the kitchen. The senior nurse stroked her head and plied her with ruddy tea. The edge of her glass chattered against her teeth.

'Well, dear, you were born under a lucky star!' said Kovalevich next morning, shaking his head. 'That chap's only just been brought in with mild gas-poisoning, and we hadn't managed to work out what's wrong with him. But the poor fellow's off his head, and do you know what sort of a mania he's got? He thinks he has to perform a sacrifice on a totally innocent human creature. And you struck him as a suitable candidate – congratulations. The sacrifice had to be bloodless – in other words, strangled. And then all the world's sins would be atoned for, and there would be eternal peace. So how on earth did you cope with him? Later on four men had a job subduing him!'

'I shouted, like a sergeant-major. And he did a left turn.'

'Well, it was obviously a conditioned reflex. And that's what saved you. What made you think of it, you clever girl?'

'It was entirely thanks to your Bunin,' laughed Anna. 'Have you noticed how he sharpens your feelings! I got this urge to turn round, just as I was reading about a dog's sense of smell . . .'

This later became a long-standing joke at the hospital, and she was called 'Anna the Innocent' – as distinct from another Anna, who was also a nurse there.

'Dear Mama, Papa and Antos! I am now in Petrograd, and at last have an address where a letter will quickly reach me. Only don't worry, I've just got a tiny scratch. A piece of shrapnel grazed my arm near the elbow, but I was very lucky: it was just a nick. I was even ashamed at being sent back to the rear for such a trifle. I'll be here for about another month, and then, I hope, I'll come home on leave. How wonderful it will be to embrace you all! But I won't be able to join you for Christmas, of course. I have a present for Antos: some real German binoculars that were a trophy given to me by our gunners. By the way, I was also awarded a Stanislav, second class, which was brought straight in to the hospital and handed to me in person. It's very beautiful, and has eagles on it. Your Anusya is now in danger of bursting with pride. What is the news of Vladek? How I've missed you all! And I would like to know about the Petrovs, and how they're getting on. You do still see them, don't you? I kiss you all, my dears! I look forward to seeing you. I will soon write in more detail. I kiss you again and again. May God keep you.'

Then came the address of the hospital. After Antos had gone

off to bed in his own room, the Teslenko parents sat embracing one another for a long time. Outside the windows there was a fog – like a milky jelly. And, as always on a foggy night, from out at sea a tolling bell and some distant hoots could be heard. They could see the gleam from the black wet branches of Anna's beloved plane tree. It was December 1916.

16

Oh, that Henrietta! Rimma never could stand her: she was always clambering to be first. She was as crass as a peasant from Bugayevka, but would roll her eyes, strike a languid pose, and then start fluttering her lips – ah, poor little birdie! The studio manager, Yakov Borisovich, was the cleverest of men, and acutely sensitive to falsity, too, but even he couldn't stand up to her. But she wouldn't get away with it this time! Who had ever heard of a woman like her singing Carmen? How could she, with her cute locks of fair hair, and her stiff, doll-like manner, play a hot-blooded Spaniard? Rimma had always kept herself in check, but today she would speak her mind. Yakov Borisovich was a champion of naturalness – so he couldn't possibly allow a wig. Carmen was dark-haired, and that was all there was to it! The author should know, after all. She could also say a thing or two about Henrietta's voice – but that wasn't such a good idea. Both she and Henrietta had their enviers among the other girls, and that would only set tongues wagging . . . Yes, that's how to do it: offer it to Lyusya. She was black-haired, and had a supple voice. True, it wasn't very resonant – but that should be left for others to say. She knew that Yakov Borisovich was on her side. But he didn't like squabbles, and made a principle of relying on the opinion of the collective. His whole idea was not to train any individual singers but rather the collective, and to get everyone working as a single organism. So why not let him rely on their opinion this time? The entire studio would make a choice between Rimma and Lyusya. Zhenya, for one, always backed Rimma to the hilt, and so did Valery . . . The others would support them, too, for the others knew that these were people to be reckoned with.

Could Rimma ever have imagined that it would all be so complicated – being a singer? For a start you had to become a singer – but that was really the least of it. Then you had to get people to sit up and notice you – specifically you. And everyone else around wanted to be noticed, too. And they were in a hurry: a singer doesn't have much time to work in. It's all very well for poets and writers – all they have to do is sit in a study and get on with their writing. Keep the door nice and firmly shut, so no one can come and spoil your mood. No manager above to worry about, and no collective, either. And no need to rush. If you aren't recognised immediately, you'll be recognised in fifty years' time. Nothing can happen to the manuscript, and, once you're dead, your talent's there for all to see. If Rimma had been a writer she would never have burnt her manuscripts – that's what came of being spoilt. And she would never have joined any of the circles and unions, as these modern-day poets seemed to go in for. Wherever there's a collective, there are also bound to be arguments – in Russia it's the only way. Yet a singer's always mixing with people, and performing to them, too. It's easier to love people from within a study: if you don't like a hero, you can re-do him, or simply have him fall under a train, like Anna Karenina. But just try having a conductor throw you out of your rhythm, or a partner that you've got to be in love with! And if you don't love them, then the audience won't believe that you do, either, and your voice will lose its fluidity. And Yakov Borisovich will say: it's getting there. Needs a bit more work. It's dreary. Shoddy. Forced. And he'd be right.

Rimma tossed back her head – like Carmen. And her fluffy headscarf became a silk shawl of burning colours, and, without bothering to warm up, she launched straight into her favourite bit – where the voice snakes dangerously about in the depths – and then instantly soared up, as though borne on six wings! The landlady's ghastly yellowy-grey wallpaper parted: this dingy little room was no setting for a voice such as hers, and the sky was no longer a Muscovite grey, with a watery, snowy slushiness, but Spanish – with large clouds and bitter on the tongue.

Cold, how cold it was . . . She had hired a room on Sretenka Street, on the first floor. Downstairs there was a sign saying 'Dressmaker and open-work clothing'. This sign had always amused Rimma, but now she found it funnier than ever. Who could possibly want any open-work clothing in a winter as awful as this? It presently never got above twelve degrees in her little room, and her landlady was forever complaining that nowhere in the whole of Moscow could any coal be found – not for love or money . . . This winter the coal was being kept down in the Donbass region: there was something the matter with the railway there. And, indeed, it was cold everywhere, and when they assembled in the hall at the studio their breath would steam. After a while, of course, their hot breath made it warmer, and they would start singing. And Rimma would laugh.

'It's cold, gentlemen, let's have an argument, shall we!'

How often she had prevented a dreadful scene with one of her quips. In the studio she was loved for her cheerfulness. Though not by everyone, of course.

It was also necessary to understand the other studio members, especially the young men. Who was exempted from military service? Students, youngest sons and performing artists. But performing artists were all so different from one another. Naturally, Shalyapin would never be called up: he sang at the imperial theatres. But the studio, although it, too, offered refuge, was less reliable. As for the girls, of course, they served art selflessly. But there was no getting away from the need for male voices, and they had to keep themselves busy with something, at least, if the studio was to go on providing that refuge. They gave concerts to the military, and in the hospitals, and to the cadets. For audiences such as these it was necessary to lower the repertoire, and how irksome that was! Just try finding anything new in art with a war on. Thank goodness that at least they weren't being forced to sing out at the front – a point on which Yakov Borisovich had been quite adamant.

'I will not allow young talents to go and ruin their voices in the freezing cold!'

Rimma was slightly late in arriving at the studio, as the tram had been too crowded and she had to wait for the next one. But she got there to find the place in the most frightful palaver, and Zhenya immediately came flying over to her.

'Rimma, have you heard? Yakov Borisovich is a genius – it's incredible what he's done!'

'Whom? Where? Whither? Why?' Rimma quoted some nonsense from a school grammar-book, and everyone burst out laughing.

It transpired that it was all about Shalyapin's hospital. Well, yes, Shalyapin did indeed maintain two hospitals at his own expense – one in 'Peter' and one here, as everyone knew. They were said to be better than the Tsarina's hospital in the Winter Palace. And now they were about to give a performance at the local hospital here in Moscow. And did Rimma know when it was fixed for? Well, it was to be in a week's time, and Shalyapin himself was coming to sing to the wounded at his hospital! He would hear us! What better chance could anyone possibly wish for? And at this point Yakov Borisovich himself had something to say.

'What it means, my dears, is this. We're changing our repertoire – we're widening our range. Nothing too academic – Shalyapin doesn't go in for that sort of stuff. But nothing too primitive, either. Some sort of folk songs – that's a must. "There is a Cliff on the Volga", for example – well, that one's for you Zhenya . . . But we'll do some classics, as well: at least a couple of arias from *Carmen*. We'll have to hurry – but it'll be well worth it. Only let's have no bickering, I beg of you – I can't stage eleven *Carmen*s at once, or we'll end up with a chorus of them . . .'

'Don't worry, Yakov Borisovich,' Rimma put in, 'even crabs need to fight, and like the odd bite – then it's peace for a day, and back to the fray!'

This relieved the atmosphere and, although it proved impossible to get by without bickering, everything went more straightforwardly than Rimma had feared. Would she have enough time to get ready? What a question! She already knew the part off by heart – every note of it! And out she came with it, not even bothering to go up on to the stage: let them see, for there, if ever, was the girl from the cigar factory. Passionate. Proud. Everyone fell quiet, listening. She did not look at them, for she knew: Carmen was hers! Hers – and no one could take it away from her!

'But those high notes are a bit off, aren't they?' Henrietta couldn't help bitching. She knew that Rimma's top notes were vulnerable, and lost no time in reminding everyone: but she'd only spited her own face. Today there were no weaknesses in her top notes, just an ardent force. Henrietta was soon pacified, and Rimma went home happy – so happy that she took a cab, heedless of the crazy expense of it. There was a heavy fur rug in the cab, and – for the first time that day – Rimma managed to warm herself up. And the snow today was so tender and warm. The snowflakes burnt her lips, as if they were kissing them. And back in her little room – had the landlady heated it up? – it was even hot. Oh, for some cold water! But she must not drink cold water: she had to take care of her throat. Well, at least she could have some lemon – now, somewhere there was still a little piece left on the saucer under a lid. Ah, there it was. Completely dried up and shrivelled, with the yellow pellicles stuck to one another. Not at all appetising. Well, so much for the lemon. Perhaps she should call her mother, and ask her for some water melon . . . But what had this to do with her mother? Her mother was in Odessa!

Am I ill? wondered Rimma with horror. Anything but that. Not now. This called for urgent measures. Even a baby knew that, if you caught cold, what you had to do was mix half a bottle of brandy with half a bottle of milk, and keep well wrapped up. That was what all singers did. She would have to ask her landlady to buy some brandy for her . . . but where could any be found now, with the dry law? Well, it must be possible somewhere . . . Other people managed to get hold of it, after all. It was said that at the taverns they poured it out of teapots, if you knew what sign to give. And fur coats, lots of fur coats . . .

But it was someone else's eyes that were looking at her from the peeling pier-glass: they were not Rimma's. They were impassioned. And terrible.

'Spanish influenza,' the doctor who had been called told the landlady. 'Half the city's down with it. What she needs is caring, caring and more caring! Is she your daughter?'

'Certainly not, doctor! She's my tenant . . . For pity's sake, I can't keep her here. They say it's such a dangerous illness!'

'Does she have any relatives?'

'She's from out of town, doctor, and I know nothing about her relatives. There's a tall fellow with curly hair that comes and sees her. He looks as if he could be from that studio she goes to. But I can't say I've bothered to ask.'

'Well, you needn't bother now,' said the doctor through his teeth.

Rimma shook her head and sang something. Spanish – of course it was Spanish! Why, they should give her a lemon – straight from the tree. And some castanets. They were some sort of shoes, weren't they?

'Well, then she'll have to go to a paupers' hospital. I'll make the necessary arrangements. Someone will come and fetch her,' said the doctor, comforting the alarmed landlady.

Rakhil just had a feeling: she had not been to market that day, and had decided to laze about at home. And then there was a ring at the door. Who could it be? Surely it was rather too early for Yakov to be home from the gymnasium. Oh Lord, he hadn't been expelled, had he? He had been in some trouble there recently . . . She went to open the door, her chest heaving with anxiety.

'Mama. Mamochka!'

'Oh, my child! Rimmochka, can this really be you? Why, you're half wasted away . . . And you haven't written, or anything. My dear child – here, let me kiss you!'

An hour later Rimma, by now fed with tea and Kattarov buns, and wrapped up in her mother's shawl, was sitting in Rakhil's embrace in the corner of the deep sofa, where it was cosiest, and shadiest, and had remained unfaded. She felt that she was drained, but she was no longer in a mood to talk, or even cry. By now her tears were all shed, her story was told, and she simply squeezed up to her mother as though she were eleven years old again, and the pogrom just over.

Moscow now seemed distant and unreal: both the studio and the hospital, and even Zhenya – had they really ever existed? Well, what of them, if she couldn't get her voice back. Now her voice was gone for good. Recovery was pointless. Now she needed no one, and no one needed her, and that was fine. How happy she had been in that delirium when she had been singing, and Shalyapin went into raptures and immediately offered to take her straight off to 'Peter'! She had loved everyone then, and had even kissed Henrietta. But then it turned out that none of this had happened – she had simply imagined it. And a month later there was lame comfort from discovering that something did, in fact, remain of her voice, and it could be enough for the drama studio. But what did she want with the drama studio? That all-important 'tiny little extra' had gone, and without it she would never be a great singer, and that meant she could never be happy. She even suppressed her joy on recovering: it was an animal feeling. At least there was something elevated in her despair, but sustaining even that proved beyond her. Life was now stupid and empty. Well, so be it. She had her mother there to kiss her, and she was warm. It was all she had left.

Rakhil had been horrified when she set eyes on the girl. She was a skeleton, a real skeleton! And her skin was even a weird sort of grey colour. What on earth could they have been feeding her on there in Moscow? And she had the look of a stray kitten. Well, don't you worry, my little daughter, Mama won't ever let you out of her sight again. Now everything's going to be all right, you just have to eat a bit more. And good riddance to the lot of them – the studios and all that music! She had already had to bury one child, and now here was a second one half-dead! To calm her spirits she heaped detailed curses on Moscow's landladies, hospitals, heartless doctors, and even the total stranger Henrietta. And, just like all true Odessan mothers, the first thing she saw to was giving the child plenty of food to eat: several times a day – and no objections, please! In a word, her mother was just the same as ever, and had not changed in the slightest.

What did surprise Rimma, however, was her brother. He had grown up, and was taller, and had a booming voice that was almost like a bass. And his hands were no longer red, and his freckles had gone. He was a young man whose appearance was, in fact, not of the worst, and he was very self-assured. He spoke calmly and with restraint, without ever sounding gullible or getting overly worked up about anything. Was it, in fact, Yakov?

The only thing that reminded her of her little madcap brother of old was his laugh. With Rimma he was tender and protective: as if the poor girl understood nothing of life. Such momentous events were unfolding – and here she was, pining over a lot of nonsense. She was lucky that she had fallen ill, or else she would have been irredeemably stupefied, mixing with those theatrical buffoons. Pure art – come off it! Once she was fully fit again, he would have to set about gradually putting her on the right road.

The newspapers still came out with their strips of white: the censors had gone utterly berserk. But, even so, everyone knew everything. In Odessa, getting hold of a copy of *The Times* was not a problem. Turn the cover page, and there it was – 'Russia's Saviours', with a photograph of Felix and Irina Yusupov. Rasputin's killers. And an article about Grand Duke Dmitry Pavlovich – he, too, was a saviour. And even those who had doubted the existence of a pro-German block in high circles believed that, seeing as even grand dukes had no qualms about killing Grishka, it must be true. And that meant that Grishka really had appointed the German Shturmer as Chairman of the Council of Ministers. And he – rascal that he was – had even taken it into his head to change his name to 'Panin'. Who was he trying to kid? But Shturmer was still there, wasn't he? And wasn't that charming little Jew-cum-Christian, the Head of the Chancellery, still there, too? And, as for the Tsarina, there must be something to that story that she had a secret direct line to Wilhelm? Or was it a fairy-tale? Well, they'd said it was a fairy-tale about Rasputin, too, but remember what Milyukov had said in his speech? He'd actually named names . . .

'Well, our newsmongers have clearly been surpassing themselves,' Rimma warily summarised when Yakov spouted the latest news to the family over evening tea.

'That horse thief's been killed, so now his killers are "saviours" . . . The grand dukes could have gone for someone higher up.'

'You mean the Tsar?' Yakov grinned. 'Under no circumstances should the Tsar be killed so simply. We'll execute the Tsar after holding a people's revolutionary tribunal. We've had enough of these piffling assassination attempts – those are half-measures. We have to ensure that not a single trace of their nest remains.'

'Yakov, what are you saying? You're in your final year at the gymnasium – do you really want that long tongue of yours to land you with a criminal record?' asked Rakhil in alarm.

'Mama, I know what to say and where to say it,' Yakov replied calmly.

What confidence, however, this boy exuded . . . And that firm 'we'. And his eyes flashed in such a way that there must be something behind that 'we'. Something big. Something menacing.

Rimma waited until they were alone together, so as not to worry their mother.

'Come on then, little brother, tell me what it is. I see that I'm politically out of touch. Who's this "we"? The Bund?'

Yakov condescendingly patted her shoulder.

'You certainly are out of touch, my dear. Here, read this for a start. I don't keep the current literature at home, but virtually one student in ten keeps a copy of the *Manifesto*. They no longer even bother about it during the searches. It's so widespread that it's become legal. Enlighten yourself – now it's time I was off to "Marusya".'

'And which "Marusya" might that be?'

'You'll find out – all in good time,' said Yakov significantly, and went on his way. The boy was coming it on a bit thick, yet there was something about him, something serious. And Rimma immersed herself in her reading.

Ivan Alexandrovich was always level-headed in his attitudes to the servants. A servant was a member of the family – of that there could be no discussion. Just take Dasha: did they really need a nanny in the house now that their youngest, Maxim, was about to finish the gymnasium? But, having been nanny to all four of the children, and become as attached to them as if they were her own, how could she possibly be expected to tear herself away from the family now? And, of course, Dasha lived with them and there was always something for her to be getting on with: now she was in charge of the cook, the maid and the coachman. Had she become a major-domo? No, when all was said and done, she was still a nanny. For her, even the master was like an unreasonable child, and she had to keep an eye on him to make sure that he ate properly.

'Well, do at least have some fruit mousse, won't you, master? It's cranberry – nice and sour! My, how you've changed, take a look at yourself. You should keep an eye on the mistress, you should, you're the head of the entire household. What you do everyone else does. You're our eagle! Well, at least have a spoonful! Zinochka will come back, our little darling will come back to us, God is merciful. I used to die of worry over my Vasenka, I did – but he came back in the end, alive and well!'

They tried to find Zina through the Land Union, sending off letter after letter. They received two identically worded replies: in the autumn of 1915 she had fallen ill with louse-borne typhus and, because she was in no condition to be transported, had been left in the care of some locals in Slonim.

That meant left to the Germans! And what did 'in no condition to be transported' mean? And how could they now set about finding her in Slonim? Good Lord, was she even alive? More than a year had gone by – and there was still no news whatsoever.

Maria Vasilyevna reproached herself that then, back in 1915, she had been more worried about Pavel, and had prayed more fervently for him. And at that very time her daughter was lying stricken with typhus – and her heart hadn't even prompted her! Her heart had not been with Zina, and now this was the price she had to pay for it.

Everyone sought to comfort her, but even Marina, even Maxim could only alleviate the pain for a while. And Marina was taking the exam to become a nurse and was about to go off and follow in Zina's footsteps. I won't let her go! No, with this one, at least, I'm not letting her go anywhere!

'Mama, I'll swear on anything you like – I'm not going away anywhere! I'll be here, at Dulchin's hospital! I'll never, ever leave you. I couldn't live a single day without you: Maxy's still at the gymnasium, and already I'm missing him because I know I've got to wait till evening before he's home again. Now what should we give Papa for Christmas, Mama – what do you think?'

Marina was already in her twentieth year, yet, of all the children, she alone was short, like her mother. And she still had childish eyes, and an open heart: she was devoted to the family – for herself she wanted nothing. Her mother would occasionally cast anxious looks at her, but no: she had no hidden thoughts, she really did like being with her mama more than with anyone else. Was that healthy for a girl? But Maria Vasilyevna banished this doubt: she knew that without Marina's little voice, without her glad and ever-ready kindness – how would they ever have managed to get through this year? Ivan had deteriorated a lot: it wasn't that he seemed to be ill with anything, but now he was walking like an old man, with a rigid back. She had never loved him so painfully, so searingly as now. But with her mean heart was she, perhaps, tearing something away from the others with this love? From Maxim. From Pavlik. She kept a jealous watch over her prayers: were they sufficiently ardent and sincere, were they said with all her soul? But that only made things worse. Every now and then she caught her thoughts wandering, and would have to start from the beginning again.

Yakov did not have to spend long as his sister's condescending enlightener. The more Rimma got to know about the Russian Social Democratic Workers' Party, the more astounded she became: where had she been all this time? With aspirations such as hers, and – ever since childhood – such dreams, too, how could she have overlooked this? How was it that, in both Moscow and Kiev, she had failed to find the right sort of people? What had she left home with? Passion: to kill the Tsar, and sacrifice her life. Yet she had allowed herself to be side-tracked by snobbish vanity – indeed, in those circles she had actually been ashamed of her provincial *naïveté*. Politics – yuck, how vulgar, one had to read Maeterlinck, and it was a disgrace not to know Leconte de Lisle.

Meanwhile the entire country was being enveloped in the subtle, but tenacious structures of the future – and what force there was in those structures, what finality. These links and chains passed through every prison, university and factory like a steel needle. And they had penetrated the press, too. And the warring army. In the midst of Russia's mayhem suddenly such a flexible, strong network had arisen, with firm discipline and clear goals. And – far from being a back-water – Odessa was one of its most important centres – far more so than Kiev!

She recovered her old fire: no, life was not over – it was only now that it was beginning. Rakhil was glad to see her daughter like this. That's what comes of proper feeding! Her spirits had picked up, and this would soon pass into her body. This modern-day fashion for skinniness annoyed her. The Odessa of her youth had valued full-bodied women, women of substance – not ones who split in half the moment anyone so much as looked at them. To be skinny was, in Rakhil's opinion, a sign either of illness or bad character. And, either way, what use was it for family life? But Rimma had a good character: just look how she laughed with Yakov, enjoying those little jokes they shared together. And she was tender with her mother, and never huffy. Now do you understand, you silly girl, what your mama is here for? Well, and high time too.

It was with some pride that Yakov introduced Rimma to the leadership when he deemed that she was sufficiently prepared. 'Fyodor the Railman' was very taken with her, and she soon had work of her own to see to. The committee needed people with a good memory, and Rimma had always been top of the class in everything.

17

The broad-shouldered second lieutenant from the artillery who was pacing over Krestovsky island clearly felt himself to be a dapper sort of fellow. That sense – at last! – of being immaculately washed and shaved, and having an even pavement beneath his feet that made his step lighter and crisper, lent him an air of naive jollity. A further notable attribute to him was his gold St. George's Cross for other ranks. But to the seasoned eye of any inhabitant of 'Peter', the second lieutenant was, of course, a manifest provincial.

Neither his cap nor his boots quite matched up to those elusive signs of tasteful military dress, as this was understood in Petrograd. The rim of his cap should, for example, have been just that bit smaller and flatter, and the cap itself was not smoothed out quite as it ought to be, and his spurs should have had a somewhat softer ring, with a slightly lower pitch. It was clear from his dark, weather-beaten face that he was fresh from the front, though of itself, of course, there was nothing surprising in that for the city of 'Peter'. People here did not share the fighting men's contempt for those who served on the staff and the ones who stayed back in the rear. And, besides, they had grown rather fed up with these permanently disgruntled men back from the front. This was no longer 1914, when every fighting man had been fêted as a hero. Now sugar was rationed, bread was scarce, and kerosene was unobtainable – in fact, what wasn't there a shortage of, except newspapers? But once they'd dinned it into their heads that back here everyone was lounging around in clover, off they went, getting all hoity-toity about it. They were, of course, the defenders of the fatherland. But press them as to how much they'd defended – and then what? Immediately they would become indignant about the idiots on the staff, and how their supplies were bungled. Well, since you acknowledge your dependence on the rear and the staff – just remember your place!

This particular individual, however, had at that moment such a jovial air that he must be straight from the front. The whinging would doubtless come in time.

Pavel, however, was truly in no mood for anything like that. If his parents' letter was a day late in coming, he would go and spend his leave in Odessa: where else? But Anna! Anna was here, in 'Peter'! He periodically kept opening the letter and checking the address of the hospital. What if he'd got it wrong? What if she wasn't there any more? He would find her in the end, of course, but even one day's delay seemed an irremediable set-back. Today. He simply had to see her today! There it was, at last, the hospital! And how typical of 'Peter' it was, too, with its Empire style and painted in ochre. It looked rather as if it might have once been a gymnasium.

'Anna Teslenko? Yes, of course I know her. She was discharged yesterday,' Pavel was informed by the first person that he asked – a bony nurse with horsy teeth.

Pavel's heart sank.

'You don't know where . . .' was all that he uttered. What could she know, the heartless blonde herring!

'Yes, I do – I do know!' she laughed. 'But it's a long way from here, almost in the centre! She's staying with my aunt, which is also where I live when I'm not on duty. We persuaded her to stay with us for a week, as she's still a bit weak. Write down the address. No, let me write it myself, or you'll only get it wrong,' she added with a crafty glance at Pavel. 'Why do you want her? A relative, are you?'

Now that was sheer mischief: this wonderful and perceptive young lady knew perfectly well that he was no relative! And he had dared to think so disrespectfully of her. Pavel bowed cordially. 'I don't know how I can ever thank you . . .'

As he walked away, Klavdia shook her head and smiled to herself. Yes, it was not unheard of for a soldier who had been awarded the St. George's Cross to come straight home from the fighting in search of his sweetheart ... Well, she obviously was his sweetheart, for who else could he have been looking for with such a crazed look in his eyes? Yes, it was not unheard of – only not in her case. She bit her lower lip and went off to the bandage-room.

An elderly woman in a blue dress and of diminutive stature – she did not even come up to Pavel's shoulder – opened a dark door with an engraved plate: half-way.

'What can I do for you?'

Pavel gave a somewhat inept explanation of what he wanted. Nevertheless, she let him in and told him to wait. He meekly sat down where he was told: by a toyish round table with a crocheted cover. He'd spent half the day running around, and now it was three o'clock, almost twilight. Could this really be the moment? Yes, yes, that was her voice ...

He sprang to his feet.

'Pavel. Is it you?'

Nadezhda Semyonovna, that same aunt of that most merciful of nursing sisters back at the hospital, was now smiling with little wrinkles radiating out from her mouth as she got herself ready to go to the baker's for some white bread: she did so hope that Pavel would be able to stay for tea? Mercy was evidently a common trait in this family. How tempting it was to stay and watch their first minutes together again: it was like snatching somebody else's happiness and warming yourself up on it – particularly at a time such as this. And it would, perhaps, not so much sully their happiness, as be like brashly reaching out and touching it, like first snow. Well, what was wrong with that? They were young, and it wouldn't do them any harm. But the wise Nadezhda Semyonovna did not succumb to temptation, and she did not return until she had waited her turn in the queue at the baker's, and then gone and bought a piece of halva with sunflower seeds and plum marmalade.

They were alone in this rather dingy little apartment, with its smell of old books. Outside the window a pale blue light could be seen shining dimly, like skimmed milk. Pavel kept kissing Anna's hands, fearing to lift his eyes: what if her face suddenly showed something he was not expecting, not that he had any right to expect anything – but it had been so long, so long ...

Anna sighed and kissed him on the head. Silly boy! As if she hadn't known all along that it was bound to come to this. It was precisely this inevitability, so wholly independent of anything she might herself do, that she had once found so frightening – way back, all that time ago. But now it no longer frightened her, now they were very brave, and if she felt like crying, then it was because it was so unexpected. My poor dear, and fancy – a moustache!

By evening tea, for which Klavdia also joined them, along with an infantry captain, who was a relative of her aunt, it had become possible to look at Anna and Pavel without fear of being tactless. Everything was decided, and Pavel, who had by now calmed down, and was radiant, sat listening to the captain's views on the opening of the Duma, though clearly without either following him or understanding what he was talking about. The captain, however, was getting more and more worked up: here, at long last, was a fresh face back from the fighting, and, with it, a chance for him to pour out his views. 'Peter', in which he had the misfortune to be stuck with his company, annoyed the captain: was it really a soldier's business to do guard duty in the rear?

'And that's what we now call an "event". First there was all that waiting, with everyone wondering what would happen once it finally opened. Can you believe it, the Preobrazhensky regiment was sent to guard it, and machine-guns were put behind the gates . . . And nothing happened – nobody so much as twitched an ear. And let me tell you – there's now this sense of numbness. A lull. And my heart tells me no good'll come of it. Something is brewing, though quite what it is, no one can say.'

'And what good can we expect to come of anything nowadays?' remarked Nadezhda Semyonovna, pursing her dry lips. 'If everyone's got so used to the idea of being disgruntled with everything the whole time? Look how het up everyone got about Rasputin. But I've no idea if so much as one hundredth of it was true . . .'

'Come on, Auntie, you're such a . . . sceptic? If that's the word I'm after?'

'Now there you have it – people are already forgetting how

to speak Russian. Incredulous, Klavdyushka, I'm incredulous! Only why do you say so?'

'But, really – the whole city knew, the whole of Russia knew! And in more detail than could have been imagined in a terrible dream. After all, he was manipulating everyone exactly as he pleased. He was appointing ministers, and dismissing them, too. And how did he treat the ladies: if he appeared in a white overall, that meant they were to kiss his hand. And they did, too, even countesses. Do you remember Sofia Andreyevna telling us?'

'I don't know,' said Nadezhda Semyonovna, cutting her off, 'I wasn't with him when he dismissed any ministers, nor have I ever kissed his hands, or been manipulated by him. Yet I know that if people want to go mad, then, sure enough, they'll find a way of doing it, and who to do it with, too. But I meant something else: so, now they've killed him, and riddled him with bullets, and shoved him through a hole in the ice – and that's no good, either! People are asking why the Tsar isn't doing something about it, and hasn't had anyone punished. He's shielding the grand dukes – that's what they say he's up to now. But if he set up an investigation and brought the matter to court, that wouldn't be any good, either: people would start moaning on about how he was out to avenge Grishka. And that's how everybody is nowadays! Everyone's saying it's no good that the war's dragging on like this, and at the same time they're accusing the Tsarina of negotiating a separate peace with the Germans. Does that mean peace is a bad thing, too?'

'Well, Auntie, you're just like everybody else – you, too, are getting disgruntled with everything!' laughed Klavdia. When she laughed, she stopped being quite such an ugly bug – and she knew it, too. Pavel, for some reason, remembered Marina: how different they were, though they would probably still have befriended one another.

'Well, you're right at that,' said her auntie, breaking into a smile, 'an old miseryguts is what I've become, too ... Now there's the samovar whistling away, offering everyone another cup, while the woman of the house prattles on about politics. Ay-yi-yi ... Pavel, can I pour you a cup?'

That same night Klavdia had a serious talk with Pavel.

'Now don't you pay any notice to Anechka smiling all the

time – you know about her wound, don't you? It was a stroke of luck that she had such a remarkable surgeon – he saved her elbow. If it weren't for him, she wouldn't even be able to bend her arm. It nearly went clean through to the nerve centre! It'll take her several months to build up her arm again, and it'll be painful! So why drag her off to Odessa? You have no idea what's going on at the moment: if it isn't the factories coming out on strike, then it's the railways . . . This isn't like the old days, when it was a matter of two days and you're there. I tell you, she's pretty weak, she's just being plucky about it.'

'What . . . is it that serious?' asked Pavel in fright.

'Now there's no cause for alarm – it could have been worse. But you must let her recover! Everyone's so used to thinking she has energy enough for two. You, at least, surely understand that she doesn't always find it so easy? A long journey is the last thing she needs now. My aunt will let you a room – so take it and stay there. I don't suppose your leave is for long, is it? Well, don't squander the time. And, as for the church . . .' Klavdia erupted in laughter, 'my aunt will find someone who can hurry things up for you. She's a great expert, she knows every priest there is.'

It was a quiet wedding, attended by only a few nurses, Anna's friends, Klavdia's cousin, a cadet from the Nikolayevsky Military College, Nadezhda Semyonovna and the infantry captain.

'Isaiah, rejoice!' sang the deacon in his booming bass, and the stony-faced cadet held the crown over the tall Pavel. It was a heavy crown, and the cadet became tired holding it up for so long, and wanted to swap it over to his other hand, but, in true military fashion, he soldiered on. The captain held the other crown over Anna's head, and Nadezhda Semyonovna kept wiping her eyes: poor children. They were marrying without parents, like orphans. She had brought a shawl for them to step on, and even gone to the trouble of seeing that the bride had a dress and veil. Why, they were so excited that it would never have even entered their heads. Thank God, the girl seemed to look all right. But she didn't cry before the wedding, and that was a bad sign. Because you ought to cry when you're about to get married, and then it's a sign that all will be well. But what did youngsters nowadays know ... Oh Lord, grant happiness to this couple, at least, for how much sorrow there is in our world! And now they were getting in a muddle over the rings ... just like almost everyone else, including herself, when she so nearly dropped the ring at her own wedding. The same ring that she had on today, although now it was a widow's ring. And her finger was wrinkled ...

Nadezhda Semyonovna did not know who to feel more sorry for: herself, or these youngsters, neither of whom were her children. God had not granted her any children of her own, although at her own wedding there had, in time-honoured manner, been prayers for an abundance of children. Well, may the Lord grant children to these two! The girl was clever, all right – but wasn't he a bit dim? Or was that because he was so happy? What a sight he was, beaming like a child by a Christmas tree. And how nice it would be to see Klavdyushka getting married one day ...

Pavel and Anna found it impossible to stay put at home: after all, it was not quite the same as being alone together, with Nadezhda Semyonovna in such a flap, fretting over the wedding dinner, and the cadet staring in awe at Pavel's St. George's Cross for other ranks, plainly longing to hear tales of derring-do, and the other guests there, too. In church there had seemed to be so few of them, but now they filled the house. And, after hurriedly changing out of her wedding dress, Anna was delighted to let Pavel snatch her away: off on their first ever trip as man and wife. Naturally, they swore that they would be back in time for dinner.

It was not, to put it mildly, ideal weather for tripping round the city. The swanky cabman kept geeing on his horse by whipping it across its damp croup, the falling snow was damp, and the sky dank and more like February. It was almost dark enough for the street-lights to be lit, though somewhere a clock could be heard striking no more than midday.

'Pavlik, look how black those clouds are!'

'Aha, vipers. Gorgons!'

'Gorgons – exactly. Do you remember 'The Song of the Host of Igor' ... All we need now is an eclipse. What a day we've picked to get married! Oh, what will our future be-e?'

'Ah, so you're afraid, are you? The only thing a wife has to fear is her husband!'

'Oh, I'm so afraid!'

And, tittering, she squeezed up to him, and the cabman smirked into his moustache: he could charge what he liked, and these two would still pay.

'Now tell me, sir! Where would you like to go next? We can't go straight on, as that's the Fontanka canal. If you like, I can take you to a certain restaurant that I know, with private rooms?'

From this 'certain restaurant' that he knew he earned a tidy bit extra that varied according to the quantity and quality of guests that he brought there. But, once again, the youngsters burst into laughter at the very thought of food: Nadezhda Semyonovna had already stuffed them full as it was, and dinner was still to come.

'I want a hat,' Anna whimsically said, playing the fool, '"with mourning feathers!"'

'So it's straight into mourning! I'd like to kill these modern poets!'

They drove to Gostiny Dvor for a hat, and Pavel meekly waited while Anna tried on some two dozen different hats. He was astonished at this zealous female rite: how choosy she was, and how utterly serious, without so much as grinning in the mirror!

'Come on, how about this one here – with the little buckle!'

'You don't understand. That one's for an old school mistress, a French teacher, some ghastly governess!'

'And for canny Polish girls, with nothing but hats on their mind, and who drive men barmy, I don't suppose they've got anything?'

'I want this one, this lilac one! I know I've got nothing to go with it, but, even so, it suits me.'

'Astonishingly well, most reverent *pani*!'

'Now that's more like it!'

Then they drove somewhere else, now with a hat-box to accompany them, and the gloomier the dank city became, the merrier they got. Oh, for a storm, and some lightning, too! And just then there was a rumble of thunder somewhere.

'We can't go down Nevsky Prospect, sir. They're rioting again,' said the cabman, turning round.

This was something peculiar to the rear, something new. It was what the captain had been talking about – as, indeed, had everyone else, too: these were troubled times, and no one knew what to expect. Now it was impossible to get on to Nevsky Prospect, and shooting could be heard. And Anna fell quiet and was looking like a little girl with wide eyes. She was his wife. At least at the front you knew who you were defending, and who you were defending them from, too. But this was like 1905 . . . And what a time they'd picked to go shooting at our own fellow-countrymen!

That evening they were greeted with the traditional cries of 'bitter!', and everyone looked on as the young couple kissed one another. They liked this custom, and the way that it openly poked fun at newly-weds. They did not find it grating, and it was nice getting used to the idea of being man and wife together. And it was just as well that they were not called upon to eat any of the food that had been put out – not that they would have been able to, anyway.

'My joy, my joy!' whispered Pavel, and Anna, still shaking with the pain of what had just happened, squeezed up to him. How firmly he held her, constantly mindful that he was her protector – yet, even so, now he had hurt her. So, it had not turned out to be so dreadful after all, there was even almost no shame to it – it was simply that she was now someone different, someone new. She was a woman. So that's what we women are like!

Now she was surprised when she saw herself in the mirror, for she had thought that her appearance was bound to change, too, and that she would go on and on changing – with each passing night, in some unknown, but miraculous way. It was a sweet horror, and it made her tremble and feel as if she were flying!

'Anechka, my dear, how pretty you've got!' laughed Nadezhda Semyonovna with all of her wrinkles, and Anna found this pleasant. But did they really have to part from one another so soon? How could that possibly be? They still had three more weeks together, and with each passing hour the time melted away. And they both felt each hour acutely, as if they were able to prolong it.

Now Pavel saw how differently the war had changed them. He had, of course, known that nurses had not been having an easy time of it, and had heard certain stories from Klavdia. So he asked Anna questions at every opportunity, urging her not to keep it all bottled up inside of her. What she must have been through, poor dear! But all this pain, and dirt, and blood had done something to her that he simply could not understand. It wasn't that they had failed to demean her, but that they had, in fact, somehow elevated her. Her entire being was radiant! Not from joy – no, it wasn't that. It was something else. Yet even when she cried, she was radiant.

'It's so pitiable, Pavlik, so pitiable! There are men lying dead beside you, and you're carrying a man who's been gassed – he's still breathing, and then all of a sudden he stops, and there's not a thing you can do about it. And then I saw these hedgehogs lying on the ground: they'd obviously been going somewhere with their young, and that's how they died – all in a line together, gassed to death. And I couldn't help crying – I'd got used to seeing people being killed, I realised, but not hedgehogs.'

And, for some reason, he was not frightened for her, although it was almost blasphemy – not to be frightened for her! After all, she had already been wounded once, and who were the ones that got killed in wartime? The very best people – of that he was quite certain. Just take his own regiment – what was now left of it? The best men had been killed off, and those who'd replaced them were 'the louche', as they would have been called in Odessa. The newcomers regarded the officers as wolves: they had spent too much time listening to the Socialists. And, as for such dependable men as were left, they were precisely the ones who had to carry out the stupid orders. Not that they were necessarily all stupid – but everyone was by now inured to the idea that no good could ever come of their commanders. How many times had they destroyed the army! All the more surprising did that then make it that they hadn't yet collapsed altogether, and were now even stronger than they had been in 1915. But how much longer could that go on for? It beggared belief, but the Tsar was the best commander-in-chief they had yet been able to come up with.

'Anusya. You know, you make me feel ashamed of myself.'

'What do you mean?'

'It's true. You do more than can be reasonably expected of a woman. But I've no idea what I'm supposed to be doing.'

'Pavlik, are you ill, or something? You're an officer, you're fighting – what do you mean, you've no idea what you're supposed to be doing?'

'That's not the point. Of course I'm fighting. That's my duty. But I went to war to try and defend Russia, and now I see everything collapsing. It's bad enough at the front – but here it's even worse. Here there are crooks and loud-mouths – and they're passing themselves off as the government. I came here thinking there might at least be some glimmer of hope, that things might be sorted out. But there's nothing. No hope whatsoever. Just political parties everywhere – and no one doing anything decent and worthwhile.'

'But what about the Tsar – have you lost hope in him, too?'

'The Tsar's the most consistent one of the lot – he's hoping for a miracle,' said Pavel, repeating a phrase that he had picked up somewhere. 'But I can't be like that. I have to see how Russia can be saved, and be involved in achieving it. I took an oath, not only to the Tsar, but also to Russia. And – I don't see how I can protect her.'

'But you're doing your duty.'

'There's a difference between "doing my duty" and ensuring that duty actually gets done. Every decent person "does his duty", but what if it later transpires that Russia's been left unprotected? What, then, is the point of it all?'

'Don't play Hamlet with me!' said Anna, losing her temper. She got up abruptly and strode over to the window.

'I've heard more than enough of this already! You all think Russia is like a fish-bowl with goldfish in it, and that at any moment it'll be smashed to bits, and no one will be able to put it back together again. But let me tell you something – Russia's big. And stronger than you realise. And she won't disappear – she'll survive! I realise things may get bad, and we may even lose the war and end up fighting amongst ourselves.'

'That would be suicide.'

'And nothing would come of that suicide! The shame would last for ever – yes. But, as far as all this talk of perishing's concerned, we won't perish. And I don't want to talk of Russia in the third person! It's the same habit that the papers have got into, whining on about Russia and her people, as if they were onlookers. So who are we then? You and I – we're Russia, and we're her people, and there's not much to marvel at, either, for there's nothing to idealise in that. Even if we're killed, there will still be others – and they're Russia, too. And they'll have children. And don't go inventing great missions for yourself – I've seen more than enough lunatics as it is.'

'Oh, and now the bluster! Just like a wild cat, and there was I thinking I'd got, not a wife, but a sweet little daisy.'

'That's because you don't know me yet. And whenever I hear these whinging generalisations, I feel like taking up smoking, like one of those Socialist women.'

'Just you try it!'

'Ah, now there's a commanding voice! That's more like it!'

Pavel burst out laughing and pulled her down on to his knees. Some things she would never understand, but, there again – wasn't that equally true of him? And now he had just caught himself at it again – burdening others with his problems. He was on edge, he was alarmed – so why shouldn't she be, too? Well, it just wasn't good enough!

He kissed her on the back of the head, burrowing his nose into her honey-coloured hair. She really was a sweet little daisy. And such a brave rabbit.

'Well, Pavlik, it's true you shouldn't go wool-gathering, isn't it? You're not a horse, and you're no poet, either – with all these funny ideas in your head. Come the time, and we'll know what to do.'

'Yes, yes, my clever girl.'

Despite the warnings of Nadezhda Semyonovna, they spent much of their time walking around the city. She was in a state of panic that disorder was about to break out, and took her place in each bread queue as though the hour of crucifixion might soon be upon her.

'You know what happened on Vyborgskaya Street? That

started because of bread, too, and then a policeman was killed, and the trams were smashed up, and the factory on Shpalernaya Street came to a standstill.'

'Nadezhda Semyonovna, what is to be done: there's always something going on here in 'Peter'. But we'll get hold of some bread, don't you worry.'

But the trams were no longer even running, although there was not quite so much shooting as there had been. Demonstrators went marching down Nevsky Prospect with red bows, and no one dispersed them. The soldiers winked at the demonstrators, as if to let them know that they wouldn't shoot at them.

Only rarely did the sun ever peep through, but even that was good for this strange city. And the light here was slightly lifeless, like in a museum, as though it came from below, or from the side. But, there again, every now and then it did pick out some highly animated little boys frolicking about on the statue of Alexander III, or a bearded man in an orator's pince-nez on a tribune made of an upturned kiosk, or women clasping the legs of some Cossack horses.

It all seemed unreal, and there wasn't even a sense of danger – evidently, nobody felt there was any. Why, for example, were so many children out on the streets? True, the schools were now closed. As, indeed, was every other educational institution. Where was a gymnasium pupil to go? Well, clearly to a rally. Here everyone had something to say, and they yelled, and whistled, and the mood was cheerful. Their parents were the ones who had let them out, after all, and that's where they went, too: now everything was happening out on the streets. And it was out on the streets that you could hear the news: the Pavlovsky regiment's mutinied. And the Moscow regiment has refused to quell them. There has been a decree dissolving the Duma – but the Duma's ignoring it, and is still in session. No, it isn't in session – it's just that they're not being allowed out. Revolutionary troops have told the members of the Duma straight to their faces, 'Take power'. The Volynsky and Litovsky regiments are with us!

There was no longer any confrontation – at last, the army and the people were together. The prisons had been thrown open after an extraordinary session of the Duma. The secret police had been routed, and the District Court was on fire. It had started! It had started!

Pavel had always thought that, if there were to be a revolution, it would throw up a leader: a man who would name the day and issue the orders. But it was obvious that this had started of its own accord. The hastily created Committee for Establishing Order stood for the Duma, whereas the Soviet of Workers' Deputies stood for the Socialists. But who had power? No one, by the look of it. The Tsar was away at the front, and was saying nothing. So who should Pavel side with? Should he get back to the front? But it was obvious that the main drama was being played out here. He decided to try to track down the captain who had been stationed somewhere outside the Duma with his company, but there was no time.

On the very next day the Tsar abdicated. An end to the monarchy! Russia was free!

Pavel and Anna made their way through the spring snow-storm, heading, like everyone else, for the Duma. The first of March was a remarkable day, both sunny and snowy. And the city looked different – it was white, with gold. There was a cheerful crowd that had decked itself out with red flags and bows. Some college girl even pinned a bow on Pavel, and someone nearby shouted, 'The second lieutenant is with us!'

Before Pavel knew what was happening, he found himself being chaired by the crowd. The entire city seemed to be like a lot of schoolchildren running away from their classes, and Pavel felt like this, too. A couple of students noisily tore down some three-coloured flags and ripped out the strips of red. Pavel, however, found that this stuck in his gullet.

'Now hold on there, gentlemen! People are fighting under that flag!'

'You're out of touch, Second Lieutenant, we've got a new flag now. The troops are taking the oath to the new government!'

And, indeed, columns of troops were filing past the Duma under red flags. Bands were playing, and waves of 'Hurrah!' kept rolling across the broad square. Oh, Pavel knew where his place was now! Not here in the crowd, of course, but with these revolutionary troops. Yes, he still had his regiment – and he would be going back to it in a couple of days' time. Now everything would be done in the new way. And who would ever have imagined that this disaffection and universal grievance and pandemonium would, like a miracle, suddenly give birth to this intoxicating sense of universal unity? So that's what revolution was: it was a miracle. If at that moment he had been told that people could fly, he would simply have nodded, but he would not have been surprised. And what of the Germans? Even under the Tsar the Germans had started being pushed back, so surely they could cope now? Now everyone was together, with none of the old enmity: soldiers and officers would be as one. Here it was, the realisation of the oath taken in his boyhood: 'always to be for the people'.

And how happily it had all coincided – youth, revolution and love. He looked into Anna's face: was she feeling the same thing? And she was imbued with such radiance, such rapture – how could he possibly doubt it!

'Pavel, it can't be chance, can it, that we're together on a day like this?'

'Of course not, my joy, of course not!'

'But let's go home now.'

'What's the matter, dear? Are you tired?'

'No. Let's go. I'll tell you later. It's very noisy here.'

Pavel suppressed a twinge of annoyance: she was not the sort of girl to start getting capricious for no reason. In a crush such as this perhaps someone had knocked her elbow, and he hadn't noticed. As they walked home, she looked very intense, and he became worried.

'You go ahead to our room, I won't be a moment . . .' She was already in the dark corridor when she said this and, hurrying off, she threw her coat into his arms.

A few minutes later, freshly washed, she came and sat down – not, as usual, on his knees, but in the armchair opposite the small sofa, and she gave him a stern look with darkened eyes.

'What's the matter, dear? Well, don't drag it out!'

'Pavlik. I'm now almost certain. I even know that it'll be a boy. Just you wait and see.'

18

Anna had worked out exactly when she would go into labour and now there were only days to go. She was still living with Nadezhda Semyonovna, and could not get over the fact that it was just eight months since Pavel had left. No, surely it was a little more than that by now . . . But to her it seemed like an eternity. If there is such a thing as eternity on this earth.

They had agreed that she was to go straight to Odessa. She was to do no more work: she was carrying their child. He was to see to the manly matters and she was now to be the mother. She was not even to work at the hospital at Odessa. Anna gladly promised not to, for by now she was sickened by the very thought of hospital smells. But leaving Petrograd proved to be not so straightforward. The railway was in the hands of the revolutionary workers. And no one could leave. It was impossible. Only some special trains were running, with the permission of some sort of committee. Nadezhda Semyonovna said that even two Duma representatives, Rodzyanko and Guchkov, had been prevented from getting a train from the Nikolaevsky station.

'It's preposterous, who ever heard of such a thing! They weren't going off on some silly nonsense or other, either – they were going to get the Tsar's abdication. But the workers wouldn't give them a carriage – and that was that. What's really so surprising is that they managed to get him to abdicate at all. You just wait a bit, till everything's calmed down. At the moment everyone seems to have gone stark raving mad – it's frightening just to go out on the street.'

This was true. That happy spirit of fraternity from the first day had proved to be as short-lived as a drunken thrill. Only a few days later Anna saw some sailors set upon a Guards lieutenant.

'Surrender your weapon!'

'Your commanding days are over, mister officer sir – now take off your sword!'

'Hang on, brothers, let's first make him salute! Atten-shun, when the working class is talking to you, you gentrified bastard!'

Before Anna had time to realise what was happening, the lieutenant had got out his Nagan and was overpowered. He managed to fire two shots. Anna was unable to take her eyes away, and she saw them tear the lieutenant's coat off and place a dead sailor on top of it, and kick the lieutenant in the head, which was now shot through – and she saw it limply lolling from right to left, like . . .

She ran home and could not stop shaking for a long time. He had not looked like Pavel, the lieutenant. But Pavel would have done exactly the same thing – of that she was quite certain. He'd managed to leave the city, thank God, he'd got away! But what if it was the same at the front? These sailors hadn't looked like sailors, swathed in machine-gun belts, and – Anna could have sworn – they had been powdered, too! For some reason, this had horrified her more than anything. Or perhaps that wasn't it. She could not be sure, but one thing was certain: she could not bear to see anything like it. At the front it had been different, and there she had not shunned the sight of blood. But now it was as though someone invisible, yet domineering, were forbidding her from hearing anyone scream. Or seeing anyone dead. Or anyone being killed and beaten up. She mustn't dare to let herself so much as think of such matters. Perhaps it was him, the little one? But the little one could not be so forceful! How she had changed: now she submitted to this incomprehensible force, and made sure to avoid such matters. She dared not do otherwise. For days on end she would not leave the apartment, though where could she have gone, anyway, as she kept having to go to the lavatory so often?

Nadezhda Semyonovna took everything on herself. She refused to take the money that Anna had received on leaving her job.

'You'll find that will come in handy one day. And, besides, it's no use to an old woman like me.'

She managed to get some milk from somewhere, and brought home some bread, and she was no longer horrified at having to stand and queue for things. Short and rather frail-looking, she appeared to be growing younger, and – virtually impossible as it was – now she held herself even more uprightly than before. At the Smolny Institute, which she had completed 'with distinction', the girls had been taught enough carriage to last them their entire lives, in fact, enough to see them through to the Day of Judgement.

'You're just like a guardian angel, Nadezhda Semyonovna,' remarked Anna in embarrassment. 'How ever have you put up with me all this time?'

'Anechka, darling, it's only with you that my heart ever relaxes, and you talk about me having to "put up" with you. You are the only normal woman in the midst of all this bedlam. You got married, and now you're expecting a child ... Not like these other girls nowadays, dashing off to the front and to rallies, like a lot of scalded cats. And don't you worry about a thing: everything will soon settle down, and then you'll be off and on your way, and I'll find out when we can get hold of some tickets for you. How lovely your hair's looking. You know how we used to brush our hair at Smolny? A hundred times in one direction, and then a hundred times in the other. Here, let me show you.'

She started brushing Anna's hair, and this was so strongly reminiscent of something that Anna burst out laughing.

'Nadezhda Semyonovna! You know who you look like? Do you remember the old sorceress in Andersen who brushed Gerda's hair and fed her on cherries to stop her from going and looking for her little brother Kai?'

'Well, cherries they may not be, but I've got some raisins for you. And, if you ever take it into your head to go flying off to the front in search of your "little brother", then I'd fetch you some cherries, and I'd also keep you under lock and key!'

All Anna knew that summer was that the revolution was something savage, a total absurdity. Everything was being destroyed, and nothing was being built. There had been a provisional government. And a soviet of workers' deputies. And they had both claimed to be the government. And how had they set about demonstrating this? By driving round the city in motor cars – the fashion now was to drive about standing up – and seizing buildings from one another. But the city, meantime, was left paralysed, although there were now two sorts of bread: 'sawdust', which was the crumbly one with the hard awns in it, and 'clay', which was the dark, damp one that was tinged with green and as heavy as the earth on a tomb. A thin slice weighed a pound. And, above all, there was the malice that seemed to have burst forth from within the earth, and there was no longer any limit to what these people who were rampaging about the city like devils might get up to.

It was a difficult pregnancy. This was strange, as she was so healthy. But her legs had already started to swell up, and the trains were all still cock-eyed, and the rumours were becoming increasingly ludicrous: Ukraine was independent and, for some reason, that meant it had gone over to the Germans. Alexander Blok was on some commission of enquiry. Now only committees and public buildings were heated. Trains were being robbed. Anarchy was 'the mother of order'. And so it went on, until October. She was stuck – that was already obvious. Nadezhda Semyonovna had a certain doctor that she knew. Giving birth in the hospital was out of the question – epidemic was rife, and even dysentery had appeared from somewhere.

It was so painful, so painful, that Anna was too dumbfounded even to moan. She knew that she was dying, that her back was about to break, that already her life was over. But then it would start all over again, and it would go on and on: lasting longer than her entire past life put together, longer than the tortures of hell. And then she was overcome by a rage that made her crumple up into an animal ball, and there was no longer any pain: now there were only the cries of somebody gasping for breath.

Something whistled past his shoulder: he had to dodge back from the narrow arrow-slit and take shelter behind the bumpy stonework. Then back to the slit.

It was coming racing towards him mounted on a dark, shaggy object, emitting screams from its flat face. He had to crane back his head and try to get at it from the side with his long spear. And down it came, still screaming – now drenched in blood.

Beneath him it was black and wet: he mustn't fall in – he had to keep a good grip of something firm.

There was light, something was twittering, and a voice was calling him. Over here. Come on – run. Fly.

It hurt. He was cold: it was a burning feeling. A face – it was a face. And it was watching him. He had to hold its gaze. Otherwise he would be borne off – there, away into the blackness.

This is Mama. He is Oleg. He's already been Oleg before some time, when his mama was someone else. But she had looked at him in exactly the same way then as she did now. And somewhere was on fire – and he had to leave his mama and get there. And she let go of his stirruped foot, and off he rode.

A child – her child, a boy! – was watching Anna with a wise and adult look, as if he knew more than she did. He was not crying, just watching – and in a way that made Anna start to feel uncomfortable. As though he were not sure if she was who she ought to be. Then he appeared to recognise her: he nuzzled up to her breast, lazily smacked his lips, and fell fast asleep. As if after a long journey.

By the next day he was already ordinary – no, of course he was extraordinary! – a baby with a dark shock of hair on his head, and blue, inane eyes. He was her first-born. Oleg Pavlovich Petrov. A strong boy, who suckled hard and lustily.

Nadezhda Semyonovna went flying about as if on wings: if she wasn't feeding Anna, she was cooing at Oleg, and kissing his pink little soles, or else dashing about tearing up old bedclothes for nappies with a loud rip. It was only a week after this that Anna learnt there had been a *coup*, and that the Bolsheviks – those same sailors who had been swathed in machine-gun belts – had taken power. The ministers of the provisional government had been arrested. Some of them were later brutally killed, or had they been put to death immediately? There were all sorts of rumours. The cadets had been slaughtered. Now they were shooting anyone they could lay their hands on. Nadezhda Semyonovna, who was enduring agonies now that Klavdia was back at the front, was forever crossing herself: to her it seemed that no place left on earth could be so dangerous as Petrograd had now become.

The firewood was all finished: the Dutch tile stove had devoured it with improbable speed. Anna kept Oleg swaddled, and both him and herself covered beneath her fluffy shawl. The tireless Nadezhda Semyonovna brought home a strapping great fellow in galoshes and a foul-smelling sheepskin coat. He installed a 'burzhuika' stove – a pot-bellied freak of a thing, with a cranked chimney shaft. Its pitch-black sides did not fit in with the apartment's dainty lace furniture covers and curtains, but, even so, it could still be stoked with newspapers, and one copy of the magazine *Niva* was enough to boil a kettle. Once the old copies of *Niva* came to an end, Nadezhda Semyonovna started on her books. First she burnt the technical ones which her husband had left her. Then it was the books from the glass-covered bookcases with gold leaf on the binding.

'Nadezhda Semyonovna! How can you burn Flaubert?'

'Ah, my sweetheart, the Golovanovs are already down to Tolstoy, and they've only got two to keep warm. But what choice have we? Olezhenka hasn't been washed for three days now. Do you know how to chop firewood, Anechka? The neighbours have a little axe, and the yard-cleaner's disappeared somewhere. Look, I've freed up an entire bookcase – that should keep us going for a month, so long as we chop it up properly.'

Month as may be, the bookcase lasted for a week. Then it was the turn of the bedside tables, with their little spindly legs.

'Klavdyushka always found it so funny, the way I keep it like a furniture shop in here,' rejoiced Nadezhda Semyonovna, 'but it's certainly coming in handy now – and the rooms are more spacious now, don't you think?'

Without mentioning anything to Anna, she was gradually selling off her family valuables: her gold chain with a medallion, her amethyst brooch, and the silver coffee-pot. It proved possible to exchange quite a number of things for food – some snub-nosed soldier even bought a threadbare fur coat in return for four loaves of bread. The girl had to eat, God forbid that her milk would dry up! The only thing that she hung on to was a sealskin overcoat. She would not go on acting as grandmother for ever, and, sooner or later, Anechka would have to leave. The very thought of it filled her with horror: she would leave, and take her baby with her – such an extraordinary, wonderful little boy, who already had a canny little smile. How could she ever get by without them, given these two were all that she lived for?

What of her parents? And where had those parents been when she was having her baby, and the boy was coming out bottom first? Once Anna's wedding candles had been burnt, Nadezhda Semyonovna burnt the two she had kept from her own wedding, but still Anna's labour dragged on. For such was the custom at birth: the wedding candles were burnt in front of an icon. This was her own girl, and it was her baby, and were it not for her they might well not be alive now. In the midst of this cold and starving city, it seemed to her that the only circle of warm light was here, around these two: she kept on feeding him, and he – round and pink little thing that he was – kept on suckling, as though the revolution had never been. But eventually they would leave – and there would be nothing but the cold and dark, and what then would be the point of living?

But she suppressed these thoughts with cruel satisfaction, and did not sell her fur coat, and prepared a bundle of things for Oleg to take with him on the journey. In Ukraine there was said to be plenty of food – why, down there they almost had cakes with cream. The boy, her boy, should not perish there. She went and visited every imaginable committee there was: surely some people must be allowed to leave the city?

Once she returned from her wanderings in a state of excitement.

'Anechka, my child, it looks as if everything will be all right! A troupe of actors is going to Kiev via Moscow. On tour. They've already received permission to go, and there's a chance of you being including with them. I've had a word with the impresario – he's ever such a nice and sensitive man, and he understands the whole situation. Only you'll have to go and see the commissar of . . . Oh, it was such a complicated name that now I've gone and forgotten it . . . Anyway, you'll have to get his personal permission, and he'll issue you with your papers. And from there you can make your own way on to Odessa.'

'Nadezhda Semyonovna, I'm not an actress!'

'Ah, who's bothered about that nowadays! The Stadnitskys said that a proof-reader at the *New Word* newspaper managed to get away with a travelling circus dressed up as a dancing bear. Now don't laugh, he sewed himself up inside a bearskin, and the soldiers even forced him to do a dance for them at the station – but the point is he got away! And in the nick of time, too, for next day they came to arrest him. I'll get some light bags ready for you – that suitcase is too heavy, and besides at the moment it's still in use . . .'

She glanced fondly over at the corner, where the suitcase was suspended from some bits of string. Inside it Oleg lay peacefully asleep, thoroughly content with his cradle. The frill of a lace Orenburg shawl was hanging down from the suitcase, and she straightened it out.

There was a pounding at the door.

'Open up in the name of the revolution! Search!'

Nadezhda Semyonovna crossed herself and went to open the door. Four men entered. The first, who was dressed all in leather and had two revolvers, appeared to be the leader. The second had on a rail-worker's cap and a beaver-skin coat with bullet holes through the waist. There was also a sailor with dreamily dilated pupils and, for some reason, a boy of about eleven, who had cheerful mousy eyes and was wearing a short fur-lined jacket and the boots of an adult.

'We're confiscating weapons and bourgeois valuables in the name of the Committee of Urban Poverty. I suggest you hand them over voluntarily.'

'Good Lord, but we haven't got anything!'

'We'll soon see about that. Mishutka, start in the kitchen – their favourite spot for hiding diamonds now is in teapots.'

The boy started rummaging round the apartment, as the first man – the one in leather – set about interrogating Anna.

'So you live here – on what grounds?'

'She's my daughter, she's an actress, and she's called in to say goodbye as she's about to go off on tour,' Nadezhda Semyonovna hastily put in.

'Hm, that's not what the yard-cleaner says. Now then, Momsy, you shut up for a moment – we'll get round to you in a minute.'

The boy had already eaten all the jam and bread that there was in the kitchen, and was now digging about in the cupboards. The man in the beaver-skin was tying the silver frames from the icons up in a bundle. Once they had been stripped of their silver, the icons were dropped on to the floor. He then stamped on them with his boots. The sailor grinned as he approached the suitcase.

'Got any weapons hidden under the baby?'

Anna raced over to her son, but the sailor had already clawed him up, like a kitten, in his enormous paw, with its tattooed heart and anchor. The boy rummaged about in the suitcase, but the sailor did not give the child back to Anna. He held Oleg up to the light, and Anna was horrified to see his little head loll about: he had only just managed to start holding it up.

'So who are you to the proletarian revolution? Bourgeois brat, or officer's pup? Answer, you little whelp!'

Anna suppressed an animal howl and an urge to bite into the sailor's throat. He was plainly high on cocaine. One false move, and there was no knowing what he might do with the child. Oh, Mother of God! Help!

Oleg turned his little head and gave the sailor a blissful toothless smile. The sailor suddenly burst out laughing.

'Why, the little rascal's grinning! Hey, the kid's one of ours. Oy, what a lovely little mug! I reckon one of our brothers came and shot his bolt with this 'ere actress – I've got a feel for these things, me. What d'you think, comrade commissar? Here, little lady, you take back your treasure. So what's he called? Oleg? Well, blow me, I'm Oleg, too – so him and me, we've got the same name. Now you listen to my revolutionary order: don't you do no harm to Olezhek here. Or I'll be ruthless on you! Comrade Commissar, what about leaving him some grub – keep him fed, I mean, a bit of grub for this little son of the revolution.'

'Calm down, Comrade Korotin,' said the man in the leather trousers disdainfully. 'We've got a lot of work to do, and you're busy amusing yourself. Mishutka! Quit fooling around!'

This last was addressed to the little lad, who had found a

brush from the corridor and had been using it to bash at a crystal chandelier that had not been used for ages. He was busily stuffing the crystal drops that he had knocked down into his pockets.

At last they left, laden with objects. By way of farewell the sailor gave Anna a smacking kiss and fired a shot from his Nagan into the ceiling. Nadezhda Semyonovna was quietly sobbing as she gathered up the discarded icons from the floor. And Anna hugged her child close to her: never again, under any circumstances, would she let him out of her arms! Neither by day, nor by night. Until they had got all this well and truly behind them.

But the very next day, after feeding the child, she had to leave him with Nadezhda Semyonovna in order to go to the commissariat for her pass. She realised that she would have to keep the child's existence secret: what troupe ever went on tour with a new-born baby? Quite how she would do it – boarding the train, which was where the passes were checked – she could not imagine. But she knew that she would manage somehow: they simply had to get out of here. Oleg was a clever little boy, and he always kept quiet when he was in her arms. He was still tiny, and she would smuggle him past under her shawl. The clinging snow champed under her shoes, which were now so wet that her feet no longer even felt the cold.

She had to wait for several hours in an unheated waiting-room, with her breasts already lactating, and from the whispers exchanged between the nervous petitioners Anna managed to ascertain that, although 'he' was 'bristlin' wi' machine-gun bullets', he was, nevertheless, not a fierce man. But there was also a 'she' – possibly his wife, possibly not his wife – and she was the brains around here, and whatever idea might find its way into her head, he did it. Evidently she loved rubies for their revolutionary colour, though she was somewhat less fond of other gems. She was a secretary there, and she wore a dress made out of a curtain.

When it finally came to Anna's turn to enter the sacred portal, she did, indeed, find herself in front of a plump woman in a lilac velvet dress. Behind her desk there was yet another door, behind which, presumably, 'he' himself sat. The woman took a sleepy look at Anna.

'Papers?'

And suddenly she seemed to wake up. Now she was no longer looking at Anna, but somewhere past her head – no, at her head! What was there? Was her hair dishevelled? No, that wasn't it, Anna realised – she was staring at her hat. It was a long time since anyone had really cared what they wore, but Anna's hat was the only one that she had – it was the same lilac one that she had bought together with Pavel. What a stroke of luck: the hat was exactly the same colour as the woman's curtain material. Anna had never had occasion to bribe anyone, and she did not know how it was done. Was she meant to say something? Or not?

She silently took off her hat and put it down on the edge of the desk. The woman in the curtain material glanced at it with approval.

'Parisian?'

'Parisian,' lied Anna with a light heart.

Two days later Nadezhda Semyonovna accompanied Anna all the way to the station platform. It was impossible to go any further, as there were soldiers there with bayonets fastened. And beyond that they were already checking people's papers.

'Now mind you take care, my child, and mind you take care of him, too,' muttered the old woman, quickly making the sign of the cross over Anna, and her shawl and her bags. She had already smothered Oleg in kisses back at home and on the way to the station. And she would have liked to do so now, but it was too dangerous to open the shawl here. So she kissed Anna.

'Look after yourself, do be sure to look after yourself . . . my golden child!'

Suddenly Anna clearly grasped that they were about to leave – and she was about to die. Alone, in a cold room. Her apartment was gone: on the day after the search Nadezhda Semyonovna's home had been 'communalised', as it was now called. She had been unceremoniously evicted into what used to be the yard-cleaner's lodge, and someone else had been moved into her apartment. And she had not been allowed to take her things with her, except a change of clothes and footwear, and some of her icons.

'There, you bourgeois – now you can stoke up on the opium of the people!'

This woman had saved both her and her child. And now, by leaving, Anna was betraying her. In order to save her son. Yet Nadezhda Semyonovna's eyes showed only gladness: they'd made it, they'd made it! They were leaving, thank God, and they would soon be in Ukraine, where there would be milk for Olezhek, and white bread rolls, too! She had no cause to grieve over herself: now that everything was settled and clear, what was there to grieve over? It was just her egoism that tormented her, but it would be easy once she'd pulled herself together again. She would go back to her little lodge – and sleep, and sleep. These had been fretful days – now they would be no more. There was no longer anyone to worry about. Oleg started fidgeting under the shawl and, after kissing the old woman for the last time, Anna made her way to her carriage.

'Don't look back! It's a bad sign!' she heard whispered from behind.

19

'For pity's sake, what's a child doing here? Yes, I recall we had an agreement – but there was no mention of a child. Of course I love children and all that sort of stuff, but we're a troupe of actors! There are going to be checks, and because of him no one will get through. You must realise – actresses don't take children on tour with them!'

The somewhat corpulent impresario was so het up that small beads of sweat had started to appear on his fleshy nose.

'Well, we're moving, thank God – from now on I'll fend for myself,' Anna answered reassuringly. 'I quite understand, and promise you I won't—'

'But how can you fend for yourself, if your name's down on a collective pass! What am I supposed to say – that one of our troupe got lost along the way? Oh, these women – no sense of responsibility whatsoever!'

Without answering, Anna changed Oleg's nappy. She hoped to wash the dirty nappies in the snow at the stops. After all, there surely would be stops, although, of course, the fewer the better. But how would she feed him? The compartment was packed solid, and there were men, too ... Nevertheless, she took out her breast, keeping both it and Oleg covered beneath her shawl. And no one seemed to mind, either – so, clearly, it did screen them from view.

The troupe, meanwhile, was still het up.

'Really, Arkady Ilyich – I had no idea you took in outsiders. And I protest!' indignantly exclaimed the roly-poly Louisa, the contralto who did the comic roles. 'I can't travel in the same compartment as a baby! With all this chirping, and these nappies

... Why, it'll be impossible to get a proper night's sleep. You promised certain conditions ...'

'Louisa, my peach! Aphrodite of my soul! Now don't go getting in a flap. She can't throw the child out on to the rails, after all! A baby brings luck. And don't you worry about comfort: you're going to have to put up with such discomfort in here that this little shrieker will be the last thing on your mind,' interjected a little man with an animated face and prominent jaws. This was Shchelkunov, the singer of comic songs, though everybody called him 'Nutcracker' – and it was a name that he gladly took to.

The others in the troupe were Raya, the soprano and reciter, Grusha, a gypsy girl who did the tragic roles and the auguries of fate, and Genrikh, the tenor and leading man. The troupe was called 'The Theatre of New Forms', and this, apparently, explained why it had two prompters: a middle-aged gentleman who looked like a lawyer, and a blond youth, almost a boy, who was so shy that he stammered. These two obviously also knew no one, and Anna realised that she was not the only 'outsider' here.

Raya and Grusha immediately started supporting the singer of comic songs.

'What a lovely baby! Such a sweetie – he's obviously a little boy.'

'What a dearie! And he's got dimples in his cheeks. Now, "Round and round the garden, like a teddy bear" ... Grusha, see how he's laughing! Don't you worry, my dear ... What's your name? Anna? Anyutochka – now don't you pay any attention to Louisa, she's always making a frightful scene, but she means well, really.'

'What do you mean, I'm "always making a frightful scene"?' snapped Louisa, seething.

'Oh, Louisa, you're incomparable! Would you like me to adopt him for you?' asked Nutcracker, flashing his teeth. 'And Genrikh will adopt him, too, won't you, Genrikh? We'll get him to do the childish parts. So what if he can't talk? By the time we finish this journey, he'll have grown up – or I know nothing about life today,' he added ominously.

The impresario merely shrugged his square palms, and Anna felt a weight lift from her heart. She even felt cheerful, for she had started to be infected by the atmosphere of this happy-go-lucky world of actors.

Despite Nutcracker's predictions, they reached Moscow without having to endure any real hardship. The train stopped twice, and everyone was ordered to get off: the first time they had, for reasons unknown, to change to a goods train, and the second time they simply had to spend six hours hanging about in the snow, huddled in a cluster. Then everyone was allowed to clamber back on. Nobody asked any questions, and everyone was happy to pretend that this was all perfectly normal and proper. They even did not turn away from the blinding lights that the soldiers flashed in their faces when checking their papers, and tried not to blink. From time to time the train erupted in shouts, when a thief had been caught in one of the carriages and there were threats to lower him head-first down under the wheels, or there was an argument over the seating in the new carriages and somebody's belongings had been flung out. But the troupe kept themselves to themselves and, with five men accompanying them, they were spared from the seething passions of the other passengers.

Shortly before reaching Moscow the train was kept waiting on a siding for nine days: rumour had it that troops were boarding. There were also rumours that the Bolsheviks were fleeing the city, but that first they meant to shoot everybody, and it was said that no one was being allowed into Ukraine any more – and a lot of other things to which Anna no longer bothered to pay any attention. She saw for herself how some of these rumours were born. It was strange how some people were still intent on frightening one another. Maybe they needed to see their neighbour more frightened than they were themselves? But Anna had given up trying to find reasons. It was obvious that the world had gone mad, that it had been jolted out of place, and everybody had been sent flying, like shreds of paper, all clueless as to where they were going. Within this madness certain complex systems operated, and Anna immediately came to understand something of them. No questions could be asked. About anything, or anybody. At best, this made people afraid, and they were disinclined to answer. But they might just as easily get furious. And you couldn't let your eyes rest on anyone:

that provoked an outburst of aggression. And rumours were not to be believed, or she would have gone mad herself.

At last the train drew into the station: here they had to make another change, and their luggage was to be checked. Word got around that items of fur were going to be confiscated, so Louisa hurriedly tore the sleeves from her fur coat: if it wasn't taken away, she could sew them back on later. From several sides a number of young and middle-aged ladies came rushing over to the impresario.

'Now then, dear, you're the one with the props! Put these in with them – they're totally worthless. They're glass trinkets, I swear, mere trinkets!'

And they thrust out shawls and blouses that were decked in suspicious-looking stones that had been hastily sewn on to them. Anna tried to keep warm by wrapping herself in Nadezhda Semyonovna's sealskin coat. The coat was a little tight, and the sleeves were too short, but, even so, what would she and little Olezhek have done without it? It was better than nothing. And there was always a chance that it wouldn't be confiscated. Olezhek took to the nomadic life with ease. Anna did not let him out of her arms for a single minute, and rightly so. They were no more than a few hours out of Petrograd when the train came to an abrupt halt: there was some fault with the points. And everything on the top berths – both people and luggage – came crashing down. A wrought-iron trunk belonging to some woman struck a pock-marked old man on the head and almost sliced his ear off. Anna bandaged him up as best she could.

She kept Oleg bound to her breast with her shawl, and so he spent the whole time hanging from her. This had certain immediate advantages: she learned to recognise the movements that he made before another nappy was added to the washing. And within a week she could almost always time it in such a way as to prevent the nappy from getting dirty. It was simpler rinsing out an empty food tin with snow, and the contents could be thrown straight out of the window from the moving train.

'Now what are you up to, you pint-sized little man! Look, Grusha, see what a stream he's letting out!' Raya felt moved to remark. 'He'll be a sharp-shooter, this one!'

The actors, being accustomed to the nomadic life, and to

striking up quick friendships, were already cracking jokes with them, and now regarded them as part of the family. On discovering that Anna had nothing but rusks and a chunk of stone-hard halva to eat, even Louisa held out some hard-boiled eggs from her own reserves.

'Come on – don't be difficult! If your milk runs out, this little shrieker will drive us all barmy with his screaming – and things are quite bad enough already!' she erupted furiously, keeping a jealous eye on Anna to ensure she ate up every single crumb of it.

The searches were conducted inside the station hall, and the impresario went off to attend to the luggage inspection, although quite how he reached agreement with the men from the Cheka remained unknown. But reach it he did, and the radiance emanating from his bald head as he returned confirmed the force of his genius.

'Anna, my dear, I can't tell you how lucky we've been! Come over here a moment. Don't push, madam, this citizen's place in this queue is right here – she'll be back in no time!'

They went over to a column, and the impresario whispered, 'Do you know what the commissar here collects? Well, let me tell you: gongs! Quick, give me that Stanislav of yours, and we'll be out of here in no time! Well, why are you looking at me like that? You're not a fetishist, I hope. And what are you going to do during the search if they start asking what a supporting actress is doing with a Stanislav?'

Anna was not a fetishist and, furthermore, up in front someone was already being stripped virtually naked, and some woman could be heard permanently screaming. During the search a group of detainees were forced up against a wall with rifle butts, and those resisting were prodded with bayonets. From the lining of her fur coat she removed the cross, with its dark red enamel, and open-work eagles, and, for the last time, she felt how agreeably hefty it was. From somewhere the middle-aged prompter had also spirited up a medal 'For work in connection with the excellent implementation of the universal mobilisation of 1914' – and the impresario gleefully rushed off into the damp darkness.

They were let through without a hitch, and even their items

of fur were not touched. Oleg passed unnoticed, and the only item to be confiscated was a theatrical sword. They were put on board a second-class carriage and, furthermore, given a pass for the onward transit of their luggage as part of the theatrical props. The train wheels rattled calmly as the indignant Louisa vainly tried to sew the sleeves back on to her fur coat.

'Grusha, you're a gypsy, aren't you – you could probably do this in your sleep, couldn't you?' she asked in exasperation. It seemed that she would have been less upset if her fur coat had, in fact, been confiscated: then they would have had to sew the sleeves back on for themselves. Anna set about helping her, and matters were soon put right.

'End of the line – everyone out!'

This was already the border station, where they had to make the most dangerous change of the journey. Anyone who was not let through into Ukraine from here would not even be making it back to Moscow. That was known. In fact, they would not be making it back anywhere. Anna followed the others and jumped down on to the wet embankment. They were in the last carriage, and it had not reached the platform. Bayonets could be seen glittering in the sweeping light of the torches, and there was a smell of dogs from the soldiers' overcoats. By now they were used to all this, but Anna also spotted a dog coming down the embankment, and it was dragging something long that was clawing at the gravel with outspread fingers. Was it a hand? She must be seeing things. But she distinctly saw those hooked fingers!

Inside the station hut the interrogation was already under way. Apart from the standard leather jacket, the commissar had also draped himself in a leather cloak. He looked like Marat and was evidently aware of it, too: he was forever striving to turn side on and show himself in profile. So he was facing sideways as he said, 'So – a theatre of new forms? With – if you please – two prompters. Now that really is a theatrical innovation.'

And then Oleg started crying from beneath the shawl.

And that was it. Exactly what the impresario had feared. Yet here, too, he was as shrewd as a snake and as meek as a dove. He convinced the commissar that a baby was absolutely essential for their revolutionary repertoire, for theirs was a theatre of symbolico-realism: which was to say that, instead of a sword, for example, they might use a piece of cardboard with an inscription saying 'sword', but that it was quite inadmissible to use a doll instead of a baby. He lied with inspiration, referring to Meyerhold and, for some reason, Chekhov, too, and finally he got the commissar to smile.

'Well, splendid. Tomorrow you can put on a show for the local proletariat. With the active participation of every single one of you. We know how to appreciate art here, too, you know. And the day after tomorrow you can be on your way again – assuming, of course, that your show has been a success. In the meantime, however, I will make arrangements for you to be put up for one night. There may be no need for you to stay a second night, as – you understand – we already have so many others to look after . . .'

They were led away to be housed with a local cobbler. Both he and his wife were terrified out of their wits. They quickly and silently evacuated a room for them and led their very quiet children off into the kitchen. Equally quietly they fetched a kettle of hot water and a pan with some pearl-barley soup for them – and disappeared. And from the kitchen not a peep further was heard.

'Come on there – cheer up! To-reador, go bra-a-vely into fight,' purred Nutcracker, spiritedly putting the soup bowls down on the table.

'Got any ideas?' asked the impresario gloomily.

'When did I ever not have any ideas? You think I've always been an actor? Well, let me tell you – before I became an actor, I was a performing artist! What's the difference, you ask? Let me explain: an actor learns his part from a piece of paper. But a performing artist is forever improvising – his entire life is a performance.'

From the embankment there came some loud howls and four short cracks.

'At least they shoot people here,' said Grusha with an unpleasant grin. 'In the western cordon, I've heard, officers have been burnt alive. How, you ask! They were doused in kerosene – and that was that.'

'Let's cut out the melan-mopies, shall we, sweetie! You ask

how I came to be a performing artist?' Nutcracker persisted, though no one had asked him any such thing. 'Well, the fact is I've been a bath-house attendant, a jockey, a tram-conductor and a card-sharp! And, after all that, the stage – now don't take this personally – is a doddle. We'll manage this show all right. I can see it already. And you take my word for it – we'll be greeted with ovations and revolutionary shots in the ceiling! Just the ceiling, I guarantee!'

The troupe bucked up, and by morning they had a clearer idea of what the show would be like. From the very first rehearsal there arose a mad hope that they really could pull it off. If only everyone remembered that to be brazen-faced was – as Nutcracker put it – 'luck for the asking'. The only person who was not at all worried before the début was Oleg – who was, therefore, the most dependable one of the whole lot of them.

Inside the wooden barrack there was a platform, some benches, and something resembling a hayloft that could even pass for a gallery. People were piled into this, too. A total of some two hundred had managed to pack themselves into the 'theatre', all of them armed. There were even some women in officers' overcoats with torn-off epaulettes and hats decorated with glass beads. And some in flat caps, too. And they were smoking cheap shag.

'Dear comrades!' Nutcracker began as compère, with a smile plastered all over his sumptuous mug. 'We are about to show you a scene of revolutionary underground figures in their brave fight with the accursed tsarist regime. You are, of course, fully aware of the idea behind the new proletarian art, but, just to be on the safe side, I shall explain it to you anyway. Here we have one prompter – he is the voice of the bourgeois press. And here, on the right, we have another with his mouth gagged – he is the voice of the people under flagrant tsarist misrule. He makes revolutionary gestures which inspire our heroes on to new heights. We shall also show you a tsarist gendarme – this man here, with the paper epaulettes. During the play you are kindly requested not to shoot at him: he is an actor of exclusively working-class origins. Should you find yourself carried away during the show, then fire at the ceiling – and be sure to join the revolutionary singing with which we will bring our show to an end. After the show is over, those who wish may have their callused palms read by the Soviet gypsy, Grusha.'

No one – not even in early 1918, not even in Russia – had ever seen a performance quite like it. The audience had simply struck it lucky – and they began to be aware of it, too. Genrikh took the part of a Putilov factory-worker, and Oleg and Anna that of his family. They were, of course, primarily engaged in distributing Bolshevik literature and storing dynamite. The villainous landlady of their apartment, Raya, brought a gendarme to carry out a search. The gendarme was none other than the impresario himself. Louisa took the part of a revolutionary-minded grandmother who abusively drove the gendarme from the apartment with her broom. But, before this, the gendarme searched for the typeset in the baby's cradle, and, with astonishing class intuition, the baby had to urinate all over his uniform. For this, the provident Nutcracker had placed a flask of water with a loose top inside his nappy.

It was the play's culminating moment, and when, on being hoisted in the arms of the gendarme-impresario, Oleg let out an entirely natural yell, the hall roared with delight.

'Look, it's alive! It's a real baby!'

As an improbably large, dark stain began to spread over the gendarme's makeshift uniform, he pulled an idiotic face, and the house hooted with laughter. No one fired any shots at the gendarme – he was merely pelted with salted cucumbers and an empty bottle. For an 'encore' Louisa wacked the gendarme eight times with her broom. And the moment Grusha started singing the 'Marseillaise', everyone joined in with her – the entire hall as one.

The commissar personally shook each of the actors by the hand, and admitted that at first he had disbelieved them, and very nearly had them marched straight off to be shot, but that they had touched his heart, and now he was even ready to let their luggage through. Indeed, so moved was he that, for 'their future success', he presented them with a couple of new gendarme's epaulettes, with the ripped threads still dangling from them. And he bashfully asked Grusha to tell him his fortune somewhere in private. Nor did the astute Grusha disappoint –

telling him all that he wanted to hear, what astonishing success he had with women, and that it would take him no more than a year to become a leading Red commander.

Ukraine! Ukraine! Now the forty-mile zone, the machine-gunning of their train by bands of one sort or another, and the rides in carts with damp hay were all behind them – and ahead lay the border check-point. It was manned by two German soldiers.

'*Heraus*! Papers.'

It transpired that they had to spend a fortnight in quarantine. The impresario busily scuttled about, but he evidently crossed the wrong palm, and the quarantine had to be observed. It was cold, though no longer as bad as it had been before: it wasn't as drafty here as it had been through the cracks of the moving carriage on the goods train. And this was the south – for goodness' sake, these couldn't be called proper frosts down here!

To Anna it seemed that the journey would never come to an end, and that the cold would last for ever, along with the angry shouting, the piercing dark, and the shooting, the shooting . . . And then suddenly she was bidding the troupe farewell at the station in Kiev, and Louisa was in tears, presenting her with a small mantle of black lace, and Nutcracker was thrusting a cockerel lollipop into Oleg's hands: and, gracious, they really were selling lollipops on the platform! And there was also a buffet, and a smell of bortsch.

Anna felt she was dreaming as she walked along the clean streets, where decently dressed people scurried from one shop to the next, and an officer – a real officer – could walk about without having anyone shoot at him. And the sunshine made it feel so much like spring . . . Olezhek was intently sucking his cockerel lollipop . . . Wasn't that bad for him? But, in any event, she was already feeding him soaked rusks – so what harm could a lollipop do? She had to get to the Andreyevsky slope, to her aunt Gelya, who was a distant relative of her mother. She knew the address: how many times had she seen it written on envelopes. But would she still be there? Was it possible that anyone was still living in their old home?

But Aunt Gelya was still there, and, on seeing Anna, she

started bubbling over with the family feelings that had been missing from her own life. She was an old spinster, with a delicate flush to her sunken cheeks, and she mainly spoke Polish – or rather that mix of Russian, Polish and Ukrainian which in Kiev was regarded as Polish. Anna immediately became Anusya, as she had been at home, and Oleg was a 'poor child', who 'understood everything', and needed to be helped to get over all the shocks that he had been through.

'Whenever there's a loud noise, he goes all quiet!'

Of course he went all quiet – to Anna it seemed normal. But even she, on seeing how overjoyed her aunt became the first time that Olezhek was naughty, felt that she was about to burst into tears. After all, it was only healthy for a child to be naughty . . . Well, no matter – it clearly wasn't too late to start.

Her aunt made her living as a hat-maker, and she obviously did very well out of it, too. Which all goes to show that sometimes there is something to these rumours, thought Anna, absent-mindedly stroking a porcelain saucer on which lay some cream cakes – those same Kievan cakes that had been the stuff of legend back in 'Peter'.

'Odessa? My child, but there are Bolsheviks there! You must have been living on the moon! Let's just suppose they were about to be driven out – you'd still be in a most frightful pickle! Don't even think of it! The last letter I had from your mother was back in September of last year. God alone knows what's going on there, they say. Wait until May, at the earliest – by then, I think, everything should have been sorted out.'

So, once again, Anna was stuck. It was a topsy-turvy Kievan summer – what with its rumours about Petlyura, and the Hetman's newspapers, from which all that could be gleaned was that they contained lies, as was usual for the newspapers, and with its cherries, sweet cherries, and lovely gardens in which it was possible to go safely walking with your child. How funnily he was now crawling, or rather running on all fours, with his knees up off the floor. Anna helped her aunt with her hats, and kept writing letter after letter to Odessa. The post was unreliable, but there were other ways in which letters could get through, and these had lately been growing more frequent. The Central Rada was said to be about to mobilise every man who was still in

Kiev, and, while there was still time, people were now heading south. But there was no reply until October. Perhaps there was no one for Anna to go and see now? And suddenly there was a letter from her mother. They were alive. She would tell her about Vladek separately, when they met. And Pavel was alive, according to the Petrovs, but she would also tell her about that separately. Why didn't Anusya come, seeing as it was relatively safe now? We can't wait to hug our grandson.

Despite Aunt Gelya's protestations, she quickly gathered her things. Heaven forbid there should be a repeat of what had happened in 'Peter'. Well, all right then – but if Anusya was to go, she couldn't possibly leave with only one small suitcase. In Odessa everything had been looted, it was said. And nowadays there was so little opportunity to send anything that Gelya would just find something to send to Anna's mother.

Kiev saw them off with a clear sky and rustling leaves. Olezhek, who was already a year old, and rather hefty, sat on Anna's arm, goggling at God's world. He stroked the tear-stained Gelya with his plump little hand, and the train started moving.

'Homeward, homeward, homeward,' clattered the wheels.

Opposite Anna there sat two women shrilly quarrelling with one another. From somewhere out in the corridor there were already cries of 'Stop thief!' And when, after eleven miles, the train came to a halt, and it became known that the Reds had machine-gunned the previous train, and that some people had been killed, Anna was no longer surprised. Who was surprised at people getting killed nowadays? The one thought on everyone's mind was: will we be kept waiting long? She knew that, if she ever did make it back home, she would never get on another train for as long as she lived.

20

Tomorrow! We begin tomorrow! Yakov and Rimma did not sleep that night. After grumbling at how wantonly they were burning the light, Rakhil went off to bed, leaving the children in the kitchen. They smiled at one another. The only way in which they looked alike was their eyes, which, like their father's, were dark brown and set slightly too close together. The 13th of January 1918 would go down in history – of this they were certain. They were in no mood to discuss the arrangements. Everything had been planned: Rimma was to act as a courier for Comrade Chizhikov and co-ordinate the reinforcements for the railway station. Yakov was to be stationed at the headquarters at Blizhnye Melnitsy, at the heart of the uprising. True, he was only to be in charge of communications, but next day that meant everything, for tomorrow their comrades were to occupy the bank, the post office, the telegraph office and the military regional headquarters. And they had to be kept in touch with the warships that had promised their support and would be helping to direct the firing. And as for the main railway station and the Odessan 'Goods Station' – they'd take the stations easily enough, with the advantage of surprise, but then the real challenge would be to hang on to them. Would they be alive tomorrow evening, or would they have added their names to the lists of the revolution's fallen heroes? Yakov tried to picture the lists, imagining them as scrolls with fiery lettering. But, instead of this, he saw a wretched schoolboy with ears that looked like his own toiling by the blackboard.

'And there's Yakov . . . er . . . Goiber . . .'

'Geiber!' came the whisper from the front desk.

'Geiber,' dolefully repeated the schoolboy of the future Soviet Russia, casting a despairing glance at the class journal over which hung the mauve numeral '1' – the lowest mark possible. Yakov snorted. He had never known how to work himself up into a dutifully sombre frame of mind, especially if he was trying. He savoured some of the tea that he had just brewed: his comrades at the port had managed to get hold of it for him. He felt clear-headed and slightly down-hearted. Maxim and Antos were at that moment sleeping – they knew nothing. Nor should they.

But what fun it had been to start distributing the literature and sticking up the leaflets together. Conspiracy was an alluring, dangerous game, and all three of them understood that what was at stake here was not just whether they would complete the gymnasium. However, when Comrade Achkanov forbade Yakov from letting the others in on any future planned activities, Yakov could see that he was right. For Maxim, all this was a lark – he was simply tagging along with his friends. But – being a spoilt young gentleman – he was incapable of holding any firm convictions.

'Kill the enemies of the revolution? Come now, surely there's no need to be quite so bloodthirsty about it . . . That's why the French Revolution came a cropper – because it indulged in excesses.'

To blurt a remark like this out to Comrade Achkanov was something that only a total idiot could ever do, and furthermore, it immediately betrayed his ignorance of the works of Lenin. Maxim really was a dim-wit – even if he was a good comrade. Yet comrade he was, evidently – up to a point. He had somehow lost his enthusiasm and now showed up increasingly rarely, even to do courier work. Antos was free of such prejudices, but he lacked self-control. All that interested him was shooting and heroics. He wasn't cut out for the painstaking work that such heroics required, for that demanded analytical capabilities. And, generally, he saw no point in studying any of the required literature, and called it faffing with paper. To go with him on even the most trivial of jobs was dangerous: with his romantic predisposition you never knew what he might spring on you. Yakov knew that he carried a Mauser round with him.

A fine dry snow was pattering against the windows, and Rimma opened the vent.

'Look, tomorrow everything will be white!'

Yet it didn't seem likely: the snow was not settling, but was being blown around the empty yard in meagre little clusters, and it was only gathering in frail mounds by the corners.

Yakov took Rimma by the shoulders and led her to the mirror out in the corridor, flicking the light on as he passed.

'What are you doing? You'll wake Mama up!'

'Have a look.'

'Well?'

'Well, you can't expect me to tell my own sister how beautiful she's looking. You know, I'd like to remember you as you are now. We may be killed, or we may get to grow old. But, either way, it won't be the same as now.'

'Sentimentality, Comrade Geiber? I would never have expected it of you.'

But Yakov could see that she was pleased.

For three days there was shooting throughout the city. Units of Ukrainian Cossacks from the Central Rada kept breaking through to the centre in armoured cars. And then being repulsed. The artillery boomed, and there was the endless, tiresome sound of the factory hooters. Then everything fell quiet: the Bolsheviks took power. Grandiose funerals for their fallen comrades started to be held. The streets were decked in red flags and black ribbons. Bands howled in mourning, orators gave speeches. Comrade Chizhikov, tall, stern, and dressed in a leather jacket, delivered a speech from the very vehicle in which he had taken the main railway station, still mounted with its rapid-fire cannon.

'Comrades. Today we are burying the finest sons of the working people. Death to the enemies of the revolution!'

'Death! Death! Death!' echoed the crowd. The entire Odessan Red Guard was there. And the metalworkers. And the revolutionary sailors. Ordinary people hid back in their homes. Well, let them – for the time being. As Comrade Chizhikov spoke, Rimma watched him in delight. She was by his side, on the same vehicle, and about to start them all singing the 'Internationale'.

On the following day they started shooting their enemies. And from then until the start of spring they got in as many as they could manage.

'The Cossacks are coming! This time it's definite, Vanda! Darling – at last!'

Once again there was shooting, and by now a boom could also be heard out in Kulikovo field. Ivan Timofeyevich, in a worn scarf and now so pinched as to appear blackened, embraced his wife and whirled her around the room. How had they managed to get through these last months? How had they survived? Engineer Teslenko was well known on the railways, and he would undoubtedly have been counted as one of the enemies of the revolution. Who was it that had opposed smashing the points? Who was it that had organised the work of the repair team during the strike? But, when they came to arrest him, he was, fortunately, at the Petrovs, and he subsequently spent most of the time in hiding with them. Vanda Kazimirovna sold some of their things to the yard-cleaner's wife and, until the trade unions were formed, Antos earned a bit extra as a stevedore – and they managed to get by!

'Are you sure it's the Cossacks? People have been saying it's a corps of Austrians . . .'

'Well, I'd welcome the devil himself!' laughed Ivan Timofeyevich, looking out of the window. Some lorries could be seen bouncing over the damp cobblestones. They were leaving, they were leaving!

'Where's Antos, Vanda?'

'He's gone for some bread.'

Vanda Kazimirovna's face slowly blanched as she looked at her husband.

'How long ago?'

'An hour.'

Whenever there was any shooting, the shops all closed – as they both knew.

Anna could hardly keep the little boy on her knees: he was squealing and kept lunging over towards the horsie. Could it really be that they were back home, in Odessa? How much the same, and how different it all was! With the bullet-pocked façades and all those windows boarded over with plywood. And there were the same old lions' heads, one now with its nose broken off. She saw a lady walking along with one foot in a galosh, and the other in a shoe. And two little boys struggling to carry a splashing bucket of water.

'Sunflower seeds! Freshly roasted sunflower seeds! Fifty carbovanets a full glass!' hollered a jolly woman in a ginger-coloured soldier's coat.

The cabman drove on down Pushkin Street and then turned into Deribasovskaya Street. At the corner there stood a cluster of soldiers in German uniform, and Anna recoiled. In Kiev their presence had somehow not been so out of place. But here, in Odessa? It was from Odessa that Pavel had gone off to fight against them. The plane trees were majestically shedding dried, intricately shaped leaves, and one fell inside the cab. Oleg immediately became fascinated by it: he invariably drew anything beautiful up to his mouth.

'Son! This is Odessa!'

'Yes-sa!' gladly responded Petrov the Younger.

Anna breathlessly made her way up the steps. Was the boy getting heavy, or was it her bag that weighed so much? And there were quite a few other things that might have taken her breath away on returning home after almost four years. Who would open the door to her? But, evidently, there is a limit to all misfortune, for it was her mother that opened the door.

'Anusya! I knew it would be today – I dreamt of you!'

And already her father was embracing her. How much older he looked, poor Papa. But her mother hadn't changed in the slightest, only her hair had greyed. Oleg, however, was embarrassed by the attention that everyone was showering on him, and he stuffed both his fists into his mouth and, just in case, sat down on the floor.

'What about Antos? Where's Antos?'

Antos was far away. Serko – the beauty – was spiritedly tramping over some feather-grass lightly topped with an overnight frost, and the steppe wind gladdened the heart as their detachment, having fought its way back virtually without loss, was now about to link up with Kotovsky's cavalry.

'Don't cry, Marusya, yet you'll be mine!' Gritsai exuberantly burst into song, whereupon the detachment took up the refrain, and the horses danced off in time to the singing. It could not have been more than half a year since Antos had suffered his chance wound in the street skirmish and been seized by the retreating Red Guards. He had struck someone as looking like the commissar's secretary, and been taken by mistake. The middle-aged doctor's assistant Stepan had brought him round again, and he certainly wasn't going to let him be shot once it became clear that they'd saved the wrong lad.

'You're not bloody well 'avin 'im! 'E's one of ours – I can see for meself!'

'What are you talking about, you fool? He's a little bourgeois – you can smell it on him! Look at them fancy boots – just my size, too. Stop blathering and turf him down off that cart!'

'But what if the little bourgeois speaks our lingo! Go on, son – let's 'ear something!'

Antos, of course, knew Ukrainian from his father. A number of different languages were spoken in the detachment, but about a third of the men were Ukrainians, including Commander Piven. He stooped awkwardly down over Antos and, drawing together his eyebrows, which almost joined in the middle, asked, 'Surname?'

'Teslenko,' Antos muttered faintly.

'Strike me – as if I'd never heard that name before! We've got four houseloads of Teslenkos back in Lyshnya! So consider him a member of our revolutionary detachment and give him a sword and a horse – that one that used to be Dovbal's. And you, Stepan, keep an eye on him – see that he recovers.'

Thus was Antos's fate decided. And a couple of months later he excelled himself on reconnaissance, displaying extreme courage, and Piven personally shook him by the hand. He could no longer imagine himself in any other capacity, and now it struck him that this was, in fact, what all his prior life had been leading up to. Why, yes, he had always backed the Reds, and now, at last, he had some real work to do – the work of a Red cavalryman. He was still growing, and had put on almost a couple of inches over the last half year.

The grey-moustachioed Stepan became very fond of him while he was recovering, and called him nothing but 'sonny' the whole time. Once, during an overnight stopover, he told Antos how Denikin's troops had beaten his own son with ramrods.

'They thrashed 'im to the bone. And they went on, even when 'e were already dead.' He spoke slowly and calmly, but the camp-fire showed his face in a different light. And there was such virulent hatred in this face that Antos felt it flow into him, too: kill the monsters. Every last one of them. Leave none alive – stamp out their entire breed.

A week later Piven was killed in an unexpected skirmish. Antos saw him slump back in his saddle, his throat streaming in red, as his horse bore the commander off into the sunset and to his death. There were also some other losses, and each one of them hardened the heart yet further: this was a fight to the death, between 'us' and 'them', and there wasn't a man among 'them' whom Antos would have spared. And he merely gave a wry smile whenever one of 'them' got caught alive, and the lads, not wishing to waste a bullet, had a bit of fun with their swords, until they got fed up with hacking at the bloody left-overs. He took no part in this himself, though not out of sentimental reasons. He was simply holding back that reserve of fury that carried him into each attack: into that happy flight of frenzy, where there was no longer any distinction between death and immortality.

The Teslenkos never saw their son again, and did not know where he was or whether or not he was alive. But he lived on for quite some time yet, until Perekop was taken. By then he had become a regimental commander, and he perished as he had dreamt: with his sword bared and galloping into battle. The fighting moved on, and the Red cavalry advanced on through Crimea, but the bay Orlik that Antos had taken as a replacement for the lame Serko lingered back, and he kept touching the lips of his prostrate master whose mouth had remained open since the attack. His master was, for some reason, getting colder and colder, and Orlik was worried and kept breathing on him, trying to warm him up. But by evening Orlik became scared: there was a strange smell coming from Antos, and now he was completely rigid, and if his hand had at that moment reached out and seized the rein, Orlik would have let out a shrill neigh and gone racing off over the steppe. He went round in a few more circles, but no longer touching his master. Then he gave a loud sigh and started wandering off – in the direction in which Antos had given him his last command.

The carbide lamp smelt foul, and, furthermore, it took up one of his hands. They had got through the passages with which he was familiar, and now it felt as if they were going down. But this was a good, broad passage, and there was hardly any need for them to keep stooping their heads. Yakov felt quietly pleased: what he couldn't stand in the catacombs was the narrow rat-holes through which you occasionally had to clamber on all fours. Whenever he felt the full weight of an arch suddenly touch against his back, Yakov had to muster all his will-power not to erupt in shrieks of hysteria. There were some people that could not work underground: they would become nervous that there was nothing to breathe, and suffer panic attacks. For people like this, it always seemed as if they were about to be buried alive, or that the way out at the top had collapsed – and now they would never get out. Yakov had himself seen a strapping sailor, who had been going along fine to begin with, suddenly later let out a scream and start banging his head against the rugged shellrock. Screaming inside the catacombs, and, even more so, banging your head against the walls, was really not a good idea: that actually could make them collapse. Even if not right above the spot where the stores were kept, there were still cases of it happening.

But Andreika made his way forward confidently, identifying where he was going from marks on the spongy walls that only he could read. This was something that Yakov really hadn't been expecting: that one day his old chum would turn up out of the blue like this. But what was so out of the ordinary about it: Odessa was a big village, so why shouldn't people bump into one another? The revolution had released Andreika from jail, where he was doing a short sentence for smuggling. Now, along with the revolution, he had gone underground. And he proved to be a real find: he knew the part of the catacombs beneath Kuyalnik as well as Yakov knew Koblevskaya Street. True, he would play the fool whenever asked to draw a map of it.

'I'm not educated – I just know what I know.'

But when it was necessary to widen the underground, he

gladly volunteered to point out the right spots, and even some new ways out. With his narrow shoulders and lithe build he could walk across an uneven surface without making any noise, and Yakov followed on behind him, not forgetting to assess whether there was enough room for the printing-presses to get through, or whether they would have to dismantle them. He suspected that Andreika was intentionally looping back round, and was all but leading him in circles. But perhaps it just seemed that way. Whenever he was underground Yakov instantly lost his sense of direction.

'There – see that? Any good?'

Yakov was so thrilled that he sucked the air in through his teeth. It was an enormous chamber, so spacious that you didn't even feel boxed in. He had to raise the lamp higher, to illuminate the arch. And it was dry, too: Yakov spotted a scrap of some old newspaper and, carefully picking it up, realised that it was not in the slightest bit damp.

'Come on – let's 'ave some light on it.'

It was the *Stock Exchange News* from 1904.

'Ideal! It's the perfect spot! Well, mate – for this you shall have unto half my kingdom!'

'Right now – or in instalments?' enquired Andreika in a businesslike manner, and they both burst out laughing. But the main surprise was yet to come. There was a small gallery that Yakov had not even noticed, with four twists and climbing steeply upwards before it came out into another, slightly smaller chamber. And inside of that chamber there was a distinct, though faint rumbling. Yakov shuddered: he, too, had visions of landslides.

'That's the sea, you weirdo. Take a look!'

Some fifty steps on down the narrow corridor – and Yakov's nostrils were assailed by a fresh, damp smell: it was a way out! And what a way out, too, coming out on to a precipice carpeted in gorse – it was a smuggler's dream! A moonlit path peacefully shimmered over the little bay: so, it was already dark.

And it was only on the way back that they spotted a few travel bags tidily stashed up against the wall of the smaller chamber.

'Are those yours, Andreika?'

'No. Looks like we've got a rival. Who else could have found this spot? Ustinych was the only other one who knew about it, but he's been dead two years now.'

Yakov opened out the top travel bag and let out a whistle. It contained a leather pouch with gold coins inside, and beneath them were yet more such pouches with roundly bulging sides.

'Stick it back and keep your mitts off!' said Andreika sternly. 'These are either serious smugglers, or Benya Krik himself and his boys. Let's get out: if they catch us in here, they'll shoot us like chickens.'

'This must be requisitioned. For Party use.'

'So you've brought a shooter, have you? If not, keep your nose out of it. Come on – let's scarper.'

That same night an armed detachment of trusted comrades set off to carry out the requisition. Andreika was right: the 'shooters' came in handy. And it was a very good night for it: moonlit, and the owners of the travel bags timed their appearance just before the requisitioning was completed. It was impossible to discover who they were. Shots simply rang out from the darkness, and back into the darkness rang the return shots. When it was all over, four people lay dead inside the little gallery: three young men in smart jackets and striped trousers, and Comrade Okhtinsky.

Andreika lay sputtering with pain on the ground: he had caught one in the thigh, although, luckily, the shot had gone clean through. It was not difficult to carry him out and dress the wound, but what were they supposed to do with him after that? They could not take him to the hospital of the Central Rada! Although – on second thoughts – why not? It was now common enough for people to be attacked by bandits out on the streets. But they would start going into the background, wanting to know which street he was shot on, and when it had happened. The Germans were a meticulous people. And then it dawned on Yakov.

Later that morning the Petrovs' doorbell sounded, and Yakov asked the sleepy Dasha to go and wake up Maxim. It could not be said that he was overjoyed on seeing his former chum. In the two months since the Bolsheviks had taken power, Yakov had hardly been back to his apartment: there had been an awful lot to do, and he had even slept at headquarters. Although, had Maxim ever come across him, he certainly wouldn't have been at a loss for a suitably sharp word in his ear. But now he had pitched up of his own accord!

'What do you need?'

'Maxim, there's no time to explain. Don't be angry – we can talk about it later. There's someone needs hiding. He's wounded, you understand?'

'I refuse to have anything more to do with the Bolsheviks.'

'But he's not a Bolshevik! Just believe me – I'll tell you all about it some time later. You remember Andreika?'

Maxim did not even have to explain anything to the family. However hostile it may feel towards the Reds, what liberal family would throw a wounded man out on to the street, even if he were a Bolshevik? Or report him to the Ukrainian-German authorities?

'Last time we were hiding a Ukrainian from the Reds, and now it's the other way round . . . Who will God send next?' chuckled Ivan Alexandrovich.

The Petrov parents remembered Andreika, Maxim's old childhood chum, perfectly well: the boisterous black-haired boy, who was plainly a street urchin, walked gingerly about the rooms in obvious embarrassment. To prevent making a fool of himself, he referred to every unfamiliar object in precisely the same way – as a 'funny little thingy'. Including Pavel's microscope, and Zina's triple mirror. And so it was that this expression of 'funny little thingy' came to be a family byword.

They delicately avoided asking this older Andreika any questions about anything, putting him in Pavel's old room, and good old Dulchin gave the necessary instructions on how to treat and cure him. Marina changed his dressing for him, and every now and then Maria Vasilyevna looked in just to check that he was not getting too bored, while Dasha took him under her wing as a child whom she remembered as having been fatherless. She delighted in feeding him with jellies and porridge, and scolded him whenever he tried to get out of bed.

The mood in the Petrov household lifted: Anna had arrived as their daughter-in-law, and with their grandson! This was Pavlik's little son – and how like his father he was! Even before, both families had been as close as relatives. They were both eaten up with exactly the same anxiety for the missing members of their families, and it was a long time since they last kept any secrets from one another concerning the ones that turned up again. When recalling Vladek, they all nodded meaningfully at one another. There was a rumour that Pavel had joined Vrangel's troops, and this, too, had been a family secret. These were uncertain times – who knew what the future might hold?

When the Germans started their hasty evacuation, carrying off certain stores with them, no one showed any surprise. By the end of 1918 it had become unseemly to show surprise in Odessa.

21

'Coat.'

Without saying anything, Rakhil took off the brown figure-hugging fur-trimmed Austrian coat that she had had ever since Moisei gave it to her. Really, what need was there for her to hang about talking with Madam Kegulikhes until dark? It was just loneliness: the children never came home nowadays, and had been foolhardly enough to go and get themselves hitched up with the Bolsheviks – so they were hiding away somewhere with their comrades. Now she really would have something to talk about: the street was black and deserted, and, even if she yelled out to the patrols on Staroportofrankovskaya Street, they still would not hear her.

'Muff. Wheels.'

Quite what 'wheels' meant, Rakhil had no idea, but there was no mistaking the fact that this villain was pointing the muzzle of his pistol down at her feet. So she had to take off the pair of shoes that were still almost as good as new. As she struggled to undo her laces, Rakhil silently mouthed a string of curses on the vile hag that had begotten such a bandit, and on all her relatives, and, with all her soul, she wished seven times seven plagues of the liver on the degenerate himself, and that he would drown at sea.

'Now gi' us a kiss!'

Rakhil brushed her lips, which were not yet cool from cursing, against his smooth-shaven snout with its smell of a perfumery.

'Right on the button – achin' for it, weren'cha!' spat out the robber with aplomb and, taking his time, he slipped off into the dark.

The patrol in the Volunteer Zone was none too pleased to stop Rakhil, now seething with indignation, beneath the street-lights shining down on the Viennese chairs that constituted the partition line.

'Pass, madam!'

'What's the matter with you – has someone put out your eyes? What sort of pass is a woman who's just had her clothing stripped off her going to have? There are robbers out on these streets, and people are supposed to carry passes around with them? Look – see what a shocking mess they've made of me!'

Rakhil lifted her naked foot in its torn stocking so that this idiot in shoulder-straps could see for himself. The patrol was already satisfied that Rakhil had her pass in the coat that she had had stolen, and was ready to let her through, but she wasn't going before giving them a full piece of her mind about the shower that called itself the city authorities and permitted a decent woman to be stripped of her clothing in broad daylight.

'Well, stick to walking about in broad daylight then,' casually retorted the young officer. 'And you were mugged in the Polish Zone – so why come pestering us about it?'

Rakhil was a fair woman, so the officer of the Volunteer Army had to listen to her views on all these French, Polish, Ethiopians, Greeks and other such riff-raff who made themselves out to look respectable while leaving bandits free to roam the city. In the end he agreed that, even for a city such as Odessa, four authorities was 'a bit much', whereupon Rakhil left him in peace.

The Petrovs and Teslenkos greeted the New Year of 1919 together. The bronze alarm clock that had been polished by Dasha went off and everyone clinked their glasses of champagne. For now it really was possible to get hold of champagne – from the French Zone!

'Well, may God grant that this year be kinder to us than the last one!' said the man of the house with feeling, robed in what was still a very presentable-looking black frock-coat. The champagne splashed on to the slightly yellowed linen table-cloth, and the women declared this to be a sign of good luck. Marina was flushed and bating Maxim: maybe he was upset at no longer being the youngest of the family?

The eighteen-year-old Maxim comically blew out his lips and pulled a face as if this was, indeed, something he was frightfully indignant about.

'We-ell, Oleg got a spinning top, but poor little Maxy got nothing . . .'

As the only young man in the family, he knew that – come what may – it would soon be for him to decide how to protect and safeguard them all. Well, he was ready for it. And it had come at the right time. Only a year ago he had still been racked with doubt as to whose side he should take. Was it really so faint-hearted to abandon his revolutionary views? Yet it was one thing to oppose the monarchy, and quite another to support the Bolsheviks. Maxim had already seen more than enough of the Bolsheviks, and since they had taken power he had been unable to forgive himself: what on earth had he been thinking of before? He had been accustomed to being an affable chap who let others play the lead roles, and, furthermore, been perfectly happy at that: after all, it wasn't as if he had to prove anything to anyone. Privately, he felt that he was more adult than both Yakov and Antos: he had long since outgrown any boyish ambitions, but he had no objection if that was how his friends wished to comfort themselves. He had always been the youngest, and everybody's darling, though apparently not taken too seriously, either. Well, so be it – that suited him fine. For the time being. Now it just strengthened his will. And for his own part, he had already made up his mind about everything.

The family were engaged in making light-hearted enquiries about where Olezhek got his stubbornness from – was it his papa or his mama? Vanda Kazimirovna was recalling Anna's waywardness, but Dasha would not let Maria Vasilyevna get a word in edgeways.

'Don't you even talk about them "thank you's", mistress. He was coming out with them as soon as he was talking, but – little sweetie that he is – he wasn't even out of nappies when he first started showing his character. And he held his little hands, not bunched up in a fist, but with his thumbs poking through his fingers: as if he were saying – that's what I think o' you lot!'

Dasha was now the only servant the Petrovs had left. For no reason the housemaid had started being obstreperous even before the Bolshevik uprising, and they had had to part ways with her – along, as it later transpired, with part of the silverware. The cook had suddenly got married – well into her forties! – to a Polish refugee: she had been very taken by the fact that, even if he was a tailor, he was still '*pan*', and she would herself be '*pani*'. The Bolsheviks had requisitioned the Petrovs' horses and carriage, and so they had also had to part with the coachman Fedko. He went off to join his brother Mykola, who lived just outside Odessa, to help him out with his fishing. 'A fish feeds itself under any regime, but, ever since they got rid of the Tsar, a horse has had nowt but suffering.'

This profound sentiment had led the indefatigable Dulchin to develop an entire theory of his own: the tsarist regime might, indeed, have only been any good for horses, but, as of now, wasn't the Russian intelligentsia proving more stupid than a horse?

'I'm told how terribly expensive everything's become,' he expanded. 'No, I reply: everything's become terribly cheap, gentlemen! What is the current value of human life? Or honour, or dignity? When any scoundrel can set up some committee with some idiotic name, and have people shot on mere suspicion? Anechka, I didn't sleep for two nights after hearing your stories, and, as for what went on here – that was really altogether indescribable. Just take those explosions back in August – do you remember, gentlemen? Everyone went racing off to the sea like a herd of animals, trammelling all over one another, and the glow hung over the city – and nobody knew what it was all about, and they weren't even interested in finding out, either. I admit it – I fled like a madman myself, and then I suddenly caught sight of an abandoned horse tethered to a post. It was looking at me inquisitively. What, it seemed to be saying, have you fine people gone and done this time? And I swear that I started to feel ashamed. So, human values have proved brittle. But all the greater has that made equine ones – by which I mean the value of oats.'

'But isn't it a good thing, mistress, that the Lord saved Pavlik from getting that cross off the Tsarina?' said Dasha from the other end of the table, in a visibly merrier frame of mind.

'What do you mean, Dasha?'

'I didn't want to say nothing about it at the time to you . . . but it wasn't for nothing that I'd heard that letter of his so many times. If the Tsarina gave the St. George's Cross to him in person, then he would have said so in his letter: she gave it to me herself, he would have said, with her own hands. And seeing as he didn't write that, I was suddenly filled with hope – I knew our darling would survive.'

'God knows what you're talking about, Dasha.'

'Maybe He do, maybe He don't – but them as what knew said that if the Tsarina ever gave the St. George's Cross to anyone with her own hands, then that were the death of 'em. A German bullet would be sure to find its way to one of them crosses, for those weren't plain crosses, mistress. She's a German through and through is that woman, and they were up to all sorts of tricks against our lads, they were. And the soldiers knew about it, too, they said – but what can you do? And as for Pavlik – you'll see, mistress, he'll come back, live and well. Well, I can't say as I'm too used to it, but this champagne 'asn't 'alf got a kick, eh? It tastes like pure compote – only stro-ong . . .'

She was already having trouble in getting her words out, and Marina put her arms round her and led her off to bed. To be out on the streets after curfew required special permission, so the Petrovs' guests all spent the night there, on sofas and chairs put together. Towards morning shooting could be heard, and now it lasted for a long time. Even Oleg woke up, and crawled down from the sofa on which he had been put the night before. It was completely dark in the room, and there was a scratching at the window. Must be a wolf, figured Oleg, freezing in horror. He should let out a scream and call for his mama – but whenever there was any shooting he always knew that he was not to scream. Without making any noise, he stamped his plump little bare soles on the cold parquet. His mother was there beside him, on the sofa. Trying not to let out a groan, he crawled over to her and got himself underneath her blanket, squeezing up close to her so as to make himself as inconspicuous as possible. He hoped that, if the wolf did dare to crawl in, it would first eat his mama.

Next morning everyone in the yard was discussing what had happened, and it was Dasha who first brought the news. It transpired that the crafty Poles had taken advantage of their neighbours' mood of festive abandon to shift the chairs that divided their own Zone from the Volunteers' – thus managing to grab themselves an extra bit of territory. The Volunteers latched on to these shenanigans, and that's when all the fuss started up.

> 'I took a snooze and woke to see
> My chair was nicked from under me.
> A Pole came up and told me straight:
> Well, there you go – it must be fate,'

the cobbler's boy sang out, and the yard chuckled. Nobody knew who had composed this little ditty, but by evening it was already being sung in all the Zones, each time with the addition of some new couplets. French battleships were anchored just outside the harbour. The city's inhabitants had been much amused by the unusual-looking black zouaves in their colourful turbans. Not to be outdone were the Greek patrols, whose horsemen sat mounted on donkeys. Petlyura's men, who had been about to cut loose once the Germans were gone, had by now left. But even the three weeks over which they had managed to get their spree in were still remembered in the city – especially by the owners of the jewellery shops. The pogrom promised by Petlyura's men did not, however, materialise: the Jewish quarters came under the protection of the criminals. And it was rumoured that Benya Krik had himself ordered his boys to keep the Moldavanka area from violence. At the time, robbery had not been looked upon as an act of violence – provided, of course, the victim had the sense not to make a fuss of it. The spoiled bandits were courteous in their robbing, cracking jokes and striking up conversations 'about the weather'. They even permitted themselves a certain nobility: when, the previous summer, the entire city had been shaken by unexplained explosions, for a period of almost two days many apartments had been left abandoned, with their doors flung wide open – but had anything been taken? Not once: the Moldavanka boys had their own moral code. Things disappeared from the apartments before and after – but not during a misfortune such as that!

The Bolsheviks had gone underground, if not too much into hiding. To some extent, they were the most law-abiding citizens of all: each comrade had a pass into any one of the Zones. It was not for nothing that the finest document-forger, the legendary 'Uncle' Zhora from Rostov, had been plying his trade there on Razumovskaya Street.

Yakov was at this time working under Comrade Lastochkin, and what a magnificent operation he had succeeded in pulling off with the French ships! Of course, not without the help of Comrade Jeanne, who was herself French. But the leaflet calling on the people of Odessa to rise up had, from its first to last line, been composed by Yakov himself, and Comrade Lastochkin had praised it and approved it without amendment. The plan was both ingenious and simple: it was to carry the propaganda campaign to the French, amongst whom there were known to be sympathisers. At the same time, the politically conscious workers were to be stirred to rise up. And then, with support from the sea, they would take back control of the city, and the comrades now positioned just outside the city were to give their support from the north-west. This would be quite a bit smarter than blowing up the artillery shell dump, as they had last August, when they managed to clobber six and a half thousand railway carriages belonging to the Ukrainian-German Directory. Ah, what an explosion that had been: it had rocked the entire city! Unfortunately, it had also caused several parts of the passages inside the catacombs to collapse – nevertheless, it left the Germans without any ammunition. It was a pity that they had not managed to take the city then: no sooner had the Germans skedaddled than the Entente came poking its nose in.

But now, even before spring was in the air, and when the nor'-easter was still blowing through the icy streets, everything was ready: it was time to begin. For the umpteenth time. But they only needed to succeed once. How sunny it was that day! And there for all the city to see from the boulevard was the red flag being hoisted above the *Mirabeau*. Come on then, you gentlemen of France, show us your metal! After all, it's all in your hands – so let's see your solidarity!

But no, the French actually put down their own men, and

nothing further came of the *Mirabeau*. Yakov ranted and raved, but Comrade Lastochkin laughed it off.

'Youth! You want nothing but victories with fanfares. But you don't see that we've won already. The French have too much on their own plate now to come bothering with us – you wait and see.'

And, indeed, on the following morning the French victoriously escorted their men down the Military Slope, where there was a detention centre for the arrested mutineers. And a week after that rumours started to circulate round Odessa that the French were about to weigh anchor and leave. It was also rumoured that the Red ataman Grigoriev was approaching the city.

'They're leaving! The French are definitely leaving!'

Maxim, who brought this news, was trying to keep calm, but it was obvious how excited he was.

'Mama and Papa, listen to me. It's madness to stay here under the Reds. Let's hurry up and pack – taking nothing but essentials. We'll need passes to board the French vessels, but I've already made arrangements for that. There will be room for the Volunteer Army and their families.'

'Well, which of us is in the Volunteer Army, Maxim dear?' asked his mother, shaking her head.

'I am, Mama. I'm sorry I didn't tell you before, but I made my mind up a long time ago. And I got accepted. Things have been looking pretty grim lately, and the army hasn't had many people joining up for it. I forced my way through to see General Tumanovsky in person, and I told him . . . and . . . and there's nothing to discuss. We've got to be there tonight.'

'You, Maxim, may have made up your mind a long time ago, but how about allowing us a bit of time to think it over?' Ivan Alexandrovich retorted angrily. 'Maybe you're right – but let me remind you that, for the time being at least I'm the eldest Petrov. Marina will be back in an hour. You'd better run over to the Teslenkos, if you don't want to waste time, and get them to come over. We're one family, we should decide this together.'

It was an unusual family council. Everyone understood that, whatever decision they now reached as to their fate, they must abide by it – there could be no rethink, no turning back. There were eight of them – it was no joke. No, there were nine: they couldn't abandon Dasha. The turbid pink sunset cast its dusty rays into the Petrovs' living-room. It made the tea in the glasses look completely red. Oleg was under the table, playing about with some empty cotton-reels. The adults looked at one another. They were silent, and everyone wanted to prolong this silence, and not to disrupt everything now, so suddenly. But a decision had to be taken, and the fragile illusion that they were protected could – even were it to continue – be dangerous.

'So, my dears, Maxim has spoken. Now I'd like you all to say what you each think,' said Ivan Alexandrovich, sitting very upright, with a wooden back. Marina cast a pleading glance at her father: couldn't he at least give her a look, or some hint, as to what he was thinking! But she realised that he would speak last. And that meant that Marina would have to risk saying what her father would not like to hear her say. She turned to face her mother, but even she was looking at her husband in exactly the same way as Marina: dreading to make some irremediable mistake.

Anna, on the other hand, had no such fear. Or doubt. She was a wife and mother. She knew how to behave, and nobody could order her about.

'Thank you, Maxim, dear, and you, Ivan Alexandrovich, for thinking about us. The best thing would be to leave now, while there's still a chance. But that isn't feasible for the boy and me. I've already tried travelling with the child, and I don't want to kill my son. God has already spared us once – and that was a miracle in itself. And, apart from that, I promised Pavel that I'd wait for him here in Odessa. I know how many families have lost one another for ever. I believe my husband's alive, and that, no matter when he comes, he'll find me here. And, after all, someone has to stay behind, so that everyone can eventually find each other again.'

She became embarrassed: this last phrase somehow sounded pompous, and, anyway, why had she jumped ahead like that?

'I'm sorry . . .' she added, blushing deeply.

'Well, then,' said the eldest Teslenko, stroking his moustache. 'You, daughter, have judged rightly, but what are we to do if the Bolsheviks do in fact manage to hang on to power? Don't forget that you're an officer's wife. Your mama and I will be here anyway – in case Antos reappears. So we can also send Pavel on to you when he shows up.'

Marina listened with her mouth slightly agape as these new complications arose to this question that had seemed so straightforward. She realised that Maxim was right. The Reds were quite simply madmen, and under them nobody would be left alive. But what right did she have to argue with Anna? She was Olezhek's mother, and she had been through the war, and managed to make the journey down here from 'Peter' during the revolution. But, as for Marina – what experience did she have? None whatsoever, she had not even lived yet!

'My dears, darlings,' she cried suddenly, 'let's go! All of us, before it's too late! We don't have to go to the ends of the earth, after all – not even to France, but just to Novorossiysk! It's our own side there – they won't let us come to any harm. And we needn't take the train – two nights and we're there!'

'But you haven't forgotten the *Portugal*, have you, Marinushka?' her mother enquired gently, stroking her shaking shoulders.

The *Portugal* was a French hospital ship that the Germans had torpedoed back in the war, when the Tsar was still on the throne. At the time it had been the talk of all Odessa: there wasn't a single survivor among either the wounded or the crew.

'Mama, the Bolsheviks have no sea power, and this is an entirely different situation!' Maxim put in hastily, but, as in his childhood, he was checked by a glance from his father.

'Here's what, my dears,' said Ivan Alexandrovich, without rushing. 'Masha, dear, do you mind if I cut this discussion short?'

Maria Vasilyevna merely nodded in silence.

'Maxim and Marina must undoubtedly go,' continued the eldest Petrov. 'I wouldn't dare tell Anna what to do, although I would recommend her to do the same thing, too. But Mother and I will stay here. I dare say these bandits may take the city, but I don't believe they'll keep it for long. And they won't be bothered about old people like us. We managed to get through those two months they were in power last time and, God willing, we'll manage this time, too. But, when everything settles down, you'll all have somewhere to return to. Maxim, let's go through to my study, I've got a bit of money saved up there. You'll need it on your journey. Marina, you go and have a wash and stop crying – you're not a little girl any more. You are, when all's said and done, a nurse, and you'll be needed there. And – that's all. That's enough tragedy – let's have some tea. Dasha, I hope you'll keep an eye on young Marina when you're there?'

Dasha flatly refused to leave: she would stay here with the mistress, and wait for Pavlik. And for her son Vasily. But the youngsters could do as they pleased: she couldn't be in two places at once. And, as for the samovar, she'd go and see to it right away: it had gone all cold without anybody there to keep an eye on it.

Now everything was decided, but there was still a certain uneasiness in the air. In their hearts they were each happy with the decision, but considered that they had chosen the easiest way out for themselves. And, in order to smooth over this uneasiness, they smiled a little more cheerily than they wanted to, and their voices sounded a little more plucky than they felt in their hearts.

It did not take the young Petrovs long to get ready, and there was still time for everyone to sit at table awhile, as of yore. They understood that the moment they got up farewells would have to be bidden, and so they were dragging the moment out. Maria Vasilyevna looked at the children, trying to banish the thought that this might be the last time that she would ever set eyes on them. Her own boy – broad-shouldered, blue-eyed and with the chiselled hands that were so typical of the Petrovs – looked so handsome when he held his guitar. He and Marina loved singing duets together, and they were singing something now – though Maria Vasilyevna's mind was already elsewhere. She simply kept watching them. And watching. Her frail, tender-hearted little girl – how would she manage without her mother? But it was, she realised, her only salvation, and there was no alternative. Ivan was right. But how painful it was! And why, why? What ferocious force was hurling her children out of the nest – one after another? Was it God's will? God could never will such a thing as this! But she could see that, although the children were saddened to be leaving, they were not as saddened as she might have expected. Their eyes were ablaze, and Marina was laughing happily, as though she had not been crying only a moment ago. She looked round at her mother and stopped laughing. And this made it all the more noticeable that she was already looking forward to the forthcoming journey. But her mother's conscience was troubled: she should have let her go on laughing for a bit longer. Only she knew how to laugh like that, in a way that brightened everyone's spirit. Maybe it would be all right? Maybe everything would turn out OK in the end?

> 'Morning misty, morning grey,
> Saddened fields lie covered in snow,
> My thoughts turn all to yesterday,
> And faces that I once did know.'

The youngsters, by now a threesome, were singing that same romantic song of which Pavel had been so fond. Their voices, which had long since blended together, sounded gentle and harmonious. The electricity in the city was now working at half-power, and the yellow light from the lamp fell across the table-cloth, their hands and faces. Dasha was sitting sadly in the corner: what sort of home would it be without the children? A little hand was tugging at the hem of her skirt. The boy, upset that no one was paying him any attention, had for a long time been puffing and panting under the table. And it was with some relief that she dragged him out to change his trousers.

Why couldn't they hurry up and go, and stop breaking her heart!

Then they were gone.

22

The harbour was deserted, and only in the distance, out beyond the lighthouse, was there one French torpedo boat left. This was called a 'blockade from the sea'. Back on land, meanwhile, there began three days of lawlessness. This was precisely the moment for which the celebrated Benya Krik, King of Moldavanka, had been waiting. If any of the bandits had until then had to make do without diamond rings, now even the lowliest of criminals and other such raff managed to come by them. Some, however, preferred opals or emeralds. It was not Benya who instilled special fear in the city's inhabitants, but rather the new and terrible bands that were now ensconced in the catacombs. Of these almost nothing was known, which made them all the more frightening.

At the beginning of March Grigoriev's Red Cavalry entered Odessa. The jolly horsemen with their enormous red bows and ribbons on their shaggy sheepskin hats came riding in to the centre of the city at a leisurely trot. The streets were almost deserted: as usual, everyone was hiding in their homes. However, a brass band that had been hastily assembled by the local Bolsheviks played outside the cathedral. The sun peeped out from behind sculptured clouds and also invited everyone to come out and celebrate. Down the long and unswept streets all sorts of rubbish was blowing about in the spring breeze: a Ukrainian newspaper would go soaring up, like a kite, or a piece of lace be pulled up and tossed over a lamppost. There were cartridge cases rolling about, with their yellow sides gleaming. And each shard of broken glass contrived to reflect and magnify even the puniest little ray. Boys whose mothers found it impossible to keep them at home were having the time of their life: they could go running behind the cavalry yelling 'Hurrah', or march in time with the band, or go running round the smashed stalls and shops, gathering up priceless treasures. These ranged from broken honey cakes to iron bed-knobs that were just right for stuffing with gunpowder and blowing up, like real bombs.

To begin with, the Reds behaved quietly: the newspaper *Izvestiya* came back, now in Bolshevik vein, and, of course, clamorous rallies were held in the squares. But, apart from this, nothing particular happened. They totalled no more than a thousand men for the entire city, although the city did not know this. Ordinary people did not understand how difficult it was for forces such as these to create the illusion of a confident government. And Yakov recalled Khenkin, the singer of comic songs: he knew how to go out alone on stage and make it seem that there was an entire crowd up there – out of nothing! Except himself. And we still have a lot, a lot of practice to do, reflected Yakov with a grin. All right, if we're to master this art – let's practise it then!

'Well, why don't they come and stay with us – it's quiet out where we are,' suggested Mykola. He had brought some fish to sell and, as usual, been round to the homes of his regular customers selling some. The rest he had to leave with the mongers at the bazaar for a pittance: it was terrible how they were now taking advantage of both the fishermen and public alike. Because of the risk. It was no joke, having to work in the bazaar at a time such as this. Mykola was an old acquaintance of the Petrovs, and his brother used to work for them. They were a scatty sort of people, but kind-hearted. Now they were discussing what best to do for Anna and the boy. Mykola knew Anna, the Petrovs' daughter-in-law: she was much nicer than your average Russian, and the way she sang Ukrainian songs was enough to make you cry. And she would help around the house, too. During the spring Khivrya was constantly complaining that her legs got 'all poorly' – his wife was getting on these days. And, besides, town-folk ate so little.

'Come on, daughter, no arguin' – get ready. We've got a goat, so there'll be milk for the little 'un.'

'What if the Reds come sticking their noses in and start asking who they are and what they're doing there? There's been a decree forbidding anyone from leaving the city without permission,' said Ivan Timofeyevich doubtfully. He was expressing doubt mainly for the sake of form: Mykola was, after all, a Ukrainian, one of their own. Who was Anna to him? Yet he had taken pity on her. He would hide her.

'They'll sooner come 'ere than our place. Out where we are, it's quiet. There's not a soul about. There's our house, the sea, and the steppe – and that's it. Who'll bother to come pokin' their nose in round our place? Well, if they do, we'll say she's our daughter. After all, she speaks like one of us.'

Anna's bundles of things were quickly tied up and, setting out beneath the tarred sail of Mykola's trusty boat, both she and the boy were carried away beyond both the Fountains – and safely away from Odessa and all that could happen there.

'Comrades, just listen, will you! There's no need to go overboard. Generally, I'm in favour of the idea, but if we do actually leave everyone with nothing but three sets of shirts and underpants, and one suit and pair of shoes – they'll start shooting at us!' said Yakov heatedly.

'Who will? Ordinary people? You have a poor understanding of crowd psychology, Comrade Geiber,' remarked Achkanov with a wry grin. 'They'll stash away an extra pair of undies, and – so long as they're not found – they'll be happy at that.'

'The entire port will rise up! All the workers! You think they've got nothing more than a change of clothes? I assure you, most of them managed to grab hold of whatever they found lying about, and now they regard it as their lawful booty! Well, let's put it to a vote then!'

This was a mistake for which Yakov was unable to forgive himself. Even supposing that he was, essentially right, he was still sure to lose out to Comrade Achkanov once it was put to a vote. But, as he had made an issue of it, he had only brought this on himself. So now he would have to remain cooped up as a clerk in the Cheka on Marazliyevskaya Street and be glad not to have been expelled from the Party. And leave it for others to work out any operations. People who knew how to curb their long tongues.

Rakhil was having the same dream more and more often. She dreamt of Isaak – still young, happy and strong, dashingly reining in his horse. And she, too, was young, and would run over to his cart with light legs – as she once had in the distant past, when there were still only the three of them.

'Come on. Let's go and get Shimek,' Isaak would say, with his shirt open at the collar, revealing his strong, tanned neck, and laughing the whole time. And Rakhil would grab him by the neck, and then – it was the same every time! – she remembered: who could she get to stay and look after Rimma and Yakov?

And, as soon as she remembered this, before she even had time to say anything, the laughter went out of Isaak's eyes.

'Well, another time then,' he would say indifferently, geeing the horse on. And, with its wheels squeaking, the cart would start rolling over the white dust, down the poplar-lined track that was shimmering in the heat – and off to the steppe. To Shimek. And, suddenly feeling heavier, she would stay behind, now unable to yell out. Unable to call him back. Until next time.

The day of the 'Peaceful Uprising' – the day appointed for the confiscation of all property belonging to the city's inhabitants, except their underpants – for the benefit of the revolution – came on the 13th of May. It had been announced on the previous day in the newspaper, but the issue of the newspaper had been wisely delayed until midday. The city had electricity, but the inhabitants were forbidden from turning it on – so it was impossible to read the newspaper in the evening. Kerosene and candles had been unavailable for a long time, and without any oil, the wick-lamps were useless. There was no point in giving the stingy inhabitants of the city time to prepare: it was better to catch them unawares. And, if anyone was not familiar with the decree, then it was their own fault.

Rakhil did not read the newspapers at all, and one fresh May morning, suspecting nothing, she took up her customary place in the queue for the tap. Fortunately, there was still water in their yard, but there was no longer enough pressure for it to reach the apartments, and, even from the tap in the yard, the water now flowed in a thin trickle. The neighbours were already queuing by the tap, as well as one or two new faces from some of the neighbouring yards. They were swapping news. Why does anyone need newspapers when there's the yard?

'Oh, Rakhilya, I see your children are already important people – so why does their mama have to come running for water!' intoned Madam Weinsbein as Rakhil drew up beside her with her bucket.

'Madam Weinsbein, it's quite true that I see little of them, but I wish you as many blessings as my children have brought me!' replied Rakhil with dignity.

'She's jealous someone's got children that've gone out into the world and even got to be commissars!' piped up the cobbler Borya the Lame from the basement.

Rakhil always 'kept face' in front of others, though this had touched on a sore point: the children spent their entire time working and working, but surely they could still come home for the night? And why was it that, if a person was at all important to the Soviet regime, they had to work virtually round the clock? And what sort of work could anyone be up to at night? Her children would drop by once a week, bringing their food rations – they couldn't be faulted there, they were very good about that! – give her a peck on the cheek and then be off before they even had time to sit with their own mother awhile. To say nothing of telling her something about what they were doing. And, as for the heartache they caused her – no, they did not understand.

And the drivel that people came out with down by that tap: why, they were saying that today the Reds were going to come and take everything away, and someone had asked Rakhil if she thought they ought to go and stay with some acquaintances out in the suburbs. But she merely brushed this aside. What funny ideas people took into their heads! And she set off to see Madam Kegulikhes. It was a long time since she had last been paid for her visits, though now, thank goodness, her need was no longer quite so pressing. Yet she had grown attached to the old woman, and, just as before, she was happy enough to go there. It was a familiar walk. There was the poster saying 'Sport for all!' on what used to be widow Voskresenskaya's house. And there was a chair standing by the entrance, with a Red Army soldier slumped on it. Guarding the people's property. Now that they had been driven from Russia, there were a lot of them here. And now it turned out that ataman Grigoriev was an enemy: he had gone off with his cavalry to join Makhno. Because he was anti-Semitic, said Yakov: he did not want any Jews in the Soviets. There were the tribunes decorated with strips of red left over from the May Day procession. Now the calendar had been changed: today ought really to have been the first of May, although, in fact, it was almost a fortnight ago. And they had put back the clocks, too: now it was three hours earlier than it used to be in the old days. They were in a hurry. This was a young regime, and its blood was up. A lorry went by, and in the back there was a student in a red scarf and some girls and sailors with rifles. Were they heading for a rally? And then there were more and more lorries.

Rakhil could already hear the shouts and shooting some way away, and she hurried to see what all the noise was.

'What are you doing? Just what – you dogs – do you think you're doing?'

Dishevelled and dressed in nothing but her night-shirt, Madam Kegulikhes was out in the yard desperately fretting over her eldest son who lay motionless on the cobbles. His gingery beard was streaming with red. Their door was flung wide open, and the sailors and girls that had overtaken her on the way here were busy taking something from the house. And feathers were flying from the bedding, just as they had at Nikolayev, and screams could be heard from the neighbouring apartments. The whole yard was in uproar, and it was terrifying.

'Help, people. The Reds are robbing us!'

'Pour boiling water on the bitch! Get your hands off!'

Again there was a crackle of gunshot, but so great was the uproar that it made it seem very quiet. Pogrom. This was a pogrom, and, losing her mind, Rakhil started running without any idea as to where she was going. She had to find someone. The boy – where was the boy? And by now the entire street was in uproar, and the city was in uproar, and the sea, too.

In the evening Yakov returned home exhausted. He had enough sense not to remind his comrades that it had turned out exactly as he had said it would. Of course, the factories had come to a standstill: everyone had gone racing home to try and protect their property, including even the Communists. Panic had spread through the city, and a riot started. Despite the threats to shoot anyone who resisted, there was someone shooting from almost every building: who in Odessa did not have their own gun nowadays? And, of course, they had to put a stop to the requisitioning. It had not even lasted half a day when, with heavy hearts, they had been forced to call off the 'Peaceful Uprising' for fear of losing control. Maybe it was really a good thing that Yakov ended up having nothing to do with it all. He had spent the entire day in bitter silence poring over some atrociously written papers and putting them into order. Sort it out yourselves, comrades. Didn't he tell them that at least the workers and Soviet staff members should be exempted from the searches? And the whole operation had been planned shambolically – they just let things take their own course. Of course, in the morning the chairman of the Cheka, Comrade Severny, had been told that some bandits were robbing the inhabitants, using forged Bolshevik warrants. It was, so to speak, a spontaneous mass action. But they should have foreseen it.

He walked past the statue of Catherine the Great, who, from head to foot, was smothered in red rags and bound in rope. Apart from feeling annoyed, there was also something else that was unpleasant: as often happens, his memory was nagging him over something that he could not put his finger on. Dombach. Where had he come across the name Dombach? He could not get it off his mind. He had seen it in the lists of people who had been shot – in that list that had included the twenty-six Black Hundreds. Earlier in the day Yakov had collated these lists in a single register for submission to Moscow. There had not been a Dombach in their class at the gymnasium, nor was there one among the neighbours. His memory was playing him up: that's what came of exhaustion, they said. The pink candles of the horse-chestnuts stood motionless in the evening air. There was not the slightest wind, the air was like spring, and Yakov flung open his jacket. He would sit with his mother awhile and drink tea with her. He had abandoned her altogether. He was sick of this Dombach, and – besides – he was dead now, anyway!

The door was open, so he did not even have to take out

his key. He heard something crunch underfoot. Stop – where was everything? The table was upturned, and the dusty corner, where the piano had been, was now empty . . . And where was his mother?

He found Rakhil on the floor in the kitchen. It was terrible to see her sitting in the twilight, with her back to the window and shaking her head.

'Mama, Mamochka, what's the matter?'

'Yakov, my child. Thank God you're here. But what about Rimma – is she alive?'

'Mama, what's up? Has somebody been here?'

'Pogrom – didn't you know there's been a pogrom? A neighbour spat in my eye out in the yard today. It's funny, I was robbed and spat at, too. My son, tell them that it wasn't you. This was ataman Grigoriev's doing, wasn't it? Or was it Petlyura that did it? Silly people, going and getting everything muddled like that. But where's Rimmochka? Ah, what a poor memory I've got – I left her with Madam Dombach.'

Yakov gasped.

Then there was a brief rumble out by the entrance, and a lorry came into the yard. It stopped directly beneath their windows, and Rakhil gave a little start. Rimma came flying in, clearly excited.

'Mama, hello! Yakov, you're here, too! Good, you can give me a hand. I've been given one or two things as a bonus, and the comrades have brought them over in the lorry. Quick – come and help me unload them. They can't hang around, they've got another two places to go to after here. Mama, what are you doing down on the floor like that? I've got such a nice coat for you: come and see! It's just the job for autumn . . .'

Rakhil wearily raised herself up and looked out of the window. By now the yard had calmed down, and by this time of the evening nobody was expecting any further to-do. But downstairs a door slammed, and the neighbouring windows were accosted by a piercing scream that kept echoing around the yard, as in a well.

'You Petlyurovite! You pogrom-maker! Damn you – damn every one of you! You Bolshevik scum! You Denikinite! May you never live to see your own children! May you pay for every drop of Jewish blood!'

Heads peered out of the dark windows. Madam Geiber – yes, it was Madam Geiber. That sweet little commissar daughter of hers had brought her mama some stolen goods. But her mama was telling her what a naughty girl she'd been. Had she really cursed her – or had they misheard?

'Madam Geiber! Say that again – it's so nice to hear it!'

Yakov managed to carry his mother back inside the apartment. She could not stop crying and shaking her head. Rimma was standing by the door in a state of bewilderment: any attempt she made to embrace her mother simply made her start screaming.

'Wait a bit, Rimma. It's just a fit of nerves. We had one or two things requisitioned ourselves while we were away. You go through to the other room for a while. Or Mama won't be able to get the pogrom off her mind. She's upset.'

'How could they possibly requisition anything from us? What were you doing? I came back into the city just an hour ago, after we'd been rounding up some performing artists from the trains. What happened here anyway?'

'What happened!' erupted Yakov. 'There was no plan, no lists – nothing! So how can we possibly now tell who was requisitioning things and who was pocketing them! Maybe it was our men acting by mistake, or maybe it was looters! And now you come here with your bonus! Get out of here, I tell you! There's some valerian in the kitchen – go and get some drops ready.'

He was so worked up that he even called his sister a fool, but this was really so uncalled for that she became understanding and took no offence.

It turned out that, in her madness, Rakhil was not so wrong after all: the following night the Red Army soldiers at the Big Fountain mutinied and went off in search of Jews to beat up. They smashed the few stalls that were still intact and killed fourteen or fifteen commissars – to say nothing of the number of ordinary Jews they killed. The fun soon spread across the steppe: off they went with torches and guns. They went searching by the cliffs, and shot the ones who threw themselves into the sea.

And all this rabble had somehow to be brought to order and restrained. And on top of that the designated contribution of 500 million still had to be exacted from the Odessan bourgeoisie. How could it be done, without taking hostages?

But then Denikin took Kharkov. The revolution was in danger! The only salvation was the Red terror! Let the bourgeoisie choke in its own blood. Let them abandon all hope that the English and the French could still come and save them. Let them know that the Bolshevik regime was powerful, and that, if the Bolsheviks did have to leave the city, they would not do so without slaughtering all their class enemies. Without understatement, *Izvestiya* was now printing the figures of those shot, mixing this with jokes: 'The carp likes to be fried in sour cream.'

Marazliyevskaya Street, where the Cheka was based, became a terrible place. Rumours started to circulate about the nightmarish Lyalka von Germgross, an investigating officer who forced people's heads down the lavatory before shooting them. And that the new chairman Kalinichenko was even more ferocious than Severny had been. And that there was some sort of revolutionary black man called Johnston, and that he actually skinned people alive. And there was also the young woman Dora Yavlinskaya, who was crazy about mass shootings, and the executioners Amur and Vikhman ... and plenty of other rumours, besides. That's the whole point of terror – to make people frightened.

But it was also necessary to get the city back to normal. And to attend to the cultural work among the masses. It turned out that the water pipes could not work without energy. It was necessary to dismantle the celebrated pier down which grain had been transported to the port. Luckily, it was a huge great construction, and it was wooden. Firewood was always needed, and anyway the port was blockaded. And it was necessary to force the unconscious citizens to come and attend the rallies, and also to recruit some performing artists. Get them to sing in between the speeches – that's what attracted the public.

The day that was to be so galling for Rimma began so well. And the weather could not have been better. And it so happened that he was to be one of the artists recruited to perform. Yura

Morfessi, the very same! The king of gypsy song, the city darling! But for Rimma – still He. Adolescent love was a lot of rubbish, of course. And her hankerings were silly, and she herself was no more than an overexcited girl. But her heart started pounding the moment she set eyes on him again. He still cut the same imposing and dashing figure, and his eyes and hair were like black fire. And now he, the idol of her youth, was about to come out in public and declare his support for the Bolsheviks! But first Rimma had to make a speech. At last, he would hear her. Would he recall the girl from the gymnasium? No matter – so we meet again, Comrade Morfessi!

Never before had she performed with such passion. She felt as though this were not an amorphous crowd, but a single man. And he had to be convinced, this man: Soviet power was young, and it was being born, like a child – in pain and blood. But this was only the start of the great road that lay ahead. And when they had won there would be no more famine, nor prisons, and the provisional need for terror would be over. They would all be brothers, and life would be as wonderful as a song.

She did not see the philistines tittering, and did not hear their whispers and mocking banter.

'Hey, it's little miss commy!'

'Go easy on them blessings – we're up to our necks as it is! What about the Red Building – time for a new colour? Or you gonna leave it like it is – as a reminder?'

This was just about the only building that the Bolsheviks had erected: a new prison that had, furthermore, been painted red. Comrade Anulov also gave a speech. He explained away the temporary hardships, and promised imminent abundance. The crowd became restless. They did not dare to disperse, but neither did they applaud. This, comrades, might not be a flop – but it wasn't doing much good, either.

'And now our Soviet entertainer Morfessi, who is already so well known to you all, will sing a song to raise the revolutionary spirit!'

And he was led out on to the tribune. The crowd stirred. Everyone realised that, like it or not, now he would have to sing something. If he launched into the 'Internationale', or perhaps the 'Marseillaise', that would mean that he really had gone over to their side. But if he sang something old, like 'The Wide Sea', for example, that would mean that he hadn't. Everyone was longing to see which side Morfessi would come down on. And out he came with the gypsy song:

> 'I tell you, boy, you're daft to go,
> You're daft to go and roam,
> With tail tucked in and head hung low
> You'll soon be heading home.'

And on he sang, right the way through to the end. Well, what of it? It was a popular gypsy song, from his gramophone repertoire. No messing around for Morfessi – this was smack in the eye! Oh, how they laughed. Oh, how they joined in the singing. Oh, what an ovation they gave him – they were beside themselves! And why not? They were applauding the show. A Soviet show. They had been told to come, and now they were applauding.

Oh, how Rimma longed to have this entire crowd of bourgeois revellers shot. If need be, with machine-guns! To ensure that not a single one of them got away. Scoundrels. There it was, a knife in the back of the revolution – from these sniggering snouts! She had never understood Dora: how ghastly it must be to shoot people with your own hand. And everyone in the Cheka considered her slightly mad. But now, it seemed, she could understand her. Or perhaps not entirely? Well, fine: at least fire above their heads, and leave each one of them standing in their own puddle. But it wasn't feasible. So she had to smile and pretend that everything was hunky-dory. And, in front of a crowd of about ten thousand people, it wasn't even possible to arrest this traitor Morfessi. But no doubt in due course Dombrovsky would intercede on his behalf. Her first love was in ruins, engulfed in flames – but Rimma went on smiling, and held her head proudly.

Commissar Dombrovsky, the Commandant of Odessa, really was a most peculiar sort of individual, with quite inexplicable sympathies for the rotten intelligentsia. It was just as Rimma suspected: he did, indeed, intercede on Morfessi's behalf, and the hooligan got off scot-free. Dombrovsky's views were, of course, later brought to light and he was shot, but Morfessi was by then out of reach: he had managed to slip away abroad. Though by then Rimma could no longer care.

Yakov was now having a hard time of it: his mother's illness was dragging on. There were times when she did not even recognise Yakov and times when she called him Shimek. It was impossible for him to give up his job at the Cheka: at a time like this it would be seen as sabotage. He had to hire a woman to come and look after Rakhil. But he did now try and come home at night. No matter how befuddled his mother might be, she still smiled whenever he was tender, and became almost like she had been before, and sometimes even stopped shaking her head. And that was another thing he mustn't put off any more: he had to go and see the Petrovs and find out how they were doing. Most importantly – how was Marina? After all, she could also be in trouble, if only for her upper-class origins. And he definitely mustn't allow that to happen.

He had never understood his attitude to Marina. He only knew that this girl was quite special. He would have liked to change everyone on earth, in order to get them to adopt the right way of thinking. Including Maxim, and all his family. They were good people, after all – they just needed their brains washed out. Marina was the only person in whom he would have changed nothing, even if he did find it impossible to imagine her as a revolutionary. But she could not be an enemy of the revolution. She was the only person he knew who could not be an enemy to anyone. And why should she be? Why not let her go on simply laughing and looking about with her grey eyes? He knew that he was not in love – there were other girls for that sort of stuff. But she was different, and he had to defend and protect her just as she was. Even if he was no longer an important figure in the Party, there were still one or two things he could do. And it was time to put an end to this foolish quarrel with Maxim. Not that they really had quarrelled, anyway – they had just fallen out over some trifle. It was ignoble waiting for someone else to take the first step. It was for him to act nobly himself. He should go and see him right away and be perfectly candid with him. And offer him help. It wasn't as if he was a stranger to them, after all – they'd known him ever since he was a little boy. But once he had come across Ivan Alexandrovich and he'd pretended not to notice him. He had clearly been embarrassed in case he might be thought to be pestering Yakov.

But there was a seal on the Petrovs' door, and – with the very worst of presentiments – he had to try and find out why.

'The Petrovs? Well, they had to move out of the main apartment. There's going to be a people's court here,' the yard-cleaner explained to Yakov, as though he had just fallen from the moon. 'That's where they are now – over in that corner, on the way down to the loo.'

Ah, so that was why Yakov hadn't seen any of them recently! He found the door down to the semi-basement and knocked. The Petrov parents opened it, both standing in the doorway.

'Hello, Ivan Alexandrovich! Maria Vasilyevna, good day!'

'Ah, Yakov. Hello. Have you come to arrest us? How nice: at least it's someone we once knew.'

Yes, they really had addressed him with the formal 'you'! They were very polite and watched him as though he were a stranger. And no matter how Yakov tried to break the ice – nothing helped. No, Marina, thank God, was not in the city. And neither was Maxim. Where were they? Well, of course the Cheka had a right to be interested. But they were happy to inform him that they did not even know themselves. Did they need any support or protection? No, thank you very much. They had already been well and truly robbed – which was evidently now called confiscation for the benefit of the people, wasn't it? They no longer had anything that could be taken, so it was hardly likely that anyone would be interested in them now. Who needed an old and destitute couple? The only conceivable reason might be to take them as bourgeois hostages. Well, that didn't frighten them, either. The old Teslenko couple had recently been shot. Well, they were lucky – they died on the same day . . .

Yakov could bear it no longer. He ran away in shame. So that was why they had been treating him like a leper! Antos's parents, who always used to receive Yakov so kindly . . . Did that mean that they had still been alive when they were covered in tarpaulin, transported out of the city, shot and thrown into a common grave? Had they stood embracing one another, or how had it been? What, in fact, did happen when people were shot? He had no idea, all he did was rewrite and correct papers like a convict, and he didn't get to see all of the papers, either. How could he go and explain that to them now? How could he exonerate himself, and claim that he knew nothing of it? And anyway he was guilty: why hadn't he pursued the matter earlier? But what could he have done?

That night Yakov got drunk and went off to Marusya. Not to the committee, as it had once been called, but to a seamstress that he knew. Everything was simple there, and Marusya smelt of laundered clothing, cheap perfume and that whiff of woman that made his nostrils dilate. And she did not ask him about anything, and spoke about nothing whatever, but immediately wound up the gramophone. To stop the neighbours from hearing.

No, the Teslenko parents had not stood embracing one another. They, like all the other hostages, had had their hands bound in wire. They had simply huddled up to one another's shoulders as the barge slowly pulled away from the shore over the pitch-black water. Their batch was not to be shot: now that Denikin was getting nearer, the Bolsheviks had already started saving on cartridges. Instead, they had simply thrown them into the water – with a stone, of course. There were plenty of stones in the bay, there was no need to save on stones.

All in all, they were lucky. And they had not been tortured: they were down in the lists, not as a family of wreckers, but as Poles. A lot of Poles had been taken hostage at the time, and that was why they had rounded them up, too – because of Vanda Kazimirovna. They were not separated for long: the Bolsheviks were now keen to hurry up and get the liquidations over with, for they did not have enough places for those facing the more serious charges. And they had found themselves next to one another on the barge: wasn't it a miracle? They had even been able to kiss and ask one another forgiveness for everything, everything. And to thank God that they were going to Him together. It was dark, and they had not been able to see one another's eyes. Soon after that the command rang out, and then came the splashes: the first, the second . . . A woman started screaming, but her screams were soon swallowed in the pervasive silence.

'Lord, save Thy people . . .' someone sang out the church refrain. That meant there was a priest there, too. Or a deacon.

They hoped that now their difference of faith would be at an end, and that the Lord would forgive them their greatest sin: that they had loved one another more than anything or anybody. More than any church, or the Poles, or the Ukrainians. And even more than their own children. Had the children ever guessed?

But they still had time to pray: for all three of them.

23

Mykola's home was a spacious, clay-walled cottage that was, in the traditional manner, whitewashed with lime both inside and out. It had an enormous stove with a stove couch and all sorts of niches and abutments that were also whitewashed. Icons draped in embroidered towels looked out from the corner. There was a table with its top scraped clean and some broad benches. There was also a frame for mending the nets on 'rotten' days. But that summer there were hardly any 'rotten', stormy days, and Mykola mended his nets outside. Anna quickly saw how she could help him. The running of the household was kept basic: the water Anna fetched from a well down in a little hollow, and there was a scrawny cock, a small brood of chickens, and a goat with a broken horn. The house itself was managed by the middle-aged, chubby and risible Khivrya. She was glad to receive Anna and her child: at least now there would be someone to chat with once in a while. Mykola was taciturn, and usually replied to all Khivrya's remarks with 'ah-hah' or 'right'. And a fine thing it is when man and wife don't argue – but it can also be dull at times. Khivrya was in the habit of talking to the goat, cursing the hens, and even shouting at the iron pots and the bowls – but it wasn't the same.

Now she 'got going' with new energy. The boy soon came to feel at home, and stamped his bare little feet on the clay floor and called Khivrya 'granny'. The way Khivrya saw it, he called for special attention because he was 'over-shy': whenever there was a loud noise he threw himself at Anna and froze, tucking his head under her arm. But Khivrya knew a cure for that, as her grandma had been a sorceress and taught Khivrya the odd thing or two. Khivrya even knew how to cast spells. Sinful as it was, that was how she had got a dashing young fisherman to marry her: all you had to do was wash the floor and wipe the sweat off your brow with a piece of bread. And then get whoever you wanted to fall in love with you to eat the bread. Mykola never knew about this, and they lived happily, and had brought up a son and a daughter. But the son had gone off to be a sailor with the Greeks and settled down in Kherson, and, as far as the daughter was concerned, she had married a decent sort of man who had taken her off to Constantinople, where they ran three coffee-houses. And now the house felt empty.

There was plenty for Khivrya to 'get going' with now, though: for a start, she had to drive the fright out of the boy. She waited till the first star appeared and brought a freshly laid egg, and then took off Oleg's shirt and started rolling the egg over his chest and tummy. As she did this, she muttered something, and Anna became rather frightened. It was, of course, sheer superstition, but it was still unsettling. Oleg was also pretty subdued, and watched her with round eyes. Then she made the sign of the cross over the child, and he immediately started balling with relief. After this she broke the egg over a bowl and held it out to Anna:

'Go and throw it away in the weeds! That's his fright gone.'

Anna could not believe her eyes: when she shook the egg the liquid inside was reluctant to come away from the shell, and it was impossible to tell the yolk from the egg-white. It had all come together in crystals, leaving a formation of sharply defined tips and edges in the bottom of the bowl.

What it was Anna could never understand, but Oleg really did stop jumping in fright whenever one of the iron pans made a loud clatter, and even the May storms had no effect on him. And out here those were the only loud noises there were. There was just the wind rustling through the weeds and the sound of the sea. Anna became tanned and grew stronger, and her clothing became permeated with the smell of thyme, which Khivrya dried in the house. Oleg ran about with nothing but his shirt on, fought with the cockerel and spiritedly helped Khivrya sweep the floor with her wormwood broom. His hair became so sunburnt that it turned white, his nose peeled, and in the evenings Khivrya smeared him with sour goat's milk to 'soothe the sunburn'. Odessa seemed far, far away, as, too, did the rest of the world. Oh, how nice it would have been to stay on that quiet coast and live like that for ever and ever. Waiting for the 'broad' wind, helping Mykola unload the quivering mackerel from his boat, and mending the nets.

As soon as he caught any mackerel they had to be sold: needles, salt, bread, kerosene, and other bits and pieces were needed. And then along came the accursed 'Moldavan' wind, and Mykola went off to the city: anyway he couldn't go fishing now. That night he did not come back, but Anna and Khivrya were not worried. Once the 'Moldavan' started blowing, it went on for three days, and sometimes a whole week.

Mykola came back looking downcast, and he said little. All that Anna managed to understand was that 'them Bolsheviks are goin' quite berserk, I tell you', and that it had become very difficult to sell fish now. Even so, Mykola did manage to bring some things home with him. He had not been to Koblevskaya Street for fear of being tailed on the way up there, and so he knew nothing about the old folk. And so life went on until August.

'Well, daughter, them Bolsheviks 'ave 'ad it this time!' Mykola brought the news from one of his regular trips to the city. 'Denikin's landed at the Big Fountain!'

For his part, Mykola expected nothing good from either the Whites or the Reds. He disliked the Whites because they were 'a load o' bloody Russians' lording about the place with their Moscow ways: the Muscovite was forever coming and 'sitting on the neck' of the Ukrainian, and, even when you did give him a ride, he was still after you with his whip. But as for the Reds, they were paupers – they'd eat the liver out of any man as could make a decent living for himself. They were trying to drive everyone into a commune, and, once there, they'd force them all to sleep under the same blanket. At least under the Whites you could sell fish without being hassled.

He ferried Anna back to the city.

'Go and see how your folk're doin' – and you can always come back to us if you want.'

He accompanied Anna to Koblevskaya Street, thinking better

of letting her go off alone with the child. And he was right. They climbed the little streets leading up from the port and found everything in pandemonium.

'Hold him, the devil! Got you now – bastard commissar!'

'Let me get at him, you people – I'll poke out his eyes!'

There was a short howl, and a cluster of people swarmed round a body that was already flat on the ground. They all wanted to get in some more kicks. They had been rounding up the Bolsheviks who had not managed to escape and were now busy meting out justice and reprisals on the spot. Anna tried to stop herself from shaking so as not to frighten the boy. It was all sickening, however understandable. Once again, the cycle of revenge was coming full circle, and it would go on and on doing so, and no one knew how to break free from it. She had seen this so often before. Men running about a square with bloody hands, and women, too. And yelling something that it was impossible to make out. Almost everybody was wearing crudely made 'woodies' on their feet – what other footwear was available in Odessa now? And the clatter of woodies on the cobbles made it seem as if a crowd of many thousands were running, although really there were no more than two or three hundred. Look, don't turn away – you have to live with these people.

After taking a closer look, Anna sighed with relief: the red wasn't blood. Blood wasn't like that, as Anna knew only too well. In fact, they had been demolishing the Cheka jail and, as there had been some overnight rain, they were now daubed in paint – red paint. As for what they found inside the jail, Anna tried not to listen. It was too dreadful. One thing was clear: they found no one alive.

A velvet hum spread over the city: it was the pealing of cathedral bells. And the closer to home that Anna got, the louder became the roars and sounds of rejoicing. Some resplendent squadrons of cavalry went riding past the cathedral to the strains of a march of the Preobrazhensky regiment. Women wept and rushed forward to kiss their stirrups.

'Colonel Tugan-Baranovsky! There he is – he's the one in front on the black horse!'

'We've made it! Oh, what duckies – that's our boys!'

But when Anna got home nobody opened the door, and neither did she come across any of the neighbours as she went down the resonant staircase. The only thing to do now was go to the Petrovs and see if her mother and father were there. But there was an unintelligible seal hanging on the Petrovs' door. Good Lord, what was it? The cool-headed Mykola told her to wait somewhere out of the way and not to fret, while he went off to find out what it meant. A few minutes later he returned.

'Didn't I tell you everything'd be all right! It's just that the Bolsheviks forced them out of the apartment.'

Maria Vasilyevna opened the door, dressed in a darned blue dress and with woodies on her feet. She immediately clasped hold of Anna and the boy, and started crying without saying a word.

This time Yakov and Rimma did not remain underground. You couldn't afford to fool around with Denikin. The Bolsheviks were hastily decamping: for the time being, at least, they had to get out. The Cheka issued Yakov with papers in a new name. Now he was a Russian, Yakov Krasnov. The change of name was vital, Yakov was told. The Whites were taking especially cruel reprisals against Jews, and treating them all as commissars. And even among the 'Red Cossacks' there were also some unconscious anti-Semites.

'But what am I supposed to do about my nose?' asked Yakov with a shrug.

They laughed, and Comrade Yakov Krasnov, the clerk in the Staff of the Fourth Red Division, set off to the battle zones of the civil war. Rimma also got a post – on a PolitDep train. They were not clear about what to do with their mother: neither of them could take her with them, but nor could they leave her to the mercy of Denikin's intelligence service. However, Borya the Lame promised to keep an eye on Rakhil – and cobblers did OK no matter what regime was in power. Yakov and Rimma left him with all the money and valuables. Borya and his wife were decent, reliable people.

The brigade commander, Gorbal, disliked commissars. Those four-eyed busybodies went poking their snouts in everywhere, and their every other word was 'discipline'. He hoped they would all choke on that discipline of theirs – this was not the tsarist army, but the Red Cossack Cavalry! What was the function of command? It had to ensure force was applied where force was needed. And to provide artillery support. And to send in the infantry, where need be, and prevent the horses from being killed. As for food and clothing – that went without saying. And, seeing as none of this was actually ever done on time, and seeing as the brigade was thrown in here, there and everywhere, and against forces that were two or three times bigger – you needed more than discipline to cope with that. This was work for the soul – you had to let your soul do the guiding. To rouse the wild beast in the boys, and the horses, too: oh, that was the life of a free fighting man! No holding back. No impediments. And don't you try and cramp our style – or we'll crush you! That was how to take a city with a single brigade. Or a railway junction. In fact, you could take anything you liked, just so long as you let the fighting man free to get on with it and avoided mucking up his pleasures with all that namby-pamby stuff.

So when he had a clerk from General Staff foisted on him, Gorbal was not overjoyed. He was not, of course, too strong on grammar himself, but someone had to write the reports to the General Staff. Although, come to think of it, who the devil needs those papers anyway? We're fighting for freedom, and what sort of freedom can we have if we're ruled by paper? Now an entire squadron in the third brigade had gone over to Makhno: sick to death of their commissars, they were – that's what that was. And, even though this Krasnov clerk didn't have a pair of specs on the end of his snout, he still had a snout that Gorbal didn't much care for. And so he slipped a wink to the commander of the first squadron: let's see this here comrade gets over to the auxiliary carts – not any old how, but with an escort of honour. To knock that Staff bumptiousness out of him and get him nice and silky.

'So where's your horse, brother?' Yakov was fondly asked by the round-faced fighter Kryzh, who was in the first squadron and had a magnificent tuft of hair flowing beneath his sheepskin hat.

'Need a horse, do I? They sent me here without one . . .'
replied Yakov in surprise, and they all howled with laughter:
the fun was starting.

'We know your real place is back with them auxiliary carts,
but – even so – this is the cavalry, not a dog's arse. You'll get
nowhere without a horse.'

'Why don't them auxiliaries let him have Grinya!'

Again they howled with laughter: Grinya was the brigade
goat, its pride and joy. And he knew how to take his vodka
when he got it, too, and went into the attack bleating wildly
and with his horns down, boosting the morale of the fighters.

But Kryzh was not going to leave it at that. Anyone working
in the auxiliaries wasn't supposed to have a horse, as he knew
perfectly well. So they had to get their fun in with this clerk
now before he managed to get to the auxiliaries!

'Know how to ride a horse?'

'I'll learn, if I have to,' said Yakov, twigging the nature of
the game and seizing his one chance.

'Attaboy! That's my kind of talk! Quit laughing, you devils –
he's going to learn! Give the man a horse, you scoundrels! Give
him that one Andrienko had before he died – bring Zhivchik!'

The 'dead' Andrienko was back in no time grinning broadly
and leading the grey, white-legged Zhivchik. Only a thorough-
going idiot could believe that this splendid-looking horse with
bands on his freshly groomed mane was a horse with no owner.
But idiotic was precisely what this clerk looked like. And when
Zhivchik reared up, he stepped back.

'Oo-ooh – what a horse!'

The boys were in for such a laugh that some lay down while
others sat so as to soften the fall, but all their faces wore an
expression of furious earnestness. Andrienko had thoughtlessly
spoiled part of the fun by bringing Zhivchik already saddled. But
no matter. Zhivchik was a lively horse, and he loved a good joke.
Zhivchik wouldn't let them down.

'Take a firm grip of the reins, and if he gives you any trouble,
give him a good whack across the withers with them,' Kryzh
instructed in a tone of concern. He even held the stirrup for the
clerk, who awkwardly jumped up on to Zhivchik on the flat of
his stomach: in his leather overcoat and high spurless boots he

looked like a crow with a big beak. He flapped his leg about, and his foot caught the other stirrup.

'Which are the reins? These straps here?' he enquired.

'Those are the ones. Grab them, brother. Take this side in one hand, and that side in the other. Oh, what a clever boy! Go-orn!'

Andrienko gave Zhivchik a light slap across his croup: go on, enjoy yourself. But Zhivchik was bewildered and remained standing still.

'So what do I do now?' asked the clerk trustingly, and they all roared with laughter.

'Like I said: whack the reins on his withers – go on!'

The clerk duly did as he was told, and the horse broke into a gallop. The unfortunate clerk was flung back like a sack, but he clung on and, wobbling about in an ungainly fashion, and swaying to right and to left, he went flying off where the horse wanted to take him – and Zhivchik was taking him to the small ravine. The boys knew that when he reached the edge of the ravine, Zhivchik would come to a sudden halt, sending the rider flying over his head into a bramble bush, and from there he would go hurling on down to the little stream where he would either cool off or break his neck. Assuming, of course, that he hadn't fallen off before he got to the little ravine. They were laughing as merrily as little children.

But Kryzh was the first to stop laughing. The clerk's cap came flying off and he turned round to grab hold of it. But somehow the cap went flying on in front. And somehow he managed to grab hold of it, the dog, and, so as to make it all the funnier, he put it back on his head crookedly, tossing his rein across from one hand to the other. And Kryzh realised that this rider had the odd trick or two up his sleeve. He was clowning about. But to do that on Zhivchik you had to know a bit more than just how to stay in the saddle. And, when he reached the edge of the little ravine and threw himself back, he did not forget, for the fun of it, to start waving one hand around in the air, while with the other hand he reined in hard – and Kryzh realised just who, in fact, was having the fun.

Yakov rode over to the boys and naively asked, 'So how do I get down, comrades?'

And once again the comrades started roaring – this time at his, Yakov's joke.

It was not as if from that moment on the brigade came to look on Yakov as 'one of the boys'. But what he learnt from Sergei Alexandrovich had spared him from this initial humiliation. Good old Sergei Alexandrovich. Yakov hung on to the reputation of the 'clerk with the tricks', and some of his mistakes were even taken as being tricks. One mistake that Yakov was quick to correct was the way he spoke. For some reason he thought he had to talk to common people in a way that was readily understandable – in other words, simply. It turned out that nothing could be further from the truth. You had to talk in a convoluted sort of way. Which he could take off Gorbal, for example.

'Our dear comrade lies in our midst, cold and lifeless. His warm heart was pierced by a bullet of the class enemy, the White Guard, that scum with golden epaulettes that we, comrades, will thrash without mercy, even though they may outnumber us and show the bravery of bandits. Back in the sunny Cossack village of Krinichnaya his old parents have now been left orphaned. His steed weeps tears of blood, and scrapes the ground with his hoof, calling for stern revolutionary vengeance for our brave and fallen fighter Terenty Pavlichenko,' said Gorbal, and a single salvo was fired over the grave. Such speeches went down well, and those who could express themselves using these unexpected turns of phrase commanded respect. Yakov quickly realised that there was no need for him to avoid words that they would find unintelligible: enigmatic expressions had a strong impression on fighters, just as on children.

But getting on with the brigade, and even with the moody Gorbal, was only half the battle. He had also to learn the ways of revolutionary ruthlessness. In theory, this was all well and good. But the practice came hard to Yakov. He found it hard enough putting down a wounded horse. And there was no need for them to run away with the idea that a clerk was good for nothing but poring over papers and writing articles for *The Red Cavalryman*. There could be no narrow specialisation during the civil war. If they were in retreat, the auxiliaries had to shoot their own hopelessly wounded. They could not be left to fall into enemy hands alive. If they advanced, and occupied some small place, or a city, then you had to identify who was, and who was not, the enemy. The Cheka would then deal with the hidden enemy, but it was their job to exterminate all possible resistance. In Zhitomir, Yakov managed to save a rabbi from being shot simply by dragging him down the street by his beard, to the raucous laughter of the Cossacks, and then dumping him in a heap of manure. The rabbi had sense enough to stay there. But he also had time enough to glance into Yakov's eyes – and in those rabbinical eyes there was a damnation so unyielding that it might have been biblical: it was like a curse unto the seventh generation.

Yakov learnt not to turn away when they were killing and raping. He learnt how to flaunt his bloodthirstiness over trifles, such as cutting a stupefied sucking-pig in half at a farm they had taken, firing his Mauser at the stained-glass windows of a Catholic church, and, above all, blathering as much as he could and showing no embarrassment over details. He had a fertile imagination, and could think up some convincing details. It was, Yakov realised, the only way.

But, together with this realisation, he was pained by a growing awareness of something else: he did not have it in him. And never would. It was not how he wanted life to be.

It was fun taking Novorossiysk, Denikin's last stronghold: by then they had heavy guns, and they started shelling earlier than the Whites had expected. The Whites who had not managed to evacuate on the English ships rushed over to the port in panic, and were chased down the streets. Here was an occasion to relish! And why shouldn't the fighters relish it, now they had come all the way to the blue sea? Yakov had nothing to do with it: this was no longer 1919, and there was no need for a clerk to be up in line with the cavalry. He came in later with the General Staff office. They had been assigned a good workplace: it was bright with high ceilings. The Whites had kept a hospital there. It was, of course, all in ruins – but that could be put right.

He found her out in a dusty garden beyond the hospital fence with all the fancy ironwork over it. There were two of them lying there, both with skirts rolled up and bared legs. It was better not to look – Yakov had already seen this sort of thing before. The lads had had their fun before killing them. All that was left of the face of one of them was her cheek and a blue eye. But they had not disfigured Marina's face. That is, not so much as to make it impossible for Yakov to recognise her. How come the Whites didn't evacuate their nurses, the bastards? Though how could a woman like Marina possibly board a ship while so much as a single wounded officer was still in the town? He did not have to close her eyes. They were already closed. What long eyelashes she had – Yakov had never previously realised quite how long they were.

And then there was Poland, and they reached the Visla. Then they retreated. But Yakov was still unable to get used to this life. The drunken excitement from blood so fresh as to be warm did not go to his head, and without this drunkenness he wasn't a fighter, but a pain – both to himself and to his comrades. Like a sober man at a drunken party.

A bare-headed woman lay on the narrow little street that looked so un-Russian with its cobbles – either wounded, or already dead, and nearby a little child was stomping about and whimpering, though he was too frightened to go up and touch her. He was afraid of dirtying his little suit, Yakov realised. His mother had told him not to get his suit dirty. They rode on, as shots could still be heard from a neighbouring street.

A week later he was wounded in the knee. Not by a bullet, but a splinter from one of the auxiliary carts when they came under fire. It wasn't serious, but it was enough for him to be sent back to the rear. He smiled to himself: he was such a pain that not even fate wanted to waste a bullet on him. They treated his leg in a hospital in Kiev for Party Staff members. It still bent. Partly. He had to take care of it. Well, so his fighting days were over. He had been a Party member since 1916, and he was a Bolshevik with a good reputation.

And one who no longer wanted to be a Bolshevik. There was not a career path in the Party that did not lie open to him – and he was not interested in a single one of them. But nor could he leave the Party – that would be suicide, leaving the Party. So who, then, was he? A Jew? Yet his documents had him down as a Russian, and besides, he did not believe in God. He was offered work in Moscow – his articles in *The Red Cavalryman* had been noticed. Sorry, but ever since his wound he'd found that he had occasional difficulty seeing properly. He had also been hit in the head. He would like to go back to Odessa. If possible, of course. He would look around, get himself back into shape and find something to apply his strength to. And he had an elderly mother there. And his old comrades there still remembered him. Ah, yes, now almost all the comrades in Odessa were new. Yakov understood. (Of these old comrades, some had proved to be enemies of the revolution, and been shot accordingly, while others had perished in the fighting, like Comrade Chizhikov.) But, even so, if possible, the place he would most like to serve the Party was Odessa.

Why refuse an invalid and a civil war hero such an easy favour? Nor did they refuse him. Reliable people were needed in Odessa, too. And Comrade Krasnov was a reliable person.

24

Under the Denikin regime the Petrovs returned to their former apartment. The first thing that Ivan Alexandrovich did was to go tearing into his study. No, it was untouched. His various knick-knacks had, of course, disappeared: the malachite paperweight, the silver ink-well . . . But the furniture had not even been moved: they had been meaning to make a people's court of the property, so why should they bother to remove the writing desk? Let it serve the proletariat regime. Ivan Alexandrovich smiled to himself and started ferreting around under the right back-hand side of his desk. The comrades hadn't sussed it! And now gently does it, as we slide out this piece of parquet behind the case . . . All the hiding-places were untouched, and in an emboldened voice the head of the family now called Maria: why not get her to come and marvel at his providence?

And they lived without trouble until February of 1920. There was even milk for Oleg, and sugar instead of saccharin. But then Kotovsky's cavalry entered the city, and it started again. With the one difference that now everyone had the feeling that this time it would last for long. Not, of course, that they thought that meant seventy years. Some hoped it would last for ever, while others gave this regime three years at the outside. Ivan Alexandrovich was a pessimist. He gave it five.

The Cheka got back to work on Marazliyevskaya Street, and the newspapers started kicking up a rumpus about the atrocities of Denikin's counter-intelligence: they used to drown living people off barges at night-time! Once again, housing committees were organised from among the conscious paupers, and the Petrovs were not at all surprised to receive visitors one night.

'Had a nice time under the Whites, eh, bourgeois? Clear the premises! By decree of the housing committee.'

This time they were forced, not into what had been the semi-basement, but out to a corner of the yard of their own house. This was luck, for they had two whole rooms on the ground floor and a door to themselves! These were the quarters in which Fedko the coachman and his wife used to live. There were three windows looking out on to the yard and a small coal cellar. Not that their predecessors had meant to leave any coal there for them: they had scuttled virtually, though not quite, all of it up. Dasha and Anna scraped around the corners and managed to gather together another three and a half buckets. Well, in four to six weeks' time they wouldn't need heating anyway – and they could hang on for a few more weeks! On their second night there, Ivan Alexandrovich went out on a little sortie, and triumphantly returned with two boards that he'd pinched off some fence. The second room, where for some reason there was a kitchen stove, was useless as far as the ventilation went. But, on the other hand, this windowless little room could be warmed from the stove. This was where everybody slept, with Oleg in the corner by the stove. The slightly bigger room, which had a door out into the yard, had for many years been known in the family as the 'cold room'. For the time being, it was unclear what they were to live on, but Anna hoped to get a job as an experienced nurse.

But things didn't quite work out that way. It transpired that you couldn't get a job without a reference from the housing committee, and why should the housing committee give a reference to some bourgeois in-law that had suddenly pitched up out of nowhere? She'd never lived here before. And who was she married to? Ah, Petrov – the eldest son? He had, it was true, gone off to war as a soldier, but after that – as the entire yard knew – he'd been made an officer! In the tsarist army. And where was he now? Ah, so he was presumed missing. Well, we all know what 'presumed missing' means. Sooner than give her any references, what they ought really to be doing was taking a closer look at Anna's background. The bread coupons were also issued by the housing committees, and it was obvious the Petrovs shouldn't bank on getting any Soviet rations. After wavering, they did, however, issue coupons to Dasha. As a downtrodden element.

'At least it'll keep the child from starving!' she rejoiced. The hold-ups with supplies meant that rations were not available every day, but, even so, there was now something to feed the boy with.

The house had a sewage system, but some of the pipes had frozen and all the neighbours now had to run out to the icy loo in the yard, comprising three little cracked wooden cabins. Either because of this, or because she had to stand and wait in the ration queues, Dasha suddenly started coughing and came down with a temperature. The Petrovs had a thermometer, but they couldn't cure her with a thermometer! They kept her wrapped up as well as possible, putting her in Olezhek's corner, and Anna went running about the city trying to find at least some sort of medicine. Dulchin was no longer in Odessa: he had managed to get on to the French ship *Dumont D'Urville*, which had taken out a group of scholars and writers. In the event, these scholars and writers had proved to be businessmen and were, for some reason, mostly Greeks and Karaites. Nevertheless, Dulchin managed to wangle his passage and before leaving he had hastily called in to bid them farewell. But the hospital, the former Evangelical Hospital, could not have come to a stop and someone must still be working there: it was impossible that she wouldn't find at least some of her old acquaintances.

However, she bumped into an old acquaintance a good deal earlier than she had anticipated: no sooner had Anna gone round the cathedral than she heard someone calling out: 'Anna-Vanna, joy of my soul!'

She gasped, but audaciously looked up at a man in a long military coat with red insignia. And he burst into laughter.

'Anyutochka! Don't you recognise me? This is my third day back, and I was just about to call in on you!'

She could not even see his hair beneath his long, cloth military cap with its blue star on the front, but his eyes sparkled so merrily and roguishly that Anna finally recognised who it was.

'Andreika!'

'The very same. Yuck, you look awful – why, you're all skin

and bone! How's the rest of the family? How's Maxy? And what about your folk? Oh, let me hug your golden little hands! It took me some time to wise up to just how good you and Marina were at changing my dressing. When I copped one down near Cherkassy, the nurse there was a right old bag: the bandage was clinging to my skin, and she ripped the whole lot off, blood 'n' all – the buzzard! And I kept on thinking of you, and how you used to soften my bandages with water to make sure it didn't hurt – God forbid! Well, are you dashing off somewhere? If not, we could call round to your place for old time's sake. I've got nowhere to invite you: I've just got this post at Proletkult. I've not fixed up my lodgings yet. But you can always count on me to get a job with supplies instead of Proletkult – and we'll have a real slap-up time of it then, eh!'

Andreika exuded such sincere and carefree joy, and his facial expression and manner were so unaltered that Anna herself felt glad that they had stumbled into one another. Well, never mind if he was a Bolshevik, and, apparently, quite a high-ranking one at that. Quite what Proletkult meant she did not know – but at least it wasn't the Cheka, and that was good enough.

'So what are you doing now – are you with the military?' she asked.

'I did a bit of fighting, but home's better. O-oh boy, was I concussed! In the end they had to discharge me,' he confided with a crafty grin. 'So how's the little brat? Growing?'

And, for no particular reason, Anna suddenly told him everything. She told him about her parents, and that Maxim and Marina had gone away, and about Dasha. For some reason, she was sure that Andreika would not shoot her with a Nagan, even if she was an officer's wife. Nor would he drag her off to the Cheka. And what sort of Bolshevik was he, anyway? He was kind-hearted. And she needed to get it all off her chest, and he was such a comforting listener.

'Come on, Anyutochka, don't cry now, don't break my heart. I can't stand to see you suffer. Ever since the front I've come over all nervy, and I can't answer for what I might do. I'll go and see that housing committee and frighten the soul out of them.'

'The soul's been abolished,' Anna smiled sadly through her tears.

'Then I'll frighten the devil out of them with this here Nagan that I got from Comrade Budyonny himself! I'll have them dancing the 'jig' – or I'm a Chinaman. You go home now, and in half an hour I'll come along with a doctor in tow.'

He tore into their wretched life like a whirlwind, and felt just as much at home and unembarrassed as before. He did come along with a doctor in tow, and from somewhere he got some milk and honey for Dasha, and procured some dry mustard. Anna smeared a thick layer of it on some rectangular strips cut from the newspapers, and covered the gasping Dasha in home-made mustard plasters. And Dasha was restored to her feet. After inflammation of the lungs, and at her age. Dasha kept making the sign of the cross, and did not know to whom she was more obliged for this miracle – the martyred Panteleimon the Healer or the Bolshevik Andrei Semyonovich? Another miracle, and one that quite definitely had nothing to do with Saint Panteleimon, was the reference from the housing committee. Andreika had gone along to their meeting in his full regalia.

'You bloody contras are asking for it! Under the Whites I bet you were cowerin' under a broom like mice, while them good people took me in and hid me!' he bellowed, brandishing his gift from Comrade Budyonny. 'Who was it that healed me when the bandits shot me? Was it you – eh, bastard? Or mebbee you? No, it was her that took care of me, with them white hands of hers!'

'White hands, comrade, are a hangover from bourgeois days. You clearly haven't quite adjusted since returning from the front,' the busybody Guskevich had the temerity to object, but Andreika turned on him with all the fury of a cavalryman.

'What – teach me, would you? And what were you doin' before seventeen? Cantor in the synagogue? And now you're suckin' up to Soviet power, eh? We'll have to look into your background, and see just what sort of hands you've got!'

Guskevich had not been a cantor – that was just Andreika's way of getting at him. He kept a little grocery stall in the New Bazaar. However, he did not like being reminded about 'before seventeen'. And, with the cherished reference to hand, Anna went and applied for a job as a nurse, and got accepted. Just to be on the safe side, Andreika accompanied her, and in the event, it was just as well that he did, too.

Anna did not earn enough to keep the family, but when Andreika did manage to fix himself up with a job in supplies and offered her a job in the People's Commissariat, she simply shook her head. Even if she could bring herself to do it, it would be silly to draw attention to herself with her background: sooner or later, they would start carping. And – working for the Bolsheviks? Working as a nurse was quite another matter: the sick were all identical. That is, they were identical to Anna, but the only people the Bolsheviks were letting into the hospitals were trade union members. Andreika shrugged his shoulders, but he didn't object. Well, we've all got our little quirks.

Dasha and Maria Vasilyevna managed to find work with a man running his own handicraft business making shawls. This desperado travelled about the local villages with his goods, exchanging shawls for foodstuffs. The job was straightforward: they had to print coloured patterns on to strips of cloth. And they could do this at home, at the same time as keeping an eye on the boy. In her youth Maria Vasilyevna had not been bad at drawing, and now she even started making patterns of her own. This brought in more money – and, oh, how that money was needed. By 1921 eggs were 600 roubles apiece, and milk one and a half thousand a bottle.

Ivan Alexandrovich now found himself in an idiotic position: the women were keeping him! Before, at least, the bourgeoisie had been set to work, either shovelling snow or carrying bricks, and he had done the allocated workload for the entire family. Dressed in his grubby summer overcoat, and with a disdainful half-smile and ineradicable upper-class air, he had loaded some sort of carts, broken ice from the road with a crowbar – and in the evening returned home, if none too steady on his feet, nevertheless knowing that there he would be fussed over, and pitied, and given a hot drink. Now he was no longer required to do such work, and with horror he realised that he had absolutely no idea what to do. He knew that it would never occur to his daughter-in-law to reproach him as a scrounger, and that, anyway, he was the head of the family and, when all was said and done, he was the one who went and pinched the firewood and chopped it up, and generally did all the manly work. Except for one thing: he was not the bread-winner.

One fine day down at the Privoz Bazaar there appeared a strange man bearing strange merchandise. For the Odessa of the twenties there was nothing out of the ordinary in the appearance of an unusual seller. Apart from the regular women mongers of fish and chicken, which now cost millions, there were also decrepit old women trying to exchange ten-year-old Easter cards and other such junk for a pinch of salt. There were cocaine dealers, furtively offering a snort. And clamorous waifs selling cigarettes. And suspicious individuals who went snooping about the rows – week in, week out – with ever the same pair of trousers slung over their arm. Indeed, there were all sorts. But this tall old man in his pince-nez and worn-looking coat still caught people's attention, as he was so obviously an upper-class gentleman. With an absent air he put his suitcase down and on top of it set out a row of little wooden boats with rag sails. Then he produced a small volume in a blue binding and immersed himself in reading as he continued standing there. Needless to say, he sold nothing, either then or on the following day. The women mongers soon grew sick of teasing him, as he never replied to anything they said, but just haughtily pursed his lips. On the third day God, who had been abolished, did, nevertheless, provide the bazaar with some entertainment.

'Hey, your worship, is that book for sale?' a couple of Red Army soldiers idly strolling around the bazaar came pestering the old man.

'No, my good sir! But the boats are.'

'What's that book? We don't need no toy boats – sell us that book there!'

'What do you want a book for, you blockhead? You can't even read,' said the old man condescendingly.

'Me – can't read? I've been readin' three years me!' the blond-haired soldier replied indignantly, with the husk of a sunflower seed on his chin. 'Now what's this meant to mean, citizens! A Red Army soldier can't buy a book – the source of knowledge – off this bourgeois trash!'

'Right – let's see what he's reading there!' yelled the other soldier in support.

'Ovid, if you must know,' replied the strange gentleman coldly. 'And I have no intention of selling it so that you scoundrels can roll your cigarettes in it.'

Well, this gent was clearly fishing for trouble and deserved to be shot on the spot – no need to trouble the revolutionary tribunal with this one. He showed no sign of humbling himself or any hint of being scared. Was that any way for a bourgeois to behave in front of a soldier nowadays? And d'you see how rude he was!

'Give 'im a slug, Mityukha – shut that big mouth for once and for all!' said the one with blond hair, getting worked up.

The second one did not take a great deal of persuasion, and he took his rifle down from his shoulder.

'Start prayin', y' old git! Here comes your pass to Dukhonin's Staff!'

The old man coldly looked up the barrel of the rifle before immersing himself in his reading again. This was outrageous: anyone in his position should be made to grovel on his knees and whimper. But what sort of fun was this?

'Uncle, that old gent's round the twist!' howled a dirty-looking urchin, and the women mongers also chimed in.

'Why pick on him? Can't you see the man's loony!'

This gave a new twist to the matter: the done thing was to leave lunatics in peace, and it was ridiculous to be offended by them. The soldiers burst into laughter.

'Come on then, old geezer, sell us your toy boat, for luck! How much d'you want? Cwo-oor – yu what? He may be loony – but he ain't daft with 'is money!'

'They're handmade,' replied the old man matter-of-factly.

This had become a question of face: they couldn't be seen haggling with a lunatic, for by now there were a good many onlookers that had come running over to see what all the fuss was about. And those were the first two boats that Ivan Alexandrovich sold. After that he came to be regarded as the 'loony gent' at the Privoz Bazaar, and people became used to him, and even took pride in him: see what a true gentleman we've got here! A real live gent, like under the old regime. He wouldn't take any nonsense from anyone, even if it was a top-ranking commissar. There was something pleasing about it: here, after all, was a man who was afraid of nothing, and whenever he put someone in their place – it was music to the ears. Whether or not his boats did bring luck, down at the bazaar they were anyway glad to make a public figure of him.

Ivan Alexandrovich made the boats in the evening, much to the delight of Oleg. He was strict with his grandson: the child needed a manly upbringing. And he only spoke French with him. Oleg called this 'Grandpa's language'. He learnt that the only way he could ever get to have a boat was by charming his grandpa in 'his language', and he prattled on in French really quite passably. Ivan Alexandrovich smiled to himself. He knew of his reputation as a loony at the Privoz Bazaar, although the family, of course, did not. But what else were people to make of a normal person in this world? He had no intention of changing himself to gratify those scoundrels. And if one day he really was going to be eliminated – as it was now called – it was not as if it would be such a tremendous loss for the family. He just felt sorry for the boy: he'd be spoilt.

Life, meantime, continued its own course: certain churches were converted into warehouses and clubs, while others had their property confiscated. The patriarch was under arrest, but still alive. Bare-legged Pioneers went marching down the streets with trumpets and drums. By the time of the fifth anniversary of the October Revolution the streets had been renamed. The unemployed thronged the labour exchange. The arrests continued at a steady pace, though no longer at the rate of the Red terror, for now they were getting more selective. Counter-revolutionaries were abbreviated to 'CRs'. This category included die-hard priests and nobles whose origins made incorrigible cases of them, as well as the more well-to-do peasants in the countryside. Officers' wives and mothers fell into the same bracket. As so many were taken in reprisal for relatives who had got away to Constantinople, this came to be known as being 'swept away for Constantinople'.

But, just as before, 'hot corn' and prawns in paper cones were sold on the street corners, people gossiped about all manner of things, and, as ever, down by the seaside the new generation of kids went on yelling: 'The water today's monkeys!'

That meant it was cold.

After changing jobs a few times, Yakov got himself fixed up as a schoolteacher. He lived with his mother, and tried to make himself as inconspicuous as possible. Rakhil was protected by the kind-hearted Borya and Rita, and in the yard she was known as 'barmy Rokhl'. However, she behaved quite normally – so long as people did not talk politics with her. If they did, however, she would start shrieking such things as God forbid people from hearing even in a whisper. She got everything muddled, and would confuse Petlyura, Trotsky and the executed Tsar Nikolai. Yakov tried not to let her go to the bazaar, but his mother was unhappy with what he bought there, and he finally accepted that he would have to let her go. There were a lot of lunatics about then, and nobody paid any particular attention to them. A man might be seen running along with a brass spittoon on his head and singing about 'cornflowers'. Or crawling about on his hands and knees, looking for a girl in the dust, muttering 'she's ever so tiny'. And it was plain to all that he was best left alone. The ones like that were harmless – it was the ones who were prone to sudden outbursts of violence that were regarded as dangerous, and these, for the most part, were veterans from the front. There didn't appear to be anything odd about them, until their frail and kindly voices suddenly erupted in a demented howl. Their lips turned blue and were flecked with foam. Sometimes they would make a lunge for someone's neck. People shied away from them. The quick-witted waifs quickly spotted an opening, and a new fashion sprang up among them.

'Come on, auntie, give some money to a syphilitic orphan! Or I might just bite you: I'm epileptic,' clear-eyed urchins of about ten would intone – and, by and large, the 'aunties' coughed up.

Yakov trusted to fate: there was little likelihood that his mother would start yelling at the bazaar or out on the street. To written slogans, placards and portraits she did not react at all – it was only if someone addressed her directly on politics. He earned enough for the two of them, and he also received a pension as a Party member invalided by the civil war. Rakhil took care of the household. And just as before, she adored her son. She never mentioned Rimma, and Yakov tried to avoid talking about his sister with her. Rimma was in Kharkov working for the Party, and once in a while she wrote. Yakov knew of her private grief: Comrade Chizhikov had been concussed in the autumn of 1919 during the fighting with the Petlyurovites. He had died in Rimma's arms and been buried in Zhitomir. Rimma had written briefly and drily about it. It appeared she was very busy. Well, work's the best medicine.

It was also work that saved Yakov. When he was with children, he felt good and calm. He was especially fond of boys up to about the age of twelve. He patiently taught them the new alphabet, how to sing the 'Internationale', and made sure that nobody was cheated out of their share of a crust of bread and jam – which was the ration at the boys' labour school that had been named in honour of some Communist or other. On his way back from work he would occasionally come across one of the Petrov family. There was no avoiding these encounters: they lived in the same yard. When it was impossible for them to slip past unseen, they would bow politely at one another. When they could, they did slip past. Andreika could not see what it was all about, and he made several attempts to reconcile them, but then he gave up. He didn't much care for these petty squabbles.

It was already 1923 when there came a knock on the Petrovs' door, and Ivan Alexandrovich, who had been getting ready to go to bed and was dressed in nothing but his underclothes, went to open the door. Petrified, Anna and Maria Vasilyevna heard a cry and some stifled sobs, and then a man's voice.

'Papa, dear, I'm sorry to spring this on you like this. I couldn't warn you.'

25

There was no sleep in apartment number twenty-nine that night. Heedless of economising, they kept the wick-lamp burning till dawn. Pavel kept on rushing over to his cases and unpacking presents from Paris, though again and again he would stop to embrace Anna or his mother and father. He no longer had a moustache, and his lips looked longer and thinner. The somewhat frail features of his face did not match his broad forehead. His eyelids were heavier, but his gaze was still the same, and his parents exchanged glances: under this gaze Anna was suddenly looking just as she had when she was a college girl.

'Pavlik! But where on earth are we going to hide you? They're shooting people who return from abroad now!'

'Come on, Papa, that's for illegal re-entry! All my papers are in order – I applied for permission, and they gave it to me. It was far easier than I thought.'

'Goodness gracious!'

'I'm not the first. Alexei Tolstoy came back – and he's a count.'

'Yes, it was in the papers. But we thought it was their usual pack of lies.'

'Well, so they lie – but every now and then they come out with the odd bit of truth, too. I was even promised help in finding a job. Apparently they're changing policies.'

'So you're banking on their policies! You crazy boy, what a risk!'

'I couldn't live without you. I had to come back. If only you knew how sick I got of living as an emigrant! Well, we can talk about that some time later. Here's a letter I brought from Maxim.'

Maria Vasilyevna, who had until now been fearing to ask about Maxim, burst into tears.

'My darling little Maxy! So he's alive?!'

'He's alive, and he's even put on weight! He's in Paris working as a chauffeur. We found one another almost immediately, and saw a lot of one another, too. And we shared the same apartment till I moved to Marseilles.'

'What about . . . ?'

'No, Mama. We looked for her, through the newspapers, and in every other way we could think of. Only so far we haven't been successful.'

'But she was with Maxim!'

'And they were meant to evacuate on the same boat together. But there was such chaos. And she was with the hospital, whereas Max was with Denikin himself. That's another story in itself: he idolises Denikin like a little boy. He was his personal aide-de-camp, and before that he acted as his secret courier. He went into the Bolshevik zones disguised as a stoker. Well, he was with his adored Commander-in-Chief, who, in the event, refused to go till the last minute. But hang on, Mama, don't get upset. A lot of people wound up in Constantinople, and from there they made it on into Czhechia, and Yugoslavia. There's not a day goes by without someone somewhere being found again. The Mirkins recently found their daughter and grandson again – in Berlin! Max will let us know if he finds anything. And we've arranged everything about how to be in touch. No, he won't come back.'

'Thank God!' said Maria Vasilyevna, making the sign of the cross.

She wanted to be on her own to read the letter from Maxim, so she took it into the 'warm room' along with a candle end that she kept saved for a special occasion. Oleg shook his head, but did not wake up. He slept just as Max had when he was little: on his back with his arms thrown above his head. Maria Vasilyevna was overcome by a marvellous sense of invulnerability. Yes, of all the children Maxim was now the only one in safety! As he would be tomorrow, and in a year's time, and always. God had punished her in so many ways – but not with this. Not with him, her blue-eyed boy. Everyone said the last child was for happiness. Over and again she kissed the enclosed photograph. He was a handsome man of twenty-three, and it was not true that he had put on weight. He was dressed as a civilian: she understood that he could not send a photograph of himself in uniform to Soviet Russia. She fell on her knees. In the darkness it was impossible to see the icon of the Mother of God, but she could still see Whom she was addressing. And she promised that, come what may, she would never grumble or complain ever again.

'So where's Dasha?' Pavel was meanwhile asking.

'She died. We had some cholera last summer,' replied Anna, as if it were her fault. 'There was nothing I could do, she was taken away immediately, off into quarantine, they said. No one else here was infected, but ever so many people died, Pavlik – you can't imagine! It was so hot, and the water supply broke down, and the city was cordoned off, and – as you know yourself – there are so few wells. I tried to get her into our hospital, but the cholera patients were taken somewhere out of the city, and there was nothing, absolutely nothing, I could do . . . I don't even know where her grave is. Olezhek cried so much, and even now he still keeps asking about Dasha. I tell him she's gone away.'

In fact, she had later found out that there was no grave: the cholera dead had been thrown into lime pits. But she did not have the heart to tell Pavel this. How often in the meetings that she had imagined having with him had she complained to him about all her woes: how back in 1921 Olezhek's hair had started to fall out from malnutrition, and how Ivan Alexandrovich had lain ill for two months, with swollen legs and a bloated stomach, and how difficult she had found it going down to the port to fetch the water with a bucket and kettle. But now she felt that she could not mention any of this. And there was probably no point, either – after all, it was no longer War Communism, but the New Economic Policy, and things were a bit easier now.

For a long, long time Pavel said nothing. He understood that this was something that he could not immediately take in: sweet

Dasha, whom he had missed no less than his own mother, was now dead. Perhaps it was a sin, but his mother had always had plenty besides the children to be busy with, whereas Dasha had belonged entirely to them. The fragrance of her flower-scented soap, her soft breast in the gaily coloured blouse on to which he had wept his childish woes, the small presents she had brought home from the bazaar for her darling, the little secrets they had shared together . . . She was his childhood, she had always been there and she should always be there. And Anna's parents were dead, too, as was the rest of that family that had inspired a veneration in Pavel that was unusual in an adolescent. But their deaths were somehow easier to understand, and were in the nature of grown-up losses. They were not the sort you cry over – rather, they came to you during sleepless nights as you stared with dry eyes up at the ceiling of a Parisian flat, or at the roof of your dug-out, or at the naked sky over your shattered, retreating detachment.

But now he had a five-year-old son, and he was there: Anna had not been wrong when she said it would be a son. In the room next door this little person on whom he had yet to set eyes lay fast asleep, and for some reason Pavel had to make an effort to go and have a look at him.

But the main thing was that he had got there in time – he'd made it! In explaining the circumstances of his return, he had told only half the truth. There was also that conversation in Paris that he had had with Maxim, and which, of course, he had no intention of relaying to his family.

'Do you trust the Bolsheviks? They'll shoot you, if not on the very day you get back, then a week later!' Maxim had declared anxiously.

'I reckon you're right. I'm not yet mad enough to trust them.'

'So why do it then? Do you think it'll make it any easier for your wife? Or for Mama and Papa? Pavel, I don't understand.'

'Exactly. That's just why I'm going. Because if I don't, they'll be arrested. At any rate, Anna will. They're going for the wives in particular. I've found this out. There are loads of cases like that. They've done with the men – and now they're after the women. There's even a special term for it in Soviet jargon: it's being 'purged for Constantinople', or something like that – I've forgotten. And, you see, I can't let that happen. I'd sooner they settled the score with me. You're an officer yourself – you must understand. For you it's different – you're single. But I left a pregnant wife with them!'

'But maybe it's already too late?'

'I hope not. God forbid.'

Maxim got up, and he made a broad sign of the cross over him. And embraced him.

The following day, when Oleg was introduced to his papa, he enquired in a business-like tone, 'How should I talk to you – normally, or in Grandpa's language?'

He was a tanned little boy who could already do the doggy-paddle and was infinitely proud of this. He kept casting critical looks at his father: perfumes came from Paris, not papas. But Pavel managed to win his respect with his ability to glue kites together. And then total adoration with his feats by the seaside: nobody else on the beach could stay underwater for so long, or swim the breast-stroke so magnificently and do 'swallow' dives from the big rock. It was true that some other men were brave enough to jump in off the rock going feet first – but his papa was the only one who could do a 'swallow' dive. Pavel caught and dried out a sea-horse for him. Nobody else in the yard had such a treasure, and Oleg endlessly showed it off to the other boys. The Petrovs were disinclined to draw attention to Pavel's return: although everything was lawful, nevertheless, God looks after those who look after themselves. Yet it was impossible to keep the child cooped up indoors in August, and the moment he was taken outside for a walk he would proudly declare to strangers and acquaintances alike: 'We've got Papa with us now!'

Pavel decided not to bother looking for work at the labour exchange. Now there was the New Economic Policy, and it was better to try and get a job through private channels. And he did get a job: at Berman's photographic studio. His youthful fascination with photography came in useful. He knew how to get even not entirely successful photographs 'up to scratch', and would come home with his sleeves stained brown from the chemicals. In the depth of his soul he did not believe that it could last long. All the happier did that make these days and nights for him and Anna. As it was a hot summer, his parents moved into the 'cold room' with Oleg. Pavel was not spoilt – two wars and his first year of living in emigration had not encouraged him to be very demanding in his standards. However, adapting to Soviet daily life and living in the house that he remembered under such different circumstances did not come easily. What with these wick-lamps, and carrot tea that was just about drinkable if taken with saccharin, and Anna having to do the washing in the wash-tub with ashes rather than soap. Good Lord, if this was called 'a bit easier' – what on earth could it have been like before?

It wasn't so bad having to go traipsing three blocks away with the buckets to fetch water as passing the cathedral each time, always with a feeling that he was walking past a reproach. The faith that he had so nearly lost had returned to him in the first war. But now it was somehow different: there was an inexpungible mixture of guilt and shame. And, as he entered the cathedral of his childhood for the first time since his return, he was struck by how unrecognisably altered it all was. Everything that could have been taken down and removed had disappeared. That was understandable. But, apart from the miracle-working icon that he had been held up to kiss as a little boy, apart from the ancient 'Maltese Trinity', and the candelabra and so on, something else, something more important had also disappeared – though quite what it was Pavel could not put his finger on. Or perhaps something out of place had been added? He remembered an angel of which he had been particularly fond on the wall above the tomb of Vorontsov – and how bright it had looked, and how effortlessly it flew up from the two dark figures beneath. When Pavel had looked at it in his boyhood he felt that he was flying up himself. But there was no flying now. Nor ever would be. Yes, something had been added, and it had infiltrated the atmosphere: it was a fear to which people had grown so inured that they no longer even noticed it. But he was not yet inured to it, and he could feel it, and he resisted it, and he tried not to let it penetrate him. The priest who had baptised Oleg as a baby and given him Communion had been shot. And the monastery had been destroyed. Many, including the Petrovs, now preferred to pray at home. And that was the least of their worries.

But Pavel found the rest of the city unrecognisable, too. At every turn there now hung these idiotic street names, bearing the names of 'revolutionary saints' – presumably as a reminder. True, no one ever actually used these names in conversation, not even the Bolsheviks. They stuck to the old names, and children were taught to do likewise. This became a self-styled shibboleth for the true Odessans, and one destined to remain for as long as Odessa itself remains standing. But how few people there were out and about now. The population had fallen by almost a third – and so many outsiders had moved in! Even so, the city looked half empty. Having gone off to war as its protector, Pavel felt this acutely. Hardly any of his old acquaintances were left. And he did not feel like making any new ones. Not that he would have had time to, anyway.

The fact that it took them two months to come and arrest him was due, as Pavel later realised, to the sluggishness of the Cheka and the fact that the passport system was not brought in until seven years later. Well, he was ready for it. He had done all that he could to prepare Anna. He had got her to promise that, if he was imprisoned rather than shot, then under no circumstance was she to try to come and visit him or send him any money transfers. There was no need to take any risks with the child. What would happen if she were arrested, too – was Oleg to end up roaming the streets a waif? And sleeping in boiler-rooms, and scrounging money on trains? Anna did not want to talk or even think about it. But when they came one night, she immediately knew who it was they had come for. There was no need to gather Pavel's things: he kept a bundle ready anyway.

'This isn't a correction home, dearies! There's no Soviet power on Solovki – any complaints and you can make 'em to the sky! Re-education starts right now. Welcome, quarantine company!' a man with an officer's bearing and a small pomaded moustache announced to the batch of new arrivals. These new arrivals, including Pavel, found it hard staying on their feet after the boat-hold. The fresh sea wind had battered their spirits. Those who survived the crossing were the stronger ones. The ones that died in the hold were thrown into the sea shortly before docking.

'Greetings, comrade captain!' exuberantly bellowed a solitary voice.

'Tambov wolf to your "comrade",' chortled the man, as he carefully brushed a speck of dust from the black cuff of his coat. 'So how come you guessed I'm a captain, eh, scum? Right: I see one of you's started down the path of correction – but the rest of you are sabotaging greeting your commander. And saboteurs get three days and nights of penalty work. And you, scum, are gonna count the circles – and mind you don't flunk it! Or I'll stick you in with that lot – and what they do then ain't none of my business.'

Penalty work consisted of dragging boulders round in a circle. The 'lesson' was six circles an hour, for ten hours. Although he found it hard, Pavel managed, but a priest who had been brought still in his cassock was already reeling after the first hour. Pavel made a move to support him, but a bullet from one of the escorts rang out against the boulder. When the priest collapsed, a horse was brought with empty shafts. Unconscious, the saboteur was fastened to them, and the sprightly captain mounted the horse and dug in his heels. Pavel heard a faint groan as the horse started to move, and the captain's laugh.

'I could spot a poser in 'is grave!'

Yes, Solovki – there was, indeed, not even Soviet power here. Order was established by former White officers who had ingratiated themselves with the Communists. And, for Pavel, these men were more loathsome than any commissar. He thought he had already seen Russian officers losing their honour. He had seen a few let themselves slip to the level of begging out on the streets. But now it transpired that he had not seen anything yet. And, as he dragged boulders, hacked at the permafrost, fell and got back up from beneath the cart to which, along with two others, he was harnessed instead of a horse – and throughout the entirety of his three years on Solovki – he no longer wanted anything. Not even to survive. Which may be why he did survive.

During his first days there he had the idea of slapping the captain in the face, or throwing himself at an escort in order to get the whole thing over and done with there and then, and he divulged this idea to the neighbour with whom he shared his plank bed.

'What's up wi' you – heathen, huh?' asked this middle-aged man, who had a peculiarly disfigured face with a squashed nose and lips as flat as a pancake, and who was plainly taken aback. He had no front teeth, and Pavel had to listen closely to make out what he was saying.

'Know what the Lord says 'bout suicide?'

'What do you mean "suicide" – I'd be shot,' replied Pavel indignantly.

'Aa-ah – same thing, if you know it's coming. Who're you trying to kid? When our Saviour was carrying His cross, He didn't hurl himself at the escort – and there's you whining on about dragging sledges! You officers all get stuck-up. Don't sin – and when the time comes the Lord will grant relief.'

'So what are you in for? Are you a CR, too?'

'I sure am. I sinned – I clobbered one of 'em young Commies when they tried to take over our church for the Pioneers. Didn't kill him, mind – but they said he lost his reason. I was upset, you see: I'm a carpenter, me, and there was a good lot of my work in that church! The interrogator was very upset I'd messed up that young Commie. So he got me boarded up. See how they smashed up my lovely little mush?'

'What do you mean "boarded up"?' asked Pavel, not understanding.

'You dunno what "boarded up" is? Well, they fasten your whole body down to a board, and then they raise up one end – and let go. Or they stand you upright and push you flat down on your face – that's what "boarding up" is. I've been working with wooden boards all me life – but I could never come up with anything like the kind o' tricks they get out of 'em.'

Three months later God 'granted relief' to this neighbour of Pavel's: he was buried with the rest of the dead, behind the women's barrack. But Pavel was not yet 'granted relief'.

After seeing him off, Anna turned completely to stone: she did not cry, but she also stopped smiling. When, with an effort, she drew back her lips in the semblance of a smile to her boy,

Maria Vasilyevna felt her heart go cold. Until Anna recovered, Maria Vasilyevna did all she could to keep the family spirits up, otherwise they would not have survived. And she made a good job of it, too.

The winter of twenty-three was cold and virtually snowless. The wind howled piercingly down the straight and blustery streets, and even the little boys lost interest in the slippery tracks that had been slopped with water and over which they had been skidding so often as to make them into solid, blackened ice. The school where Yakov worked was heated, but, even so, some of the children sat in coats, and others in their mothers' cardigans. When he was at work Yakov himself did not take off his fluffy green scarf. He grew tired of writing silly reports, and with each innovation he was supposed to write yet more of them. If it wasn't the complex method of teaching, then it was the working-group method, or there was some sudden campaign to identify defective pupils – the devil alone knew what that was meant to imply. Just to be on the safe side, he declared there to be no 'defectives' among his own pupils, and received a stern rebuke from his superiors for failing to conduct some of the idiotic tests that had come down 'from above'. Irritated and in a foul mood, he went out into the cold entrance hall with its portraits of Lenin and Trotsky and started smoking by the window over which there was a semicircle resembling a slice of lemon.

'Uncle boss, need a cleaner?' he heard, feeling a tug at the elbow.

It was a creature hidden away inside a shawl and a tattered cardigan, and from the little he could see of her face, Yakov guessed that she was about sixteen. Was she a waif?

'No, thanks,' Yakov replied briefly. The school already had a cleaner of its own, and, besides, nobody would offer a job to anybody off the street. People either got, or failed to get, work at the labour exchange, providing they had an identity card from the housing committee. And, even if there had been a job going, she would still have to go and see the headmaster about it, rather than an ordinary teacher. Yakov did not bother to explain all this to the girl. But the dark eyes on that grubby little face had such a look of despair that Yakov fished in his pocket and gave her half a bread roll. The next day she came back with the same question. And again, the day after.

'What do you keep coming back for?' asked Yakov in exasperation. 'I've already told you—'

'It's so cold outside,' replied the girl ingenuously. 'Don't kick me out, uncle – I just want to get warm, and then I'll go. That's what I ask everywhere I go. It's warm inside official buildings, and you can warm up before they nab you.'

'Where do you sleep?'

At this question the girl merely started blinking, as though she were afraid that Yakov might be about to arrest her there and then.

'How old are you?'

'Just gone eighteen.'

Either she was lying, or the shawl made it impossible to tell what age she was. And anyway what the hell prompted Yakov to ask her all these questions? In any event he couldn't help her: these days there were loads of these kind of people hanging around the markets and railway stations. But now those dark enormous eyes were looking at him with such hope, as if this 'uncle' was about to issue her with food rations, fix her up with a job and pack her off to live in the former apartment of Vera Kholodnaya.

Cursing himself as a total idiot, Yakov took her home and let her sleep on top of a trunk in the kitchen. Next day he would go and have a word with Andreika – maybe he could fix her up with something. He had heard that the Nansen mission at the German consulate was taking on some couriers. Or possibly something else would crop up . . .

But Andreika was away, and for a week Yakov got nowhere. And, even if he did strike it lucky, the girl still needed to have some papers drawn up for her. And how was he going to do that, when the only thing that he had managed to get out of her was that she was called Musya? In answer to questions about where she was from, where she had been born and so on, she simply stared in fright, and when Yakov started asking her about her parents, she broke down altogether.

At this point, Rakhil suddenly grew indignant. 'Let the girl be! She's got a Jewish heart – what more do you want of her?

She's such a lovely child – why do you have to go and make her cry!'

Yakov simply whistled between his teeth, instantly getting from his mother, 'Don't whistle indoors – or there'll be no money in the house!'

It looked as if, while Yakov had been away working, Rakhil and Musya had been striking up some sort of relationship together. He looked around the kitchen. Everything was washed and spotlessly clean: his mother hadn't the strength to do that. Disorder was something to which he had got used, and he had stopped noticing it – but order was something that he did notice. Only why a Jewish heart? This Musya did not look like a Jewish girl, and her hair was, if anything, fair. Could it be nothing more than the look in her eyes? Well, what difference did it make if she was or wasn't Jewish! This was something which, unlike his mother, Yakov regarded as an obsolete prejudice. But there was no way he could throw her back out on to the streets now. So, for the time being, why not let her help about the house – and take it from there.

When Andreika returned and heard the entire story, he gave Yakov a crafty wink. 'Hey, kiddo, you're no mug! Where d'you manage to dig up such a little beaut? Wey-hey, lucky bugger!'

Yakov looked at his friend in bewilderment. This girl – 'little beaut'? However, she had by now tidied herself up, and Rakhil had forced her to throw her old rags away and given her one or two things from the trunk that she'd made into her own size.

Andreika burst out laughing. 'Ah, you monk in devil's trousers! Hey, I get it: at twenty-four you reckon you're too crocked for the girls! You're the spas' invalid – the poor wasted kid! Listen, what if I do manage to fix her up with something? How about letting me have the hussy as a favour for an old mate?'

'Get lost! What do you think she is – a horse? I asked you to help someone, and all you can think of is bonking!'

'Come on – there's no need to get het up about it! OK, OK, say no more. But if I don't have a right old piss-up at your wedding – then I'm a Chinaman!'

Yakov shrugged. Andreika occasionally got some weird ideas into his head. Well, at least he'd promised to do something.

When he got back from school the following day Musya was washing the floor in the corridor. And singing. Yakov had never heard her sing before, and he had not heard her say all that much, either.

"Neath the hill and down the dell, There is a lake, I love it well,' her clear little voice sang effortlessly and without gasping for breath. It was as though she were not washing the floor, but out walking in a garden. She saw Yakov was back and immediately clammed up, as if she had done something wrong. Her bare feet, which were the colour of a peeled apple, stood firmly and stolidly – with toes bunched – on the damp floor-boards. Over her calf muscles there was a tender down of gold on which drops of dirty water were quivering. She saw that he was watching. And quietly grinned to herself.

Rimma arrived in the spring, coming to take a break at a rest-home. For the first time in half a year Rakhil suffered a breakdown: once again she started shouting about pogroms, and Rimma turned round and went out. After more or less managing to quieten his mother down, Yakov caught up with his sister out on the street. No, she wasn't offended. Poor Yakov, was it always like that living with a sick woman? But hadn't he tried to have her cured? Although how could he possibly have told anyone about the background of her illness? Why didn't he come and see her at the Fountain, the former villa of Renault?

The tram took Yakov along a familiar route, with its boxwood hedges, now unkempt, and the lions' heads that Yakov had loved to count in his childhood going all the way down the long, grey wall. The shadows from the branches of the plane trees were still patchy: the leaves had only just started coming into blossom. But it was already warm, and Yakov narrowed his eyes as he savoured the smell of spring. Here, out of the city, the smell was stronger and it was intoxicating.

They drank cheap white wine with biscuits of some kind and smiled at one another. Rimma, who was dressed in a stern blue suit, looked tired and thin. And there were those shadows under her eyes . . . His sister was no longer the little girl she had been, but a thirty-year-old woman who made no attempt to hide a single one of her years. She had become somehow more abrupt, and now she was a smoker. But how good it was to see her again! Unable to remain sitting in the quiet and emptiness of the rest-home, they went down to the sea. The shore was deserted – the season had not yet started. The bright water splashed lazily, and only further out to sea did it become green and azure. Rimma gnawed at a juniper twig that she had snatched on their way down. She loved the astringent taste of the little cones, with their blue film and funny buckled hornlets. Yakov stood on a stone and dipped his hand in the water.

'Monkeys!'

They both laughed.

'Anyway, Yakov, how are you? How's work, how are your comrades? You've written so little that I hardly know anything. And the tone of your letters is – I'm sorry, but it's so decadent. I understand it's hard for you with Mama, but even so . . .'

'Actually, living with Mama is easy. It's not often she's like that, and I'm used to it now, anyway.'

'But you've changed. I'll be blunt – I didn't recognise you. You're sort of lifeless – and now, at a time like this!'

'Lifeless is just what I am. Rimma, I didn't want to talk about this, but now you've raised it yourself . . . I don't see how I can go on living.'

'You mean materially?'

'No, that's not what I mean. Do you remember when you came back from Moscow, from that studio of yours? Well, I'm in the same position now.'

'But that was ages ago! And it was you who helped me to get my bearings, and you were already a Bolshevik yourself. Don't forget you were on the right track before I was!'

'But what if it now strikes me as the wrong track? If everything fine that I ever had belongs to the past, and can never be brought back?'

'You mean the New Economic Policy? I understand – a lot of people are unhappy about that. Was that what we fought the civil war for – so that we could now watch these NEP men stuff their ugly mugs! Yet you know perfectly well that it's only temporary, while we liquidate the war ruin. But in due course we'll crush them with a hand of iron . . .'

'That's exactly what I'm afraid of – that hand of iron. You see, now I know that I'm not made of iron. We've got Dzerzhinsky who's made of iron – but I'm not.'

'What are you getting at?'

Yakov explained as well as he could, and Rimma remained silent for a long time. Was it possible that her own brother considered Comrade Trotsky a scoundrel? Particularly now, after Lenin had died, when Trotsky was the only hope left for them, and everyone that was truly faithful to the Party should be rallying round him? Was it possible that he, Yakov, had lost his faith in the Communist future? Was it possible that he had become, in essence, an enemy of Soviet power, concealing his true identity beneath a Party ticket? Well, if that were so . . . She was so pained by this that she suddenly realised how much she loved her inept brother, and always had loved him, and – even if he did now hold such views – she could not stop loving him. She wanted to hit him in the face, to yell out, to do anything – to stop him being like this. He was watching a seagull that kept looking as if it meant to settle on the water but was unable to make up its mind. He was standing with his head flung back, like a blind man.

By now it was evening and, having both calmed down, they were ending the conversation and discussing a point they had not yet touched upon.

'Well, could you do it yourself? If the revolution needed Anna, Zina, or any of your other old friends shot? Would you personally . . .'

'No,' Rimma replied honestly. 'I would try and do something for them. But why take such extreme cases? The revolution knows who to shoot!'

'Because it doesn't know! Because they're always extreme cases! And because nothing can be done about it, and you know it! But that's not what I mean. You see, for you, too, the best is now behind, and those friendships are more important than the revolution.'

'Bunkum! You always did turn everything on its head, Yakov. And anyway, that's enough. We're already arguing like Russians!'

And there really was no point in their arguing. It was better simply to make the most of being together. Rimma hoped that

Yakov was in a temporary depression – he had, after all, been concussed. For herself, she could not imagine life outside the Party. She did not seek personal happiness: the only man she had ever truly loved now lay in the Zhitomir cemetery beneath a tin five-pointed star. She kept a portrait of Makar in a black crêpe frame in her study. His merry eyes smiled out from the frame: hero of the revolution Comrade Chizhikov had not liked miserable people.

Yakov introduced Rimma to his wife. She took a liking to Musya: she was modest and easygoing – yet, at the same time, cheerful. She was a happy housewife, enjoying a silly chintzy happiness that Rimma could never understand, but was highly sensitive to in others. She found it pleasant that Musya was shy with her. And she was so young . . . No, she was all right. Just what Yakov needed. It was better that he should at least feel himself to be a man, or else he'd crack up altogether. It was, however, strange that he didn't know whether or not she was Jewish. Or was he just pretending not to know? Well, no matter. It looked as if in about six months' time Yakov would already be coddling a baby. Rimma knew that she would never have any children of her own. It had nothing to do with her mother's curse. And, besides, her mother had been ill when she yelled at her. Rimma simply felt that some women did have children, but that this wasn't her fate.

Semyon Yakovlevich Krasnov was born precisely when he was expected. He had the same brown eyes as his grandfather Isaak, and Yakov was touched to see that his little body was covered in golden down. He felt sorry when this down came off. But by then he already adored his first-born shrieker with all his soul. Rakhil, of course, insisted on circumcision. But Yakov refused with a fury that surprised even himself. Apart from its being politically risky, he could not even think of inflicting any pain on this helpless, warm and wet little creature with tomato-coloured cheeks.

PART THREE

It was 1933 when, almost without limping, Yakov got down on to the platform at Kiev. He had on a grey summer overcoat and a soft hat with a crease down the middle: he looked like a low-ranking Party official or a writer, but in any event an intellectual who was doing modestly well. He looked older than his thirty-four years: already there were wrinkles round his eyes stretching slightly up towards his temples, and round his mouth a complex picture had formed, as though it were a mouth that was grudgingly amused by something the whole time. His chin was somewhat too pointed for a successful man, and raised a little too high for a man free of worry. In his suitcase, which, though not new, looked presentable, there was the usual assortment of items taken by a man travelling on business: two shirts, a razor, the food that Musya had packed for him rolled up in a newspaper, a hand-written report that he was to deliver at the teachers' conference, and a still unread copy of the magazine *Ogonyok*. Yakov read magazines starting from the end: the back page was kept for humour. Gradually working his way backwards, he would come to the leading article. The leading articles were compulsory reading, especially for a worker on the ideological front. And it was into this category that schoolteachers fell.

The conference could hardly have come at a more awkward time: after a nine-year gap Musya was about to give birth again, and at a time like this it would have been better for Yakov to be at home. But he hoped to get it over with by the end of the week. Revelling in spring, a Kievan sparrow flew chirruping past him, all but brushing against his new hat. Yakov grinned and proceeded into the pompous building of the railway station, with its columns and sculpted wheat sheaves. From here he was due to go to the House of the Collective Farmer, which was where the conference delegates were due to be put up. He bought a pea-pie. The woman who sold it to him looked at him with unseeing eyes, and, as he was walking away, behind his back Yakov heard 'Hey, Yid!' He turned round. No, it could not have been the pie-seller: she was already busy seeing to a woman in a shawl. Behind him there was a little queue. Was it someone there? But what difference did it make who said it? Why, 'n' a warm hello to you, city of Kiev.

In the room where he was put four beds remained unoccupied, though the two by the window had been taken by a couple of new arrivals. They were talking about something, but when Yakov came in, they immediately fell silent. Yakov knew when people fell silent like that. He said hello. And received a polite reply. But, although Yakov related a few innocuous jokes the conversation never took off.

And throughout the four days of the conference Yakov could sense – not with his ears, but rather his back – that short word, the same one with which his acquaintance with real life had begun in 1905. It could not be said that he hadn't been expecting this. He knew that this was currently the national policy: there were a lot of Jews in the Ukrainian OGPU – the former NKVD – the former Cheka. Perhaps not actually a majority, but enough for Kiev, with its permanent ethos of anti-Semitism, to single them out for attention. And why should anyone like the OGPU? Especially in Kiev, which had stronger links with the Ukrainian countryside than Odessa had. The rumours of what was now happening in the countryside were so dreadful that even Yakov, who was ready to expect anything from 'these people', disbelieved them. Well, yes, it was true that the countryside had been slightly squeezed in order to stop food from being hoarded: there had been a newspaper campaign about it. And with collectivisation now under way, measures had to be taken against stubborn opponents. And, yes, it was true that no one could now leave the countryside for the towns: the passport system had been introduced, and they were scarcely going to issue passports to the peasants. But to claim that villages were cordoned off with troops? And to claim that people were dying – in the countryside – of hunger, and had even been reduced to cannibalism? No, excuse me, those must be fibs. Especially in Ukraine, with its black earth region, groaning with food.

However, his passport was checked before he had even time to get out of the station. And it was impossible to buy a return ticket without a passport. And at the Kiev Hay Market he again saw something that he had not seen for so long that he had forgotten about it: women pleading for bread in deadened voices. Manifestly country women. And there were round-ups at ·the Hay Market, and papers were checked. He was caught up in such a round-up, but they had only to glance at him before the militiaman in red piping said, 'You can go.' Yakov looked unmistakably urban. Like everyone else in the round-up, he behaved in a pointedly conscious manner, and both his movements and his facial expression displayed a disposition to unquestioning obedience. But, at the same time, his face also showed uncomprehending innocence: surely it went without saying he had nothing to do with any of 'that sort of thing'. And he was ready to wait patiently until this little misunderstanding had been cleared up. The scale of the misunderstanding somehow diminished of its own into what was, essentially, no more than a trifle. Later on, in the hotel, and in the Red conference hall with its bust of the leader, he moaned through his nose, writhing at the recollection of the idiotic, animal pleasure that he had derived from that brief 'you can go'. And at how he had walked away: half-side on and with his back half-turned, once again displaying that readiness to return immediately if they suddenly had any doubts and called him back.

He felt relief on leaving the subdued city of Kiev, with its hidden mysteries, tensions and hatred. Odessa could never be subdued, no matter what. Even the Odessan trams, erupting in tantrums mingled with jokes, sounded more like a musical comedy and had a southern air of carefreeness to them. In the Kievan trams people jostled in silence and resentment. In this copiously green city, shaded by its wet April foliage, there was an atmosphere of such accumulated malice that, come the evening, Yakov found his neck muscles stiffening. And, whoever may have been guilty of this malice, Yakov guessed on whom – given the chance – it would be taken out. And just what did those idiot Jews think they were up to clamouring to get into the OGPU? Didn't they even have any pity on their own children? That bastard Kaganovich. A lot of good he'd done, that was for sure.

On the way back the train came to a halt. Not even at a small station, but simply out in the middle of nowhere. It must be some sort of hitch, thought Yakov absent-mindedly, supping his ruddy tea from one of the train glasses. The glass-holder was beautiful, with its whorls and depiction of the Kremlin. But the train remained stationary, and Yakov decided to go out on to the embankment and stretch his legs. His fellow-passengers, immersed in their newspapers and eating their hard-boiled eggs, moved their legs out of the way to let him past.

Yakov had got out a cigarette before even jumping down on to the gravel, but he immediately forgot all about it. Towards the train there came, half-walking, half-crawling, some sort of people with grey and bloated faces. They were feebly clambering up on to the embankment, then stumbling and crawling back down again, and Yakov heard the nagging groan: 'Bread. Bread.'

Someone had already got up to the footboard and was trying to crawl into the carriage. Yakov's sleeve was grabbed by some fingers clenched into a bird's foot, but he had no bread on him – he had left it in his suitcase. He made a move to run back to the carriage to get it, but then the peasant woman with purulent eyes who had grabbed him thrust something into his hands and collapsed. Face down. She kissed his shoe, her face grovelling in the oil stains down on the gravel.

'Petrik. This is my Petrik. Take him, uncle, for Christ's sake!'

Yakov was so dumbfounded that he did not even have time to recoil, and then the train started moving, and the carriage attendant came running through the carriage yelling, 'Stand clear of the doors!'

A youth was hanging on to the footboard, but he lacked the strength to maintain his grip, and as the carriage attendant ran past, he kicked him off, bellowing at Yakov, 'Want to stay behind, citizen?'

It was not until Yakov was back inside the carriage that he recovered his senses, as the train was gathering speed and the wheels got back to their busy clatter. In his arms he held a bundle of dirty linen. He drew back the edge and saw a pinky-grey little face about the size of a large apple. The eyes in the little face were half-open – they were the turbid blue of a new-born baby. Its tiny mouth gaped like a fish's, without making any sound. Yakov was seized by a fury that he had not experienced for a long time. He knew this feeling, and also knew that he was incapable of controlling it. It was in this state of fury that he had nearly killed a man – a fighter from their own detachment – back in Poland, down a narrow little street in a village they had taken. It was in this state of fury that he had pounded on the desk of the Odessan First Secretary when insisting that a colony of waifs should be given some food rations. And so, too, when he had yelled at the headmaster of his own school after the ten-year-old hooligan Dotsenko had been expelled from the Pioneers. It happened rarely, but when it did, Yakov did not know what it might bring him to. And now it was happening again – and he did not know where it might take him. But this Petrik would not die of hunger. He was in Yakov's arms – and he would live!

Yakov had no idea how he would arrange it. If he took the baby into the compartment, everyone would immediately realise what was going on, and what would happen then? Yakov would flatten the first person who so much as opened his mouth. He would take the child to Odessa, and play it from there.

He took a better grip of the weightless bundle and went back inside his compartment. Three faces looked up as he entered. He had not previously paid any attention to these faces. After Kiev, he had no desire to hob-nob with his fellow-passengers. There was a young woman in a boa. And a middle-aged man with a little moustache like a cockroach who looked like an accountant. And a fat woman with knees akimbo and a cheesy face. She had just finished guzzling some food, and had not yet brushed the crumbs off her knees. All of them had mouths shaped like the letter 'O', and inquisitive eyes. Well, who's first?

The fat woman threw up her arms and went waddling out sideways into the corridor. This was something that Yakov was not ready for: should he seize hold of her and not let her go till they reached Odessa? And force everyone else to stay in the compartment, too? What else was there to do? She had, after all, gone scampering off to peach on him, the bitch. And what then? Would the carriage attendants come running up, bind him up and hand him over to the militia? But he wasn't breaking the law. For a baby, no passport was required. But a birth certificate was. And this baby was meant to be left to die at a breast that had withered like a rag – so what right did he have to interfere? Step on up, and I'll show you what right!

At this point the woman returned and silently held a small bottle of milk out to Yakov. She pushed down on the throat of the bottle with her thumb, but Yakov was slow to react, and milk splashed on to his trousers as the train jogged. The woman, who appeared to be dumb, simply rolled her eyes to the ceiling and took the bottle back. From her expansive sides she produced some sort of rag and deftly rolled it up, stopping the throat of the bottle in such a way that the end of the rag protruded from it in a cone, and then thrust it into the fish's little mouth. The baby sneezed and tried to spit it out, but she stroked her finger over its velvety cheek, and the little mouth diffidently began sucking.

Without altering her frightened expression, the young woman in the boa started digging about in her little travel-bag and pulled out a couple of towels. On hearing the steps of the carriage attendant, the moustachioed cockroach-accountant started whistling a foolish little ditty and stood in the door with his hands thrust into his pockets. He was dreamily gazing out of the window, barring the narrow compartment door with his Cheviot-jacketed back. Nobody said a word – Yakov had evidently come across some very quiet travel companions. There was just a radio playing, and it was playing loudly, too. It was impossible to turn it off in the compartment, and this was something that always irritated Yakov in trains. But now it proved handy.

To the strains of the song 'The Lass Bade the Fighter Farewell' the child was fed, and to the strains of Pioneers' songs his nappy was changed. Evidently his navel had not yet healed. So he was two days old, at the outside. The baby feebly wiggled his little heels, and, without thinking for long, the young woman in the boa kissed these little heels one after the other, just as Musya had kissed Semyon's. Only this woman did not add: 'Come on – it's time you were on your feet!'

During the journey the baby twice came down with diarrhoea: could that be the effect of cow's milk? By the time they reached Odessa they were all left without either towels or handkerchiefs. But the canny travelling companions smiled at one another and exchanged winks, and the accountant kept trying to amuse the baby with his imitations of a horned goat.

Yakov managed to get home without any further adventures. The child, who was swaddled quite presentably, did not attract anyone's attention, except Yakov did become the butt of certain jokes in the tram: so, a breast-feeding papa, eh? Still touched by the illicit kindness of his neighbours in the train compartment, Yakov went down Koblevskaya, now Podbelsky Street, feeling calm and at peace with the world. It was already dark, and on either side of the road, the yellow street-lights suddenly flared up in the mauve evening.

'Sh-sh, sh-sh,' Yakov kept saying to the whimpering bundle. And just as he passed through the entrance to his yard he heard a piercing shriek. Yakov's hands broke out in sweat: the cries were coming from his window. Musya, Musya, dear girl! He ran the last few steps and, with a shaking hand, he reached across to his other pocket and got out his key. Abandoning his case by the door, though managing not to drop the bundle, he flew into the flat just as the shrieking subsided. Rakhil and Rita, the wife of Borya the cobbler, were swarming about over Musya's bed. Yakov saw her head thrown back, with the veins on her neck still bulging from strain. Rita raised something grey and motionless up on its little feet and gave it a resounding slap on its tiny buttocks. A creature that looked more like a disembowelled hare started twitching and shrieking. And a good, lusty shriek it was, too.

'Ah, so now the man of the house gets here,' laughed Rita. 'Congratulations, Yakov Isakych – you have a daughter!'

Musya's face was slowly returning to its normal colour, and Yakov kissed her on her damp temple.

'I couldn't wait any longer.' She smiled weakly. 'The seizures came on all of a sudden. Give her to me!'

Rita placed the child on her sunken stomach and busied about so deftly and knowledgeably that Yakov stopped worrying. Everything was finished within half an hour, and the swaddled baby girl was already lying by Musya's swollen breast. Rakhil went out to accompany Rita home, constantly reiterating how grateful they were, and then she told Borya what a golden wife he had. While she was there she also woke up the nine-year-old Semyon, who had been left with Borya when it all began, and took him back home with her.

'Semyon, look – a little sister!' she said, leading a freckly boy in a Pioneers' tie and with a sleepy pink cheek up to the bedside.

'Which one?' reasonably enquired Semyon.

Rakhil could not believe her eyes, for in her arms Musya was holding two bundles with quite identical mops of blackish damp fur on their little heads.

'So what got into you, Mama – going off with Rita like that before it was all over!' grinned Yakov. 'And what took you so long? While you were gone another little boy popped out!'

Dumbfounded, Rakhil could do nothing but clutch her head. For a minute she thought this was some trick being played on her, but what trick could it be if – no matter how often she wiped her eyes – there were two little faces, rather than one, both lolling there, clumsily nuzzling Musya's brown nipples.

'Poor girl,' she cried out, and set about removing the swaddling from the second acquisition, but Musya gently pushed her away.

'Hang on, Mama, let them suckle.'

The doctor who was called did not come until noon the following day, and he registered the birth of twins, a boy and a girl. The boy was smaller, but that was not surprising as he was born second. Semyon boasted to everyone at school that he had a little brother and sister – Petrik and Manya. Yakov went to work with eyes reddened from lack of sleep: if one of the little treasures wasn't balling, then it was the other that was shrieking away. It looked as if this little couple were as bent on keeping the wailing up as the Roman vestal virgins had been determined to keep the fire going. However, Musya had enough milk, and it became possible to look upon the sleepless nights as one of the joys of family life. Funniest of all was that the children really did look alike, with their brown eyes, black hair and pointed little noses. Features that are common among both Jews and Ukrainians. Which made it all the easier to keep the secret. Yakov and Musya promised one another that the children would never know anything of what had happened. And this promise was to remain unbroken until just over thirty years later.

Oleg Petrov had stayed behind at the circle of model aeroplane enthusiasts. Van Sanych had managed to get hold of some real india-rubber for the gliders – an acquisition whose value was beyond the comprehension of the uninitiated. There was, of course, not enough of it to go round for everyone. Which meant that only those whom the circle selected for the regional competition could have any. And the whole matter had been fully gone into. And Oleg, with his luck, had, of course, been chosen as a reserve. That was despite the fact that only a week before Van Sanych had himself said that his model was just about the best of all. Now he was left without either any india-rubber or the slightest chance of glory. That is, he had a tiny chance if any of the team had any last-minute hitch with their contraptions, and they had to call on the reserve. Now in high dudgeon, however, Oleg brushed aside this chance so as not to make light of his sense of grievance.

In any event he could not now invite Tanya to the competition. Because, if she did come, then it was certain that no one would have any last-minute hitches, and he would have to remain a useless reserve sitting with his model on some peeling park bench. And, even if it did have red stars on the wings, this model still wouldn't be allowed to fly in the competition. And Tanya, in her short brown jacket with her Young Communist badge, would watch enraptured as his lucky rivals sent their small and meticulously made aeroplanes whirling through the air.

Did he ever have any luck in his life, like other people had! Why couldn't he be like everyone else was? Like that Borka the activist, or Tanya? She was the first in the class to be accepted into the Young Communist League, and her father had nothing to do with it. He was a helmsman on a cargo boat, and not even a Communist. She was just that sort of person. Brave, open, cheerful. Look her in the eyes and you could see how totally frank she was: she had no secret thoughts whatsoever. Yet he was already nearly fifteen – and what did he have to show for himself? At the age of fifteen the writer Arkady Gaidar was in charge of a regiment. Everyone knew that.

What if, just supposing, he came first in this competition – then, perhaps, he really would make up his mind and apply to join the Young Communist League? Already he could feel the hefty chunk of metal with its red enamel in the palm of his hand – the coveted badge of the Young Communists. And how he would stick it into his jacket and secure it tightly on – so that it could never, ever get lost. Anyway, even if he did come first – would he really go ahead and do it? They might turn him down because of his origins, although, there again, they might not. But at least there would be an end to this silly uncertainty. And he would take it like a man. Yet here he was, latching on to this uncertainty. He was a drip. A coward.

He walked over the Stroganovsky Bridge. From here the early evening sea came into view. At any moment now the lighthouse would come on. The October chill was already intensifying, but the sky was clear, and the weather would hold for about another fortnight. He wanted a nor'-easter to come blowing in rain on the day of the competition. Steady now – fine way that is for a comrade to think! If I were a good comrade, he thought bitterly, I would live for the interests of the circle, rather than my own personal interests. Only this did not, for some reason, make his desire for rain go away, but had the opposite effect.

He went up to the railing and looked down. Below solid shadows had already settled, and the salient girder could scarcely be seen. He knew he was not going to throw himself off. But it was nice to think that he might. This gave his sense of grievance over his unsuccessful life a rather sweet, liquorice taste.

And there was no one, no one with whom he could have a heart-to-heart talk! Now he would go back home, and immediately be transported into that isolated little world with its five people, and he would become its sixth. His mother would already be home, and he would kiss her hand – as ever, and how unthinkable it would be to have to do this in front of other people. Her hand would smell of hospital carbolic and household washing, and he would almost be pained by something for which the word hadn't even been thought up.

He had realised that he was a two-faced individual two years before, when, for some reason, the class had started to discuss whether or not it was possible to love your parents more than Stalin. And it wasn't even a discussion, for the answer was too obvious for everyone, including himself. But, ever since then, he had known that he loved Stalin more than anything on earth – whether he was at school, his circle, or anywhere else. Yet at home it was the opposite, and the mandatory portrait of the leader that hung in every home made him uneasy – if only for what it reminded him of. At home his grandpa was right to be sarcastic, as was his father, too, walking about in that way that made it so unmistakably plain to everyone that he was a White Guard, and that scalded Oleg with a forbidden, joyous pride: that's who we Petrovs are! There, on Koblevskaya Street, it was natural that they should read the tales of Perrault in French to that two-year-old imp Alyosha, his little brother. And that there should be many things of which they never spoke, even though they did occasionally speak in hints, and that after coming back from Solovki his father should have ordered his prison sack not to be hidden far away. And even when that grime came off his face and he started to look more like the father whom Oleg remembered, even then, Oleg knew, he was waiting to be arrested again. And so was everyone else, and so, till it happened, they would pretend to be simply getting on with their life, just like everyone else.

His father was on the night-shift that day, and by now he would have probably already left home. They would not see one another until the following day. But when they did, they would talk about model aeroplanes, about the radio, about frigates and clippers, but not about that. Sometimes Oleg dreamt that one day his father would (for some reason he always imagined that this conversation would be held late at night) say to him, 'Let's have a talk, son. Man to man.'

And he would tell him everything and explain what sort of a man he, Oleg, should be. It wouldn't matter if he told him to believe in God. It wouldn't matter if he told him to kill Stalin.

It wouldn't matter if it turned out to be a conspiracy against Soviet power – and his father made Oleg take an oath and drew him into the conspiracy. Or if he said that he was guilty, and renounced his past, and ordered Oleg to become a true Communist, even to leave the house, but let him start a new life that was no longer split in two like this.

But no such conversation took place. Either because his father thought him still too young, or unworthy of his trust. He never explained anything at all to Oleg, apart from mathematics if his son was having some difficulty with it at school. That was how he brought him up – not explaining anything. About three years before, Oleg had come home in a state of excitement, and had joyously announced how they, the Pioneers, had disrupted evensong at a church on Pushkin Street. It had been such fun, as the whole gang of them went bursting into the half-dark with its smell of burning candles and forbidden, alien atmosphere – and there gone caterwauling and jumping about in the knowledge that this was not hooliganism, but something that had to be done: it was the struggle against religion. And how funny it had been that the silly old women could do nothing but wag their fingers and hiss, which only made it all the more fun teasing them. His father let him get to the end of his story and, without uttering a word, he put him down on the sofa and thrashed him with his belt. Only later, when his son got back up on his still shaky legs, had he deigned to say, 'Get to be a human being – and then you'll understand what that was for.'

Perhaps he thought that Oleg still didn't understand, even now?

He had already turned into Koblevskaya Street, but had not yet reached number forty, where he lived. He was stopped outside number thirty-eight.

'There 'e is – out strollin'. I'll 'ave yer out strollin'. I'll 'ave yer breathin' good 'n' deep – only first you gotta lie down. Stretch yourself out, like. What 'ave you bastards done with Murochka?'

This was Vitka the Snake, who was endeavouring to live up to his distinguished nickname. Oleg was glad. For one thing he'd left his model back at the circle, and now he had his hands free. But also because he relished the forthcoming fight. Having a fight with the Snake, and, what was more, in front of witnesses, was something well worth a go: even if the Snake won, it could still do nothing but bolster Oleg's prestige. But if Oleg did manage to land a decent blow on the Snake, then it would be talked of for half a year to come. Even the Snake himself realised this, but someone had lured Murochka – the best of his pigeons – away from his flock. OK, even if Oleg didn't have any pigeons of his own, he still sometimes hung out with Filya's crowd. And it was Filya that was really the Snake's main suspect: there were then three flocks on the loose – the Snake's, Filya's and Syunchik-Shtymp's from way down on Port Street. Shtymp he could deal with some other time, but, in the meantime, now that the Snake had bumped into Oleg like this, what else could he do but straighten the record with him?

Oleg permitted himself to forgo etiquette. The convention was to start by whipping each other into a state of fury with an exchange of insults, and then perhaps retire to a somewhat quieter spot and get down to business there. But he knew the Snake. And with a clear conscience he decided not to hang about: he got stuck in right away – with an upper cut to his nose, and no holding back, either. Something made a lovely crunching sound: either Oleg's knuckles, or something they'd come up against. The Snake was blinded and he was hitting out inaccurately, and Oleg saw that he had a chance. He felt no pain when he fought – only fury and an animal thrill. The onlookers yelled their approval: it wasn't often that the Snake's gang got to see someone having the better of him, and it was a spectacle they none of them minded.

But they were both already exhausted, and when someone yelled 'Scarper!', they weren't about to start quibbling over whether this was a false alarm or not. Oleg, trying to keep his balance, set off back home to number forty. Out of the corner of his eye he could see that the Snake couldn't walk away without being helped. Serve 'im right, too. It was not until he reached the arch of the entrance that he was overcome with pain. But from there he had only a few more steps to go before reaching the tap, and by the tap it was dark. Sobbing from the release of tension, he washed his battered face and ran his tongue over his teeth. No, everything seemed all right there. He wetted his handkerchief and put it to his eye. There was a familiar pinch. The cold water soothed the pain, and made the skin draw tight. He got himself back into shape as best as he could, using the same handkerchief to brush down his jacket before dragging his fingers through his hair. The Snake had given him a heavy kick on the shin, but at least it wasn't his knee. The bone was intact, and the rest would heal.

Oleg had his own key, and he hoped to get through to the wash-stand before any of his family could see him. They never made a fuss over his fighting: 'The boy goes out on to the street, and anything can happen there.' But should he ever take it into his head to come to table in a dirty jacket, or with his hair in a mess, that was regarded as outrageous. His father had returned from Solovki looking more like a corpse, but as soon as his hair had grown back, he reverted to keeping an immaculate parting in it.

After his fight with the Snake, Oleg felt better, as he always did after any contact with real life. The depression that had been building up seemed silly and a figment of his imagination. Like in the summer when, stupefied by the ringing heat of day and the diving, you wash your feet in the evening under a stream of cold fresh water. And the stream, and the tap, and the enamel wash-bowl that's as clean as from a hospital seem so small and unreal. And the only real thing is the ringing of the sea and the oppressive sun in your ears, and the bygone day, as enormous as a water-melon.

His arrival back home was noticed immediately.

'Olezhek, at last! Grandma's been calling you!'

Without noticing his appearance, his mother grabbed him by the shoulders, and so the two of them went into the 'warm room' and up to his grandparents' bed with its knobs on the bed-head. His grandma was no longer calling him. She cast a distracted look at Oleg, as though she were seeing him from a distance. With large, large eyes, and very calmly. Then, looking as if she were straining to recall something, she drew her eyebrows together and made a move of her hand. Oleg took her hand in bewilderment, but his grandma made a sign with her eyes, indicating that this wasn't what she meant, and he let go of her hand. She made the sign of the cross over him, diligently and sternly, and slightly drew in her lips in the beginning of a smile. Only then did Oleg understand that she had, in fact, recognised him. However unexpected, he knew that she was about to die, and that nothing could be done about it. And Grandpa knew, and so did Mama.

But she was certainly taking her time over it, and he sat on the floor by the head of her bed. He was ashamed that he could feel nothing. Grandpa was now holding both of Grandma's hands and muttering, 'My darling, my darling!'

Get on with it then, thought Oleg, so unbearable was it to see his grandpa like this. And, as if in answer to this blasphemous thought, his grandpa suddenly let out a cry and let his head fall down on his grandma.

Maria Vasilyevna was given a church funeral. A real-life priest, in a cassock and with a cross on a chain, sang in that very church on Pushkin Street in which Oleg had already once been. And he wafted the censer about. Taut little puffs of blue smoke sprinkled out from the censer. That was incense, Oleg realised. The smell was somehow familiar. And he was not even surprised. This sort of thing occasionally did happen to him: he might suddenly recall an unfamiliar street as though he had previously walked down it some time. Or a little stairway that he had never before seen leading down to the sea would seem familiar right the way down to the last step, and before getting there Oleg might be able to picture a dusty side-street that he had never been in, but was in fact just round the next corner.

Like everyone else, he held a yellow candle. And, also like everyone else, he went up to the priest to get his blessing. He did not find it strange kissing the priest's hand, even though it was in front of others. And there were a lot of people in the church: both those who once used to come and visit them at home, and those that his grandma used to greet out on the street, and some that were total strangers. Throughout the service his father stood with an expressionless face. And his grandfather tried not to stoop, and to focus his bewildered gaze. Oleg wanted to touch his father's hand, but he did not dare to in church.

That came only later, when the coffin was taken down the steps. His father looked up briefly, and with his eyes he indicated his mother. Oleg took her by the elbow, and she leaned on his arm, as though he were a man. And so the young Petrov led her out of church holding her by the arm. He did not give a damn who noticed. He even wanted to be noticed. Let there be a scandal at school, let them brand him at the meeting and all the rest of it. And if Tanya did likewise – then that was fine, too. Amongst them, the Petrovs, there were no traitors.

Yakov had not seen Rimma for two years, since the time their mother was buried. She had only come for two days then, and had remained wrapped up in herself and remote. Yakov realised that she would find the burial difficult – more so than he would himself. And it was plain that she had prepared herself for this: she was going to shut out whatever uninvited callers offering their condolences might have to say, and be insensitive to their looks. Were it not for Musya, with her violent and heartfelt sobbing, she would not have known how to behave even in the house, and would not have emerged from the wall of defence that she had come surrounded with. But Musya, who, in her simplicity, had no understanding of the complex history of family relationships, threw herself on Rimma's neck almost the moment she stepped over the threshold. And, sobbing, she told her that Yakov was away at work, and related how Mamochka (as she called Rakhil) had suddenly clutched her heart and collapsed right on to the kitchen table. And how her lips and face went blue. But Semyon – God grant health to his headmaster for expelling him for a week for something he'd been up to there at school – happened to be home, and he ran off to get an ambulance. But by the time they got there it was already too late. And it had been hot enough to drive you out of your mind, just like it was now. And Mamochka had been down to the bazaar only that very morning, and brought back two water-melons so big that not even a stevedore could have lifted them. How could her heart possibly take that? And it was all her, Musya's, fault: she should never have let Mamochka go to the bazaar on her own like that.

Yakov was relieved to see how, under the heartfelt torrent of Musya's lamentations, Rimma melted. Musya, meanwhile, kept tormenting herself over what a golden person Mamochka had been, mixing this with complaints against 'these bureaucrats'.

'Can you believe it, Rimma, it took them three days of fiddling about with papers before giving a death certificate – and in August! But you can't bury anyone without a certificate, so I told Yakov: you slip them a bribe, I said. He's ever so unpractical like that . . .'

She somehow managed to combine tactless day-to-day details with an open, childish grief and naturally drawing Rimma into this grief. That's women all over – God alone knows how they manage it. They both cried together, and Rimma kept muttering how beautiful their mama had been in her youth, and about some song she used to sing to Rimma and Yakov – all about a goat, some raisins and an almond. And they cried some more – this time over the song.

But in the yard, when the coffin had been carried out and they were waiting for the two funeral horses, as some old Jewish band members were lazily tuning up, knowing from experience that it would be some while before things started – once again Rimma turned to stone. And with some reason. 'Barmy Rokhl' was loved in the yard, and even those who had no intention of following the coffin to the Jewish cemetery had come out in quite some number. And, of course, whispers started to be exchanged. They all centred on the person of Rimma: so, even she had come. The accursed daughter. Taking advantage of the fact that her mother wouldn't rise up out of her coffin. Look at her – all tarted up with her fashionable shoulder pads. Heartless creature. And look at Musya – she was just the daughter-in-law, but that still didn't stop her from looking all weepy.

According to the lore of the women of the yard – at any rate, those of the women who established such lore – Rimma should be beating her fists on the coffin, pulling out her hair and crying, 'Forgive me, Mamochka!' But Rimma remained silent, and the yard felt that there was a defiance in this silence: it was as if she meant to deny it, the yard, from seeing this spectacle. The backchat grew louder. As if to let Rimma know: come on, it's time you started. Don't be so proud, woman. And, had she in fact started crying out then those same scandal-mongers would have raced forward and wholeheartedly comforted her, and persuaded her that she had done no wrong, and that her mama was fine now, and that she had, of course, already forgiven her everything, and that, anyway, there was nothing to forgive – for such were the times. In times such as these everyone behaved like lunatics, and who, really, was to blame for it?

But none of this happened, and after a while Yakov forgot to keep an eye on Rimma. For he, too, was human, and it was his own mother that he was burying. And her hands, and the soft stomach against which he had snuggled in his childhood, and the hardened lips that had once sung him the song about the little goat.

Rimma's visit that time had not drawn them any closer to one another. And now, when she came in December of thirty-six, as they stayed up until late in the kitchen, they both felt that there was nothing on which they could see eye to eye. It began with something innocuous: Yakov was a great lover of jokes. Of course, these were times when it was better not to get too carried away with them – but surely it was all right to tell this one to his sister? And, besides, it was an old joke, one that was almost harmless now.

'A little boy asks: "What's stronger, the kebab or the garlic?"' Yakov had scarcely begun. But, for no good reason at all, Rimma suddenly flew off the handle, and then it started.

'Don't you find anything sacred!' Rimma furiously snapped, trying to keep her voice down.

'Sacred? I thought all that stuff was abolished back in seventeen?'

'Don't try and look innocent – you know perfectly well what I mean! Philistine!'

'OK, I'm a philistine! With a potted geranium and a canary! But I don't mind telling you that I haven't killed a single person, or made anyone unhappy.'

'Really?'

'Really – not since I came to my senses, I haven't. And as for what went before, it's not for you to judge – like you told me yourself. One hell of an agitprop train that is – with machine-guns!'

'And you call that coming to your senses, do you? All you've done is turn into an enemy of Soviet power! And a hidden one, too! You haven't even got the guts to—'

'No, I haven't! If you mean I ought to go and report myself to the authorities – just remember, I've got a family. And I've never much gone for suicide, either.'

'And a man like you is working in a Soviet school!'

'And working in a school is more than enough for anyone to see the price of all this folly! One minute it's self-rule, and marks are forbidden. Then it's the team method, and marks are awarded to the collective. Then there's a campaign to fight this and that, and one of my top girl pupils is drummed out of the Pioneers for having a doll at home! Then they're purging children's libraries and getting rid of all the fairy-tales! And how many years were Christmas trees banned for? And why have they suddenly removed that phrase from the primers – the one that Soviet power launched its struggle against illiteracy with? Remember: "We are no slaves – no slaves are we." Well, even if it was a bit of a tongue-twister, it was still no worse than "Mama bakes cakes". Now it's disappeared though. You think what that means. But forget the primers – I'd gladly shoot every one of our leaders just for the struggle against the waifs, if others hadn't taken that in hand without me!'

'Firstly, it's not against the waifs – it's against the fact that they're getting out of control.'

'What do you know about it! Your business is to sit in Kharkov and send out directives. But do you know what they did in Kiev when some of those kids were being rounded up? They drove them out of the city, to a field – it was minus twenty! – and ditched them right there. I knew one of them myself – I later found him a place in a children's home. He was eleven, and old enough to make it to the nearest village. But the rest of those kids were left there to die. And at the time you were signing papers authorising that same struggle and offering up prayers to that scoundrel Trotsky of yours. And now it's Stalin you pray to!'

'Leave Trotsky out of this. After Lenin he was the only

man who would have refused to allow the Party line to be distorted.'

'Ah, so you admit—'

'With Trotsky, it was a tragic mistake. But the Party will still put it right – I'm sure of it! And, incidentally, under Trotsky there wouldn't have been any of this latent anti-Semitism. You're buried away in that school of yours – with dolls! – so don't pass judgement on what you don't know about. But how often – even at regional level – do we have to fight against creeping chauvinism!'

'Well, you know, the chauvinism of others is most often spoken of by people that suffer from it themselves! Trotsky did the Jews no favours with his Bolshevism. And neither did we.'

'If that . . . If that's how it is – then you and I really have got nothing to talk about!'

'Well, we can agree on that. Let's go to sleep. Musya's made a bed up for you.'

The following morning Rimma left, after refusing even to have breakfast, greatly to the disappointment of Musya. It was this that Yakov had found finally infuriating, and he did nothing to persuade her to stay. He was ready to put up with any difference of views, but – getting to the stage of their causing a family rift? Well, anyway, what does the Second Secretary of the Kharkov regional committee of the Party want with a piffling relative like me? he reflected bitterly.

It was already the school New Year holidays, the most wonderful period of winter. All the fuss with the end-of-term tests and results was over and done with, the New Year morning party had passed off perfectly satisfactorily, and Yakov was enjoying a few days well-earned break from school. Once again fir trees were now allowed in the schools, and even in the Kremlin – for children. So, just like every other teacher, Yakov also had a fir tree at home: when the lorry came bringing round the large fir trees for the schools' New Year parties, before getting their school's tree put up in its wooden frame, the smart school administrator Silych had put aside some of the nicer-looking ones for the school staff.

There had been no Christmas trees in Yakov's childhood

(it was a point on which his mother had been strict), and he regarded the smell of conifers and the delicate shards of broken glass baubles as a fleeting joy that he had needlessly been forbidden. He had gone to the Petrovs as they were preparing their Christmas tree, and there they had joked and squirted one another with slices of orange, and danced about and chewed nuts. And how lovely it had been to paint the nuts gold, and wrap themselves in the fine gold threads as they got everything ready before hanging it up at the Christmas tree party itself! He remembered how Marina started untangling him before suddenly spinning him off round the room and brushing off the newspapers that were spread out over the table. And they – the two of them – had themselves ended in these threads of quivering gold, laughing as they called Zina and Maxim to come and help them out!

Now he was glad not to deprive his own children of all this, and he shared in the enjoyment with them. Manya and Petrik, who were not yet four, obediently repeated the little children's commandment about the tree: 'Eyes can look – but hands can't touch.' Yet their hands still reached out to it, and Musya laughed as she shook the silvery fragments off some Grandfather Frost from Petrik's bed. Semyon, who had completed the term with top marks, got the camera that his father had promised him, and he did not take off its wholesome-smelling leather casing even when he sat down to table. Soon he would be thirteen – and that was virtually the start of adult life. Yakov had even promised that he would no longer make him go to bed at ten o'clock.

Now he pointedly went straight to bed the moment his parents looked at the clock. First, because there wasn't long to go now, and second because he'd found a way of reading under the blanket with his pocket dynamo-torch. And having to keep squeezing it all the time built up his wrists, and no one could see him. The torch did, however, hum, though his parents thought they had a cricket in the house.

'Our cricket's gone to sleep,' Yakov grinned when the humming from next door had died down.

'Won't he ruin his eyes though?' asked Musya in alarm as she dried the forks. But this was just for form's sake as they had already discussed this topic on several previous occasions.

'No, it can't harm him. You should be glad the boy's reading. I've left a copy of Hugo lying around for him. Stolen goods are sweeter.'

He drew Musya close, and her body, now rather fuller than before, softened for an instant, but then it assumed a vigilant stiffness.

'At least let me finish the drying-up, you madman!'

'And I say no.'

'And I say you'll get belted with a wet cloth! Hooligan!'

'Milady, I pine for thee. Permit me a hug!'

Musya grinned and put the cloth to one side. Then the doorbell rang.

'Who is it?' asked Musya in alarm.

'Telegram – has to be signed for,' came the answer from the other side of the door.

In thirty-seven no one needed telling what the delivery of a telegram at this sort of time meant.

'Divorce me, denounce me, do what you like – but keep the children safe!' Yakov said sternly as he looked into Musya's frightened eyes. And, without hurrying, he kissed her hard, annoyed that this was all he had time for. By now there were impatient knocks at the door, and Yakov went to open it.

Being a respected person, Rimma Isakovna was invited into the study of the First Secretary in order that she might be privately informed of what had happened.

'It transpires that your brother is a Trotskyite, Comrade Geiber. We do understand that this is in another city, and that he has a different surname from you. But, even so, you must react in some way. You must – as a matter of principle – dissociate yourself from him. Otherwise things could get nasty – bearing in mind the position that you hold.'

So. That meant they had uncovered their kinship. They had worked quickly. As regards her position – that was a hint that otherwise they would not have hung on ceremony. She knew how she was supposed now to dissociate herself – by writing a newspaper article and making a speech at a meeting. Or at several meetings and in several newspapers. And it was imperative that she should incriminate her criminal brother, and so confirm the charge. And this while the investigation was still under way. And so push Yakov closer to where they wanted him.

'I . . . I appreciate your concern. I must think.'

'What is there to think about, Rimma Isakovna? But you go ahead and think about it. Think hard.'

Comrade Omelnichenko could hardly conceal his delight: whatever you might think up now, my dear, your time as Second Secretary's up. We've spent more than enough time wondering how to undermine you – but let's see you try and wriggle out of this one.

For Rimma, however, there was nothing to wriggle out of. And she had no intention of trying. Without hurrying, she gathered up all the papers on her desk. She liked the smell of the new cardboard files. She always kept some new ones in reserve, with their patterned borders and sturdy note-labels. Having completed her working day, she did not, as she usually did, stay on. What was the point now? She told her driver he could go, and took pleasure in strolling off on foot. The snow was just as she liked it: fluffy, and muffling every sound. All that could be heard was the mournful ringing of infrequent trams, while off in the little side-streets it was utterly still. A yellow light could be seen burning up in someone's windows – just like a little gingerbread house. She was in no rush. It was mild and pleasant like this, and the frost wasn't severe.

She did not want to think about anything – neither about herself, nor her brother. For some reason the studio and Moscow sprang to mind. Maybe because of the snow. She recalled the bluey-grey Moscow back streets, the frozen green sky, and the erect columns of smoke climbing up into it, making it appear as if it were these columns that held up the sky.

She was arrested four days later. Already she was tired out with waiting. And it happened at work, though she had left everything that she had got ready back at home. When your luck's out, it's out. She had, for some reason, thought that an arrest began in the interrogator's office. And she was ready: she would behave with dignity and be courteous, but firm. Like the women revolutionaries of former times. But the arrest started with a search in her office: they searched the pockets of both her suit and coat, all but turning them inside out. And in the investigational 'isolator' she was ordered – oh, the shame of it! – to strip naked. She took it into her head to protest, but was impassively told that she would be stripped forcibly.

'Open your mouth. Bend over. Open your buttocks. Remove your hairpins.'

Dumbfounded and crushed, Rimma did not resist. She only hoped that she would not burst into tears from the powerless humiliation of it. Then she was led away to a cell in which there were already fifteen women – all dressed as they had been at the time of their arrest, and one even in evening dress. There was a foul smell in the cell. After looking round, Rimma realised where it came from: it was a metallic barrel-like object that was covered with a strip of cardboard. This was the lavatory. Or the 'parasha', as it was called. Inside the cell there were already certain complicated rules and relationships in existence, but Rimma knew nothing of these, and she did not want to know: it was enough that she was sharing a cell with a group of women criminals. She did not talk to anyone, or answer any questions. She silently sat down on the bunk indicated by the guard. She was seized by a sudden hope that her case would be cleared up. She would not be here for long. Because it was so utterly absurd. Her – and this cell. And she had no toothbrush, or anything, apart from a handkerchief. She tried not to listen to what the others were saying and to avoid looking at anyone. But from the bunk over by the window there came a viscous groan, and out of the corner of her eye Rimma saw a middle-aged woman fiddling about with a little huckaback towel.

'What are you gawping at, newcomer? Still in shock? That's Linda – she's a Baptist. She wasn't carried back in from interrogation till lunch-time,' remarked a shaggy, large-busted woman who looked like a speculator, catching her glance.

Rimma made no reply. Five days went by before her first interrogation, and in that time Rimma had – like it or not – to make herself familiar with the prison ways. People really were carried back in from interrogation. But not everyone. The woman who looked like a speculator came back on her own feet, and without looking beaten up. Three of the women in the cell pointedly kept their distance from the others. They were Party workers, one of whom Rimma knew: she had been the editor of a local newspaper. Rimma became the fourth of these women. They found her a toothbrush and a spare pair of knickers – even if they were a bit too big. But knickers always had to be tied round the waist anyway, as the prisoners were forbidden elastic and had it removed from them. These women were friendly in a selective way. Communists had to help one another. With each one of them there had been some mistake – but the Party mustn't be blamed for that! They would be cleared – and then discharged. In the meantime, however, they shared their parcels, food and even cigarettes with Rimma. Rimma did not expect any parcels from anyone, but within their circle everything was shared.

Her heart pounded when she was called out. She had not been told where she was going, but as they had not said 'with your things', that meant she was being taken for interrogation. There was nothing terrifying about this clean study. And the interrogator was young and ruddy-cheeked, and he smiled at Rimma as though she were an old acquaintance. Rimma readily replied to his smile and, obeying his gesture, she sat down on a little stool screwed to the floor. On his desk the interrogator had a new file with patterned borders. Rimma saw that it already contained some papers.

She answered to her name, year and place of birth, and current job. She confirmed that she had a brother called Yakov Isakovich Krasnov.

'And what is your attitude to the fact that your brother has proved to be a malicious Trotskyite?'

'Comrade interrogator . . .'

'It would be more appropriate for you to call me "citizen interrogator",' the man behind the desk gently corrected her.

Rimma bit her lip. How could she have forgotten that? Well, she should be grateful that he hadn't turned round and said 'I'm no comrade of yours'. After all, she was a suspect.

'Citizen interrogator,' she began, obediently adopting the correction, 'I am sure that this is a misunderstanding. I only see my brother very, very rarely, but—'

'You did, however, go and see him only recently – last month, in fact.'

'Yes, I did. And I know exactly what his attitude to Trotsky is. It isn't just negative, but extremely negative. He gets very heated when he argues about him.'

'And who was he arguing about Trotsky with?' asked the interrogator with interest.

Rimma realised her blunder. She feverishly sought an answer that would save the situation, but the interrogator gave her no time.

'Was it you?'

'Yes,' Rimma admitted.

'But if he has a negative attitude to Trotsky, and you argued with him – that must mean your attitude is positive?'

That was it, Rimma realised. Now her one difference with the Party had been brought out into the open. But perhaps it was for the good. At any rate she would shield Yakov, that scape-grace father with all those children of his. Want a Trotskyite? Fine. She would give them one.

'Yes, I do take a positive view of Trotsky's work. Both his practical and theoretical work. That is what my brother and I were arguing about. He was trying to make me change my mind.'

'Interesting. Yet his own testimony here does not corroborate that. Here it is: "My sister, Rimma Isakovna Geiber, and I discussed purely family matters. For the most part we remembered the civil war and discussed the upbringing of my children. I know that my sister is wholeheartedly devoted to the Party, and I have never discussed political matters with her, as I know her opinion on any matter in advance." Curious, wouldn't you say, Citizen Geiber? It means that he must have been lying at his interrogation in order to protect you? Or that you are now lying in order to protect him?'

'Citizen interrogator, I am ready to set out my views frankly and in writing. And then you can judge for yourself.'

The interrogator readily gave her a pen and paper, and she set out her views. This interrogation was taking quite some time: the young interrogator pointedly looked at his watch, and then started to hurry her, but Rimma kept on writing.

'Let me write it all down, otherwise my testimony will be incomplete.'

This is becoming amusing, she thought, the accused is writing out the case against herself, while the interrogator tries to restrain her. Was he in a hurry to be off to some tryst? Never you mind, young man – work is more important. You can wait – both you and your girl. And, as the Party to which she had utterly devoted herself was treating her in this way, Rimma wrote down everything. It was the last thing that she could do for the Party – to point out its mistakes. She addressed her testimony unconventionally – it was a letter to Comrade Stalin. All case documents had to be filed together – the rules were the same for everyone. Should this interrogator dare to mislay them, then he was really in deep water. He, too, had someone watching over him. And she managed to get it all down: that Yakov was no Trotskyite – owing to his lack of political acumen – that the denunciation of Comrade Trotsky was an intrigue of the Kamenev-Zinoviev block, and that the mass arrests of devoted Communists was the Party's suicide. Someone had to keep the country on the right, Bolshevik path!

When he saw the heading, the interrogator frowned. But he did not start to argue, and sent her back to her cell. Rimma did not sleep that night, and she kept on remembering the other things that she should have written down. Or other ways she might have put it. OK, she was not naive. So this letter probably wasn't about to go landing on Stalin's desk. But in due course someone would eventually get to read the minutes of the interrogations, and they would see that she was right! And so, after all, she would not die in vain. She would perish defending the interests of the Party from its enemies who lurked inside the Kremlin itself. Whether from excitement (she was shivering), or something else, she kept having to rush to the 'parasha'. Maybe her bladder was chilled? It was cold in there. Ah, so what! How nice not to have to worry about your body any more!

Two hours after getting-up time it finally started to turn grey beyond the pea-soup-coloured screen that shielded the window. Rimma listened indifferently to an exchange of insults between the speculator, who called the screen a muzzle, and the

Communist Klavdia Mironovna, who forbade her from using such a word. It had an official name – it was a cover-shield, and any other word for it was a mockery of the investigative organs. That Klavdia's always overcooking it, thought Rimma, without caring. And she was surprised at herself: she was reasoning like Yakov. Not that it mattered, really. She had already done all that she could, and now she had no further duties to discharge. Not even to the Party.

She was surprised when they gave her only fifteen years. The investigation did not take long, and she was not beaten up. But it was a pity the journey to camp had to be in springtime! They were forever doing something with them: endlessly lining them up, counting them, transporting them in closed railway trucks. But spring penetrated the cracks of these trucks, with its subtle, subtle smell. And how powerful that smell was: even through the stench of the trucks it managed to excite the nostrils. And there was a stop at which, drowning even the cries of the waterless prisoners, could be heard the tender call of a cuckoo. Maybe that call was what started that riot in the neighbouring carriage, when the guards started shooting until everything died down again. Rimma was not surprised: that cuckoo was enough to drive anyone mad. She suddenly felt how furiously her doomed body wanted to live. She had to make an effort not to hurl herself against the wooden boards of the truck. The others plainly felt the same way, too. In any event, they all cursed each other, and two women criminals grabbed hold of one another's hair with a howl.

This springtime ordeal of the transport was worse than starvation and the horrors of prison. Not that there was any shortage of vileness now. Rimma was glad not to have any of her things with her: anyway they would have been taken from her during the transport. But those disinfections at the transit points, when you had to stand naked while some oaf of a medical orderly took a brush smeared with green soap and, with the cold-bloodedness of a machine, shoved it between your legs! And those hideous dogs that were released and came snapping at the laggers the moment the column dawdled! And the most terrible transit point, the last one – when you're already there.

The women's transport's made it! And as for what they got up to with them before packing them off to the different camps – Rimma knew that she could never tell anyone about that. She could not forgive herself for the fact that she was still alive. But at Kolyma this presented no problem: if you don't want to live – then don't block the light. Others do want to. Rimma did not compete with those others in trying to get work either on the sick-bay, or in the kitchen, or in the recreational groups, where there was, nevertheless, some chance of surviving. She simply marvelled in silence: could anyone honestly wish to survive here?

The Communists helped one another even here. There were opportunities to get one of the easier jobs. But by autumn Rimma, with her indomitable character, had already been assigned to wood-felling. The prisoners covered the tarpaulin tents with snow, and the packed crust kept in the warmth well. Only the teams that had fulfilled their norm were allowed to go and warm themselves up by the camp-fires. But Rimma ended up in a team of 'stiffs': they hardly ever fulfilled the norm. And – either because her rations were reduced, or because she was getting to the end of her strength, beyond which she recognised no further change of mind would be possible – once again her body revolted. It yearned to be properly fed, and warm, and free of lice, and – for some reason – to have some little juniper cones to chew on. Yearned to a point of stupefaction, to a point of shameful self-pity. So it was no bad thing when a guard helped out: when they were lined up he kicked her in the small of the back with his felt boot as he went by. And heaped however many obscenities on her as she got up from the snow.

After that it got easier. It was early November, and soon the first real frosts would set in, and it wouldn't be long then . . . The pine trees struck her as astonishingly beautiful in the downy hoar-frost, as did the wonderful sky – it was bright, brighter than in the south. And green, and pink and mauve – and every other colour, too. With calm fondness she recalled Yakov, and his wonderful little son, Semyon – the clear-eyed Pioneer who looked as if he'd jumped off a magazine cover. And even the pair of spoilt twins. Their antics and their eternal howling had annoyed her when she stayed at Yakov's. But now they seemed amusing and endearing. And she recalled her mama – positively, fondly, without banishing the thought of her, as she once had. It was possible to envy the believers: after all, they hoped to meet again some time. And how wonderful that would be. Only she knew too much to believe in that.

It was not quite the end of November when Rimma's teeth started falling out. After pulling out the first one, she looked at it in surprise and for some reason had an urge to hide it somewhere. But then she laughed this off and threw it in the snow. Next day she started giving half her bread ration to a Jewish girl in the same team as her. She was so small that it was hard to believe she was nineteen. She was a Jewish black-eyed child, torn away from her mother. In all likelihood back home she had never held anything heavier than a violin in her hands. But even so, she objected: 'Come on, Auntie Rimma – you need it yourself!'

Any other of the women would not have objected. She was a decent girl. If there were a God, surely He'd protect this one, at least. Rimma pulled back her lips in a smile.

'I don't need it any more. Live, Mariam!'

And, as she looked at this smile – and saw how cracked Auntie Rimma's lips were, although there was no sign of blood on the cracks – Mariam believed that she really didn't need it any more. So she took the bread. On her last day Rimma gave her her entire ration.

Mariam survived, and even married. She called her first daughter Rimma. Her husband, who was a former camp doctor and later became a well-known gynaecologist in Irkutsk, did not argue. It's a beautiful name.

28

Pavel was taken in August of thirty-seven. Although they tried not to wake him, the seven-year-old Alyosha heard everything. He did not go back to sleep again until morning, crying, not so much out of sorrow, of which he was not yet aware, but because he felt slighted: his papa had said goodbye to Oleg, but not to him! And he had told Oleg: 'Look after your mother.'

But to him he had said nothing, absolutely nothing. Well, all right, he would show them all. They would see who could look after their mother better, Oleg or him, Alyosha. He would not say a word to anyone. Until Papa got back. And then they would all be ashamed themselves.

The following morning, when his mama told him that Papa had had to go off on a long journey on a construction job and would not be home for a long time, he merely nodded. But it came as a surprise when, a few days later, he was hurriedly made to learn the fable about the vixen off by heart, and his mama took him to school to try and get him registered there. After all, it was only a short while ago that, much to his disappointment, they had decided to put this off for another year – until he was eight. They said it wasn't compulsory before that age, and what good would it do him there, anyway? At this, Alyosha had all but burst with indignation: what good would it do him? Slavka who lived down in the basement was only half a year older, and he was going to school and had already been bought a uniform, and a belt with a buckle, and a satchel with wonderful hasps, and a wooden pencil-case with the Soviet banner burnt into it, and a star, and the hammer and sickle. So why did Alyosha have to go on hanging out with the younger kids in the yard? And listen to Slavka's insufferable boasting?

Out on the street he took his sweaty palm from his mother's hand: he wasn't a little boy. Anna smiled. Her son was trying to look taller, and doing his utmost to hold his little head high. She should have given him a shorter haircut – but there was still plenty of time for that. It was a pity to have to cut off his blond locks: after all, she could only ever enjoy them while he was little. And for all the trouble she'd had with Oleg, Alyosha had been an easy child right from the word go. Both the pregnancy and the birth had been easy, and she hardly even noticed him growing up. That was what it meant to have his father there. Yet she and Pavel were always so busy that they had been unable to pay the child any attention. Back in thirty-one she had been switched from nurse to hospital orderly, and for this she was grateful. They could very well have dismissed her altogether. Pavel worked at Gena's former factory as a lorry-driver. She would arrive home from work with her arms dropping off, but the moment she got back she would be greeted by such a radiant scene, with Alyosha's happy little face looking like an angel in a picture. He was calm and always content with everything, and he could keep himself entertained. Naturally, it was the grandparents that rescued them: for as long as they were still alive Anna did not have to spend all her time looking after the boy. And she knew that he would be fed and put to bed on time and, without fail, taken out for a walk. She cursed herself as a bad mother, but there was nothing she could do about it: quitting her job was out of the question. Later on, when Maria Vasilyevna died, Alyosha came under the charge of his grandpa. And she had no reason to reproach herself for this, either: it was thanks entirely to Alyosha that the old man, who had instantly become subdued and lifeless, lived on for another year and a half. Ivan Alexandrovich was overhasty with the boy, Anna saw, but she did nothing to stop him. There was no point in depriving the old man of the last meaning and light in his life. Shortly before he died he put Alyosha on the table, and, almost without faltering, the little boy read out the last pages of his primer to his mama and papa: it was a great surprise for Pavel's name-day. By the age of three and a half he was already so independent that he could tie his own shoe-laces and had mastered all the niceties of getting dressed. Apart from needing help with the buttons at the back of his vest that did up to his stockings.

Anna was utterly at a loss when her father-in-law died. She was unsuccessful with her efforts to get Alyosha into the kindergarten. She tried taking the boy to work with her, but it came to nothing: the senior nurse was a pernickety sort of woman, and she discovered the irregularity in no time. And Anna was in no position to get herself into trouble. It was Tsilya from their yard that rescued her. Her husband was a small and quiet man, and he had some sort of job at the tram depot, and the yard would have known hardly anything about him had not Tsilya spoken of 'my Fima' every other word. However, he evidently got back from work with bags of energy still inside him. At any rate, Tsilya's fertility was fabled throughout the quarter: if she wasn't pregnant with the next of her progeny, she was busy breast-feeding the last. Dishevelled, loud and indestructibly healthy, her entire gang kicked up a racket in the yard from morning till night, with Tsilya keeping vigilant watch over them. Acknowledged as the 'yard mama', the moment a fight or any dangerous bit of tomfoolery began, Tsilya dished out generous slaps to her own and other people's children alike. For a modest sum she gladly agreed to keep an eye on Alyosha as well, thus preventing him from having to stay at home on his own. The boy was not capricious about this either, and he adapted quickly. After a few weeks he had already started talking with a Jewish lilt to his voice. But on sensing that for some reason, this annoyed his papa, he easily adjusted between his manners at home and those out in the yard. When he wanted to rub his father up the right way, he would sing the French songs that he had learned from his grandpa, and needlessly wipe his nose with his handkerchief. The rest of the time he made do with his sleeve, just like any other normal Odessan child.

Anna had no doubt that he would be accepted at the school. Particularly now, when Nikolai Ilyich, who was being treated for an ulcer at her hospital, was still headmaster. But who knew what it might be like in a year's time? Everyone was being 'swept away', good Lord, everyone. What would come of the boy if she, too, were taken? Oleg was already grown up, and he had a job. Any moment now he would be off in the army – and would Alyosha then have to go to a children's home? And not an ordinary home, either, but a special one for children of enemies of the people. There were rumours of what sort of things they did with the children there, though nobody knew exactly what went on. And that was the most terrible thing of all. She snapped herself out of it: what's this, getting to be a scaredy-cat, are we? What people fear is what happens to them. There was the boy looking radiant, already on his best behaviour and thrilled to bits. She could not possibly spoil her son's great day.

They celebrated that day, not only by buying a school uniform and satchel, but also an ice-cream, sitting at a shiny marble table at what used to be Fanconi's café. If you're going to celebrate, celebrate! She would have to go and borrow some money from Nina, but she wouldn't refuse her. Last year she had herself borrowed some from Anna.

By the time mother and son returned home it was already a rubicund summer evening. Alyosha could not, of course, sit still for even five minutes: he raced away to show off his brand-new school items to Manya and Petrik. Oleg had not yet returned. The apartment was clean, cool and empty. Anna went up to the greenish mirror in its heavy carved frame: Pavel had redeemed it from the wife of the chairman of the housing committee when the chairman lost his post. Anna remembered this mirror – it was the same one that used to be in the Petrovs' hallway. It stood on the marble pier-glass table with its grey veins and bulging, heavy legs, which were also carved. She and Zina used to prance about in front of it when they were still girls in school-hats, and Pavel would tease them whenever he caught them at it. The reflection now showed a tired woman with pronounced streaks of grey in her short-cropped fair hair. Her chin drooped, the ends of her lips looked as if they were sealed together and were already arching down. She was forty-three. By the time Pavel was out she would be fifty-three. She must not think about it! All she wanted was for him to stay alive – then it wouldn't matter if she looked as if she were seventy. Unlike the first time, now she could cope. Thanks to Maria Vasilyevna, who had then so put her to shame. Without saying a single word, as only she knew how. Anna smiled in the twilit glass, as though at that moment Pavel could see her. Now that's more like it.

'Mama, can Petrik and Manya come and have tea here? It's two hours since Aunt Musya said she'd be back soon!' she heard Alyosha's voice from the hallway, which now also served as the kitchen.

'All right, fine. Alyosha, leave that primus alone, I'll light it myself!' said Anna, bestirring herself. She loved it when Alyosha brought home these amusing five-year-olds with their enormous prune-brown eyes. It was funny watching her son share his things with tiny Manya in such knightly fashion. As he saw it, this meant everyone had to go halves on everything, and that Manya was also to have half his biscuits or sweets. He even scrupulously ensured giving her a bite from his sugar lump, and she, as a young woman, would accept this as her due. In one of their usual bedtime chats, Alyosha told his mama that Manya was a princess on whom a sorcerer had cast his spell, and that her real name was Marianna. Anna was flattered to be so trusted, and only hoped that her little prince was not about to discover that he might break the spell upon his Marianna with a kiss. It was much better having the children in front of her eyes. And it was just as well there was still some apricot jam left.

They had already been herded back into their barrack, and Yakov, cursing from the pain in his damned knee, had clambered up on to his top plank bed. He made himself cosy with a needle and thread, with one leg drawn up and the other resting out in front of him. Prisoners were not allowed needles, and thus he cherished this one that the deceased Styopych had given him with particular fondness. It was Styopych who had taught him how to keep a needle hidden from any search. Now whenever Yakov sewed his trousers he knew that before he'd even finished doing his own he would be beset with favours from others needing their overcoat mending, or their shirt. 'Got no hands, or something?' he would grumble, though this was just for form, as there was no dodging out of it and he would end up sewing them anyway.

Out of the corner of his eye he noticed that on the lower plank bed, down in the best and warmest corner that had been occupied once and for all by the privileged criminal fraternity, there was a buzz of excitement. That meant the criminals were about to start one of their periodic settling-ups: either someone had lost at cards and was not paying, or else someone had broken the criminals' 'law'. All that was clear was that later that night there was going to be a bust-up with bloodshed, and – sure as you like – the entire barrack would be put on defaults.

Inside the camps the criminals were an even more noticeable force than the camp authorities. They thought nothing of playing cards for a tooth or an eye of a 'frayer' – one of the non-criminal prisoners – and the loser had immediately to go and knock out the tooth or eye of the frayer in question. The intended victim knew absolutely nothing of either the game or his role in it – although he was the one that ended up on the receiving end. Robbing the frayers, especially the 'fascists' convicted under the political article 58, was a matter of natural course. The authorities tacitly encouraged the criminals, and everyone knew this. But there was little likelihood that today's settle-up would affect Yakov personally. He enjoyed a special status. The criminals' ringleader, who was known as 'the Eye', even called him Isakych, rather than a fascist.

'Isakych, sing us a song from Odessa!'

'Isakych, let's have a story!' they had pestered him even back at the transit points.

And it was with this reputation that he had arrived at the camp, and now he was here, he made it a point of honour to hang on to it. The subtle art of telling a gripping story that compelled its listeners to forget all about hunger and other such camp miseries – including the camp itself – was far from being as straightforward as it sounded.

'All right – I'll tell you what happened to me once!' some greenhorn would pipe up, imagining his life to be one of uncommon interest. And he would be bitterly disappointed when he was cut short before even getting to the end.

With Yakov it was different. Zeks, after all, were like children. A story could have all sorts of lies, exaggeration, and dreadful though unexpected details, and they should, preferably, be funny. Yakov knew all this with the unerring instinct of an Odessan – no matter if he had been born in Nikolayev. Besides which he had one further rare quality: he had a flair for making up jokes. During his time in the camp, he introduced an endless series of jokes about bone-headed 'screws'. And to the end of his life, as he heard his own jokes being recounted, by that time readapted as a series about militiamen, he would enjoy the sweet glory of an anonymous artist.

'Why don't militiamen eat pickled cucumbers?'

'Well?'

'Because their heads won't fit in the jar!'

His listeners would howl with delight, and the narrator, intoxicated with success and old enough to be Yakov's son, would continue. 'Why do militiamen always go round in threes?'

'Well?'

'One can read, and one can write. And the third's there to keep an eye on the two intellectuals.'

Yakov chuckled as might a grandfather at his own grandchildren. But that was years later, and, for the time being, getting through the day was of itself no mean undertaking. And best fitted to succeed in this was the man who was cheerful and carefree. Or who managed to look as if he was.

Like now, when no sooner had he threaded his needle than from the lower plank bed there came the call: 'Isakych, sing us a song about Odessa!'

> 'Mama, Mama, what'll we do
> When winter's come and we've gone blue?
> We've got neither a scarf nor a coat –
> Instead we'll have a darn sore throat!'

Yakov sang with comic concern, fondly recalling the satirical couplets of Khenkin. But on this occasion he was only able to give his barrack the benefit of a further three such verses. The lock clattered, and in small clouds of icy air the duty screws came bursting in. No, he had not misheard – it was his number they were yelling.

'With your things to the exit!'

Still unable to take it in, Yakov found himself travelling in what was indubitably a free passenger compartment, gradually becoming accustomed – and yet not daring to become accustomed – to the fact that he was himself a free man. He could ask the carriage attendant for some tea. He could get off the train. He could – oh, how non-zeks undervalue this blessing! – run to the lavatory as and when he pleased. He understood absolutely nothing when, back in the study of the camp governor, some unfamiliar but correctly mannered comrades in civvies had informed him that his case had been reviewed, and that he was to be released without any further delay. They were about to issue him with money for the journey back to Odessa, as well as a money transfer from his wife. That meant – Yakov eventually twigged – that that crazy Musya had not started divorce proceedings against him. She had even sent him some money. She must be off her head. The rest passed him by altogether. To serve only eleven months of a ten-year term? It was unheard of! And who had ever heard of the Bolsheviks reviewing anybody's case? He was courteously informed that, immediately upon his return, he would be reinstated in the Party, and told where to send his application. That was just what Yakov could have done without. But, he realised, there could be no getting away from it now.

What Yakov did not know was that in thirty-eight, following the dismissal of the almighty Yezhov, in place of the massive flow into the camps there was now a modest and unexpected counter-flow, including releases such as his own. This went on for a year in all, and then the counter-flow dried up just as mysteriously as it had started. One way or another, Yakov fluked his way into being caught up in it. And now – like a man back from the dead – he was returning home. The money transfer had been quite sizeable, and it turned out that his travel expenses were more than he needed. Maybe it was silly to spend it, maybe Musya had contracted debts and sent him the last of what she had? Ah, tosh! He'd get his job back. They'd manage somehow. And with the abandon of a zek he bought himself a decent suit and hat at Leningrad's Gostiny Dvor. He would have found it unbearable to turn up home in a shabby overcoat still showing the stitching from his numbers and soused in the foul, bitter stench of prison. And he bought some hefty bars of chocolate with the bronze horseman on the gilded wrapping paper.

It was morning as the train drew into Odessa. Heedless of the indignant rumpus from the passengers waiting outside for the lavatory, and even the banging on the door, Yakov shaved with particular care, put on some eau-de-Cologne and attentively inspected the pale strip of scar on his chin. He had copped this back at one of the transit points – and not in a fight, either. An improbably large boil had simply swollen up, and a seasoned zek from their train had magnanimously cut it out with a razor-sharp knife. And no bones about it – a generous slash he'd made of it, too. Well, no matter: a scar merely made a man all the better looking. It was a pity his hair was 'à la Mayakovsky' – but how could it possibly have grown in eleven days? Yakov suddenly laughed and screwed up his face. He was familiar with this intoxication of returning home. It's the same even when your train's simply pulling into the station after a business trip, or any other kind of journey. Once you've got to the Odessan Goods Station it's child's play, and you get an urge to talk gibberish, and, for some reason, you're almost expecting to be greeted with fireworks. But out you get – and everything's as downbeat as ever, and there's an orphan rain falling. And you feel like an orphan yourself, coming back to your own native patch without any shoes on, and your feet battered and bleeding.

'Shame on you, citizen!' a corpulent woman who was desperate with waiting outside justly laid into him when he finally emerged from the carriage lavatory.

Yakov guiltily pressed his hand to his heart, blew a bit of fluff from his jacket and, accompanied by unflattering wishes, proceeded on through to his compartment to get his raincoat and hat. He did not remember how he got home. Following the superstitious habit of his childhood, he spent the whole time counting the lions outside the houses and on top of the stone walls. And, just as in his childhood, he cheated, adding on the sculptured lion and lioness from the city gardens, although, in fact, the tram window, on to which someone had stuck one of his 'lucky-number' tickets, was so steamed over that he was unable to see them.

Had he been right not sending Musya a telegram? Bloody egoist, lover of effects. He had no keys, and what if no one was home? Then he'd have to dance about outside his own door, the husband back from the dead, left out under the slushy December snow. But what kind of problem was that – he wouldn't mind spending the whole day dancing about under the snow! In the camp he had tried not to think about Musya and the children, otherwise he would never have coped. But now it all came welling up inside. He remembered Musya's favourite joke. Ever since thirty-three, no matter where he was going, even if it was on a Pioneers' field trip, as she was preparing his things, she would be sure peevishly to repeat: 'And you can tell that stork we don't need no more babies!'

In fact, not only Musya was home, and immediately clung to him with endless tears, but so, too, for some reason, was Anna Teslenko. She, of course, had the delicacy to leave immediately. But her strange presence added to Yakov's unease about the manner of his return, which, he felt, was already peculiar enough anyway.

It was not until later that evening – when the children, dazed by events and their presents from Leningrad, had been put to bed, and Musya, by now coming to terms with it all and no longer continually clutching at his sleeve – that Yakov heard the explanation. 'Anechka? She's our neighbour from apartment twenty-nine! You hardly even know her. But I can't tell you what a wonderful, wonderful woman she is. I don't know what I would have done without her. And her husband's such an extraordinary man. After you were taken, I nearly went mad. Who'd give me a job as the wife of a Trotskyite – and, as for our savings account, you know how little we had in there yourself. So I was stuck at home, howling like an idiot, and Semyon was howling with me: he got expelled from the Pioneers at school. I packed the little ones off to Tsilya and howled.'

Yakov stroked her shoulders and hair and listened to how Musya and Anna had 'got to know one another through the children', what a well-educated boy their Alyosha was and how out in the yard he had protected Manya and Petrik, and how Anna and Pavel had immediately lent her some money and refused any repayment, and how they had 'made her see sense', convincing her that there was no point in despairing and that she had to go on living. And what a life it had been: Andrei Semyonych had helped her to get a job at the laundry – the one just on the corner, and a month later had himself been arrested. But she'd still been upset that he was so stand-offish about it and had been in such a hurry to wash his hands of anything to do with her. Probably he already had a feeling that he was about to be arrested, and she, the fool, had not realised. But they had not dismissed her at the laundry. And now, even if she wanted to, there was no getting away from it, as no one could change jobs nowadays. It was the law. What did Yakov know about it – he knew nothing! They'd brought in such strict rules these days: if you were twenty minutes late then – by decree – you were up in court! Borya's elder son had been done like that: the tram-track had been blocked with snow, and the trams stopped running, but he still had to get all the way out to the Marti factory! He had been late, of course. More than twenty of the others who had to get there from the city were late, too, and there was a trial – a show case. They'd all been sentenced. As saboteurs. It had turned Rita into an old woman – why, you couldn't even recognise her.

And what had happened to Semyon! At school he'd been told to denounce Yakov, and they had arranged an assembly for the next day. He'd come home and started preparing his speech – no kidding! They'd managed to din it into his head that his father was an enemy.

'And – then what?' asked Yakov, bracing himself and doing his best to make it appear that he would take a 'quite right he was, too!' view of the situation.

'I smacked him round the gob with a towel: don't you dare, you little scamp, denounce your own father! And he started shaking all over, and got ever so cheeky, you know, telling me: "The young Spanish Communists were beaten far worse than that!" Can you believe it! And off he went, complaining about how we'd always been wrong, and how Auntie Rimma was right, and claiming that she'd understand him, and how he'd run away and go and live with her in Kharkov. Well, I didn't want to – but then I told him where his Auntie Rimma is now. That had him in tears, all right, and after that I had no more nonsense out of him. Everywhere he went he took your photo with him. And did you see how he cuddled up to you? That means the boy's got a clear conscience.'

'So where is Rimma?' asked Yakov, fearing to guess.

'I tried to find out, Yashenka – but I still don't know where she's gone. She got fifteen years with no right of correspondence. Straight after you – I thought you knew . . .'

No, Yakov did not know. Nor did either of them know that Rimma was no longer alive at the time of this conversation, nor would they know for a long, long time to come.

Next day, after waiting until Anna got back from work, Yakov went and rang her doorbell. He already knew about Pavel. And, even if she drove him away, he still had to go and see her. And say thank you. For what she had done for Musya and the children. He was not surprised that Anna had told Musya nothing of her and Yakov's previous acquaintanceship. He had said nothing of it himself. His reason, however, had been to preserve his self-esteem – but what about Anna? Anna's concern was probably not his self-esteem so much as Musya's, and preventing it from looking as if she bore a grudge. And she had always been like that. No matter if it were 1908 or 1938. And now, out of all their childhood acquaintances, only the two of them were left. Counting Pavel and Rimma, that made four. And God grant that the four of them were, indeed, still alive. And there was nothing to be ashamed of: yesterday a zek himself, now he was going to see the wife of another zek. He'd had four teeth knocked out at the interrogation, and he was forever telling himself that this was for Dombach. For Dombach. And he hoped she would forgive him: for Dombach, and for Marina, and for that rabbi. And for the fact that he was alive and free. And had to be restored to the Party. Who else was now entitled to grant forgiveness, if not zeks' wives?

Having not even had time to take off her scarf, Anna opened the door. They looked one another in the eye. And Yakov realised that she would not drive him away. And when he kissed her outheld hand she drew it back, not out of enmity, but simply because she was embarrassed. It was something to which she had become unaccustomed.

29

> 'My sweetheart's gr-rave I sought to find
> Though where it lies no man doth know,
> With br-roken heart I long have pined,'

sang Petrik, lingering on the 'r's' that he had only recently managed to pronounce properly, before continuing with relief: 'Where art thou, oh my Suliko?'

'You sing well, son,' said Yakov approvingly, holding back a smile. It was the first time that he had ever paid any attention to the words of this song that it now seemed all but impossible to get away from. There was his boy, not even school age yet, with an innocent face and singing all about a grave: it wasn't the most childish repertoire, to put it mildly. But he had to encourage it. Because the last thing that Manya and Petrik had brought home was that maddening:

> 'Two crooks said okey-dokey
> And jumped Odessa's poky,'

a song which, incidentally, not only came from the underworld, but was also illegal to sing in public. In fact, children did not have full criminal responsibility until the age of twelve, and these two were both only six. But if they'd been twelve, then they could, perhaps, have been shot – though what about when children didn't have full responsibility? Well, it was said that a boy had written 'Stalin' in the snow, and his father got ten years. God alone knew why: maybe the boy had written it near a lavatory? It was just as well that snow was such a rare thing in Odessa. Oh, you couldn't keep too close an eye on children!

Pleased with his papa's approval, Petrik was babbling on about the May Day morning party at the kindergarten at which he was due to sing this song. Because he sang better than anyone else in his group. And if his papa didn't believe him, he could ask Ksenia Mikhailovna.

But when he heard the words 'morning party' Yakov suddenly fell to thinking what would happen at quite another 'morning party', and he stopped listening to his son, and only nodded. He knew what would happen. There was going to be the May Day schools' music competition – throughout the entire city. With great pomp and senior-ranking Party guests. And some friendly foreigners had been invited, too. The former Sibiryakov Theatre, now the Ukrainian Theatre, could hold about a hundred thousand people! Yakov was the master responsible for their school's entry. He had, of course, been over the repertoire a hundred times: it definitely had nothing that could be construed as either untoward or out of line. And, of course, the repertoire included 'Suliko'. The beloved song of the beloved leader. Misha Zilberg was going to sing it. And the audience was meant to sing along with him, for everyone knew it off by heart. Splendid. But he realised there would be fifteen of the best schools taking part, and they were no less clued-up than his own school. Fifteen times – he would stake his life on it – 'Suliko' would sound forth from the stage. But that was rather a lot, when all was said and done. If only the foreign guests knew Russian, or had the song translated for them – then the foreign newspapers would later write that the favourite song of Soviet children was all about a sweetheart's grave. Some grave that, for some reason, 'no man knoweth' how to find. It could look awkward.

But, on the other hand, what headmaster would agree to the removal of this song from the programme? Perhaps he could suggest it should be sung by a collective choir, with all the schools joining in together right at the end? He would have to make some quick phone calls: for a start to his own headmaster!

'Yakov, can't you hear me? Tell him!' he heard Musya's voice, already sounding somewhat irritated.

'Come on, Mama, that isn't for rubbish. I heard it – that's for kerosene!' said Semyon moodily.

'And I'm telling you it's for rubbish! Get a move on!'

They were lucky if the rubbish-cart came twice a week, and its arrival was heralded by the ringing of a handbell. By that time the rubbish buckets of every apartment would be brimming over, and the occupants would rush over to empty them into the cart. But a handbell was also rung when the kerosene was brought. So long as an elephant had not trodden on your ear, it was easy to tell the bells apart from one another. Only Semyon was never sent to go and get the kerosene. Because it was said that when a girl from Preobrazhenskaya Street had been sent to get some, a hooligan had thrown a match into her can, and the girl was burnt to death. It was, however, Semyon's duty to take out the rubbish. And the canny lad claimed that it was his mother, rather than himself, who was tone-deaf and unable to tell which bell was which.

'Any more out of you and I'll belt you . . .' Yakov obediently responded to Musya's appeal to paternal authority.

'Rubbish! Rubbish!' squealed Manya's happy voice outside the window. She was conscientiously running round the yard in a circle, trying to prolong the excitement. The 'uncle' rubbishman had finally let her ring the bell! He always let the boys ring it, but today she had thought of what to say.

'Girls are better than boys! The pilot Grizodubova got her medal from Stalin himself in the Kremlin – and I'm going to be a pilot, too!'

And the 'uncle' rubbishman arched his eyebrows so funnily, and handed her the heavy bell that had ever such a loud ring to it – not to say quite a bit of dirt, though that didn't matter.

'Well, go on, pilot – off you go!'

Grumbling at his treacherous sister, Semyon started clattering the rubbish buckets, and Yakov returned to his reflections. What was it that he had been meaning to do? Why did he have to try and outsmart everybody else? Well, if he started making those telephone calls right away, it would look as if he were trying to scupper 'Suliko'. So – evidently Stalin liked it, and Soviet radio could not get enough of it, either. Everyone liked it. Would it look as if Yakov were the only person who didn't like it? When would he finally wise up? What, didn't he care what the bourgeois newspapers said about this abroad? Well, it was for others to answer for that – his job was to answer for his school. He would arrange it so that his school came on first. Nobody wanted to come on first, because the children were nervous and might get flustered on stage. So the others would be glad to let him go first. But his eagles wouldn't get flustered. And then every one of them, even Stolyarsky's celebrated school, would have to imitate them: and if they had to sing 'Suliko' another fourteen times, then so be it.

Now content, he gave Semyon some money for an ice-cream – in gratitude for distracting his attention at the right time and thus preventing him from doing something stupid. But he did not, of course, bother to explain this to him. So, in all fairness, he should cough up some more money for the little ones, too.

Well, use your wits and you can always get by. No matter what the regime. He had a quick look through *Pravda*, glancing at the headlines. He had his own system of reading, and it was both simple and effective. By looking at the newspapers you could always tell who was in for it. There was collectivisation – they'd gone for the peasants: some had been starved to death, and others were accused of being kulaks and sent to Siberia. There was industrialisation, when they'd started imprisoning the engineers and held that spate of wreckers' trials. Consolidating the leading role of the Party – that meant the Communists were in for it. Consolidating the nation's army and navy – that meant the military was in for it. To consolidate, they imprisoned. This was the system that he now followed as he read through the newspapers.

The government and the Party were concerned about Soviet cinema . . . poor film directors . . . Youth, learn how to fly! . . . The model milkmaids . . . Ah, this sounded more ominous: there was concern about the flourishing of the culture of the country's different nationalities. How was that to be taken? Well, it was obvious how it was to be taken – but which nationalities did it mean? He made a mental note of this and continued. As far as

Soviet schools were concerned there was no sign of a campaign. Well, thank you for that, at least.

Yakov was not surprised when, shortly after this, they started deporting the Black Sea Greeks. With a mixture of relief and shame at his relief he discovered that the Poles and Germans were also being deported. For the time being, presumably, there were no instructions on the Jews. The trains would depart with their cargo during the night. For obvious reasons, nobody was there to see them off. Now the Kostupolo family from their yard were gone. When the school year started on the first of September there was no sign of his best pupil, the school's mathematics star, Lena Antaro. Semyon lost his school-chum Kostya Bazili. The city's population was thinning out: there had always been a lot of Greeks in Odessa.

There were still the Greek verandas in the old yards, and, just as before, the housewives fried the Black Sea plaice and sprats *à la grecque* outside on these verandas. And there, too, as the primus stoves hissed and the women squabbled and laughed, babies crawled and ran about with red potty marks on their naked bottoms. And ornamental vines, as old as the city itself, twined around these rickety living quarters. By the autumn of thirty-nine they were, as ever, changing their colours: from green to yellowy-pink, and red to violet. But already there were certain notes missing from the dissonant uproar of the yard. And, in any event, now that autumn was here the verandas were gradually getting more and more deserted anyway. In winter this was where the bikes, collapsible summer chairs and other bits and pieces were kept. But now people no longer lived there – they had gone back indoors. The rooms vacated by those who had gone were occupied in the twinkling of an eye. But this did not make it feel any more spacious.

> 'Planes will soar
> Machine-guns roar,
> And iron tanks roll forward,
> Our infantry break through, and sappers, too,
> As machine-gun carts race onward . . .'

sang Five 'A' in martial fashion. Yakov, who had taken on these thirty schoolkids only a month earlier after bidding farewell to his leavers' class, was beating out the time. It was all right – it did not look as if they were about to make fools of themselves at the next school parade. They were kids, just like any other kids – they'd be OK. He had yet to discover any with a particular gift for mathematics, but in time he would din that into them. There's no such thing as children who are no good at maths – it's the adults that are no good at it. But they had done a good job of gathering scrap metal, and had not let their class leader, Yakov Isakych, down. Already the little devils were trying not to let the side down.

And aeroplanes really were soaring – already, in this day and age. And machine-guns were roaring. Western Ukraine had expressed its happiness at being reunited. Anyone failing to express such sentiments would be reunited, not with eastern Ukraine, but eastern Siberia. The Baltic Republics had cheerfully merged into the friendly family of peoples. The newspapers reported that it was Finland itself that launched the attack: they must have gone out of their minds. Well, they'd chosen a very good time for it: anyway the borders had to be pushed back from Leningrad.

Anna was not sure whether to be glad or worried that they were in no hurry to take Oleg in the army. It was true that there had been a decree putting back the call-up age to twenty. But he already was twenty! And what did it mean if they didn't take someone? It meant that he was not trusted. It meant that he was earmarked for a camp under that catch-all phrase of 'child-avengers', applied to the sons and daughters of people who had been shot or imprisoned. And the fact that his application to join the aeroplane club had been refused without any explanation made this look even more likely. He plainly did not belong to that same youth who were being called upon to learn to fly. And when his call-up papers finally did arrive, Anna was thrown from one dread to another: here it was – but would it be worse than ever now? What would come of the boy? It was like falling into an abyss: there was no longer anything, anything that could be done to help him or keep him safe.

He put on some scruffy clothes, as if he were about to go

and work with the voluntary Saturday workers. The army would issue him with a uniform. He had a crew-cut. Anna's heart started when she saw him: how like Pavel he looked – good heavens, it was astonishing! The same Pavel that had come back from Solovki – also with a crew-cut. Only he did not have any virile folds round his mouth. He already had the same eyes as Pavel, but his lips were boyish and plump. Just right for kissing girls.

And her son went and fought in the Finnish war. At least it wasn't the camp. 'Grant that nobody kill him, and that he kill nobody himself,' prayed Anna. But her prayer was not heeded. In any event, not the second part.

Their company was thrown into the attack at night-time after a flare was fired. Oleg, who was on skis and in white camouflage, did not feel the cold: just before going into the attack they had been given vodka. But in this dark and snowy forest he did not immediately know where he was supposed to be firing. And neither did the others. Because they were not being fired at from in front, where the snow lay untouched. Goodness knew where they were being fired at from. But Lyoshka let out a somehow strange rasp and fell over, and so did some of the other lads at Oleg's side. Oleg raced on, feeling that at any moment he would also be hit. Someone was watching him. Taking aim at that very moment. And the camouflage would do nothing to fool him. He skied off to the side and brushed against a broad fir tree – two shots immediately rang out from the snow-laden branches, and more snow came tumbling down. Ah, there he was! Oleg managed to spot where another little snow-slide started to tumble down: was it from that pine tree over there, or what was that moving over there? And now he was aiming there: he took a shot – yanked back – and shot again. Ah, so that's where the Finn was! He was in white, too. Only for some reason he hadn't fallen, but remained hanging there. Stay hanging, you bastard – that's for Lyoshka. If it weren't for the picturesque, grotesque radiant light of the full moon, there was no telling how the attack by their company might have ended. They would most likely have been slaughtered like chickens. But now it was clear that the Finnish snipers had been up in the trees waiting for them. And from a snow-laden tree, you couldn't shoot without at least some snow flaking down. So look for that – and then shoot. Shoot, and don't dither. Dither – and you're dead.

By morning half their company was alive, and they had taken the little forest. It was dreadful to see their own dead: for Oleg it was the first time. The medical orderlies went round gathering them up. But the Finnish snipers were left hanging in the trees in the pink frosty mist. And that was the most frightening thing of all: the still, still forest. With the Finns hanging there from their chains. They had been chained to the spot before the fighting. Chained to their own pine and birch trees. To stop them from retreating. Some of them were still alive, and muffled cracks could be heard, like a finger-nail over a newspaper. They were being polished off by those men brought up from the NKVD squads in the rear.

When the mobile kitchen arrived towards midday, Oleg thought that he could not eat. But he cursed himself for being such a woman and forced himself to have something. Lyoshka the accordionist had been shot in the throat. Lyoshka could not eat any more. But he, Oleg, could. And he could shoot, too. And from now on that's just what he meant to do.

His letter was short: he was alive and well. He was happy with the army. He sent his greetings for the New Year. He had joined the Young Communist League. He had stopped smoking. He kissed his mama and his little brother Alyosha. And wished them all happiness.

Well, of course, how could she be anything other than happy at receiving such a letter? And he was alive. And not wounded. She was so happy that she felt like crying. And he had been accepted into the Young Communist League – did that mean there was now nothing to stop him from going on to university after the army? And he had stopped smoking – now that was a surprise. He had been smoking for a long time: on the sly when his father had been at home, but then, after his arrest, he smoked openly, and she had said nothing about it. And now suddenly this, and, what was more, in the army . . . Perhaps he was hinting at something? Well, if so she had no idea what. That evening Musya and Yakov called in to see her, and she showed them the letter. All three of them racked their brains – but could come up with nothing.

'You're trying to read too much into it!' said Alyosha with a shrug of his shoulders when he got back from the baker's. 'It doesn't mean anything in particular. A lot of people pack in smoking there – Rudik told me. Because of the "cuckoos".'

'First of all, don't shrug your shoulders like that – it's rude! And what are you talking about cuckoos for?' asked Anna in bewilderment.

'The "cuckoos" are the Finnish snipers – that's what the soldiers call them. And they perch up in trees or on roof-tops. They can shoot a fly – no sweat. And when it's dark they fire at a cigarette – you know how easy it is to spot the light? So, as soon as anyone lights up, the Finn's on to him – bang! And up there it's dark just about the whole time during the winter – isn't that right, Uncle Yakov? Because it's the north,' Alyosha patiently explained to his mother, who was so ignorant of manly matters.

'Hey, brother, you're quite some military expert!' Yakov drawled with respect.

Alyosha would not have minded flaunting some of the other things he knew, but it was hopeless in front of his mother. She could not abide anything like that, and would immediately cut him short: 'Stop boasting!' Other mothers would have been quite the opposite: come on, recite some poetry to the guests, and show them your school mark-book – assuming, of course, it was worth showing. But with her it was always 'Don't!' Well, maybe it wasn't such a bad thing after all: the minute anyone showed up at Slavka's place he was forced to get out his violin, and he was already at his wits' end. And he went to school like a puppy, with a little velvet bow tied round his neck. Because he didn't go to any old school, but Stolyarsky's, which was supposed to bring out prize-winning international musicians. For his parents it was a pleasure, but for Slavka it was an ordeal: he had to take such care of his fingers that he couldn't even fight. And, of course, he was teased in the yard.

'Slavochka, don't pick your nose, or you'll break your finger – and what would you play your violin with then?'

It was a dog's life. He wondered if anyone had any normal

parents. Ones that didn't actually show off themselves, but didn't stop their children from doing so. Anyway, good for Oleg. He was obviously in the front line, seeing as he'd packed in smoking. Maybe he'd have the sense to bring back something from the war – even an unused cartridge would do. Only he still had a long time to serve. Even if the war ended, it would still be another two years.

30

Pavel found his second time in the camp harder than the first. Had it come straight away, he would not have had time to get used to hoping that they might never come for him. But, really, they'd left him in peace for so many years . . . He kept on reminding himself that it could end at any moment. But either he failed to do this often enough, or conversely, he did it too often. One way or another, the prospect of a second term had receded into the realm of abstract ideas, and for this arrest he was, for no good reason at all, shamefully unready.

And the camps were changed now. For all its horrors, the Solovki of the twenties now looked like nothing more than a Pioneers' recreation party. Back then it was people that killed, tortured and mocked the zeks. Specific individuals that you could hate and feel contempt for. There was that bastard, and this one, and that one. What could be worse than human tyranny and the refined arts of the executioner? Well, now there was the conveyor. It was a machine. There was not even anyone to hit out at: they were all petty officials – each with their own little duty to see to. That captain had alternated his sadistic enjoyment with fits of humour that were worthy of a convict and bouts of hard drinking. After these bouts the captain slept it off, and then you had a break.

Here there were no breaks. Just as a machine-tool doesn't stop when someone's hand gets caught in the cutter, neither did this machine ever stop. It had not even been built as a special form of mockery – it simply worked day and night. Using not humans, but numbers. Sleep, clothing and the other natural requirements of the numbers were simply not allowed for. What was allowed for was fuel: the bread ration. Because numbers had to work. On the great construction sites of Communism – fulfilling the plan. But plans had to be overfulfilled, whereas fuel had to be spared. And, in both cases, according to a specific percentage: the machine had to meet its own figures. And numbers turned into camp dust, and then, in order to fulfil the plan, the machine ensured that the conveyor got new numbers. Pavel was simply one such number, and his job was to carry one end of a board laden with concrete. If he dropped dead, the movement of the board would not come to a halt, it would simply be up to the next number to take over from him.

Nevertheless, dying was the one thing that Pavel did not want to do. He was still so alive, and he fastened discarded tyres round his worn boots, and chewed pine needles on top of his ration. There was not a single one of the zeks' little tricks for survival that he neglected, and he studied them in fine detail and stubbornly hoped to survive throughout all of his ten years. And to get back out, and return to Anna and the boys. But such thoughts were dangerous. Such thoughts could make a man overheat inside, for where there was hope, there was also fear.

'You're crackin' up, boy,' his team-mate, the seasoned brick-layer Trifon reasoned with him. 'Don't crack up – take it easy. Everyone finds their second term hardest, but once that's over – it's a doddle. Take my word: third time in 'n' you won't bat an eyelid. You're still young – you've got your whole sentence ahead o' you.'

This Trifon had been a sergeant-major in the war of fourteen, and now he loved teaching the raw newcomers, just as in his day he had taught raw soldiers.

'Look like an eagle, walk like a man! Even flies die of moping!'

Pavel appreciated the value of this advice, and it made him feel ashamed. Did he really give the appearance of someone who went round licking out soup-bowls or cadging dog-ends off strangers? What was Trifon doing instructing him like this, as if Pavel were about to buckle? But that meant he obviously looked as if he actually was cracking up. He couldn't banish his thoughts, but surely he could keep a closer watch on how he behaved in front of others? He imagined that Alyosha was at that very moment watching him – 'Papa's monkey', as Anna laughingly called him. He was seized by a young and cheerful recklessness: come on, son! Look like an eagle!

From that day on, without knowing it himself, he became a real zek. And one with a real chance of surviving, and – if it came to dying – then he would do so cheerfully. It turned out that his fellow-prisoners were most interesting people, each with his own form of worldly wisdom, and occasionally ideas so outlandish that it was a joy to listen to them. It was never dull. Why had he never noticed that before?

Just take Mikhail Borisovich, Pavel's workmate on the board! Already well into middle age, it was thanks to the sick-bay that he had managed to stay alive, for without it he wouldn't have lasted a single year at this sort of work. He would take a week off in the sick-bay, and then come out again. Then he'd do a bit of work – and then go off sick again. But to get into sick-bay you had to have a temperature of thirty-eight, otherwise the matron wouldn't even look at you. Yet a temperature was precisely what a weakened man hardly ever got, for a temperature was what the organism hurled its last strength at. Assuming it had any left to hurl. Mikhail Borisovich, who, for such an obvious Jew, had the peculiar surname of Katsenko, felt sympathy for Pavel because of the way he was carrying the board. For there were ways and ways of carrying a concrete board: if you were going uphill, the bulk of the weight fell on the man behind, whereas if you were going downhill, it fell on the man in front. And there were ways and ways of loading them, too. Pavel was stronger. And, according to the code of the camp, that meant that he could either beat up or simply threaten his weak workmate, and so force him to do the 'slog'. And save his strength for surviving that bit longer. Pavel, of course, figured things differently, and he saw it as the duty of the stronger to take the bulk of the weight himself. Out of gratitude, Mikhail Borisovich shared certain secrets with him.

It turned out that the nurse in the sick-bay was a Latvian called Emma. And she felt sorry for the zeks. Inject a cubic centimetre of turps under your skin, and you were in business: your temperature was touching forty. And you could get the same result by injecting milk. How to get milk, though? Why, for the right sort of person the sick-bay had everything. Naturally, you couldn't do it too often. You had to be very careful, and make sure no one noticed what you were up to. If things got dodgy for Pavel, he should remember. Not a word to anyone, mind – otherwise our Emma's had it.

In the early days of the revolution this Mikhail Borisovich had, Pavel realised from his stories, been nicely fixed up in Vienna. And he had managed to transfer all his business and quite a sizeable amount of money from Russia, too. Well, sure there had also been a war going on there, but, even so, there was no comparison. However, he had got moving before the war broke out, and got his family out, too. Yes, he still had a wife and grown son over there – and quite all right they were, too. For Mikhail Borisovich was a man with a flair for business. And only once in his life had this flair ever let him down: when Russia launched the New Economic Policy, and, like a fool, he had started trading here. And very successful he had been, too, to start with: supplying rubber was like striking gold! And with his languages and knowledge of the business he had been the ideal middleman. On his first trip he was well received – so he made another . . . But from one of these trips he never made it back. No, he certainly hadn't been arrested immediately. Well, that was a story in itself. If he wrote down his life, it would sound more like a novel. There had been ups, and there had been downs. Some time he'd tell Pavel the whole tale – and give him a good laugh while he was about it.

And yet, to Pavel's amazement, Mikhail Borisovich turned out to be a convinced Stalinist. Pavel thought he was joking – but no, he was utterly serious!

'No, Communism's got nothing to do with it – how blind you are! So what if I admire power? Do you think I'm the only one? I don't know what justice is, or what you're supposed to eat it with. I've never seen it and I've got my doubts about it. But what do I see? The enormous power of an enormous country – and all so that one man can do whatever he likes. You think that's a high price to pay? Certainly not! Throughout the whole of history this is the first time it's ever happened. Don't talk to me about the pharaohs – this goes way beyond their wildest dreams! They couldn't do this, they couldn't do that, they couldn't even give God a new name. But he can do anything! Do you understand – anything! Can't you get that into your head? Well, in that case I don't understand which of us is Russian.

'You wonder why people love him: from little kids to people that are his right-hand man one minute and in jug the next? Propaganda, you say – but what's propaganda got to do with it? It's always been there, and it always will be. It's simply that people love absolute power. Whether you're imprisoned or released – it's entirely as he pleases. If he pleases, he'll make you into a top writer or singer. You know what's happened to some people? Zek today, academician tomorrow!'

'And the day after that – back to zek?' asked Pavel, grinning.

'Well, maybe so, and what of it? That's the game, and those are the stakes! What if they came in here now and told you that you can go – you're a former officer, for goodness' sake! – your life would be transformed, and in a week's time you could be a marshal. It's an enormous, enormous power, and we're part of it, it's us that actually make up this power – from a marshal right the way down to the last zek! That's enough to intoxicate anyone! Absolutely!'

'And then comes the hangover?'

'Well, so what? Have you never been drunk, or something? What are you looking at me like that for – think I'm mad, do you? Nothing of the sort, I simply understand the times we live in. That's how it is now, and it has a charm all of its own. And, in his own way, Stalin is a great man. He wouldn't get through a single day if he didn't know how to command people's respect. That's what he's good at.'

'I won't even bother to argue,' said Pavel, shrugging his shoulders.

'Well, you don't think I'll go racing off and snitch on you, do you? Or have I offended your national feelings? Well, if I weren't a Russian at heart, how would I understand the scale of such extremes? So cut out the feeble bath-house jokes . . .'

'What was that?' asked Pavel, not understanding.

'Well, all this "Take off your cross or put on your underpants" kind of guff . . . Believe you me, I'm sick and tired of it. But that doesn't make me change my attitude. What else could have possibly drawn me back to Russia?'

They had no time to argue it out. It was not often that zeks had the chance to hold such long conversations. And a couple of days later Mikhail Borisovich once again skived off to the sick-bay, only this time he did not come back. Either he died, or he got lucky and was able to 'stick around' there, just as he had hoped. Pavel later racked his brain trying to recall whether he had heard his name before somewhere, or even seen his face somewhere a long while ago. But he could not remember anything. Now he was carrying the board with another man, a somewhat bumptious young whipper-snapper from Rostov. And he saw that the youngster was constantly sizing up whether or not to have a go at him. Well, fine – he didn't mind being sized up that way. Without any ado, Pavel made sure that the weight was spread evenly. He knew that fights were invariably won by whoever was more ready to take things right to the limit. And, if it came to a scrap, the man that had fought at the front would have the edge over this little spiv.

'Mama, look! See how big they are! Can we make them into a risotto? Can we?'

Alyosha proudly shook his day's catch of mussels out of his fishing bag. They smelt of iodine, and scrawny strands of reddish seaweed that had not yet dried were still clinging to their mauve sides.

'They're enormous! Where ever did you get them?' asked Anna in delight.

'At station sixteen. There's a rock there, you see – on one side the mussels are a bit titchy, but on the other they're huge! The only trouble is it's hard swimming back to the top if the waves get too high. Once I was too slow – and the wave sent me crashing into the rock with a right old wallop!'

'You take care now, son,' said Anna, who had nothing left but to heave a sigh. Alyosha was already nine that summer, and it was unthinkable for her to keep him cooped up at home all summer long. Anna had allowed him the freedom to go to the seaside on his own, and she had not even been unduly worried: he had learnt how to swim when Pavel was still with them. In the evenings she smeared his sunburnt face and shoulders with sour cream, listened to his riveting tales of what enormous gobies Petka – whom she had never met – had reeled in and guessed that she knew far from everything about the adventures of her independent son. She cooked the risotto just as he liked it: half rice, half mussels.

'Mam, let's do it in style!'

That meant that while it was still hot the risotto had to be put inside one half of the washed mussel shells before being covered over with the other. Anna served up the steaming shells on the chipped dish, with its gilded rim, and Alyosha was already jumping up and down by the door.

'Mam, why don't I go and ask Manya and Petrik over?'

'Ask them all over,' replied Anna, and with a patter of sandals her little provider went scampering over the yard asphalt.

The two of them had been living together for almost a year now, and Anna was finding it unusually easy: her housekeeping chores were somehow negligible. She had grown used to being constantly mindful of the requirements of a household of six, and getting everything done right on time, which meant working without ever stopping. If it wasn't one thing, then it was another – but it lasted all the time, except when she slept, and even then there would be something that she had not yet done, and for which she would reproach herself. How could it be difficult when she was doing it for people she loved – it was nothing but a pleasure! But her loved ones had left the home – one after the other, no matter what she did about it. And now the only one left was Alyosha. And it turned out that there was almost nothing for her to do. Cleaning, cooking, washing and sewing for two was almost too easy. It left her with loads of time on her hands, as in her childhood. She and Alyosha could go off for an entire day at weekends, taking a sandwich lunch with them. They loved wandering round the city – going wherever the fancy took them, without any plans or objectives. They swung together on the chains by Voronstov's statue, dropped by to see how Alyosha's favourite little griffins were getting on, and went running down the steep steps leading to the sea. Once they found a kitten meowing in a gorse thicket, and they called it Murzik and took it home with them.

Work went on, much as ever – Anna was paid as a hospital orderly, though the nurses were only too glad to have her do many of their own duties. But she held the job down, and being irreplaceable had its advantages. Nobody was keen to have Anna leave the surgical department, and nobody cavilled with her. Not even with the fact that she kept quiet during the general meetings. Although you weren't meant to keep quiet. You were meant – depending on the subject of the meeting – to call for the death sentence for enemies, or criticise whoever ought to be criticised, or rapturously applaud. Well, what was to be expected from a virtually illiterate hospital orderly! So they turned a blind eye. To Anna it seemed that her work at the hospital was cushy: she was not expected to work round the clock, as she had been during the war. Come the end of the working day – and it was off home. And once she got there, Alyosha would be pleased to see her. Then it was back to her department, where the patients would be smiling. It was fine.

There, out in the big world, somewhere far away, a war was being fought. The Germans had already taken Paris, and Molotov had congratulated them on their success – on behalf of the Soviet government. Loudspeakers resounded with speeches and songs, and newspapers were either calling for something to be done or else threatening someone. There was an air of expectation, like before a storm.

Meanwhile the two of them went on living together on Koblevskaya Street, finding joy in each other. They were both worried about Pavel and gathered parcels for him, and they were both looking forward to having Oleg back home on leave: he was hoping to get a week or ten days off in the autumn. Together they counted the days till her next pay-day, and, if she received a state loan instead of money, together they would figure out how to make ends meet. What right had a zek's wife to be happy? If she was not heartless, she ought to be worried about her husband and lie awake at nights. And she should be worried about her elder son: the Finnish war was over, but her heart told her that another one was about to begin. And she should also be worried about her younger son: what if he went too far with his seaside adventures at station sixteen? And what if she were arrested herself? And how could she ever afford to buy a new pair of shoes for Alyosha in time for autumn – it was frightful how enormous his feet were getting. There was an eternal shortage of money, yet she had to send something to Pavel: on this she simply refused to listen to him. And the greater her reason to be frightened and worried, the sweeter was the illicit joy of simply being with Alyosha.

Only now did Anna understand that they had been too clever with Oleg: how much thought they had given to what to discuss with him, and what not to discuss. What if he blurted it all out at school? What if it kept him from establishing relationships with children of the same age? What if he was too young for such discussions, or they harmed him in some way – bearing in mind the times. But with Alyosha she avoided trying to be clever: anyway, she would not live for ever. She kept nothing hidden from him. Following an amazing childish instinct he adapted easily: he knew where and about what to keep his mouth shut. And he stayed clear of trouble, despite all her worries about letting him go off to school. Needless worries, too, as it transpired: were they really the only family like this in the entire city?

'Do you remember Papa?' she would ask from time to time. And she was surprised at how far back he could actually remember. Well, how old must he have been in May of thirty-six? Surely he was too young to remember. But he told her how, when the booming started, Papa had taken him and Oleg and led them round the corner, and ordered them never to forget what they saw.

'You were at work then, Mama. You probably couldn't even hear it. But how loud it was – and the dust flew, and then the bell-tower came crashing down, the whole thing collapsed in a heap, and made a sort of explosion. And then the large cupola came down, and there was absolutely nothing left to see of it, and Papa seemed to be shaking all over. And he kept saying: look, and don't ever forget. That was the cathedral where he fell in love with you, wasn't it?'

'I don't know where he fell in love with me. I don't think it was in the cathedral, though. But we both used to go there. And Oleg was christened there, and so were you.'

'Then why have you never taken me there?'

'It was closed in thirty-two.'

'They were bad people that blew it up, weren't they?'

'Yes, they must have been. Or stupid. But Christ ordered us not to sit in judgement over others.'

'But also not to imprison anyone, isn't that right? So it's wrong that they're forever sitting in courts and judging people?'

'Yes, it is. But there's no need to shout about it.'

'Do you think I'm still little, Mam? Let's go to the circus when it opens. It won't be long now – just as soon as the holidays are over. We'll go to the circus and buy some cream pastries, and we'll take Manya and Petrik with us. And then we'll scrimp and save. We'll drink tea with dry bread biscuits, all right?'

And when the circus opened that is what they did. Japes such as these they gave the Polish name of *vycieczki*. They were happy-go-lucky sort of people, and the bread, if it was dried with cinnamon, made for some jolly tasty biscuits. The autumn of forty was cold and early. But Alyosha had a coat that suited him very well, one that Semyon had outgrown ages ago and Musya kept in the sofa along with some other useful bits and pieces. It simply needed shortening and for the buttons to be straightened out. Yakov and Musya had been close to the family for a long time now, and there was no need to stand on ceremony with them. Petrik was himself running around in the shoes that had been Alyosha's last year. The children spent their days and nights at whichever apartment happened to be the more suitable at the time. And, at this, Anna, who occasionally had to go and work on the night shift, was only glad.

31

'Who's teaching Kuzin – you or me?' asked Yakov furiously, pulling the would-be assailants back by the ear.

They were better off giving Yakov Isakych a straight answer. Yakov Isakych did not stand on ceremony with his pupils: he might well clout them.

'You are, Yakov Isakych,' muttered the miscreants.

'Just what do you think you're up to – two against one like this?'

'But what if he's dragging the whole class down? He'll make us lose the competition ...'

'Okay, I'll ask you again: who's teaching him?'

Yakov had sweated blood over this wretched competition. Whoever thought up such things? But these little fools were trying their utmost: understandably enough, as after the exams the best class at the best school was going to Moscow! For a whole week! And there they would see the Exhibition of Achievements of the National Economy, and the Kremlin, and possibly even Stalin himself! It was known that he sometimes gave Pioneers a talk. And the children had been in a state of tension throughout the entire year, with having to keep on getting top marks – collecting more scrap metal than anyone else, coming first in the Pioneers parades ... Not that the question of who was going in any way depended on this, however. What did best school mean? The City Department of the People's Education would decide that as it saw fit, and the children had absolutely nothing to do with it. What had everything to do with it was CDPE's assessment of the school administration.

But Yakov's class, by now already in the sixth form, had been flogging themselves to death and shown themselves incapable of any restraint. When collecting scrap, they had managed to go and get forty metres of piping from a building-site – an incident which had subsequently caused Yakov no small trouble. They had caught a spy – and dragged him straight off to the NKVD, on what used to be the Jewish Street. He turned out to be a construction student who had been learning how to survey with a theodolite. Kuzin was about to be beaten up for getting a '2' – who had ever heard of such a reason for boys to be fighting! Well, it was, of course, heard of: it was the Makarenko method. A Soviet teacher did not beat his pupils. But, in order to keep discipline, there were activists among the pupils themselves. And if a wrongdoer got beaten up in some quiet little corner – what had that to do with the teacher? It wasn't as if the beaten-up pupil was about to go and complain about it. It was, furthermore, a method known to have achieved some significant results.

Only Yakov would not permit such methods in his class. He preferred sticking to the old ways. His kids had plenty of chance to grow up being scoundrels as it was. If anyone needed clouting it was better that he should do it himself – assuming it was a boy, of course. It wasn't quite following the rule-book, and he would never say that it was. Only the parents were not opposed to it, they were even thankful. They knew their own little madcaps, and all but prayed for a strict teacher. And the kids didn't mind, either. Why, not long ago Korytin had been to see him – now he was a strapping great chap. The extent to which he had worn down Yakov's nerves as a pupil is not a matter that we need now go into. But somehow or other that hooligan had got into university to study mathematics! And now he came along, booming out in his bass voice:

'Yakov Isakych, I got a real easy card for my oral, but for the written exam I had to do a graph. And that's it, I thought, I couldn't remember what to do – whether to do a symmetrical diagram of sine or cosine. Well, I thought I was done for – and then it was as if someone knocked me on the head: it was an uneven function, mutton-head! Uneven! And do you remember clouting me when you showed me how to do it up on the board that time?'

By the time of the exams his Six 'A' class were looking worn out – either from cramming or preparing their crib-sheets. Yakov, who was not indifferent to this genre, had a collection of crib-sheets, and over the years he had been teaching he had accumulated what was little short of a museum of them. There were pencils with formulae intricately burnt into the sides, and complex constructions held in place by pins and rubber bands that recoiled back into the sleeve, and exercise-books the size of a postage stamp covered in minute writing as if they were intended for reading with a microscope. The most brilliant crib-sheet of all he had been unable to take home, though he had photographed it: before one exam the tenth class had quite simply written all the formulae out on the ceiling – in enormous letters! Who ever looked at the ceiling? And the rascals had done remarkably well. Later on, however, knowing Yakov Isakych's susceptibility to such matters, they owned up – so that he could also share in the pleasure. But not until after the exam results had been published.

Like any other teacher, all Yakov's vases and glass jars were brimming over with peonies and roses these days. It was customary to bring flowers to the exams. Which was why Semyon came to hate these smells from earliest childhood: peonies meant exam-time.

To the delight of Six 'A' the complex calculations of the City Department of the People's Education culminated in their school being chosen. And as for which was the best class in their school – that was obvious. And Yakov, with his usual luck, now had to take this mob off to Moscow to attend a Pioneers rally. Taking a week out of his holiday – and, he understood, without getting any compensation for the week, either. Naturally, it was such an honour. Very well then! It had to be done. As he looked at these radiant faces, what choice did he have, other than to smile in reply? But he immediately took advantage of this moment when they were ready to promise him anything, and made them give their 'word as Pioneers' to keep iron discipline and be angelically obedient.

And on the 19th of June they set off: thirty schoolkids in red

Spanish forage caps, each in full Pioneers uniform, with Sonya as Pioneer Leader, and Yakov Isakych. They conscientiously waved as their mothers stood on the platform shouting their last-minute exhortations. There was a bit of a scuffle over the upper berths in the carriage, they drank an incredible amount of tea with flat little packets of railway sugar and filled the entire train with virtually non-stop singing. They even managed to drown out the radio.

It was just as they were making their way to Red Square that the loudspeakers started booming. Everything on the streets came to a halt, even the traffic. And the pedestrians stood very still and quiet. And Yakov saw his children dissolve in this silence and the menacing voice emerging from the black speaker, and all that remained of the children was their eyes. Enormous eyes on thin little legs.

'This is an all-stations broadcast . . . Perfidious attack by Hitler's Germany . . . On the 22nd of June, at four o'clock in the morning . . .'

And the music: how on earth could they have found time to write the song?

> 'Arise, enormous country,
> Arise for mortal fight . . .'

rolled out in wave after wave from one loudspeaker to the next. And then they came into Red Square. Because that was where everyone else was making for, and there were already a lot of people gathered there. And they stood, and waited. For some reason everyone was certain that Stalin was about to appear. He would come out and deliver a speech that would make it clear that they were about to repel the attack, and that they would be victorious. Or perhaps they had won already? Since four o'clock in the morning! There were films and books showing that, if anyone did come looking for trouble, their reply would be as quick as lightning, and the enemy would be repulsed in a matter of hours. Only it felt as if everything was going differently. This was no longer books – it was reality. This was something big and terrible. Yet still there was no sign of Stalin.

It was a further eleven days before he delivered a speech, and when he did, it was on the radio. By that time there were already broadcasts giving the names of the cities that they had abandoned. And all the time more and more of these names kept being added. After the initial excitement, the children became very obedient, and it required no effort from Yakov to keep them all together, in one group and never out of his sight. They were already pressing up close to him as it was. And he realised that they were stuck there. There was no longer any passenger travel: all the railways were crammed with trainloads of troops. He was unable to get through to Odessa on the telephone. He went round various departments enquiring what he was to do with the children. Eleven girls and nineteen boys. The week was coming to an end, and what then? Good grief, back in Odessa they must all be going out of their minds! He tried not even to think of Musya. She was a brick, she would cope. But how about the parents whose children were up in Moscow?

All he managed to do was to get them put up in some rest-home just outside Moscow, where they were fed and ordered to wait. They would be seen to later, for now nobody had any time to see to them. Letters were written to their home addresses and then put in a letter-box. After that they could only wait. Yakov made a short speech to the class, announcing that they were all now mobilised for war. As Pioneers in time of war it was now their duty to work, work and work. He hoped this would keep them from tearful hankering after their mothers. But they were already twelve- to thirteen-year-olds. They were not little. Yakov tried to keep them busy all the time. They taped over all the windows, as everyone now had to, criss-crossing them with strips of paper. In case of aerial attack. It was also necessary to ensure that the black-out was observed: not a single ray of light should be visible! The rest-home also took in some other groups that had been stranded, from Ternopol and some other place. But they, the Odessan Pioneers, had, of course, to be the best of the lot.

Pavel was travelling in a troop train wearing the same black overcoat as all the other zeks who had only yesterday been in camp. They had been issued with tarpaulin boots and forage caps. For the time being without any stars on them. They would get their weapons later, after taking their oath. They were to take the oath on reaching their destination. For the time being they were travelling under guard. He could not believe his ears when they had been lined up and the announcement was made. Here it was, that change of fate about which his strange workmate had spoken! Now it struck Pavel that this was precisely what he had foretold: word for word. He had not even immediately understood what it meant. Only a few days later he caught wind of the communiqués about the abandoned cities. Remembering the map, he realised how quickly the front line was changing. At this rate, what would come of Odessa in a month's time? But, to begin with, it simply burst upon him: this was it. It was real. And again men could be men. How long had they been taught not to think as men! To be frightened of their own shadow – if they were free. To forget even their own names – if they were in camp. But now they could not manage without them. And old Whiskers himself was now calling them his 'Brothers and sisters!'

He understood that this was exactly what the 'black tops' were there for – to be thrown into the most perilous fighting spots. And that they had virtually been sentenced to death. But, even so, it was a welcome ray of hope. If he had to perish, then he would not do so humiliatingly as a zek, but as a soldier. Fighting for Russia. As for dealing with their own scum, they could get round to that some time later – and with weapons to hand! Right now though – how easy it was to forget about all that. For now there was one enemy, the Germans. Hans and Fritz.

'Now then, lads – let's pulverise these bastards, shall we?' they were cordially greeted by a military figure with a large rhomboid insignia on his chest as soon as they had been disembarked at some siding.

'Let's pulverise 'em!' roared the echelon in reply.

And along the entire length of the hastily formed columns of 'black tops' the cry was taken up: 'Hurra-a-ah! Let's pulverise 'em!'

Musya was hastily getting everything ready for Semyon's departure. A year ago he had put his name down for military college, hoping to get a place there once he'd finished school. A lot of other boys had their names down for it, too. Before finishing school, with one year still to go. He was only seventeen. But it was clear that there was no point in waiting. He had to report to the college right away, without waiting to be called up. He would make his way to Moscow, and from there they would all be sent straight to the front – and who's going to bother checking if you're one year too young? figured Semyon. Thank God the college in Moscow is at least a good way back from the front. They won't surrender Moscow, though the front is getting closer and closer to Odessa, figured Musya. And – Semyon could be proud – she had helped him to gather his things and papers without a single objection. Not like the other mothers, who as soon as the call-up papers arrived started crying as though their sons were dead already.

Semyon divided his boyish goods between Petrik and Manya. How miserable these valuables of bygone days seemed now that he was a grown man! The fishing tackle he gave to Petrik, and the torch with the dynamo to Manya. The stamps went to Petrik, and the Greek coin with the Medusa to Manya. As for the camera, that should be left for his mother to sell: they were facing a hard future. He kissed his mama and the little ones. He tossed his bag over his shoulder like a true soldier. Musya did not accompany him to the station: he did not have a ticket for his journey. He would find some way of getting round that once he was at the station. He knew there were still goods trains running to Moscow. He'd manage somehow.

They had packed in such a hurry that there were still some bits and pieces and papers lying about on the floor. Musya sat down heavily on the sofa, putting her arms around Petrik and Manya. Now they were all she had left. But how could children be expected to understand that? There they were, jumping around as though they had ants in their pants: they were longing to be out in the yard. Alyosha was out there playing at war with Slavka – now that was something they did understand. Well, it was only natural for eight-year-olds.

When she got back from the hospital, Anna found her howling in the half-light that the summer twilight had cast through the apartment.

'I'm so frightened, Anechka, so frightened!' she sobbed, as

Anna embraced and comforted her. Now she was no longer alone, it was not so awful, and, as she listened to Anna, she started to believe that Yakov would come back, and that, for the time being, Semyon would study in Moscow, and that she and the children would not be lost, and somehow they would cope.

In the evening, after carefully drawing the black blinds, Anna and Musya put the children all together in the broad bed with knobs. And then they went and sat at the table in the 'cold room'. The tea had gone cold, and they did not feel like boiling the kettle again. From behind the closed door giggling and muffled blows could be heard: there was obviously a pillow-fight going on. Manya and Petrik adored these overnight stays with the Petrovs, and they were happy that today Aunt Anya had come and brought them all to her home. From behind the door someone let out a screech, and then started arguing that it wasn't fair to use a sandal.

'Musya, can you remember if they washed their feet?' Anna pondered out loud, and, as though by magic, the noise died down.

Musya stifled her laughter, squeezing out, 'No, I don't think so.'

'Ah, the little rascals! I'll go and get them to do it this minute.'

Convincing snores started to emerge from the 'warm room'.

'All right – if they're asleep, you'd better leave them.'

Exhausted by the hot day, the three children were, indeed, soon fast asleep. They had great plans for tomorrow: today they had found a way into the catacombs! Straight from their yard! In order to try out the dynamo torch they had run down to that quiet corner of the yard where hardly anyone ever went, unless on a call of nature. There was a narrow path in between the tall buildings, where it was always dark and rather frightening. And from up above there were shouts of 'Woo-ooh! Woo-ooh!' the whole time. It was the cooing of the pigeons resonantly echoing between the walls. But the older boys assured them that it wasn't pigeons at all, but dead Galya, who had hung herself in her room five years ago. There, over by the yard lavatory, there were some cellars with coal and all sorts of rubbish. And there, as they flicked on the dynamo torch, they spotted something that they had never noticed before. When they moved back the wooden boards, there was a dark chute, but, instead of smelling like a cellar, a rather frightening draft came blowing out of it.

The catacombs! So that was it! This were where Yakov had said it was so easy to get lost and never be seen again, and in which there were countless treasures hidden by Greek pirates and smugglers. And he said that absolutely no one knew everything about them, as they were so big and tangly. The friends, of course, did not go down inside. They put the mouldy boards tidily back in place and cleared off before anyone noticed them. In his time, Yakov had drawn a map of the catacombs, and they knew that, ever since the civil war, this map had been kept out of reach up on the high wall-shelves out in the communal corridor along with some old books. What they needed now was to get the map down and, without hurrying, get themselves thoroughly prepared for a sortie inside! They could make a compass out of a needle: the magnetising could even work on a thread. And take a flask and some food. Yakov said that during the war the catacombs were simply irreplaceable! Assuming, of course, you knew your way about them. Tomorrow they would go on a reccy, keeping it secret from their mothers.

And both women – one slightly older than the other – remained sitting, constantly listening to the sounds of the night. An aeroplane flew by . . . No, it was all right. That droning came from the direction of the sea: the port was now working day and night.

'Tsilya, you've a light showing!' came a yell from out in the yard.

'Any better?' Tsilya shouted back.

'Now it's the other side!'

Then everything fell quiet: evidently Tsilya had sorted her blinds out. All that could be heard was the ticking of the tin wall-clock and the faint screeching of mosquitoes. Goodness, they'd even got in through the darkened blinds. Musya settled down on the sofa with the cat Murzik. The room was stuffy, and, after turning off the light, Anna opened the blinds and the windows. From the tiny front garden beneath their windows came the smell of gillyflower and nicotiana. The 'beauty of the night', however, was not yet in bloom. It needed watering, but she could not be bothered to move.

Now they were whispering quietly, so as not to wake the children. About what – nobody heard. Was it that they had to buy in some groats while they were still available? Or about their husbands: where they were now, and what the future might bring? Or about Oleg's last letter – the one that he had written before the war? Or quite possibly about something else, like childbirth, or the sort of hats they used to wear. Who's to say with women, and what they talk about with one another?

Summer nights are short. And, in the south, dark. Just as it once had in the times before electricity, the moonlight mingily outlined the still warm stone fences and walls, basking in the shadows of the ornamental vines on the verandas and turning the outspread plumes of an acacia into palm leaves. Closer to daybreak the foliage started to murmur, and then there was a sigh through the branches and in such places as there were weather-vanes they started squeaking. The 'broad' wind had started blowing.

Alyosha smiled in his sleep and turned over on to his side, all but pushing Petrik out of bed. Anna went up to them and, after groping for the blanket in the dark, she straightened it out again. There was a clatter as she trod on top of someone's tinful of treasures lying discarded among the sandals. But nobody woke up. The three of them were breathing evenly through their noses, filling the small room with a cubbish warmth.

What will come of them, Lord, what will come of us all?

Anna did not know. She waited for a moment, as though she were expecting an answer. Was it worth knowing?

And, reckoning that anyway she and Musya would no longer be able to get off to sleep now, she went out into the hallway: to make some tea.